WHEN

YOU

DISAPPEARED

ALSO BY JOHN MARRS

Welcome to Wherever You Are

The One

WHEN

YOU

DISAPPEARED

JOHN MARRS

Previously self-published as *The Wronged Sons* in Great Britain in 2014.

Published by Thomas & Mercer, Seattle

www.apub.com

Amazon, the Amazon logo, and Thomas & Mercer are trademarks of Amazon.com, Inc., or its affiliates.

ISBN-13: 9781611097511
ISBN-10: 1611097517

Cover design by Mark Swan

Printed in the United States of America

'There are some things one can only achieve by a deliberate leap in the opposite direction.'

—*Franz Kafka*

'Life always waits for some crisis to occur before revealing itself at its most brilliant.'

—*Paulo Coelho*

PROLOGUE

Northampton, today

8.20 a.m.

The thick tread of the Mercedes' tyres barely made a sound as it pulled over to the curb.

The passenger sat nervously in the rear, tapping his lips with his forefinger as his gaze met the cottage.

'That's twenty-two pounds, mate,' muttered the driver in a regional dialect he couldn't place. Most of the accents he'd heard in the past few years were those of commentators on the British sports channels his satellite dish picked up. He fumbled with his deerskin wallet, separating the euros and the sterling that were bunched together.

'Keep the change,' he replied as he offered a ten- and a twenty-pound note.

The driver responded, but the passenger wasn't listening. He opened the door and carefully placed both feet on the pavement, steadying himself with his hand on the frame before settling the door closed and stepping away from the vehicle. He patted out the creases in his bespoke suit while the security blanket of the car disappeared as silently as it had arrived.

Minutes passed by but he remained rooted to the ground. Hypnotised by the white cottage, he allowed waves of long-buried memories to wash over him. This had been their first and only home together. A family home. A home and a family he'd relinquished twenty-five long years ago.

The pink rosebushes he'd planted for her beneath the kitchen window had gone, but for a second he imagined he could still smell their sweet scent in the air. Where once there lay a sandpit he'd dug for the children, now stood a shed adorned with swirls and speckles of jade-and-white ivy slowly changing its form.

Suddenly the front door opened and a young woman appeared, bringing him back to the present with a start. He'd not anticipated another visitor.

'See you later!' she shouted, closing the door behind her. She threw the strap of her handbag over her shoulder and smiled as she passed him. It wasn't *her* though – this girl could only be in her late twenties. For a moment he wondered if it could've been her daughter and he reciprocated with his own polite smile, then watched her until she walked out of view. But the sight of her had given him butterflies.

James had told him that she'd remained living in the same home, but that conversation had been a year earlier, so there was a chance her circumstances had changed. There was only one way to find out. His heart raced as he drew a deep breath that he didn't release until he reached the end of the gravel path. He raised his head to look up at what had once been their bedroom.

That's where you killed me, he thought, then closed his eyes and knocked on the door.

CHAPTER ONE
CATHERINE

Northampton, twenty-five years earlier

4 June, 6 a.m.

'Simon, tell your dog to bugger off,' I mumbled, and brushed away a moist tongue burrowing its way into my ear.

They both ignored me so I pushed Oscar's wiry head to one side. Then he plonked his bum defiantly on the floorboards and whined until I gave in. Simon could have slept through World War Three – or worse, our kids jumping all over us like we were trampolines and demanding breakfast. I wasn't so lucky. My once cherished lie-ins had become a luxury dependent on the needs of three under-nines and a hungry mongrel.

Oscar's stomach contained a built-in alarm clock that woke him up at six on the dot every morning. Simon could walk him and throw tennis balls for him to fetch, but it was me he wanted to feed his greedy belly. It wasn't fair.

I rolled towards my husband and realised his half of the bed was already empty.

'Oh, do it yourself, Catherine,' I grumbled, and cursed Simon for going on one of his insanely early morning runs. I dragged myself out of bed, threw on my dressing gown, shuffled across the landing and quietly opened bedroom doors to check on the sleeping kids. However, one door always remained closed because I still couldn't bring myself to open it. *One day at a time*, I told myself. *One day at a time*.

I went down to the kitchen and filled Oscar's bowl with that hideous-smelling tinned meat he'd wolf down in seconds. But when I turned to put it on the floor, I was alone.

'Oscar?' I whispered, not wanting the kids to barrel downstairs just yet. 'Oscar?'

I found him in the porch, pacing in an agitated fashion by the front door. I opened it to let him out for a wee, but he stayed by the doormat, staring out towards the woods down by the lane.

'Please yourself,' I sighed. Annoyed he'd woken me up for nothing, I traipsed back to bed to steal another precious hour of sleep for myself.

7.45 a.m.

'Leave your brother alone and help me feed Emily,' I warned James, who roared as he chased an excited Robbie around the kitchen table with a plastic Tyrannosaurus Rex. 'Now!' I warned. They knew they were treading a fine line when I used that tone.

Moving the kids from bedroom to bathroom to kitchen was like chasing reluctant chickens back into a henhouse – as frustrating as hell. Some of the school mums claimed to love the chaos of family breakfasts together. I just wanted my rabble out of the house and into the classroom for some peace and quiet.

James poured his younger sister a bowl of cornflakes as I cut the crusts off their Marmite sandwiches and packed their lunch boxes. Then I slathered Simon's in Branston Pickle, sliced the bread horizontally – as requested – and wrapped them in cling film and left them on the fridge shelf.

'You've got fifteen minutes until we go,' I warned, and stuffed their lunches into the carelessly hung satchels on the coat rack.

I'd long given up leaving the house with a full face of make-up on just to take the kids to school, but to make sure I didn't look like a scarecrow, I scraped my hair into a ponytail and stepped back to check myself in the mirror. Oscar yelped as I trod on his paw – I hadn't noticed that he'd been oblivious to the breakfast bedlam and hadn't moved from the doormat.

'Are you feeling poorly, boy?' I asked, and bent down to scratch under his beardy chin. I'd give him until the afternoon to perk up, and then perhaps I'd call the vet, just to be on the safe side.

9.30 a.m.

With James and Robbie at school and Emily quietly playing on the sofa, I was up to my elbows ironing Simon's work shirts and singing along to Boyz II Men's 'End of the Road' on the radio when the phone rang.

'Simon's not here,' I told Steven when he asked to speak to him. 'Isn't he with you?' I'd presumed he'd taken his work clothes with him in a backpack and gone straight to the office after his run like he often did.

'No, he's bloody not,' Steven snapped. He could be a real grumpy sod when he wanted to be. 'I've been trying to convince the client I've been stalling for half an hour that even though we're a small company, we're just as professional as the majors. How can he take me seriously when half of us can't even turn up for a hotel breakfast meeting on time?'

'He's probably lost track of the time. You know what he's like sometimes.'

'When you see him, tell him to get his arse down to the Hilton quickly before he screws this up.'

'I will, but if you see him first, could you ask him to call me, please?'

Steven muttered something unintelligible and hung up without saying goodbye. I was glad I wouldn't be in Simon's shoes when he did turn up.

11.30 a.m.

Seventeen ironed work and school shirts and two cups of coffee passed by before I realised Simon hadn't called me back.

I wondered if Steven and I were mistaken, and that he hadn't been for a run but actually had a meeting of his own to go to. But when I popped my head around the garage door, his Volvo was still parked there. Back in the living room, his house keys sat on the record player lid; above them, a montage of photos from our tenth-wedding-anniversary party hung from the wall.

As another hour went by, a niggling doubt began to irritate me. For the first time in almost twenty years, I couldn't feel Simon's presence around me. No matter where he was or how far we were apart, I always felt his presence.

I shook my head to make the doubts disappear and scolded myself for being daft. *Too much coffee, Kitty*, I told myself, and vowed decaf was the way forward. I put the coffee jar back in the cupboard and sighed at the mountain of washing-up waiting for me.

1.00 p.m.

Three and a half hours after Steven's phone call and I felt jittery.

I'd called the office, and when Steven admitted he still hadn't heard anything, I began to panic. Before long, I'd convinced myself Simon had been out for a run and had been hit by a car. That he'd been carelessly tossed to the side of a road by a hunk of metal and a driver without a conscience.

I strapped Emily into the stroller she was too old and too big for, as it was quicker than walking with her, attached the lead to Oscar's collar and dashed off to find my husband. I asked in the newsagent's if Simon had popped in earlier, but he hadn't. Neither had our neighbours, nor Mrs Jenkins from behind her twitching net curtains.

As we walked the route Simon normally ran, I made a game of it, explaining to Emily we were hunting for snaggle-waggles – the mythical bedtime creatures he'd created to ease them to sleep. I told her they loved to hide in wet muddy ditches, so we'd have to look carefully in each one.

We covered a mile and a half and found nothing before we began walking towards Simon's office. Steven was no longer angry with Simon, which bothered me further. It meant he was worried about him. He tried to reassure me Simon was probably okay, and suggested that maybe he was on a site visit. But when we checked his diary, his day was clear of all appointments.

'He'll come home tonight pissed as a fart after being at the pub all afternoon, and we'll all be laughing about this later,' added Steven. But with no definitive proof as to where he was, neither of us was really convinced.

On our way home, Emily and I took the dirt track past Harpole Woods, where Simon sometimes ran. I hid from Emily how worried I was, but when she dropped Flopsy, a now-threadbare toy bunny he'd bought her, onto the path, I'm ashamed to admit I lost my temper and shouted at her for being careless. Her face scrunched up and she bawled, refusing to accept my apology until I carried her home.

Even Oscar had grown sick of being walked, and dragged his heels behind us. I must have been a strange sight: a perspiring mother with a screaming child in one arm, dragging a knackered dog and a stroller behind me, all the time searching for snaggle-waggles and my husband's dead body.

5.50 p.m.

Six o'clock, I told myself. *All will be okay at six o'clock because that's when he always comes home.*

It was Simon's favourite time of the day, when he could help bathe the kids, put them to bed and read them stories about Mr Tickle and Mr Bump. They were too young to sense the distance and sadness that remained between Simon and me. I'd come to terms with the fact things might never get back to how they'd been, no matter what we did or said. Instead, we were adjusting to a new kind of normal in the best way we could.

I'd picked up James and Robbie from school earlier. As I threw some breaded fish under the grill and set the table for dinner, James tried to explain something about his friend Nicky and a Lego car, but I wasn't listening. I was too on edge. Every couple of minutes, my eyes made their way towards the clock on the wall. When six o'clock came and went, I could have cried. I left my food untouched and stared out of the window, into the garden.

In those gorgeous summer months, we often finished the day on the patio, poured ourselves a couple of glasses of red wine and tried to enjoy the life we'd made for ourselves. We'd talk about the funny things the children had said, how his architectural business was coming on, and how one day we'd have enough money to buy an Italian villa and live half our year here and half over there. In fact, we'd talk about anything except for what had happened that day over a year ago which had left our relationship so exposed.

I hurried the children through their bedtime routines and explained that Daddy was sorry he couldn't be there but he'd gone away for work and wouldn't be home till late.

'Without his wallet?' asked James as I tucked him in.

I paused.

'Daddy's wallet is on the sideboard. I saw it,' he continued.

I tried to think of a reason why he wouldn't need it. There wasn't one. 'Yes, silly Daddy forgot it.'

'Silly Daddy,' he tutted, before wrapping himself in his sheets.

I dashed downstairs to check if he was right and realised I must have passed it countless times throughout the day. It was always the one thing Simon took before leaving the house, even when going out for a jog.

And it was in that moment I knew for sure something was wrong. *Really, really* wrong.

I called his friends to see if he'd gone to one of their houses. I was sure the click of each receiver was followed by me being the subject of their pity once more, even if it always came from a place of kindness. I flicked through the phone book for the numbers of local hospitals. I called all twelve of them, asking if he'd been taken in. It pained me to think he could have been lying in a hospital bed all day without anyone even knowing who he was.

I anxiously tapped my pen on my thigh as receptionists trawled though admittance forms in search of his name, but there was nothing. I left them with his description, just in case he turned up later, unable to speak for himself.

My last resort was to phone his dad and his stepmum, Shirley. When she confirmed he wasn't there either, I made up another excuse and told her I must have mixed my days up, as I thought he was popping over. Of course, she didn't believe me. Simon wasn't the 'popping over' type, at least where they were concerned.

I was so desperate I even contemplated trying to contact . . . *him*. But it had been three years since his name was last mentioned in our house, and I wasn't even sure how to find him, anyway.

My fears were interrupted by the phone's ring. I banged my elbow on the sideboard and swore as I raced to pick up the receiver, and then let out a disappointed sigh when Steven's wife, Baishali, spoke.

'Is there anything I can do? Do you want me to come round?' she asked.

I said no, and she told me she'd call in later. But it was my husband I wanted to hear from, not my friend. All I could think about was that Simon had been gone for the whole day and nobody knew where he was. I was angry with myself for not being alarmed when Steven had first called in the morning.

What kind of wife was I? I hoped Simon would forgive me when we found him.

9.00 p.m.

By the time Roger and Paula arrived soon after my call, the day had suddenly caught up with me. My body and brain were frazzled.

The first thing they saw when the front door opened was me bursting into tears. Paula hugged me and walked me back into the living room, where I'd spent most of the evening waiting by the phone. Roger had known Simon since infant school but had switched hats from family friend to his job as a detective sergeant in the police force. Even so, it was Paula, who'd always been the bossy type, who led the way as we tried to piece together how he might have spent his final moments in the house.

'Right, let's start at the beginning and work out where that bloody idiot's been all day,' she ordered. 'When I see him again I'm going to give him hell for what he's putting you through.'

We exhausted every possible scenario as to where he could have gone and who with. But when it came down to it, none of us had the first clue. Reluctantly, we resigned ourselves to the fact he'd vanished.

Thinking that on my own was hard; hearing his friend echo my thoughts was harder. And making it official made it all the worse. Police protocol meant we had to wait twenty-four hours before we could report Simon missing, but Roger was willing to bend the rules and called his station to explain.

'God, Paula, what's happened to him?' I asked, my voice trembling.

She couldn't give me an answer, so she did what she always did when I needed a best friend, and told me what I wanted to hear. 'They'll find him, Catherine, I promise,' she whispered, and hugged me again.

I was trapped in a horrible nightmare that happened to other people, not to me. Not to my family and not to my husband.

◆ ◆ ◆

SIMON

Northampton, twenty-five years earlier

4 June, 5.30 a.m.

I rolled onto my side and glanced at the pearly white face of the alarm clock on the bedside table. Half past five, it read. It had been fifteen months since I'd last managed to sleep any later than that.

Our backs were connected by barely an inch of flesh but I still felt the delicate rise and fall of her spine as she slept. I pushed myself away from her. I watched as a fragile sliver of creamy orange light gently illuminated the bedroom through a curtain crack.

I pulled the cotton sheet from my chest and gazed at the sun as it rose over the cornfields, enshrouding the bleakness of our cottage with a golden blanket. I dressed in clothes thrown over a chair and opened the wardrobe, careful to ensure the creak of its hinges didn't wake her.

I fumbled for the watch that had spent most of its life hidden in a green box on a dusty shelf, and fastened it to my wrist. It pinched, but I'd become familiar with discomfort. I left the box where it was.

I moved carefully across the floorboards and closed the door with little more than a whisper. I paused outside the bedroom door that always remained closed. I turned the handle and began to open it before stopping myself. I couldn't do it. It would do me no favours to go back to that day.

The staircase groaned under my footsteps and startled the slumbering dog. Oscar's amber eyes opened wide and he struggled to coordinate his sleepy limbs as he lolloped towards me.

'Not today, boy,' I told him, offering an apologetic smile. His head tilted to one side, confused then disappointed at being deprived of his daily walk. He let out a deflated sigh and returned to his bed in a huff, burying his head under his tartan blanket.

I unlocked the front door and gently closed it behind me. I chose the quiet of the lawn over the crunch of the gravel pathway, opened the rusty metal gate and began to walk. There was no final stroke of a child's hair, no delicate kiss planted on my wife's forehead or a last glance at the home we'd built together. There was only one direction for me to go. Their world was still in sleep but I had woken up.

And by the time they roused, there would be one less tortured soul amongst them hanging on by his fingertips.

6.10 a.m.

The house behind me had already faded into my past by the time I reached the dirt-track lane that would carry me into Harpole Woods.

My thoughts were blank but my legs were preprogrammed to take me to where I needed to be. They led me beyond the perimeter of the horse chestnut trees, through the stubbly bracken that tried to tear the legs of my jeans and into the woodland's belly, to where the faded blue rope had lain for years as a marker on the ground's sunken basin. There had been a pond there once, and the rope had been tied to a tree for the local children to swing over it. But the water had long since evaporated, leaving the rope without a use.

I picked it up from the ground and repeated the familiar process of tugging it until it was taut. The elements hadn't eroded its strength and I wished I had remained that tough.

Then I sat on a long felled oak trunk and looked above, earmarking the strongest branch in the canopy.

7.15 a.m.

I couldn't remember when I'd last been engulfed in such beautiful silence.

Almost two hours had passed since I'd removed myself from the chaos of my life. No children clattered around my feet. No radio blared pop songs from the kitchen windowsill. There was no constant spin of the washing machine drum on another endless cycle. Nothing to distract me from my thoughts – just the gentle hum of motorway traffic in the distance.

I knew it wouldn't have mattered if I'd remained in that house another week, month or for the next fifty years. After all the punches and kicks I'd taken and inflicted, I could not return.

I picked at clumps of moss flourishing on the trunk's damp bark and recalled the day it all became too much for me to bear. I'd been standing motionless in the bathroom as the echo of her grief escaped from behind our closed bedroom door. Her sobbing had become louder and sharper until it pierced my skin and barrelled its way through my veins and up into my head. It felt ready to burst, so I clamped my sweating palms over my ears as if to stop it. But all I heard was the rapid beat of my own wretched heart – a hollow, despicable ticking inside a soulless carcass.

Then it hit me with a force so sudden that I collapsed to the bathroom floor. *There is a way out of all of this.* I could rid myself of my torment if I accepted my life had run its course and committed suicide.

Immediately, the throbbing in my head had begun to ease.

If I'd forgiven her or she'd forgiven me or if we'd made a Faustian pact to forget everything and everyone that had come between us, it wouldn't have mattered. It was simply too late; we were irreparable. Stones had been cast and glasshouses lay in shards all around us. Inside I was dead; it was time for my exterior to follow suit.

I'd let out a long breath I wasn't aware I was holding and left the bathroom. A decision of such magnitude would be perceived as drastic to most, but to the desperate, it was obvious. It would mean I could finally gain control of my life, even if it was only to end it. And now that I understood the sole purpose for living was the planning of my death, I felt my burden rise from my shoulders.

Like her, I had mourned, but silently and for different reasons. I'd wept for what she had done to us all; I'd wept for the future we should have enjoyed together and for the past she had worked so hard to destroy. We had wept together and apart for so long, grieving for contradictory losses. Now she would weep alone.

Over the following months, I wore my supportive husband, stable parent and loyal friend masks convincingly. But, underneath, I remained preoccupied with being the master of my own demise. Searching for the right time, the right place and the right means to my end became an obsession. I mulled over options, from an exhaust fume–filled garage to acquiring a shotgun licence, from leaping off a motorway bridge to tying breeze blocks around my ankles and throwing myself into the Blisworth canal.

But for the sake of the children, first I had to tend to her, as she needed to regain the tools to resume her journey before the wind was knocked out of her sails again. So I took control of the day-to-day nurturing and support of our family until her physical and mental health gradually improved. And as she began to blossom, my decay continued.

There would never be a good time for her to discover her husband had taken his own life. But I knew even at her lowest point, she was stronger than me. Eventually she would rise from my ashes to raise our children to the best of her ability. What she would tell them of my death would be for her to decide. I had loved them dearly, but they weren't wise enough to see who their father really was or to identify his flaws. I hoped she might keep it that way.

Meanwhile I'd settled on a method, and a location I knew like the back of my hand. A place where one of my darkest secrets lay buried – the woods near to our home.

My plan was simple. I would climb a tree, loop the four metres of rope over the branch and affix a noose around my neck. Then I'd let myself drop and pray the severing of my spinal cord would accelerate the speed of the inevitable. I hoped my life wouldn't slowly drain away from its stranglehold instead.

It was what I had to do. What I had planned to do. What I had been to the woods many times to do.

Only, when it came to the crunch, the end result was always the same. I couldn't do it. Five attempts over two weeks had finished with me facing the canopy of trees with the rope in my hand but unable to take that final, fatal step. And, after a time, I'd return home to her as broken as when I'd left.

Now, here I was again.

It wasn't the act of killing myself I feared, because there was little in the world left to scare or scar me. Nor was it guilt at leaving my children without a father, because I'd already disconnected myself from them without anyone noticing.

What terrified me was the fear of not knowing what lay beyond my life. My best hope was the perpetual nothingness of purgatory. The worst was a continuation of how I was living now, only with flames scorching my heels. I wanted death to remove me from my misery and not replace it with something equally as ghastly.

But how could I be sure it would? There was no guidebook or wise old sage to confirm I wouldn't be jumping from the frying pan into the fire. So my only escape route was a risk I had become too afraid to take. But was it the only escape route?

'What if you just walked away?' The voice came so suddenly and so unexpectedly, I thought it belonged to somebody else. I looked around, but the woods remained empty.

'Your death doesn't necessarily have to be as a result of a physical act,' the voice continued, almost singsong-like. 'What if you just erased the last thirty-three years and simply disappeared?'

I nodded slowly.

'You can never be part of the lives of anyone you know again. You'll have to force yourself not to worry about them or contact them. She'll assume you've had an accident but can't be found, and then eventually she'll come to terms with her loss and move on. It'll be better for all of you in the long run.'

While I couldn't kill myself, I could do all of that. I wondered why I hadn't considered it earlier. But when you're sinking in the depths of depression and think you've found an escape route, you stop searching for an alternative.

'What's stopping you from going right now? You've wasted enough time already.'

Yes, you're right, I thought. I had already whispered goodbye to every significant person in my life, blowing all but one into the air like dandelion seed heads. So before alarm bells rang, I took a deep breath, released my clenched fists and picked myself up from the tree trunk with a renewed sense of hope.

I placed the rope back in its rightful place and left the woods as a man who no longer existed.

1.15 p.m.

It's remarkable how much ground you can cover by walking without purpose. With no direction in mind or inner compass to guide me one way or the other, I resolved just to keep moving.

I followed the bright globe in the sky, across fields, pastures and sprawling housing estates, through tiny hamlets and over dual carriageway bridges. I passed a sign that read YOU ARE NOW LEAVING NORTHAMPTONSHIRE, THANK YOU FOR VISITING, and smiled. That's just what I'd been for all my years – a visitor.

Suffused with optimism, I recognised I'd always been too self-involved to absorb the world around me, or to appreciate its entirety. I'd never taken pleasure from simple delights like picking raspberries from roadside bushes, eating apples from orchards or drinking fresh water from brooks.

But modern life wasn't like the Mark Twain novels I'd read as a boy. Pollution had embittered the taste of the raspberries, the apples were sour and water doesn't really taste like water unless it's mixed with fluoride and flows from a tap.

None of that bothered me. My new life was just beginning and I was here to learn, to understand and to enjoy. By retreating I could advance. I had nowhere and everywhere to go. I would start afresh as the man I wanted to be, and not the man she had made me.

4.00 p.m.

The sun began to weigh heavy on my shoulders and my forehead was sore to the touch, so I untied my shirt from around my waist and used it to cover my head. A road sign ahead revealed I was a mile and a half from the Happy Acres holiday park we'd once driven past on our way to somewhere else to play happy family.

Ramshackle and surrounded by barbed-wire fencing, on the surface its name appeared ironic. She'd said then that it reminded her of a documentary we'd watched on Auschwitz. But the families staying in its shabby holiday homes obviously didn't share her view.

I entered through the open gates, held together by brown, flaked paint scraps and rust. Thirty or so static caravans were positioned in a large arc. Others had been thrown around like afterthoughts into more remote locations amongst overgrown hedgerows. Children filled the air with squeals; mums and dads played cricket with them; and grandparents sat listening to crackly medium-wave stations on portable transistor radios. I envied the simplicity of their happiness.

A small café kiosk caught my eye, bordered by sun-faded plastic tables and chairs. Checking my pockets for change, I grinned when I found a crumpled twenty-pound note that must have survived the washday. Already the new Simon was proving luckier than the last. I ordered a cola from an uninterested girl behind the counter, who rolled her eyes as my change cleared out her cash register.

I remained in my plastic chair well into the evening as a spectator, studying the holidaymakers like it was my first visit to earth. I'd forgotten what family life could be like – the way we were before she disembodied me.

I stopped myself. I would not think about her and the repercussions of her actions. I was no longer a bit-part player in her pantomime.

8.35 p.m.

The smell of barbecues and scented candles wafted through the caravan park as night approached. I presumed I'd been invisible to everyone's radar until a bare-chested, middle-aged man ambled towards my seat at the café. He explained his wife had spotted me throughout the afternoon sitting alone, and invited me to join his family for some grilled food.

I gratefully obliged and filled my stomach with charred hotdogs until my belt buckle pinched my belly. I listened more than I spoke. And when they asked questions about my origins and my length of stay, I lied. I explained I'd been inspired by a celebrity sportsman who'd recently completed a sponsored charity walk from John o' Groats to Land's End. Now I was doing the same, for the homeless.

I quickly learned how easy it was to be dishonest, especially to people who were willing to accept you at face value. No wonder my wife and my mother had found it so easy.

My hosts were impressed, and when they offered me a ten-pound note for my chosen charity, I neither felt guilty nor the need to explain how my charity began and ended at home.

Thanking them, I made my excuses and headed towards a cluster of caravans on the perimeter of the field. It wasn't hard to fathom which lay empty, and after a quick flip of a metal latch on a rear window, I discreetly climbed inside one.

The air was stale, the pillow was lumpy and stained with the sweat of strangers, and the starched woollen blanket scratched my chest. But I'd found myself a bed for the night. I wiped dirt from the inside of the window, looked out at my new surroundings, and smiled at the gifts a life without complication was bringing me.

Both my body and my mind were shattered. My calf muscles and heels throbbed, my forehead was singed and my lower back ached. But I paid scant attention to temporary pain.

Instead, I slept as soundly as a newborn baby that night. I had no dreams, no plans and most importantly, no regrets.

◆ ◆ ◆

Northampton, today

8.25 a.m.

Catherine sat in the dining room with her laptop computer resting on the mahogany table. She moved it slightly to look at the photograph of New York's Fifth Avenue printed on the placemat underneath and smiled. She hoped they'd find the time to return there before the year was out.

According to the date on the message, James's most recent email had been sent in the early hours of that morning. It had been a month since her eldest son had last flown home to visit, but travelling around the world was part and parcel of his life now, and she'd grown accustomed to it. Despite the demands of his career, he regularly kept her up to speed on his antics. And when he couldn't find time to jot down a few lines, even just to say hello or that he'd write more later, she'd log on to his website or Facebook profile to read his updates. Robbie had tried to demonstrate how easy it was to Skype and FaceTime, but she'd only just mastered how to record the soaps on the TV. One thing at a time, she'd told him.

The act of picking up a fountain pen and writing a letter was something she missed. She was disappointed that most people found it too time-consuming or old-fashioned to put pen to paper instead of finger to keyboard. But it had been years since she'd last sat down and written anything herself, apart from her signature on business contracts.

Emily had only just left the house and would be back in the evening to collect her for dinner. That gave her ample time to reply to James and order those biographies she'd been meaning to buy from Amazon. But before she could begin any of that, a knock at the door interrupted her. She removed her reading glasses, closed the lid of her laptop and went to answer it.

'Have you forgotten your purse again, darling?' she shouted as she pushed down the handle. But when the door opened, Emily wasn't standing there. It was an older gentleman.

She smiled. 'Oh, I'm sorry, I thought you were my daughter.'

The man smiled back, removed his fedora and slicked back some of the stray grey hairs the brim had loosened.

'Can I help you?' she asked.

He didn't reply but held her gaze and waited, patiently. She noted the quality of his three-piece tailored suit and his Mediterranean tan, and she was quite sure from just a cursory glance that his pale-blue tie was pure silk.

Although his continued silence was a little awkward, she didn't feel threatened. He was attractive, well groomed, and something about him felt familiar. Maybe she'd met him in Europe on a buying trip, but then how would he have known where to find her? *No, that's just silly*, she thought.

'What can I do for you?' she asked, politely.

After another pause, the man opened his mouth and began to speak.

'Hello, Kitty, it's been a long time.'

She was puzzled. *Nobody called me Kitty except for my father and . . .*

Her stomach dropped like she'd fallen thirty storeys in a split second.

CHAPTER TWO
CATHERINE

Northampton, twenty-five years earlier

5 June, 4.45 a.m.

My eyes stung like they'd been splashed with vinegar. In the space of twenty-four hours, I'd barely closed them. My whole life revolved around waiting for Simon to come home.

I'd gone to bed at midnight in the same clothes I'd worn all day, as if putting on my pyjamas would mean accepting it had drawn to a close without him. And as willing as I was for it to end, the thought of living through a second day like that frightened me.

I'd left our bedroom door ajar so I wouldn't miss the sound of the telephone's ring or a policeman's knock. And I lay perfectly still on top of the quilt, because being trapped between sheets and blankets might cost precious seconds in the race to get downstairs. I desperately wanted to sleep, but I was so anxious that the slightest crack or creak had me on tenterhooks, in case Simon was dashing across the landing to tell me it'd all been a silly misunderstanding.

I imagined how he'd hold me tighter than I'd ever been held before, and those horrible twenty-four hours would become a bad memory. Those long, long hours since I'd last shared my bed with him. Already, I missed hearing him whistling 'Hotel California' to himself as he mowed the lawn, or watching him catch ladybirds in marmalade jars with Robbie. I missed feeling his warm breath on my neck as he slept. Where was the man who'd hugged me as I cried myself to sleep and begged God to bring back my little boy?

My eyes were still open when dawn broke. It was a new day but I still ached from the torture of the last.

8.10 a.m.

'Where's Daddy?' asked James suddenly, his eyes looking past the kitchen door and towards the hallway.

'Um, he's gone to work early,' I lied, and swiftly changed the subject.

I'd tried my best to pretend everything was normal when the kids woke up. But as they finished their toast and packed books inside bags, my hugs lasted longer than usual as I tried to feel Simon inside them. Paula had volunteered to take them to school for me while I poured my fourth coffee of the morning and waited for Roger.

'That's just going to put you more on edge,' she said, pointing to the mug then wagging her finger like a schoolma'am.

'It's the only thing keeping me sane,' I replied, and paused to stare at my hands to see if they were still wobbling. 'What if he doesn't come back, Paula?' I whispered out of James's earshot. 'How can I carry on without him?'

'Hey, hey, hey, I will not allow you to think like that,' she replied, holding my hand firmly. 'After the hell the two of you have been through, Roger will move heaven and earth to bring him home.'

'But what if he can't?'

'You mark my words, they will find him.'

I nodded because I knew she was right.

'I'll take Emily with me as well if you like,' she suggested, already pulling the pink stroller from the cupboard under the stairs.

'Thank you,' I replied gratefully, just as Roger arrived, accompanied by a stern-looking uniformed policewoman he introduced as WPC Williams. Paula ushered the kids out of the back door before they saw my visitors. We sat at the kitchen table and they took out their pens and pocket notebooks.

'When was the last time you saw your husband, Mrs Nicholson?' WPC Williams began. I didn't like her scowl when she said 'your husband'.

'Two nights ago. He wanted to watch *News at Ten* but I was tired, so I kissed him goodnight and went to bed.'

'Do you remember what time he joined you?'

'No, but I know he was there.'

'How? Did you see him or talk to him?'

'No, I'm just sure he was.'

'But it's possible he might not have been? I mean, he could have actually left that night?'

'Well, I suppose so, yes.' I wracked my brains to recall if I'd felt Simon at all during the night, but I drew a blank. Then WPC Williams changed her direction.

'Was everything all right with your marriage?'

'Of course,' I replied, defensively.

'Did Simon have any money problems? Did he show signs of stress at work?'

'No, nothing at all.' I didn't appreciate the way she referred to him in the past tense.

'You haven't considered the possibility there might be someone else?'

That caught me by surprise. It had never crossed my mind, not even for a second. 'No, he wouldn't do that.'

'I think Catherine's right,' added Roger. 'Simon's not that kind of guy. Family means everything to him.'

'Only it happens more often than you think—'

I cut her off forcefully. 'I told you, no. My husband does not have affairs.'

'Has he ever disappeared before?'

'No.'

'Even just for a few hours?'

'No.'

'Has he ever threatened to leave?'

'No!' My hackles were up and my head buzzed. I glanced at the digital clock on the oven and hoped the questions would end soon.

'Have there been any family problems lately?'

Roger and I glanced at each other and I felt my throat tighten.

'Only what I told you about in the car,' Roger replied for me.

'Right. And how did Simon deal with that?'

I swallowed hard. 'It's been a tough fifteen months for all of us, but we've managed to get through it. He was very supportive.'

'I can only imagine. But you don't think it has anything to do with why Simon left?'

'Stop saying he's left!' I snapped. 'My husband has gone missing.'

'That's not what Yvette meant,' Roger replied, glaring at his tactless colleague. 'I'm sorry, Catherine, we just need to look at all possibilities.'

'You mean you think it's a possibility he could have walked out on us?'

'No, no, I don't. But please bear with us. We're almost done.'

The questions finished after a long half-hour, when all the avenues we'd explored ended in cul-de-sacs. Roger asked for a recent photograph of Simon, so I pulled out a padded envelope of pictures I'd yet to place into albums from the kitchen drawer.

I'd taken them two Christmases ago, the last time our family was complete. When it was all of us together, not six minus one. Now I was terrified it was about to become minus two.

The photo was from early on Christmas Day, when James had been dancing and miming to his new Michael Jackson CD while Robbie was in his own prehistoric world, with a Diplodocus and something else with a spiny back fighting for power. Emily had been making herself giggle popping bubble wrap with her feet.

I recalled how Simon seemed oblivious to the wonderful chaos. Instead, he'd looked around at the family he'd helped create like he'd never seen them before. In one picture, he seemed fixated by the face in the high chair smiling back at him. There was something blank about his expression that wasn't the Simon I remembered. So I picked another photo instead: all smiles. That's how I wanted people to see him, as my Simon. Because that's the Simon I desperately needed to come home.

12.45 p.m.

Word of Simon's disappearance spread like wildfire because it had to. If he was lying injured somewhere, then time was of the essence to find him. So, under police supervision, our friends in the village formed a search party.

Dozens of people of all ages, along with neighbours we'd never met, hunted for him in fields, along country roads, in copses and church grounds. Police divers tackled streams, ponds and canals.

I stood by the fence in the back garden with my arms wrapped around myself, willing my tremors to stop. I watched as blurred figures fanned out across the fields. I dreaded hearing a voice suddenly shouting that they'd found something. But the sound of their feet trampling the crops was all the wind carried back to me.

Later, I joined Roger and WPC Williams in searching the house from top to bottom for anything out of the ordinary. It was invasive, but I gritted my teeth and accepted it because I knew they had a job to do.

We searched through the antique writing bureau, paper by paper, folder by folder, ploughing through old bank statements and phone bills for 'signs of unusual activity'. Simon's passport, chequebook and bank card were in their usual place in the drawer, next to mine. I examined each of the scores of receipts he kept in shoeboxes, dating back years.

Elsewhere, police checked his records with his doctor and trawled through his office paperwork with Steven. Neighbours were questioned, and even the milkman and our poor paperboy were given the third degree. But Simon simply hadn't been seen.

WPC Williams asked me to narrow down what he might have been wearing, so I rummaged through his wardrobe. Suddenly I recalled Oscar waiting nervously by the front door the day before. It hadn't registered at the time, but Simon's running shoes had been by the dog's side. This puzzled me. It meant he hadn't, as I'd presumed, gone for a jog. So WPC Williams was right: he could have disappeared during the night. But where had he gone so late, or so early, and why? And why hadn't he taken his wallet or keys?

'How are you getting on there, Mrs Nicholson?' yelled WPC Williams from the foot of the stairs. 'Have you found anything?'

'No, I'll be down in a minute,' I lied, and perched on the ottoman trying to fathom out the unfathomable. I don't know why, but I felt it best to keep my realisation to myself. She doubted him already and I wasn't keen to prove the smug cow right.

With the arrival of a *Herald & Post* reporter came police reinforcements in a transit van. Three handlers with barking German shepherd sniffer dogs came into the house to pick up a scent from Simon's clothes. Oscar cowered in the pantry, unable to understand why his world had become such a confusing, noisy place.

'I know how you feel,' I whispered, and bent down to kiss his head.

5.15 p.m.

I'd had no choice but to lie to the children again when I'd picked them up from school in the car. Robbie and James punched their fists in the air when I said I was taking them to the cinema to see a new Disney film.

I'd accepted Roger's advice and got them out of the village so they wouldn't ask why so many people were in the streets and fields on a weekday. I wanted to keep them in a world of cartoon make-believe before reality hit them. As they crammed in as much popcorn and as many iced lollipops as their mouths allowed, I casually mentioned that Daddy had been home at lunchtime to pick up some fresh clothes.

'He's flying to a different country for work, in a huge plane, like the one we flew in to Spain,' I said. 'He'll only be gone for a few days.'

They loved the thought of him on a big adventure somewhere across the sea. Robbie said it made him sound like Indiana Jones.

'And Daddy asked me to take you all to the cinema for a treat and to remind you he loves you very much and he'll be home soon.'

'Thanks, Daddy!' shouted James, lifting his head up to the sky to wave to an imaginary aeroplane.

As soon as the film's opening credits began, I wondered if an early evening out to cover up a gigantic lie was the right thing to do. But how could I expect them to understand their dad had vanished when I didn't understand it myself? I couldn't tell them the truth because I didn't know what the truth was.

I stared at the screen for an hour and a half, not taking in a single word or animated image. I couldn't stop thinking about Simon's running shoes. If he hadn't gone for a run when he left the house, then where had he gone? And why? I went round in so many circles I began to feel queasy.

But amongst the confusion, I was still certain of one thing. Simon hadn't left us of his own free will.

8.40 p.m.

I pulled into the drive soon after fading daylight forced the search party to come to a halt. A tired Robbie and James trudged up the staircase and into the bathroom to brush their teeth. I hurried into the kitchen and found Steven and Baishali, who'd brought Emily back from Paula's house.

'Have you heard anything?' I asked hopefully.

'Sorry,' she replied, and I felt my bottom lip quiver. She looked at me apologetically and rose to her feet to hug me. But I put my hands up to form a barrier.

'I'm okay, honestly. I'd better check on the kids.'

'I wasn't sure whether to tell you this,' she began, and then stopped.

'Tell me what?' As much as I loved her, Baishali's fear of saying the wrong thing could be frustrating at times, especially now, when all I needed was the truth.

'You had a couple of visitors earlier.'

'Who?'

'Arthur and Shirley,' she replied, then stared at the floor like a guilty child.

I sighed. In the chaos of those twenty-four hours, I'd asked Roger to fill in Simon's father and stepmother, and then promptly forgot about them. I was too tired to go into battle tonight.

'I wouldn't keep them waiting for too long,' added Baishali, reading my mind. 'You know Shirley's like a dog with a bone if she thinks someone's not telling her something.'

I nodded, scared that if I spoke, my voice might crack. She could tell, and this time, I let her hug me.

'Try not to worry. Simon will be back soon.' She leaned back from me and gave me an encouraging smile. But all I could wonder was how many times people would tell me that before it came true.

◆ ◆ ◆

SIMON

Luton, twenty-five years earlier

5 June, 8.40 a.m.

Cars and lorries thundered past the motorway slip road as my feet sank into the soggy grass verge.

With little money and no alternative means, hitchhiking would be the best way to reach London, provided I could persuade a driver to take pity on me. But both man and machine appeared deliberately oblivious to my optimistic thumb. However, I had patience on my side.

After a restful night in my tatty caravan, a family car with a roof rack strapped full of weathered plastic suitcases had parked by my side early in the morning. With minimum fuss, I'd grabbed my clothes and scrambled out of the rear window like a fugitive, dressing as I ran.

My pace slowed when I reached the gates, then I paused at the sound of a child's scream. One of the new arrivals, a little boy of no more than three years, was unable to contain his excitement and had run eagerly towards the caravan. He must have tripped and taken the brunt of the impact on his knees.

As I watched, his mum discarded her handbag, ran around the car and scooped him up in her arms. Fatherhood had taught me the difference between genuine and exaggerated tears. The boy knew what he was about. The longer he made his pain visible, the longer he'd remain her priority.

Not that this had ever worked for me with my own mother. The last time I'd seen her had been some twenty years earlier – when I'd longed for her death.

My father, Arthur, was a loyal but weak man whose only mistake in his mediocre life had been to offer his heart to a transient soul.

Doreen was his polar opposite – a flighty, part-time wife and parent who sauntered in and out of our lives through her own set of revolving doors.

When she gave us her attention, she was fun, attentive and loving. You could feel her presence long before she made her entrance into a room. Her infectious laughter filled corners my father and I couldn't reach. She and I would giggle as we built dens in the living room using polyester bedsheets draped over the sofa. We'd crawl inside to escape the world, and pick at crumbled digestive biscuits from the tin filled with cast-offs from the supermarket's damaged-goods shelf.

But Arthur and I only ever had the woman we loved on loan. It never mattered how long she remained in our company – a month, six months, maybe a year if we were fortunate – we always kept one eye on the clock, waiting for the inevitable.

Doreen's extramarital liaisons were both frequent and humiliating. Sometimes it only took a stranger's wink and a sniff of greener grass and she'd dig her way out to the other side. Once she absconded with the local pub landlord to work in his new premises in Sunderland. Then a Pan Am pilot with an American twang promised to show her the world: she reached as far as Birmingham before he cast her aside.

And there were her extended stays in London with the one my parents only argued about when they thought I was sleeping. Doreen was terrified of being happy, but equally frightened of being alone. Anytime she reached the middle ground, she ran either from us or to us. Just because I grew accustomed to it, didn't mean it made sense.

'I get suffocated, Simon,' she once strived to explain. I'd caught her one Saturday teatime trying to slip away without being noticed. She knelt with her suitcase in one hand and my hand in the other, talking to a six-year-old like he knew how to navigate the trenches of the heart.

'I love you and your dad, but I need more,' she cried, then closed the front door and disappeared in a stranger's blue Austin Healey.

We always forgave her dramatic vignettes. Eventually her departures came as a relief, as anticipating the melancholy they induced was far worse than the actual rejection. When I wished her dead, it was only to force the merry-go-round to stop.

Even today, as a grown man about to embark on a brand-new life, a small part of me still ached for my mother's love, despite myself. After all the promises she'd broken and the tears I'd shed, I needed her to know she was forgiven before I moved on. And London was her last known location.

The heavens opened and the rain poured down just as a car's indicator flashed and it pulled over up ahead. I ran towards it.

My wife's actions had made me understand there were times when there was no other option but to leave everything behind, and to hell with the ramifications. And I had a better reason to leave my family than Doreen ever believed she'd had.

Hemel Hempstead

1.10 p.m.

After being dropped off a few miles south of Luton, I attached myself to a metal chair in a motorway service station and waited patiently for the rain to stop.

I was sitting near an oil heater to help dry my damp clothes. I wedged a bunch of napkins under the table leg to stop it from rocking on the uneven floor tiles. A stocky man in a red cap and apron behind the counter frequently took pity on me, refilling my mug with hot tea for no charge.

I mulled over what I might say to my mother when I found her. I'd followed her once before. I'd been thirteen years old when she suddenly began writing me letters from her new home in London. She'd reassure me I was never far from her thoughts – words I'd longed to hear in the five months since she'd last left. And I read each sentence again and again until I knew them off by heart.

I'd missed her too, and even though it wasn't something I felt I could share with my father, I suspected he felt the same. So I kept our correspondence covert. I'd intercept the postman and squirrel away her letters between books about building designs on my bedroom shelf. I'd reply hastily, recounting my day-to-day activities, life at my senior school and the things I'd do with my friends. I even told her about a wonderful girl I'd met.

Then, out of the blue, Doreen asked me to visit her. She told me she was sharing a house with a friend and had a spare room. It was mine to use if I wanted it. Doreen was working in a nearby restaurant and had saved some money, so offered to send me the train fare.

I wrestled with my conscience before I broached the subject with my father. He was surprised, and probably a little disgruntled to learn it wasn't just his wife who kept secrets from him. He tried to make increasingly flimsy excuses as to why I shouldn't go, warning me she would only hurt me again.

'I had a full head of hair when I met her – look at me now,' he said, clutching at straws and pointing to his shiny dome. 'She'll do the same to you, Simon.'

But we both knew his reluctance was because he was scared I'd prefer to stay with my mysterious, occasional mother over my pedestrian, full-time, bald father. I reassured him it wasn't the case, but I admit, I briefly considered it. Although Arthur had yet to fail me, Doreen Nicholson's secret life held an overpowering allure.

I imagined her living in a beautifully furnished home where she spent her nights dressed up to the nines, holding glamorous parties for London's elite. And I needed to experience first-hand just how that world took preference over mine. Eventually my father had relented and let me go, but he insisted on paying for the ticket himself – making sure it was a return.

As a grown man, I now recognised Doreen's and my reasons for craving new lives were at odds, but our actions mimicked each other's. I was beginning to understand her like I'd never understood anyone else before.

London

5.30 p.m.

I was sandwiched between four snoozing Yorkshire terriers in the back seat of a Morris Minor when I reached the outskirts of London. I'd approached an elderly couple by the service station's petrol pumps and they'd agreed to deliver me to the capital. An eight-track played *John Denver's Greatest Hits* on a loop while they trundled along the motorway at no more than forty-five miles an hour. I only realised the irony of my singing along to 'Take Me Home, Country Roads' by the second chorus.

I absent-mindedly fumbled with the rotating bezel on my watch – the only gift Doreen had given me that I'd kept – and stared through the window at a train bursting out from a tunnel in the distance.

I remembered my mother standing, waiting for my train twenty years earlier, taking nervous drags from an unfiltered cigarette as it pulled into the platform. Nicotine and lavender perfume clung to my coat as she pulled me to her chest, her falling tears glistening on her cheeks and bouncing off my lapels.

'It's so good to see my baby,' she cried. 'You have no idea.'

I did, because I felt exactly the same.

We perched on the top deck of a red double-decker bus as we made our way to her home in East London's Bromley-by-Bow. Doreen draped an arm around my shoulders and intermittently kissed the top of my head as the wind raced through my hair. I'd always had a fascination with buildings, and was as hypnotised by the architecture we passed as by the woman who held me. I sketched notable landmarks like the Houses of Parliament and St Paul's Cathedral in my jotter to show Steven when I returned home. He shared my obsession with creatively designed, historic buildings. They had dominated the city for generations, ever-present fixtures that wouldn't uproot themselves if a better location made itself known.

'We're here,' my mother finally announced with a nervous smile, as if to encourage mine in return. But I struggled to find any enthusiasm for the cramped little terraced house on the square before me. It was squeezed in between dozens more, like a concertina, in an austere backstreet square. I knew my disappointment secretly mirrored hers. *It doesn't matter*, I tried to convince myself, *I'm with my mum*.

She unlocked the front door, and as the sun struck her face, I saw the tears she'd wept had made her make-up drip like ink. Behind her heavily disguised eyes lay the ghost of a purple bruise.

And as she lifted up my suitcase and walked into the corridor, the sleeves of her floral dress rose a little to reveal yellow and blue circular blotches scattered randomly about her wrists. I didn't mention them.

Inside, Doreen's house was neat but sparsely furnished, and hadn't seen a lick of paint since the last war. Strips of wallpaper had once made futile attempts to escape by peeling themselves from the walls, but sticky tape secured them back into place. Cigarette smoke had stained the ceiling above a blanched armchair from which stuffing leaked. A large pair of scuffed men's boots lay tossed to the side in front of her white stilettos.

'Whose are those?' I asked.

'Oh, they belong to a friend,' she replied.

And before I could delve any further, a monster appeared.

◆ ◆ ◆

Northampton, today

8.27 a.m.

'Simon . . .'

She whispered his name, as though the word was trapped in her last breath and she could barely find the strength to shape her lips around it.

'Yes, Kitty,' came his measured reply.

She gripped the door handle like a life belt. She was terrified that if she let go, her legs would buckle beneath her and she'd drown in emotions she'd cast adrift decades ago.

In the few moments she took to regain her composure, her mind raced nineteen to the dozen. At first, she considered she might be having a stroke, and that her brain was playing tricks on her. Then she wondered if the disease they'd told her she'd beaten had returned to play one final, callous joke. She focused on the olive-green eyes before her, eyes that had once given her everything she'd ever wanted, then cruelly snatched it away.

'Are you all right?' he asked. He'd anticipated his reappearance would be likely to shock her, but he was concerned he might have to catch her if she fainted.

Meanwhile she was snapping out of her thoughts. No, he definitely wasn't a figment of her imagination. He was very real. The man who'd fallen from the branches of their family tree twenty-five years ago; the man she had loved then lost; the man who had been no more than a ghost for so long was standing on her doorstep.

She cleared her throat and her voice reappeared, albeit as little more than a croak. The word she produced was one that had preceded so many of her unuttered questions, past and present.

'Why?' she asked.

'May I come in?' he replied, having faith that her answer would be yes. Instead, she said nothing and stood firm. He tried to read the expression on a face he no longer knew, until eventually she turned aside and allowed him through the porch and into the living room.

As he moved inside, her eyes looked beyond the front garden to see if anyone else had witnessed his resurrection. But, like the day he had vanished, he was invisible. She inhaled all the fresh air her lungs would allow before she breathed in that belonging to the dead.

Then she quietly closed the door.

CHAPTER THREE

SIMON

London, twenty-five years earlier

6 June, 5.20 a.m.

Street-sweepers brushed discarded soft drink cans and polystyrene fast-food boxes from London's pavements into black plastic bin bags. The previous day's rainstorm had washed away the stale, humid air and brought with it an early-morning chill. I pulled my shirt cuffs down over my cold hands, perched on the wall outside the British Library and leaned back on the railings, hoping it would be warmer inside when it opened later. I'd spent the night in a homeless shelter at a church, but awoke early to get a head start on my day.

Now I passed the time by staring at the blank faces of the daybreak workers who sleepwalked past me. Any one of them over a certain age could have been Kenneth Jagger.

My first recollection of the monster that lived with my mother was of his iron-girder legs pounding down Doreen's stairs. The solid brick walls had seemed to quake under each footstep. Then, when he reached us, Kenneth briefly eyed me up and down, and without saying a word, lumbered into another room. I looked at my mother quizzically. She answered with a forced smile.

My loathing of Kenneth was immediate, intense and plainly reciprocated. I had never been in close proximity to such an intimidating presence. He wore a thick, black moustache and his receding hairline was poorly disguised with a limp Brylcreem quiff. Dark hairs crawled across his broad shoulders like spider's legs and poked out of the holes in his dirty white T-shirt.

A chequered history was etched across his gnarly face – a portrait of his environment. A collection of clumsily self-inked gun and knife tattoos on his forearms and the backs of his hands warned he preferred to be feared, not befriended. A crimson heart with a black dagger penetrating the name 'Doreen' sat off-centre on his left bicep. Its faded colouring indicated he had been a part of her life a lot longer than I.

As Doreen began to pull him aside into their tiny concrete backyard, I noted a scrapbook lying on the sideboard. He saw me looking and nodded his head as if to say 'open it up'. It was more an order than a request.

Inside was a potted history of the man in the form of newspaper cuttings.

Kenneth Jagger – or 'Jagger the Dagger', as the press had branded him – was a gangster of sorts – enough of a wrong'un to earn vibrant stories every time the police questioned him in connection with armed robberies. Knives were his weapon of choice. His was a wasted life, blighted by sporadic stays at Her Majesty's pleasure, but never a punishment so harsh as to encourage him to see the error of his ways.

By the mid-1960s, Kenneth had remained a small fish in a crowded pond. As a career criminal, he had seen meagre returns. All he had under his control were his aspirations, and Doreen. According to one report about his conviction for beating and robbing a postmaster, he'd been released from prison shortly after my mother had last walked away from us. I realised he must have been the one my parents argued about behind closed doors.

Kenneth and Doreen returned to find me engrossed in his criminal CV. If he thought something like that might impress me, he'd already misjudged me. And Doreen's apprehensive expression told me she, too, sensed the atmosphere that hung thick in the air like her cigarette smoke.

'Right, let's get the tea on,' she offered in an overly chirpy voice, like Barbara Windsor in a *Carry On* film. She nervously tapped her bottom lip with her finger. 'Do you want to give me a hand, Simon?'

'How do you know him?' I whispered as she bustled me into the kitchenette.

'Kenny's an old friend,' she continued without making eye contact, and focused on peeling potatoes and dropping them into a deep-fat fryer.

'But why is he here? With us?'

'He lives here, Simon.'

I glared at her, waiting for a better explanation, but there was none. I scowled at Doreen, unable to reconcile the carefree life she'd led in my imagination with the squalid reality before me. The silence loomed heavy between us as we made our first, and last, meal together.

1.50 p.m.

I'd sifted through mountains of electoral registers in the library dating back two decades, but drew a blank in trying to find any trace of Doreen. It was possible – and given her history, quite likely – she had moved on from East London. But the pain etched into her face the night my father and I turned her away from our door for the first time had told me she'd resigned herself to her fate. And that lay with Kenneth.

So I relied on my hazy memory, a London street map I'd smuggled out under my shirt, and several buses to get me to Bromley-by-Bow.

I recalled Doreen's futile attempts to gloss over the sour mood between Kenneth and me that day by talking incessantly. He'd had little to say, and stared menacingly at me to relay his feelings instead. I all but ignored him, frightened to even make eye contact. She'd had everything she could possibly have needed with my father and me, but had discarded it for a pitiful existence with a worthless man. It made no sense.

'How long's he here for?' Kenneth suddenly spat, then stuffed his face with another chip sandwich. Tomato ketchup trickled down his chin like lava.

'Don't be like that, Kenny,' Doreen replied gently. Around my father she was the life and soul of the house, but around Kenneth, she was subservient. I didn't like this version of her.

Doreen asked me about school and I explained how I planned to go to university and study architecture. She smiled warmly. Kenneth just laughed.

'Poncey load of crap,' he roared. 'University. Load of bollocks.'

'Why?' I asked – the first time I'd dared to speak to him.

'You should get a proper job. Get out there and work instead of learning rubbish.'

'I'm thirteen, and I can't train to be an architect if I don't pass my exams.'

'Listen, kid, I was in the boxing ring and earning money working on the markets when I was your age, not wasting my time.'

'Well, my dad doesn't think it's a waste of time.' I directed this at Doreen. Her eyes remained fixed on the table.

'What does that pussy know? Someone needs to make a man of you.'

I was aware cockiness probably wasn't the best way forward with a man like Kenneth, but my brain wasn't listening. 'Like you?'

'What did you say?'

'Nothing.' I looked down at my plate.

'You think you're better than me, don't you?' he continued, a volcano preparing to erupt. 'Coming down here with your big bloody ideas. Well, you'll never be better than me – you're fuck all.'

I looked to Doreen for support, but she said nothing. Then my ability to self-censor completely evaporated.

'So I should stab someone and waste my life in prison, then – would that be better, Kenny?'

He banged both fists on the table. 'You know what I've got? Respect. And you can't buy that.'

And before I could process what was happening, he'd thrown his chair to one side, and I was six inches off the ground, pinned to a wall by an arm the size of an anchor. His cheeks had exploded in a rainbow of reds.

'You ever look down your nose at me again and I swear to God, I'll fucking kill you,' he shouted, as bread and potato bullets flew from his mouth and sprayed my face.

'Kenny, no!' shouted Doreen finally. She came towards us and tried to grab his arm. He swivelled around and her cheek took the brunt of the back of his hand. It sent her sprawling to the bare floorboards.

'Leave her alone, you bastard!' I yelled before he punched me in the stomach, winding me, and then clamped me tighter so I struggled to breathe.

'Stop it, you're hurting him,' pleaded Doreen, smearing a trickle of blood from her lip across a ghostly pale face.

'Maybe this'll teach him a lesson,' he replied, pulling his arm back to punch me again.

'You can't do that to your own son!' she screamed.

He hesitated for a moment before letting me drop to a heap on the floor.

'I told you then to get rid of him,' he fired back before storming out of the dining room. The front door slammed as I fought for breath, and time temporarily stood still.

'Why did you say that?' I gasped at last, utterly confused.

'I'm sorry,' she sobbed.

'He isn't my father – Arthur's my dad.'

'You have two, Simon. I just wanted you to get to know each other.'

Doreen attempted an explanation but I refused to listen. The truth was out, and so was I. I hadn't even unpacked my suitcase when I picked it up and left. She ran up the street behind me, begging me to stay, naively believing Kenneth and I could work through our differences. But, as always, she was fooling herself.

Arthur knew something had gone terribly wrong when I called from a telephone box at Northampton station, begging him to pick me up the same day he'd dropped me off. But he never enquired as to what had happened and I never volunteered a reason why. I think he knew but, secretly, he was just grateful I'd returned to him.

I didn't reveal to anyone the truth of my heritage. I locked Kenneth in a box inside my head and I only thought about him again when Doreen reappeared a few months later on the eve of my fourteenth birthday. As three disconnected souls gathered in our hallway, Arthur and I knew we were too exhausted to go through the charade again.

I ran to hide in my bedroom without speaking to her and sat on the floor, my back pressed against the door, listening. Downstairs, Arthur turned down her request for forgiveness. She begged with all her heart, but for the first time, he refused to relent. Eventually the front door closed and he retired to the kitchen, quietly weeping.

Later that night, I left the house and found Doreen waiting for me at the end of the garden. She thrust a green box into my hand.

'This is for you,' she said calmly, and tried to force a smile. 'Always remember your mum loves you, no matter how stupid she is.' Inside the box lay a handsome gold Rolex watch. By the time I looked up, Doreen was already walking away. I didn't try to stop her.

4.40 p.m.

My feet must have grazed every road and cobbled avenue in the East End before I chanced upon where my mother once lived. But the square's name wasn't the only thing to have changed over time.

A looming tower of concrete flats had ousted her row of dilapidated houses, casting a bleak shadow over an already grey landscape. Everything I'd deplored during my fateful last visit had been demolished and replaced by a more contemporary, but equally hideous, version of the same thing.

Disappointed, I gravitated towards a greasy spoon café to contrive a new plan of action. I ordered, and an elderly waitress with a raven-black beehive and a soup-stained apron carried a cup of tea to my table.

'Excuse me, are you from around here?' I asked as she shuffled away.

'All my life, darlin',' she muttered over her shoulder.

'I don't suppose you remember a woman who used to live in a house where those flats are now? Doreen Nicholson?'

She stopped, turned around. 'Hmm.' She thought. 'I knew a Doreen, but Nicholson weren't her last name. What does she look like?'

My father had never taken a photograph of my mother – well, if he had, none had ever hung on a wall inside our house. I could remember how she smelled, sounded, laughed and sang. I could picture the hint of grey hiding in the roots of her hair, how her large gold earrings made her lobes droop and the Bardot-like gap between her two front teeth. But for years I had struggled to put the pieces of a mental photofit together to create a whole woman.

'Ash-blonde hair, around five foot four, olive-green eyes, quite a loud laugh. She lived here about twenty years ago.'

The waitress headed towards a wall of framed photographs behind the counter, and unhooked one from the wall. 'This her?' she asked, handing it to me. Instantly I recognised one of the four women standing in their uniforms around a table.

'Yes, that's her.' I smiled and swallowed hard.

'Yeah, darlin', I knew old Dor. She lived around the square on and off for a while. Worked here with me, ooh, a good few years back now. Poor cow.'

Goosebumps spread across my arms. 'Did something happen to her?'

'Yeah, she passed away, darlin'. About fifteen years back.'

'What happened to her?'

'That bloody fella of hers gave her one pasting too many. Bounced her head off the walls, the Old Bill said. He was a vicious bastard . . . Gave her brain damage. She was in a coma and on machines for weeks before she went.'

I closed my eyes and exhaled as I muttered his name. 'Kenneth.'

'Yeah, that's the one. How did you know her then?'

'She was my mother.'

The waitress put on the glasses hanging from a copper chain around her neck and squinted. Then she sat herself down opposite me with a thump.

'Well, blow me, of course you are . . . You're Simon, ain't you? You have her eyes.' I was surprised she knew of my existence, let alone my name. 'Ooh darlin', Dor said you was a handsome little bugger,' she cackled as I offered an embarrassed smile.

'She talked about you a lot, you know. She had a baby photo of you in a little locket round her neck. Well, she did till he made her pawn it. Never forgave herself for letting you go.'

For a fleeting moment, I felt warm inside.

'What happened to Kenneth?'

'Locked him up again, didn't they? Told the coppers she went for him and it were self-defence, but the jury didn't believe him. Got banged up in the Scrubs for life this time.'

The waitress introduced herself as Maisy, and lit an unfiltered roll-up cigarette as she filled me in on the missing pieces of my mother's life. She recalled how Doreen and Kenneth began courting in their teens. When she fell pregnant with me, her parents and Kenneth had insisted she have an abortion. But when Doreen stubbornly refused, he pummelled her in the hope nature would force her to miscarry. Even then, I was a resilient soul.

The first of her many swift exits began with a stay at a cousin's house in the Midlands. There, Doreen met Arthur and he fell hopelessly in love with her. And aware she was pregnant with another man's child, he offered to take care of us both. It was all the security an unwed mother-to-be with a bastard inside her needed. Doreen had love for her new husband, but he was unable to capture the heart of a conflicted creature. And after I was born, she knew a sedentary family life would never equal a passionate one.

So she returned to Kenneth, alone. The abuse continued, and when it became intolerable, she rotated between the two men in her life.

'Please don't blame her, luv, she couldn't stop herself,' added Maisy, despairingly. 'She was a smashing girl, but she had a self-destructive streak. I got a feeling her old dad messed with her when she was a little 'un, if you know what I mean. I don't reckon she thought she deserved to be loved. She tried so hard to make Kenny a better fella, but he was born evil. You can't change nature.'

No, Maisy, you can't, I thought, catching my reflection in the café window.

Doreen reappeared in London for her final swansong, soon after we'd rejected her. 'She had nowhere left to go,' said Maisy. 'She knew Kenneth was gonna be the death of her, so she just held on as long as she could.'

And after the inevitable happened, her friends were unaware of where Arthur and I lived. With no savings to pay for a funeral, they clubbed together to offer her a respectable send-off instead of a pauper's grave.

'I still think about your old mum,' added Maisy, her eyes moistening. 'Always wished I could have done more to help her.'

'So do I, Maisy; so do I.'

7.50 p.m.

The grounds of Bow Cemetery were laid out in square blocks, making my mother's plot easy to locate. Her name, the years of her birth and death, and 'God Bless' were all her substitute family could afford to have engraved on the concrete headstone. 'Laing,' I repeated out loud. I hadn't even known her surname.

I tore out buttercups and long grasses and smoothed down stray pebbles with my hands. Then I lay on a bench close to her and soaked up the troubled tranquillity around me. I made up my mind to keep her company that night – my mother had spent too many evenings on her own.

My two fathers lived in contradictory worlds, but shared common ground when it came to her. They'd loved her too much but had handled her rejection in very different ways.

Doreen and Kenneth. I'd fought to be so different from the people who'd created me, but I'd ended up exactly the same.

8 June, 3.10 p.m.

'What the fuck do you want?' he began with a derisive snort.

I didn't reply. I sat calm and motionless, my palms face down on the table, staring at him, unafraid.

'Well? You expecting an apology or something? 'Cos you ain't gonna get one.'

Kenneth Jagger had planted himself behind a metal table in the visitors' room in Wormwood Scrubs prison, his arms folded defiantly. Only there was little for him to be defiant about, because he was a different man to the one I'd last encountered.

A merciless cancer had ravaged his bones and cut his body weight in half. His cheeks were sunken and hollow and chemotherapy had reduced his teeth to brown crumbs. The tattoos that once shone proudly on his tough, leathery skin had blurred and sagged as the muscles beneath them deflated. Doreen's name and the heart were barely distinguishable under a layer of raised welts, like he'd tried to cut her out of him with a blade. Eyes that once craved esteem were now drained of hope.

'Don't waste my time,' he spat.

'You don't have much left,' I replied.

He shot me a look that would have petrified the thirteen-year-old me. 'Last chance. Why are you here?'

I was there because I wanted to know if my rotten apple hadn't fallen far from his decaying tree. I'd dedicated much energy to trying to erase our biological link, but in the end, I was a chip off the old block.

'What did it feel like, killing my mother?' I asked.

He paused. Of all the things I could have asked, that wasn't the question he'd expected. 'Why did you do it?' or 'What's wrong with you?' possibly. But not an enquiry into the emotions involved in severing a human life.

'It was self-defence,' he finally replied. 'The bitch tried to knife me.'

'That wasn't what I asked.'

He frowned, puzzled as to what to make of his flesh and blood. So I repeated myself.

'I asked you what it felt like to kill my mother.'

'Why do you wanna know?'

'I just do.'

His faded, squinting eyes burrowed deep into mine. 'What happened to you?' he asked.

'I'm not scared of you anymore.'

'Well, you fucking should be.'

I shook my head. 'Kenneth, look at you – you're no threat to anyone. Your time has been and gone. You're a pathetic, dying old man who'll only ever be remembered for bringing misery to people's lives. Now answer my question please. What did it feel like, killing my mother?'

At first, he tried to pretend my words hadn't rung true, but his fallen expression betrayed him. From the corner of my eye, I watched the second hand of a wall clock rotate twice before he spoke again. And when he did, his bravado crumpled like a house of cards. His shoulders slumped and his arms unfolded. It was as if suddenly he was too tired to fight against the world any longer, like he'd realised I was the only person left who cared what he had to say. And he was almost grateful for my ear.

'It was the worst feeling in the world,' he said at last, his voice ravaged. 'And I've done a lot of bad shit in my time.' He cleared his throat and raised his eyes to mine. 'It was like someone else was killing her and I was watching but I couldn't stop them. I loved her so much, but I never really had her. She was gonna leave me again and find you.'

'Why?'

'It tore her up not being part of your life. I told her she weren't going, but she wouldn't listen. My Dor never bloody listened. She started packing her bags instead.' His eyes became watery but no tears fell. 'I grabbed her and pulled her away, but she reckoned she'd "wasted too much of her life" on me. She was always saying it, but this time she meant it. So I smacked her one, and once I started, I just kept going. I couldn't let you have her.'

I sat in silence and digested Kenneth's words. I felt no anger towards him – I'd invested too much time in hating the woman I'd built a life with to have any spare. Instead, I understood him.

'Thank you,' I said, finally. 'I have something for you.'

I glanced around the room to ensure I wouldn't be seen by a guard, then rolled up my shirtsleeve, unclasped the watch Doreen had once given me and pushed it across the table towards him. He covered it with his hand.

'Take it.'

'I don't want it.'

'She bought it for you, correct?'

'No, I got it myself.' I assumed that meant he'd stolen it.

'And she took it, without you knowing, to give to me.'

His head fell and he looked away. I realised I'd been wrong to presume.

'You wanted her to give it to me?' I asked. He remained inert. 'But you disliked me . . . You wanted her to terminate me.'

'I didn't wanna kid because I didn't wanna turn them into someone like me. I ain't got anything to show for my life but you. You're the only thing I've ever done that was any good.'

I allowed him to embrace that illusion briefly before I spoke again.

'You're wrong, Kenneth.'

Then I leaned across the table to whisper something in his ear that no one else in the room could hear. I sat back on my chair while he scowled at me, confused and dismayed.

'So now you know the only good thing you ever did isn't just a little like his father,' I said. 'He's worse.'

'You fucking monster,' he muttered.

'Like father, like son. Keep your watch and I hope they bury you with it sooner rather than later.'

Then I turned my back on my father and left the room.

◆ ◆ ◆

CATHERINE

Northampton, twenty-five years earlier

6 June, 8.45 a.m.

I unscrewed the lid from a bottle of wine and poured it into a dirty mug, which had been lying in the kitchen sink along with the rest of the unwashed dishes. I opened the kitchen cupboard, took three aspirin from a bottle on the top shelf and swallowed them in the hope they'd get rid of the pounding headache brought on by a second sleepless night. The bottle rattled when I shook it. It sounded nearly full, and for a moment I wondered how many pills it might take to kill a person.

I glanced wearily around the room and sighed at the mess it had so quickly become. It was in good company. The rest of the house was a mess, the past two days had been a mess and I was a mess.

I tried so hard to be positive in front of everyone else, but when I was alone, the doubts set in. I couldn't tell anyone how sick I felt each time I thought about what might have happened to Simon, that I jumped with every ring of the phone or footstep on the path, or how I was surviving on adrenaline and caffeine, my brain fighting against a body begging to go back to bed.

The only part of me keeping sane was the part that put the children's needs before mine. Everyone knew Simon was missing except for his own flesh and blood, and it was my job to keep it that way. But it was hard, because many of their friends' parents had taken time off work to join the second day of the search. It was only a matter of time before the kids found out. Then what would I tell them? Parents are supposed to be the ones with all the answers, but I had none.

According to Roger, the first seventy-two hours are the most important in the search for a missing person, as that's the time frame within which most turn up. Any longer than that and hope begins to fade. Simon's clock was ticking.

So I clenched my fists and prayed it would be the day they found him. I swear WPC Williams had stifled a smile when she warned me that if they'd not turned up anything by nightfall, they'd have to call off the search. I wondered how many loved ones I'd have to lose in my lifetime before God gave me a break.

Suddenly I was aware I still had hold of the aspirin bottle, so I threw it back in the cupboard, ashamed of something I'd never do. I finished the rest of my wine, put the mug back in the sink and headed upstairs to shower.

As I stood under the warm jet, I crumbled. I cried and cried until I couldn't tell whether my body was wet with water or tears.

3.35 p.m.

It may have been inevitable but it still caught me off guard.

'Amelia Jones says Daddy's lost,' cried James as he ran to meet me at the school gates. 'Is he?' His green eyes were wide and troubled. Robbie, too, looked as anxious as I'd ever seen him. I knew they deserved my honesty.

'When we get home, let's find your fishing nets from the garage and we'll go to the stream,' I replied calmly. 'And then we'll have a chat.'

The late-afternoon sun hid behind a large dragon-shaped cloud as the four of us and Oscar walked in single file towards a wooden bridge over the water.

I chose a place they associated with their daddy, as if it might soften the blow a little. It was somewhere he'd taken them many times to pretend to fish. They'd catch imaginary minnows and crayfish, throw them inside pretend buckets and bring them home to me, where I'd play along and pretend to be amazed by their haul.

We sat down, cast our imaginary lines and skimmed the surface with nets while I gently explained we might not see him for a while.

'Where has he gone?' asked James, his brow narrowing like his father's did when he couldn't make sense of something.

'I don't know.'

'When will he be back?'

'I can't tell you, honey.'

'Why?'

'Because I can't. All I know is that Daddy's gone away for a bit and hopefully he'll come home soon.'

'Why don't you know?' pushed James.

'I just don't, I'm sorry. We don't know how to find him. But I know he's thinking about us all.'

'But when we don't tell you where we're going, you tell us off,' reasoned Robbie. I nodded. 'So are you going to tell Daddy off?'

'Yes,' I lied, but I wouldn't tell him off. Instead I'd wrap myself around him and hold on for dear life.

'Has he gone to see Billy?' asked Robbie, his face beginning to crumple.

I swallowed hard. 'No, he hasn't.' I knew he hadn't. I prayed he hadn't.

'But how do you know?' scowled James.

I looked into the distance where the stream melted into the fields and said nothing. The fishing continued in silence and they caught nothing while their little brains digested what I'd said, as best they could. None of us wanted to imagine a life without him.

8.10 p.m.

I sat on a patio chair, wrapped in Simon's navy-blue chunky Aran sweater, and waited for the day to merge into dusk. The cordless phone I'd asked Paula to buy for me was never more than a foot away. But it was as silent as the world around me. Only the moths clamouring around a candle's flame in the Moroccan lantern kept me company. Directionless and unsteady, we had a lot in common.

I tried to cheer myself up by thinking about all the silly things he used to do to make me smile, like giving the dog a voice, dancing around the kitchen with me to old Wham! songs, or putting on one of my dresses to make our friends laugh in the middle of a dinner party. He could be so silly sometimes, and I desperately wanted that man back.

I poured the last trickle from a bottle of red wine into my glass and waited. That's all I'd done for three days – wait.

When I was inside our house I was homesick for a place I'd never left. But it had become claustrophobic without Simon, and I dreaded the nights. Because without the interruptions of friends stopping by or me trying to put a smile on the glum faces of the confused kids, I had even more time to think about him. I missed him, yet inside I raged at him too, for leaving me like this.

I didn't care what WPC Williams had said: I knew Simon too well to ever consider he'd walked out on us. The strength and support he'd shown me during the worst thing that could ever happen to a parent had proved he was a fantastic husband and dad, and I desperately needed to believe that he was still alive. Fifteen months had passed since we'd last been united in grief, and there I was again, but this time I was on my own and grieving for a man whose fate was unknown.

◆　◆　◆

Northampton, today

8.30 a.m.

He knew his fingers would tear through the soft felt brim of his fedora if he clutched it any tighter. But he wasn't ready to let go just yet.

He watched as she turned back from closing the door and noted how she avoided his gaze when she walked towards the centre of the living room. Time hadn't eroded her natural grace. The crow's feet around the cool flint of her eyes were new to him, and the narrow lines across her forehead stretched further than he remembered, but none of it mattered. Her loveliness was altered, but not in the least bit dimmed. Her grey hairs were like perfectly placed brushstrokes in an oil painting, all the better for not being disguised by artificial colouring. Her bloom had far from faded, and that made him feel awkward and dusty in comparison.

For Catherine's part, she had so much to say but nowhere to begin. So she remained silent and knotted her fingers together tightly so he couldn't see them shake. Try as she might, she did not want to look at him, but it was a struggle. Eventually she allowed her eyes to cautiously run over him.

His face had filled out, leaving his cheeks jowlier. His waistline had expanded, but was kept under restraint by his leather belt. His feet looked larger, which she realised was a peculiar thing to focus on.

Then her eyes became glued to him, fearing that if they became unstuck, he would vanish. And if he was to disappear again, she wanted to be there to see it. It had been years since she'd last glimpsed his image in any of the few remaining photographs left hidden in the attic. She'd forgotten how handsome he was. How handsome he was even now, she admitted, then immediately chastised herself for thinking that.

He stood awkwardly and surveyed the living room, trying to recall what had been where when he was last inside it. The layout appeared familiar, albeit with fresh wallpaper, carpets and furnishings. But it felt so small in comparison to what he now called home.

'Do you mind if I sit?' he asked.

She didn't reply, so he did so anyway.

There were pictures of people in frames scattered across the sideboard, but without his reading glasses, their faces were blurs. It was the same when he'd tried to remember what his children looked like – clouds always masked the finer details. Well, all apart from James. He knew the man James had become, and he'd never forget that.

The silence between them lasted longer than either noticed. As the uninvited visitor, he felt the need to begin.

'How are you? You look well.'

She gave him a look of disdain, but it failed to unsettle him. He was prepared for that.

'I like what you've done with the cottage,' he continued.

Again, nothing.

He scanned the sandstone chimney breast and the wood-burning stove they'd had a devil of a time installing soon after they'd moved in. He smiled. 'Is that old thing still working? Do you remember when we almost set the chimney alight because we hadn't cleaned it out before—'

'Don't.' Her curt response prevented him from reaching the end of memory lane.

'Sorry, it's just being in this room after so long brought it back . . .'

'I said don't. You do not turn up at my house after twenty-five years and begin speaking to me like we're old friends.'

'I'm sorry.'

An uneasy, foggy quiet filled the room.

'What do you want?' she asked.

'What do I want?'

'That's what I asked. What do you want from me?'

'I don't want anything from you, Kitty.' It was a partial truth.

'Don't call me that. You lost any right to call me that a long time ago.'

He nodded.

His voice sounded a little raspier and deeper than back then, and contained traces of an accent she couldn't place.

'And spare me your apologies,' she continued. 'They're a little late in the day and unwelcome.'

He'd played out this opening scenario dozens of times in his imagination before Luca had booked his flights over the Internet. Would she remain in shock or slap him, embrace him, yell at him, cry or just refuse to let him in? There were countless reactions she could have had, but somehow he'd failed to anticipate this icy hostility. He didn't know how to respond to it.

'Where did you go?' she asked. 'While I was out searching for your dead body, where the hell were you?'

CHAPTER FOUR

SIMON

Calais, France, twenty-five years earlier

10 June

I'd not made acquaintance with motion sickness before last night, locked in the back of the truck. I'd lost track of how often I vomited. My stomach had become nothing more than a hollow trunk.

The driver had warned me the crossing would take about an hour and a half, but the festering storm outside soon put paid to his estimate. An uncaring English Channel picked up our ferry and tossed it around like a rag doll. I felt my way around in the pitch black and wedged myself behind two packing cases strapped in place to the sides of the truck.

I'd buried my history with my mother's bones, but to truly shed my skin, an unfettered, unspoiled me could only thrive far away from the past. France's geographical location made for an obvious starting point. Reaching it without a passport or money was, however, an obstacle. But a haggard truck driver with a nicotine-stained moustache and disdain for authority offered me a solution.

Earlier in the day, he'd picked me up near Maidstone and we'd enjoyed a rapport over the state of British football and the Conservative government's penchant for privatising anything and everything. At no point did he enquire as to my hidden motives when I explained where I was headed and how my lack of means might hamper me. However, he'd come to his own conclusions.

'I did a bit of prison time back in the day,' he began, rolling a cigarette as he steered. 'As long as you ain't murdered anyone or touched any kids, I'll get you over there.'

Minutes before he drove through the customs checkpoint, he locked the trailer doors behind me, leaving me hidden behind wooden boxes with a torch, a can of supermarket beer and his homemade cheese and chutney sandwich. But neither the food nor the drink remained inside me once the storm exploded into life.

The conditions outside were clearly too chancy for us to dock, so we remained mid-Channel until the white squall played out. With each dip, my stomach touched my toes until the ferry finally docked safely in the port.

'Look at the state of you!' the driver laughed when he set me free in the car park of a French hypermarket.

He helped my unsteady feet back onto land and I shed my vomit-stained clothes behind the truck, throwing them into a bin. I climbed into his cab in just my underwear and changed into new clothes I'd taken from someone else's bag at a homeless shelter I'd slept at in London.

'This is as far as I can take you,' he said back outside. 'Good luck, son.'

'Thank you. By the way, I didn't catch your name?'

'Just call me Moses,' he chuckled, and slowly pulled away.

As his truck disappeared out of sight, I counted the fistful of French francs I'd stolen from the wallet on his dashboard.

Saint-Jean-de-Luz, France

17 June

Waves from an inclement Atlantic Ocean lapped at my feet and made the hairs on my toes sway like a sea urchin's spines. The rotating beams from a pair of lighthouses sliced through a bruised sky as night swept in. Three concrete walls framed the harbour and prevented the water and horizon from ever meeting. Unable to catch a breeze in their sails, a handful of windsurfers straddled their boards and paddled to the shore.

I was unsure how long my journey from the north to the south of France had taken, as without Doreen's watch, time neither existed nor mattered. Hours blended into each other like colours in a tie-dyed T-shirt.

I'd spent long stretches of time hovering by French roadsides searching for a friendly smile behind a moving windscreen. Sometimes I found myself hiding in train carriage toilets avoiding ticket inspectors.

It was during my days of near solitude when the faces of those I'd left behind drifted in and out of my head. I questioned how she was coping without me. Had she presumed I was dead like I'd hoped, or was she still holding on to faint hope of my return? Because I wanted to fade from all of their memories quickly.

However, my rational side knew I had to nip these thoughts in the bud. If I allowed them to become more frequent, they'd only hamper me. So I began to train myself to think only of the future and not of the past – and, specifically, her. It wasn't easy, especially with copious amounts of time on my hands.

Manipulating one's thoughts is relatively simple for a few moments. But the part of your brain that holds in its core everything that's amiss about one's self doesn't appreciate being contained for long. The longer I dwelled on the badness, the harder it would be to anticipate the good times ahead. But I had freedom to choose and I could, if I wanted to, reject those thoughts.

So as soon as something detrimental came into my mind, I snatched it mid-air and quashed it. I reminded myself those memories belonged to a person who no longer existed.

Of course, I couldn't control everything I thought about, but I learned to manage and compartmentalise much of it. And by the time I disembarked at the beach in Saint-Jean-de-Luz in the south-west, the wheels were already in motion. The key was to remain conscious of and fixed upon only the present and the future. To assist in that project, I created new memories by focusing on what I saw and sensed from the moment I arrived.

I began by inhaling the salty sea mist and the smells carried by the wind from the surrounding gastronomy. I appreciated how the beach's harbour resembled a huge toothless grin, and I found myself smiling back at it. I was impressed at how the historic architecture of Saint-Jean-de-Luz had been kept so pristine. I could see a Basque church and longed to go inside it.

Ahead of me lay the ocean; to the left, the Spanish border and the mighty Pyrenees; behind me, the body of France. I could run in any direction and no one would catch me. It was the place I could begin again.

My personal hygiene had been restricted to washing myself in stained basins at truck stops and train stations, so my first priority was to walk down the concrete steps, strip off my musty-smelling clothes and run into the water in just my underwear.

The salt stung my eyes when I lay face down, grasping a seabed that slipped through my fingers. I swam towards a white metal buoy bobbing along under the spell of the ebb and flow. Linking an arm through its scaffolding, I took in the coastline.

I threw myself under the water and the sound of the waves tussling against the tide tore through my ears. I held my head under until my baptism was complete.

The harbour was a popular dock for boats and trawlers that ended a day's fishing in picture-postcard comfort. The gentle vibrations of their engines gave satisfying tingles up and down my arms and legs as my nerves sprang back to life. Closing my eyes, I flipped onto my back and slowly paddled towards the beach to dry my new skin in the setting sun's rays.

Instinctively I believed my new life had the potential to be perfect.

28 June

Fumes from the Gauloise had fused with the burning cannabis resin and floated up through my nostrils then deep into my lungs. I leaned back on my elbows, sank further into the sand and savoured the high before exhaling.

'Good shit, man,' said Bradley, who sat next to me, cross-legged.

'Yep,' I replied without looking at him, my eyes like crescent moons.

With the aid of my pidgin French and helpful locals, I'd been directed towards a backpacking hostel on Rue du Jean. The beachfront buildings were exquisite, but the Routard International was hidden three streets back, under a shroud of dirt and dilapidation. Its cream and olive-green facade had flaked, chipped and fallen like dandruff onto the pavement.

Inside, framed sepia photographs arranged carelessly on its reception walls revealed its previous incarnation as the Hôtel Près de la Côte – a glowing, three-storey art deco hotel. Its geometric shapes were now muddied and barely visible behind a hodgepodge of cheap, modern bookcases and dressers. And its former elegance and stylish modernism had all but vanished.

Marble tiles had dropped from the ballroom's walls and lay shattered around a grand piano, felled by two fractured legs. It had downgraded from a luxurious destination to an ad hoc home for fly-by-nights with limited means.

The remainder of Moses's money just about stretched to a dormitory bed for the week. The nights I'd spent in a homeless shelter in London had quickly acclimatised me to others' sleep-talking, snoring, and the smells produced by six bodies in a confined space.

It was mainly young European travellers, keen to explore beaches away from the glamour of Cannes and Saint-Tropez, who inhabited the hostel. I had more years on me than most, but I'd never looked my age. This allowed me to shave a decade from my date of birth. My hitchhiker's tan gave me a healthy sheen and masked the weight I'd lost by irregular eating.

I made the acquaintance of small pockets of people who spoke in tongues I often couldn't understand. But through botched German, Italian, French and plenty of exaggerated hand signals, we muddled along until we caught each other's drifts.

I spent my first few days seeking potential employment, from menial and unskilled work pot-washing in café kitchens to being a trawlerman's assistant. But the town looked after its own, and there was no place for an Englishman yet to prove his worth.

So I filled my time by familiarising myself with my adopted home through exploratory field trips. My fascination with architecture remained and there was much to absorb, like William Marcel's pre-First World War Hôtel du Golf, and the ochre-red country club in Chantaco I'd read about in my father's *Reader's Digest* magazines.

My evenings were occupied by listening to hostellers reminiscing about their pre-travelling lives, while offering little about my own background. My scant smokescreen involved leaving university to spend a couple of years being part of the world, not merely studying it from the sidelines.

It was a plausible story that I repeated so often, I'd begun to believe it myself.

30 June

'You should've told me you're looking for a job,' said Bradley, the American-born hostel manager. He was an amiable man in his late thirties with shoulder-length, salt-and-pepper hair and Elvis-sized sideburns. His surfer's saline tan etched deep white lines into his face and aged him prematurely.

'Yes, do you know of one?' I asked hopefully.

'Well, it's not much, but we need a janitor. Someone who can check people in and out too, and do odd jobs. It doesn't pay much, but you'll get your bed and board for free.'

It sounded ideal and I began the next day. The role offered extra perks I hadn't accounted for. I could raid the cupboard of forgotten clothes, read literature in the 'Take a book, leave a book' library and practise my language skills with other travellers.

I gave walls fresh licks of paint, hammered loose floorboards, wiped vomit from bathroom toilets and welcomed new guests. Ample free time and reliable surf enabled me to learn the skills of wave riding, thanks to Bradley's patient lessons and his collection of colourful surfboards. Once I'd mastered the basics, scuba diving became my next challenge, followed by horse-trekking excursions through the neighbouring mountain foothills.

My evenings were golden – the day of work followed by an hour on the beach watching the sun set over a joint or two with Bradley, and finally shots of Jack Daniels and Coke at one of the local bistros.

I adapted to my new way of life with gusto. And with my baggage consigned to sealed boxes in my head, I was at ease living in a way I'd never dared to dream of. To the eyes of a stranger, and even myself, I had no discernible essence.

CATHERINE

Northampton, twenty-five years earlier

17 June

'Just tell us where he is!' Shirley yelled as I grabbed her shoulder and shoved her out the front door.

'Get out now!' I screamed back.

Shirley's exasperated voice echoed around the house as I gave her and Arthur their marching orders.

For half an hour, Simon's dad and stepmother had subjected me to a bitter barrage of questions and accusations, and I'd had enough. My nerves were already in tatters without them sticking their oars in. I'd expected them to turn up on our doorstep sooner, but they'd clearly been too busy spending their days festering over how he could've vanished into thin air. And they were convinced I must have had something to do with it.

When they'd arrived, I'd made the most of the light summer night and sent the children into the garden to play. Then I took a deep breath and slowly walked the green mile to the living room. There, Arthur and Shirley sat side by side, their arms and legs crossed.

'I'm sorry I didn't tell you about Simon,' I began, 'but I didn't want to worry you.'

'You think it's acceptable for us to hear from the police that our son is missing?' barked Shirley. 'We should have been told immediately.'

'Yes, I know, and I apologise. But I asked Roger to keep you informed, and he's Simon's closest friend, so it wasn't like you were told by a total stranger. And I'd really rather not get into an argument with you about it right now. It's been a hideous couple of weeks.'

'Yes, so I've heard. It must be quite stressful spending afternoons with the children at the cinema while their father might be lying dead somewhere,' she sniped.

'Shirley, it wasn't like that. It was one afternoon, and on Roger's advice. And they're my children, so I'll decide what's best for them, not you.'

She shouldn't have dragged the kids into it, especially since their grandparents barely even played a supporting role in their lives. They lived in the next village but rarely offered to babysit or pick them up from school. A stranger would be forgiven for assuming they had no grandchildren.

After the funeral, they'd hardly bothered to offer either of us help, or a shoulder to cry on. I'm sure that must have hurt Simon, but he'd not admitted it.

I'd always presumed their lack of interest in us was my fault. They remembered a boy who was once infatuated by Alan Whicker's travel documentaries and who'd dreamed of exploring the world's architecture. Then, by twenty-three, he was a married man and later, saddled with his own family. Even before we walked up the aisle, he tried to convince them that all he'd ever wanted was his own normal, loving family, but they wanted more for him than that.

I recalled his relationship with Shirley wasn't easy. She was a big, bottle-blonde hurricane of a woman who burst into Arthur's life a couple of years after he'd kicked Doreen out. I remembered how, when we were teenagers, Simon often moaned about how she'd order him to do his homework and tell him off for smoking. But then she'd clean up his bedroom and cook him meals, and all without expecting anything in return. He might never have loved her, but she showed him what a mum was capable of. I never admitted it, but I'd been envious he had parents who cared.

They were at a loss to understand why, after all Doreen had put Simon through, he would do the same to his own family. With no proof to the contrary, they'd decided I'd driven him away.

'Were you pressuring him to do better at work?' began Arthur, awkwardly.

'No.'

'Were you giving him the support he needed?' Shirley demanded to know.

'Yes, of course I was.'

'Did he really want all those little ones so soon?'

'Yes, Shirley. I didn't get pregnant by myself.'

'You could have tricked him. A lot of women do, to get what they want.'

'What, four times?'

'Well, why did he leave then?'

'He hasn't left, he's disappeared. And it has nothing to do with our children!'

'That doesn't rule you out as the cause though, does it, dear?'

I rolled my eyes as we went round in circles. I took a bottle of wine from the cupboard and poured myself a glass without offering them one. They looked at each other with disapproval but I didn't care. I took an extra-large gulp to make a point.

'Are you sure you don't know where he is?' asked Shirley.

'What kind of question is that?' I replied, taken aback. 'Do you think we'd be sitting here having this conversation if I did?'

'Now's the time to tell us, Catherine. Just put us all out of our misery. Does Simon have another woman? Is that what it is? Is he with her now? You're hurting our grandchildren if you're putting your own pride first and pretending he's just disappeared.'

'This is ridiculous! Of course he doesn't. And how could you think I'd not put my kids first?'

'Plenty of women struggle to keep a marriage together,' Arthur chipped in. 'They don't try and save face by kicking up a fuss and claiming he disappeared when he's walked out.'

'That's rich coming from you! Weren't you the one who told everyone Doreen left to become a bloody missionary in Ethiopia? I don't recall you mentioning anything about you booting her out.'

His face flamed red.

'And if Simon had done that to me, then why hasn't he been in touch with you?' I continued. 'If he left me, he left you too.'

'Did he leave a note saying why he went?' asked Shirley.

I let out a groan. 'You've not listened to a word I've said, have you? Let me spell it out for you: Simon did not leave. He has *gone missing*. The police are treating him as a missing person. What more evidence do you need?'

Shirley rose to her feet. 'I'm sorry I have to ask this, Catherine, but did you do something to him?'

That threw me. 'Like what?' I asked, genuinely confused.

'Maybe you had an argument that got out of hand, you might have hurt him, then panicked, I'm not saying you meant to, but . . .'

'What, then I got the kids to help me wrap his body up in an old carpet and buried him in the garden? You've been watching too much *Murder She Wrote.*'

'We deserve to know the truth! He's our son!' she growled.

'He's not your son, Shirley,' I snarled back. 'But he is my husband and it's me and my children who are suffering the most. And how are you helping? By accusing their mother of murder? What kind of monster do you think I am?'

Their silence spoke volumes.

'If he's not dead, then he's abandoned you,' Shirley responded matter-of-factly. 'And frankly, I'm not surprised.' Ever her faithful lapdog, Arthur nodded in agreement.

'I'm only surprised it didn't happen sooner,' she continued. 'I've always said you can never repair damaged goods.'

Despite the cruelty of her words, it still took a glimpse of a bewildered Robbie sitting on the bottom stair listening intently as his mother was torn to pieces before I snapped.

'Just leave!' I bellowed, lurching towards Shirley and grabbing her by the arm. 'Get the hell out of my house.'

'Just tell us where he is!' Shirley yelled as I grabbed her shoulder and shoved her out the front door.

Arthur shuffled awkwardly behind us.

'Get out now!' I screamed, and physically pushed them onto the path then slammed the door, locking and chaining it behind me. I took a moment to gather myself before approaching my son with my broken heart still racing.

'Doesn't Daddy love us anymore?' he asked, brushing away stray blond hairs stuck to his wet cheeks. 'Is that why he ran away?'

I wanted to slap his grandparents for putting that idea into his head. Instead, I knelt down, placed his hands in mine and looked him straight in the eye.

'I promise you, Robbie, no matter where your daddy is or what has happened to him, he hasn't run away. He loves us with all his heart.'

He peered at me cautiously, stood up and climbed the stairs. 'You're a liar,' he said quietly as he retreated to the safety of his bedroom. 'You made Daddy run away.'

I could just about take what Arthur and Shirley had said. But hearing my little boy doubt his mother for the first time in his life was crushing. I should have gone after him and tried to explain Simon hadn't been driven away by anybody. But Arthur and Shirley had sapped my strength.

Instead, I poured myself another glass of wine, sat in the kitchen with my head in my hands and fought the urge to break every dish in the sink.

25 June

I knew by the way the orange vase on the sideboard vibrated that a police car was pulling up outside our house. Their engines had an urgent, distinctive throb I'd grown used to and one which made the joints under the floorboards rattle. Then the panic would creep up my spine, terrified of what they were about to tell me.

It was usually just an update on the investigation or to ask me yet more questions I couldn't answer. But the visits that scared me the most were when they brought me plastic bags containing pieces of stray clothing they'd found strewn somewhere. A handkerchief, a hat, a sock, a shoe . . . the list of items for me to identify went on and on.

Each time, I barely spoke as I sifted through them, but nothing ever belonged to Simon. The officers tried to hide their frustration at each dead end, as a positive result would be one step closer to solving the case. But he wasn't just a case to me: he was my husband.

And gradually the catwalk of the orphaned clothes petered out along with their visits.

30 June

James was eight, Robbie was five and a half and Emily was approaching four, and they showed no more understanding of our new life than their equally confused mum.

They barely let me out of their sight in case I vanished too. From behind the kitchen curtains, I'd feel three pairs of eyes glued to me, even when I walked to the end of the path to put the rubbish out. I constantly reassured them I wasn't going anywhere, but they didn't believe me.

Daddies were supposed to stay, and once they learned that wasn't necessarily the case, they became worried that mummies wouldn't always stay either. I hated myself for thinking it, but part of me wished I could have told them Simon had gone to see Billy when they'd asked. They might have made sense of that more easily. But it was more important than ever that I pretended to be the constantly upbeat parent, no matter how I really felt.

Emily was aware something had made her world topsy-turvy, but it didn't seem to trouble her much. In fact, she loved the extra cuddles she received from our friends as they came to the house. It was difficult for them not to melt at the sight of her huge baby-blue eyes and goofy smile, especially when she'd point to a photograph of Simon on the sideboard and sing: '*Daddy's gone. No Daddy.*' I'd nod my head sympathetically, then distract her with Flopsy or a Barbie doll.

Robbie took it the hardest. He and our dog Oscar spent more and more time together, feeding off each other's confusion. I'd well up watching them as they sat together in the back garden, staring across the fields, waiting for Simon to reappear like he'd been part of a magic trick that had gone horribly wrong. Each night when I put them all to bed, I'd leave Robbie's door ajar so Oscar could sneak inside to sleep at the foot of his bed.

James was the spitting image of his father, from the brown waves in his hair to the sparkle in his green eyes and his infectious laugh. One night, he scattered his collection of white and brown seashells he'd found on the beach in Benidorm across his bedroom floor. His friend Alex had told him that if he put one to his ear and listened carefully, he could hear the sound of the sea.

Every now and again he'd pick one up to try and catch Simon's voice, in case he was lost at the seaside and needed his help to find his way home. I tried it myself once, but I heard nothing but the echo of my emptiness.

◆ ◆ ◆

Northampton, today

8.55 a.m.

She glared at him with unflinching venom she'd only felt for one other man. But she'd long buried that person in her past – along with her husband.

71

Her forehead was so furrowed it felt sore. It was difficult to find the words to respond to what he'd recalled about his first few weeks without them. Of all the possible outcomes she'd considered – and there had been many – she hadn't envisaged he'd simply taken a holiday. While she'd been frantic with worry, he'd been lying on a beach.

She wanted him to understand how their lives had fallen to pieces when he disappeared. She needed him to know that while he was creating a whole new persona, her destiny hadn't been one of choice. But if she could have conveyed to him even a small sense of what she'd gone through, it was apparent that he still couldn't comprehend how the agony of a missing soulmate felt. That he could so easily disregard the first thirty-three years of his life, and those who were an integral part of it, beggared belief.

'Did even a tiny bit of you consider what it might have been like for us here, while you were getting stoned with a bunch of teenagers?' she asked.

'It wasn't like that, but at the time, I suppose not,' he replied with brutal honesty. 'I assumed you thought I'd had an accident but couldn't find my body.'

'And please correct me if I'm wrong here, but you actually made yourself forget we even existed?'

He nodded.

'What about birthdays, or anniversaries?' she persisted, hoping to find a glimpse of remorse. 'Did you ever think of us then?'

'Not at first, no, but I had no choice. It was the only way I could move on.'

'That's the difference between you and me, Simon. I'd never have wanted to move anywhere if it wasn't with you and the children.'

'I had to get away, I was suffocating.'

'Oh, spare me the melodrama,' she snapped. 'You could have asked for a separation if you didn't want to be married to me anymore. I'd have been heartbroken, of course, but I'd have worked through it eventually. And leaving me was one thing, but your children? I will never understand that.'

Feeling her voice begin to crack, she swallowed hard. She had vowed many years ago not to shed another tear over him and she wasn't going back on her word now.

'You asked me where I went, so I told you,' he replied quietly. 'I'm not responsible if you don't like what you've heard.'

She rolled her eyes. 'No, you're right. Responsibility isn't a word you're familiar with, is it?'

'I'm not here to argue with you,' he said with maddening calm.

'Then why *are* you here? Because I've got a lot of anger in me that I'm trying my damnedest to contain. Only you're not making it easy when you tell me how you just put us out of your mind.'

'Of course I thought about you. I thought about you all – in time. What I'm saying is that it wasn't beneficial for me to dwell on the past straight away. I had to block you all out to carry on. I apologise if that sounds callous, but at the time I did what I thought was best.'

She shook her head in disbelief and ran her hands across her cheeks. They were burning up. She walked over to the window and unlatched the lever arch to release the claustrophobia from the room.

As the light hit her hair and revealed her scalp, he thought he noticed what looked like a crescent-shaped scar on the side of her head.

She turned around quickly. 'Were you sick of us all, or was it just me? What did I do to make you not want me anymore? Did you get a better offer from someone else?'

He looked towards the fireplace, not yet ready to explain his reasons. He recognised a familiar object. 'Is that the one Baishali and Steven bought us for our wedding present?' he asked, pointing to a round orange vase.

His change of subject threw her, but she nodded regardless.

'How is he? Has he retired yet?'

'Yes, he has. One of his sons runs the business you threw away. Then he and Baishali retired to the south of France. Funny he didn't bump into you on the beach. You'd have had so much to catch up on.'

He didn't ask about Roger. Now wasn't the right time.

'Anyway, I doubt you've risen from the grave to make small talk,' she continued. 'So either tell me why you're here or go back to where you came from.'

'You need to know the full story first.'

'What, more riveting tales from Club 18–30? I don't have time for this.' She walked towards the porch as if to open the front door, but she knew it was an empty gesture. She had waited too many years for answers for it to end now.

'Please, Catherine. I need you to know what became of my life. And I want to know what you did with yours.'

'You don't deserve to know a thing about me.'

'I know I don't have any right to, but it's been a long time. We both need closure.'

Sod closure, she thought. All she wanted to know was why. Even after all this time, she still felt she had to be to blame. The puzzle was missing key pieces she couldn't place by herself. So she told herself that while she'd indulge him, she wouldn't make it easy for him – whatever happened that day.

CHAPTER FIVE
CATHERINE

Northampton, twenty-five years earlier

17 July

A long, loud knock on the front door woke me up at sunrise with a jolt, scaring the life out of me. I jumped out of bed, looked nervously out of the landing window and saw Roger's unmarked police car and a van parked by the curb. My mouth was dry.

I threw on my dressing gown and felt my legs wobble as I dashed downstairs, hoping the noise hadn't woken the children. *They've found your body. I've really lost him.*

Roger stood awkwardly with his head bowed, unable to look me in the eye.

'I know what you're going to say,' I began.

'Can I come in?'

'You've found him, haven't you? You can tell me.'

'No, we haven't, Catherine. But I need to talk to you.'

Roger entered, while a handful of officers carrying torches and wearing overalls and boots wrapped in blue polythene bags stayed by the garden gate. None of them looked at me.

'I'm really sorry about this, but it's out of my hands,' he began apologetically. 'We've been offered an alternate line of enquiry that my chief inspector's ordered me to follow up.'

'I don't understand.'

He paused. 'We've received a tip-off that suggested we need to examine your garden for . . . signs of recent disturbance.'

'Signs of recent disturbance,' I repeated. 'What does that mean?'

'There's no easy way to say it, but there's a suggestion Simon's remains may be buried here.'

'Is this some kind of joke?'

'I only wish it was, but I have a search warrant.' He pulled out a document from his jacket pocket and handed it to me. I threw it back at him without reading it all, choking at the absurdity of it.

'You seriously believe I buried my husband in the garden?'

'No, of course I don't, but we have to follow up all leads, even if they come from crackpots.'

'Tell me who this crackpot is, Roger,' I demanded.

'I'm not allowed to say.'

'This is me you're talking to. I have a right to know.'

'I'm sorry, Catherine, I can't.'

I paused. 'Wait a minute, you said crackpots, as in there's more than one. Who would . . . '

My voice trailed off and I shut my eyes when I realised who was responsible.

'Arthur and Shirley!' I fumed. 'I'm going round there now to sort this out once and for all.' I'd vowed never to speak to them again after our last confrontation, but I was furious enough to make an exception.

'No, you're not,' Roger replied firmly. 'You're going to stay in the house and let me do my job. We're not going to find anything, but the quicker we can get this over with, the quicker we can leave before your kids and neighbours wake up.'

I glared at him in both frustration and disgust, scared that even a tiny piece of him might believe my poisonous in-laws. But there was nothing but embarrassment in his eyes.

'Just do it, then go away,' I fired back, and left him to it. Then I hid, ashamed and humiliated, behind the dining room curtains as officers silently searched the rear garden, Simon's shed, and prised up random patio slabs around the pond.

They bagged samples of ashes from his bonfire heap, trawled through the boot of his car using special sticky tape to lift fibres, and sieved earth in the borders by the front lawn. But when they focused their attention on the pink rosebushes he'd planted for me during the depths of my depression, I couldn't contain my anger any longer.

'What the hell are you doing?' I yelled, running towards them. 'You don't know what they mean to me!'

'The ground's freshly dug, so we have to check,' a faceless man in uniform replied.

I grabbed the spade from his hand and threw it across the lawn. 'That's what you *do* in a garden – dig soil and plant things, you bloody idiot!'

I stomped back into the kitchen and finished off a half-empty bottle of wine in the fridge, then hurled it against the wall. A frightened Oscar scarpered for safety into the living room.

I let the children sleep in longer than normal, and two and a half hours after their arrival, the police put their tools in the back of the van and Roger reappeared on the doorstep.

'We've finished. As I said, we didn't expect to find anything. I'm so sorry for putting you through this, Catherine.'

'So am I,' I replied, and slammed the door on him.

14 August

'Simon is not dead,' I told my reflection in the bathroom-cabinet mirror. 'He is not dead. He is not dead.'

Each time a shadow of a doubt crossed my mind, I'd say the same thing out loud over and over until I believed it again. But as each week passed, it was getting harder and harder to believe.

I peered inside the cabinet to make sure everything was where it should be for when he came home. I did that a lot. His razor, shaving cream, brush, comb, cotton buds and deodorant stick were still lined up neatly, and all as redundant as me.

I closed the doors and commiserated with the haunted face staring back at me. I asked myself if I'd been unfair by offering the kids false hope that he was still alive. I may have stopped feeling his presence, but intuition told me he wouldn't be gone forever. Was that enough? And besides, what lessons would I be teaching them if I gave up on their dad so quickly?

Simon was my first and final thought each day, and probably every other thought in between. Each night in bed I'd tell him about my day, but he never replied. Still, I was sure he was out there somewhere, waiting to be found. But I felt like I was in a shrinking minority.

It was subtle at first, but I began to see a change in our friends. No one actually had the guts to put it into words, but I began to pick up on little signs of doubt when I brought his name up. Steven seldom mentioned his name unless it involved the business. Baishali would tug awkwardly at the dark curls touching her neck and then change the subject. Even my ever-reliable Paula began to look at me like I was naive for not considering he could've just walked away.

Without her knowing it, she hurt me more than anyone else because we were so close and she didn't trust my instincts. And it made me ask myself if I shouldn't be talking about Simon so much. But why should

I stop? He was my husband and it wasn't his fault he'd been taken away from us. Why couldn't everyone else see that?

I became resentful towards anyone whose sole focus wasn't to help find him. I knew people had their own lives to live and I envied them, but their doubt frustrated the hell out of me. I wanted to tell them all to sod off. But I needed their help to keep myself together, so I got my support from a bottle of red wine instead. It understood what I needed more than any friend did.

I led a double life as one foot sank in quicksand and the other flailed around desperately, seeking enough solid ground to keep myself stable.

Family dinners became subdued affairs. I'd entice the kids into talking or give them something to focus on like empty promises of fun holidays, and birthdays and Christmases to come. But it didn't matter what I said. All they wanted was their father. So, most nights, we'd sit quietly, shuffling chicken Kievs around our plates like chess pieces, trying to stop ourselves from staring at the empty chair at the dining room table.

In the end, I moved the chair into the garage. It made no difference. We'd gawp at the empty space instead.

2 September

It took an eight-year-old boy to shame his mother into action.

'Look what I've made, Mummy,' said James proudly as he pushed a piece of paper into my chest.

My heart bled when he showed me a drawing of his dad with a reward of his fifty-pence pocket money for the person who found him.

'We can put it in the window,' he suggested helpfully. It was the kick up the backside I needed.

Three months after Simon's disappearance, Roger admitted the police investigation had drawn a blank. I'd let them do their job, even if it meant searching my house or digging up my garden for his remains. But there was only so much I could take of feeling stupid when the children and neighbours asked me for updates and I couldn't give them answers.

I'd fallen into a vicious circle of feeling sorry for myself and relying on others to find him. And then I'd get frustrated when they hadn't. James's reward poster reminded me there was nothing stopping me from finding Simon myself.

I sprang into action with a second wind and called our local newspaper, which sent a reporter to the house for a renewed appeal. And once the interview made it to print, regional news programme *Countywide* asked to come to our house and film a segment. I can't say I was proud of it, but I used our children's anxiety to tug at viewers' heartstrings.

'Mummy's trying to make people feel sorry for us,' I whispered to James and Robbie out of earshot of the cameraman.

'Why?' asked Robbie.

'Because if someone knows where Daddy is but hasn't said anything yet, then they'll see us on the TV and realise how much we're missing him and they might tell us where to find him. But we all have to pretend to look sad when they start filming us.'

'But we don't have to pretend,' replied a puzzled James. 'We *are* sad.'

Of course they were. I paused to ask myself if I was exploiting their pain to prove something to myself or to help our family as a whole. Would parading them publicly heap more psychological damage on what they'd already suffered? Or did the end justify the means?

I didn't see I had much of a choice, so I shoved them into the living room wearing long faces. I was a terrible mother. But, fired up by a breath of fresh interest in us, I blanketed surrounding villages, bus and train stations, hospitals, libraries and community centres with posters I'd had printed with my husband's photograph and description.

I delivered them to each place by hand so they'd be less inclined to throw them away, having seen my worried and desperate face in person. And I wrote three dozen letters and sent his photo to homeless shelters and Salvation Army centres around the country, in case he'd turned up confused. Being proactive gave me a lift I'd not felt in a while. I was optimistic and in control. When I'd completed every bit of outreach I could think of, I told myself that all I had to do was wait.

The police received thirty or so calls after the TV appeal, but none of the leads came to anything. I drew a blank with the Salvation Army, and only one shelter in London recalled seeing someone with a vague similarity to Simon. But that person had left months ago.

By the end of September, I was back to square one.

It's funny what the mind can do when it's grasping at straws and only touching nettles. Down to either wine or desperation, I began coming up with ludicrous theories to explain his absence. If it offered a faint glimmer of hope, I latched on to it.

I scanned through newspapers on the library's microfiche to see if there were any serial killers on the loose he might have fallen victim to. I asked Roger if there was any possibility he could've been forced into a police witness protection programme. I spoke to a very sympathetic woman at MI6 to ask if he'd been leading a double life for years as a spy, and was now on a mission somewhere in the world. She couldn't, or wouldn't, confirm or deny it.

I spent a day reading interviews with people who claimed they'd been abducted by aliens and experimented on. Simon hated his doctor prodding and poking him, so in a rare moment of self-amusement, I pictured his face as E.T. tried to stick a long finger up his backside.

I even visited a friend of Paula's mother, a psychic who frowned when she held Simon's comb in one hand and photo in the other. She closed her eyes and hummed.

'Well, he's not passed to the other side yet, dear,' she began, to my relief. 'I'm sensing that he's safe and well, but far away. Somewhere sandy. I'm getting mountains and people speaking in funny accents. He's smiling a lot. He seems very happy.'

I stormed out before she finished, cursing myself for throwing money at a fraud.

Back home, I walked through our front door, slumped across the kitchen table and, without taking my coat off, finished off a glass of wine I'd left earlier.

Four months had passed since Simon had vanished, and I was back to the morning of June the fourth – without him, and none the wiser as to why.

7 October

I went to bed early and turned off the lights, hoping the wine would knock me out quickly. It didn't. My stomach rumbled but I couldn't be bothered even to make myself a sandwich.

I'd long ceased closing the curtains, so that I could stare out of the window during my frequent bouts of insomnia. The moon was brighter than I'd ever seen it, as were the stars. I stared at clusters of them and tried to fit them together to form Simon's face.

It wasn't anything in particular that set me off, but I'd spent most of the day at a new low. It doesn't matter if you're holding the hand of a loved one as the death rattle slowly dissolves into a rasp, or if the police turn up on your doorstep to tell you there's been an accident. No matter how death happens, the pain is hideous.

Some people build barriers to hide from themselves or those who share their pain. Some shut down completely, and others dedicate the rest of their lives to mourning. The brave ones simply get on with it.

I couldn't do any of that. Because when someone simply disappears into thin air with no reason, no explanation and no closure, all you're left with is an interminable void. A gaping, aching chasm that can't be filled with the love, sympathy or strength of others.

Nobody knew my heart was now a black hole, swirling with the debris of unanswerable questions. Until physical proof of Simon's death came along, I would never, ever, truly be able to let him go.

I had no funeral to arrange; no body to bury; no one to blame; no autopsy to offer a medical answer or suicide note to explain a reason; no nothing. Just months of absolute nothingness.

And as everyone else's lives carried on beyond our garden gate, I was stuck in purgatory and feeling so very, very alone.

◆ ◆ ◆

SIMON

Saint-Jean-de-Luz, twenty-five years earlier

14 July

There was an emptiness in my belly that needed to be filled. My imagination was hungry and I craved a project to sink my teeth into. Even as a boy I'd had an urge to construct. Birdhouses, dens, rabbit hutches, dams in streams – it didn't matter so long as it was a tangible object I could build from scratch and be proud of.

My life in France was content and free of stress. But while I'd shaken most of the trappings of my past, living in a hostel that was once so splendid and now cried out for help made my desire to design and actualize impossible to ignore. It was what I did. I made things. I created things. I restored things.

And the more time I spent under its roof, the more familiar I'd become with its personality. I knew which floorboards creaked and which had barely enough strength to support my weight. I knew the windows to keep closed, or risk the rotting frames disintegrating. I knew on which side of the attic the mice preferred to nest. I knew the rooms to avoid in a heavy downpour and the places to find maximum sunlight for Bradley's indoor garden of cannabis plants to thrive.

I'd fallen in love with its every delight and failing. I'd accepted its flaws in a way I couldn't do with a person. I also knew that papering over the cracks of something couldn't disguise its deeper issues. I longed to transform the Routard International back into the Hôtel Près de la Côte.

Local folklore had it that the hotel had seemed to appear from nowhere in the mid-1920s. It had been designed by a promising Bordeaux architect who'd only ever made two visits to his project – once as they broke ground, and again when the doors were declared open to paying guests. Nobody could remember his name.

He'd been commissioned to design it for a wealthy Jewish German family who, after the First World War, feared their country might implode again. So they fortuitously made their property investments abroad. But when Germany crumbled for a second time, their hotel remained while they disappeared from the face of the earth. Their legacy was intact, but the hotel was orphaned and, with no owners to trace, the manager at the time retained it as his own. Upon his death, its fate lay in the hands of a succession of distant relatives who cumulatively did little to prevent it from falling into rack and ruin.

I was dismayed at how something once so treasured could have been wilfully abandoned, before recognising the irony. But I related more to buildings than to people. If you gave structures time, detail and attention, they would protect you. You would be safe beneath their roofs. People never truly offered such guarantees. So I made it my mission to give it the help it had given me.

Bradley put me in contact with its entrepreneurial Dutch owner, who admitted he'd blindly purchased it through auction on description alone. I wrote him a detailed, twelve-page proposition, explaining who

I was, my feelings towards his property, my qualifications and skills that would enable me to resuscitate it.

I listed the work it required and an approximate timescale and costing. Then I crossed my fingers and waited. A fortnight later, Bradley approached me over breakfast.

'I don't know what you said but the usually cheap bastard is on board.' He smiled, and offered me a congratulatory handshake.

'Really?' I replied, genuinely surprised I'd been taken seriously.

'Yep. He's wiring the money into the hostel's bank account on Monday, so you can get started when you like. He'll probably sell it once you're done, though.'

At that point, I did not care. The news delighted and excited me in equal measure, as for the first time in months, I had something to focus my attention on other than myself.

13 August

The work the hotel required gave me lots of time to spend alone. And with each acquaintance I made at the Routard International, I reflected more on the ones I'd cast aside.

I thought back to not long before Catherine and I became a couple, and the childhood friends who helped to shape me, specifically my best friend, Dougie Reynolds.

He'd moved some five hundred miles from Inverness, Scotland to Northamptonshire with his family, after his policeman father accepted a transfer to take charge of a new unit. They uprooted to the street next to mine.

Our friendship wasn't instant. Roger, Steven and I glared at the lanky, sapling-armed boy ambling into the classroom with his auburn hair and coarse, unintelligible accent, like he'd just fallen from a spaceship. During his first few days in our territory, he was given a wide, discerning berth. But he paid frustratingly little heed to our feigned lack of interest.

I'd just reached a personal best of twenty-five keepy-uppies with a football on the village green when he wandered over to me.

'Bet you I can do more,' he said with a grin, and struck a defiant, comic-book superhero pose with his hands on his hips.

'Go on then,' I sniffed, and deliberately threw the ball too hard at his chest. By the time he'd reached fifty with ease, he'd claimed victory and headed it back to me. A little humiliated, I began to walk away.

'Arch your back a little,' he said suddenly. 'Put your arms out for balance and focus on the centre of the ball.'

I reluctantly followed his advice, and it was only when my bare thigh smarted from the repetition of skin against cheap leather that I stopped at fifty-one. I concealed my smile, but that was all it took to cement the foundations of a friendship.

I was unsure whether it was his affable personality or his stable family life that captivated me the most. Dougie belonged to the perfect family, compared to mine, at least. A mother, a father, a brother and a sister – everything I'd have killed for.

Dougie Senior greeted his wife Elaine with a kiss to the cheek on his arrival home each evening. And she'd respond with an infinite supply of hotpot dishes and mouth-watering casseroles. Their family banter filled the dining room as Michael, Isla and Dougie each told their parents all they'd done that day. No detail was too insignificant to be included.

My friends all adored Elaine, and I think found her sexy before they knew what sexy meant. Her curls glowed like a Christmas tangerine, her skin was milky and freckled and she possessed a Monroe-like hourglass figure. She never asked me about Doreen, but I'm sure Dougie had explained to her my mother's irregular presence in my life. I wouldn't have been bothered if she'd pitied my circumstances at home. I was just grateful for the attention from a mother, even if it wasn't my own. Later, Shirley would try her best to mother me, but by then, I no longer wanted a matriarch.

Dougie's parents treated me like a part-time son. My place was set at the dining room table regardless of my presence. My sleeping bag remained on a camp bed in Dougie's bedroom and they'd even bought me my own toothbrush and facecloth. All the Reynolds children were encouraged to invite their friends over, and their house resembled a youth club with the number of children passing through its doors. But I believe Elaine took a special shine to me.

As an only child, I was fascinated by the unfamiliar world of sibling relationships – how they played, learned and fought with each other. They taught me the definition of family. But watching them also bred resentment in me towards my father. The head of Dougie's house was not a ghost of a man too overtly consumed with his louche wife to notice his own neglected son.

I questioned what was missing in my father's make-up that rendered him unable to keep hold of Doreen. Why didn't she love him like Elaine loved her husband? What did he lack that drove my mother into the arms of other men? He lacked nothing, of course. My negativity merely masked what I felt were my own failings as her son. I knew the man who offered me as much as he could also had his limitations. So what I couldn't get from him, I stole from the Reynoldses.

But the most important lesson I learned from spending time with them came years later. And it was that, if you scratch the surface of something perfect, you'll always find something rotten hidden beneath.

1 September

While neither Bradley nor I trespassed too far into each other's pasts, my gut instinct was that he was a reliable sort. My history was as irrelevant to me as it was to anyone else, so I would never have voluntarily revealed my true colours to him.

Such aloofness was a self-defence mechanism born out of bad experiences. Because the more you trust in someone, the more opportunities you give them to shatter your illusions about them. But as much as I cared to think of myself as a solitary unit – and as much as it was against my better judgement – I still needed a Dougie Reynolds in my life. Bradley came close to filling that vacancy.

It was during a lock-in at the village pub a decade earlier, and with several pints of Guinness loosening our lips, that Dougie had revealed the disease running through his family. Out of the blue, he confessed his father was a violent wife-beater who regularly knocked the living daylights out of Elaine.

Sometimes he'd hone his skills in front of his family, but for the most part, he kept his hobby behind the bedroom door. Dougie explained it was why she had encouraged his friends to spend time at their house. Because if left alone, some minor incident would likely occur and inspire Dougie Senior to hurt her again. Our friendship offered them a temporary stay of execution. He'd used me.

I masked my ever-increasing dismay while he tearfully recalled his family's swift departure from Scotland. Elaine had been attacked so badly that she'd been hospitalised for a fortnight – her husband's lightning-bolt blows broke her jaw and five ribs. Instead of offering their support to Elaine, Dougie Senior's colleagues encouraged her not to press charges against one of their own, and offered them a fresh start elsewhere.

But my disappointment wasn't directed at the culprit – it was towards his son. Dougie had urged me to buy into his idyllic home, knowing full well what it had meant to me. Any sympathy or understanding he should have expected as a result of his disclosure was greeted by stone-faced, silent selfishness instead. The snow globe in which I'd placed the Reynoldses had been shaken so vigorously, the contents would never settle again. He'd cheated me out of the only stability I had known. Ignorance was bliss, and I'd liked bliss.

I was also disappointed with Elaine's failure to remove herself from the side of a sadist. At least my mother had had the strength to leave us for a reason, no matter how weak it was. Elaine had plenty of them but she'd stayed and she'd lied, like all women do.

Eventually, Dougie must have read my expressionless face and realised my lack of compassion meant he'd confided in the wrong friend. So the conversation petered out, was brushed under the carpet and never discussed again.

Years later, I learned Dougie wasn't all he seemed, either. If I allowed myself the opportunity to know Bradley better, he'd probably disappoint me too, so I kept him at arm's length. It was better to remain on my island than drown in somebody else's sea.

7 October

'He's dead, man. Shit.'

Bradley gently rolled Darren's rigid body onto his back. He lay there with his eyes clammed shut. His forehead was as pale as a frosty morning and just as cold.

'He certainly is,' I sighed, then pulled a patchwork blanket up over his bare chest and covered the face devoid of expression. 'He looks quite peaceful. It doesn't look like he suffered.'

'My grandpa looked the same when he died of a heart attack in his sleep. Good way to go, right? Bet that's what happened to our guy. Better call the doc, then.' Bradley picked himself up and walked towards the reception's payphone.

With my eyes fixed on my friend's movements, my hands darted under the dead man's bed to find his backpack. I relied on touch to open the metal fasteners and fumbled around until I found my prize. I crammed it into my pocket just as Bradley hung up the receiver and turned around.

'Doc's on his way,' he shouted.

Darren Glasper had appeared on our doorstep a month or so before his sudden demise. Our hostel was cheerful and – most importantly for the traveller on a budget – inexpensive. And like myself, the intoxicating lure of the town's unfettered, relaxed anonymity was all it took to persuade Darren to remain there longer than first planned.

He told me over supper one night that, as the youngest of a family of eight, his motivation was to discover his own identity away from those who'd shaped it. At first, he'd succumbed to family convention by leaving school and becoming immersed in an unrewarding career in Sheffield's steel mills and foundries. But Darren craved more than a lifetime of manual labour in a job he despised. So, to his loved ones' surprise, he announced he was leaving to travel the world and educate himself, before returning home to educate others as a trainee teacher.

Despite his family's inevitable attempts to persuade him he was being foolish, he upped and left. Nevertheless, he beamed with pride when he spoke of them, and the wall behind his bunk bed was plastered with family photographs. He'd arranged them like a protective halo around his head and introduced me to them one by one. They all looked so much like one another – even, somehow, his parents.

Summer was a fertile period for the hostel and it had been filled to bursting with guests. However, the closing days of the season were quieter and allowed the building to loosen its belt and exhale. It gave me space to sink my teeth into my renovation work, and Darren and others were more than willing to act as my labourers.

He'd been afforded a four-bedroom dormitory to himself, but when neither Bradley nor I had seen him that day, his lack of presence concerned us.

At some point, Darren had checked out of the world he was so keen to be a part of.

The town's doctor arrived within the hour to officially pronounce him dead from a suspected heart attack. I'd joined Darren's smiling family in keeping his body company while we awaited the police and an ambulance to take him to the morgue for an autopsy.

I wondered how his family's lives would be affected by his death. I pitied them when I realised they'd probably never come to terms with being robbed of the opportunity to say goodbye to a son and brother, or apologise to him for arguing against his wanderlust.

For a moment, I contemplated how Catherine had coped when I too had followed my heart. But my thoughts were interrupted by the arrival of two officers, so I left the room and wandered into the courtyard for a cigarette.

Alone, I put my hand into my pocket and removed Darren's passport. His need to leave his old world behind would live on through me. I was enjoying my time at the hostel, using it as a place of redemption and healing. But I knew I'd develop itchy feet when I eventually finished my project. And possessing no passport or international identification meant that leaving for fresh pastures would be problematic. But not now.

Darren and I shared similar almond-shaped eyes, hairstyle and facial bone structure. A cursory glance at his passport's photograph confirmed that. As long as I avoided a razor for a couple of weeks, I'd match his light beard and gain the potential to explore wherever I liked.

The moral issues raised by assuming the identity of a man who'd yet to be laid out on a mortician's slab were complex – so I put them aside. No other issues presented themselves, especially as I alone knew that Darren had lost his wallet in Algeria. Without his passport, there would be no speedy way of tracking down his relatives.

I told the police his Christian name and his nationality and left them to fill in the blanks. It would buy me time. I stubbed out my cigarette and returned to the building to watch in respectful silence as his body was stretchered away.

Darren and I were both freer from those who'd held us back than we'd ever been before.

◆ ◆ ◆

Northampton, today

9.50 a.m.

'When did I ever hold you back?' Catherine roared. 'How dare you!
I did nothing but support you and encourage you. I believed in you!'

As each new revelation fell from his lips, her mood darkened, shade
by shade, until all she saw was black. She questioned whether the man
sitting before her was indeed the same one who'd promised to love her
until death do they part so long ago. It looked like him; it sounded like
him. Even his mannerisms remained, like the way he absent-mindedly
scratched the print of his thumb with his middle finger. Or when he
tapped his bottom lip to mask his anxiety.

But she heard no one she recognised in his recollections of his life
after discarding his family. Had it really been in him all along to live
without a conscience? How could she have failed to recognise such
deplorable deceit and opportunism in him? Her love really had been
blind.

'And you stole a dead man's passport?' she continued, perplexed.
'That's deplorable.'

He shuffled uncomfortably in his seat, like the devil was poking
him with a pitchfork. 'It's not something I'm proud of, but I did what
I had to do. I had no choice.'

She drew deeply from a reservoir of anger. 'Oh, here we go again
with those bloody words. *You had no choice.* Please, spare me. It was the
children and I who had no choice, no choice but to carry on trying to
live without you. No choice but to do all we could to try and find you.'

'In all honesty, I didn't expect you to be so persistent. I hoped you'd
give up after a few weeks.'

'But that's what love is, Simon. It's never giving up on the person
you've given your heart to. It's having faith that no matter how tough
things get, that person will always be looking for you.'

She shook her head at her own stupidity in dedicating so much time trying to find a man who'd long left the country. They stared at each other until she stopped waiting for him to defend himself. Her victory felt hollow.

He wasn't ready to explain in full why he, her husband, the stranger, had suddenly elbowed his way back into her life. It wasn't a revelation he could suddenly blurt out or casually slip into the conversation. He had to make clear to her why he had made his choices before he could reveal the role she'd played in pushing him away.

Only then, when she realised her culpability, could he drop the first of his bombshells. Otherwise all she would hear when it detonated was the deafening sound of the truth ricocheting around the room. She would not pause to reflect, and his appearance would be over as quickly as it began.

For her part, his refusal to answer even her most basic of questions frustrated her. She deserved to know the truth – all of the truth. But against her better judgement, she also had a growing curiosity as to just how he'd filled his ocean of time.

She hoped he'd lived a miserable, depressing existence filled with regret, longing and woe. But none of that was evident in the suntanned, healthy-looking man who'd invaded her home. And all she'd heard so far were his thinly disguised boasts of a much better life abroad – without her.

He rose to his feet and made his way over to the French doors in the dining room to look over the garden he'd once toiled to shape. The corners of his mouth rose when he spotted the patio where they'd spent many long evenings planning their future. He hadn't thought about those nights in years, and for a moment, he acknowledged there had been good times after all.

She'd since had a brick barbecue built and a wooden pagoda erected, where bright green grapevines hung. He knew from experience they'd never make a decent wine. A child's yellow plastic bike was propped up against a crab-apple tree he'd planted in the corner by the firs. He wondered where and who the bike's owner was.

'I am glad you kept our house,' he said softly.

'My house,' she corrected quickly. 'It's my house. And I nearly lost it because of you.'

CHAPTER SIX

CATHERINE

Northampton, twenty-five years earlier

14 October

'You bloody idiot,' I muttered.

My heart had sunk when I'd read the letter. Eight weeks was all we had left in our home before the bank repossessed it. I'd been ignoring the stack of brown envelopes addressed to Simon and crammed them into the kitchen drawer, out of sight and out of mind. And I hadn't given any thought to checking the balance in our account.

Money wasn't something I'd ever needed to take responsibility for. I'd been more than happy to let him deal with our finances. I'd presumed he'd make sure we were okay, and as long as we kept a roof over our heads that was all that mattered. Silly old me.

So I'd only known there was a problem when the first cheque bounced. It rebounded off the doormat and back into my hand a few days after I gave it to a petrol station cashier. Two more soon tumbled through the letterbox from our gas and electricity suppliers.

But it wasn't until my debit card was declined at the supermarket checkout that I knew I had to pull my red face out of the sand to see just how much trouble I was in. The fridge was almost bare, and the only food we had was waiting to be paid for in an abandoned trolley.

So I plucked up the courage to look at the bank statement and, through squinted eyes, regretted it straight away. I was up to my neck in an emergency overdraft I hadn't known had been activated. Simon's wages had always covered the utilities, but there was never much left to siphon off into a rainy-day account.

He and Steven had agreed that until the firm reached a certain profit, they'd only pay themselves a basic sum. But now, with only half the work being done, Steven had barely enough to cover his own expenses, let alone mine. There was little in the way of spare cash, and certainly not enough to survive a drought. And after three months of natural erosion, the reservoir was dry.

Despite the turmoil it had seen, our house was as much a part of the family as the people who lived under its roof. But unless my fairy godmother waved her magic wand, we were going to lose it.

I wasn't stupid. I loved a little gossip as much as the next person. So I knew many people in the village were talking about me. I'd see them looking away when they spotted me in the street, unsure of what to say. I heard whispers at the school gates from the other mums. I had my suspicions they thought Simon had walked out on me, only because I'd have probably thought the same thing if I was them.

So I played my rumoured 'abandoned wife' status to my advantage and pleaded ignorance to my debts during an appointment with our bank manager. I even felt a twinge of guilt when I turned on the waterworks in his office with surprising ease to prove how hard I was finding it to cope. But it worked.

He offered me a further eight-week stay of execution, giving me a total of four months to climb out of arrears before his hands became tied and we lost our home. I could have kissed him, but instead I skulked back home, ashamed of how I'd let things slide. Then I decamped into the dining room and faced the reality of my money woes on a table littered with old statements and red letters. A bottle of wine gave me support as I watched figures on reams of pages twirl around like whirling dervishes, daring me to take a closer look at the mischief they'd created while I was distracted. Eventually, I calculated my outgoings were triple my incomings. No matter where I thought I could make some savings, the debts were still going to mount up.

The fact that Simon had, as far as the authorities were aware, not actually died but gone AWOL made it much harder to claim welfare support. I'd slipped into a grey area that wasn't recognised by black-and-white regulations. I wouldn't receive a widow's allowance, as there was no proof he was dead, and I'd not been 'actively seeking work', so I couldn't claim unemployment benefits. I was allowed family support, but that fortnightly payment didn't stretch far. I was caught between a rock and a hard place.

Frustrated, I poured myself another drink while my eyes filled up faster than the glass. I was both angry with him for leaving me like this and at myself for being in denial. Something had to change. It was time to remove myself from my pity party and start being the breadwinner.

I began by selling the family car I rarely used, then reluctantly pawning my jewellery, including my gorgeous wedding and engagement rings. Never in all our years together had I taken either of them off. Not even when we'd spent all our waking hours glossing doors and staining floorboards or lifting concrete slabs. If I scuffed my rings, it didn't matter – they'd be reminders of what we'd built together. Even when four pregnancies made my fingers puffy, they remained where I could see them at all times. Now Simon's disappearance had made them the saddest objects I owned. The only thing stopping another round of tears was the knowledge that when we found him, I'd be able to buy them back.

A house clearance firm I found in the telephone directory made up the rest of the mortgage shortfall. I begged them to come late in the evening, as I was too embarrassed for the neighbours to see strange men taking our worldly goods away in the back of a truck.

I sold the Welsh dresser from the kitchen; a sofa and television we barely used from the den; Simon's writing bureau; two bookshelves; three wardrobes; the dishwasher; a chest of drawers, dressing table and sideboard; lamps and crockery we'd been given as wedding presents. And while it killed me to do it, I even sold the children's bikes. By the time the removal men left an hour later, I still had a home but barely anything left to fill it.

I sat broken-hearted, gazing at the empty floors and empty walls in our empty shell. And as I nursed my wine and glanced at my empty finger, I felt like a hopeless failure, as a wife and as a mum. It seemed like it might be harder than I thought to leave my pity party early.

21 October

My children gave me an unselfish, beautiful, organic love that grew as they grew. But the love Simon had given me was something altogether different. It had made me feel desired, appreciated, respected and needed. And I missed that; I missed it so much. He took with him something I didn't believe I could hurt so badly for.

But as each week passed, I gradually figured out I shouldn't need another person to validate my life, no matter how much I had loved or now longed for it. It was something I could do myself and it began in our local supermarket, of all places.

I knew checkout assistant and shelf stacker wasn't the greatest job in the world when I saw it advertised in the window. But this beggar couldn't afford to be a chooser, so I gagged my inner snob and applied for it.

I stared into the staffroom mirror that first morning and barely recognised myself. I was a thirty-three-year-old bag of nerves dressed in an ill-fitting, brown Crimplene uniform and wearing a 'Trainee' badge.

I'd become used to mirrors tormenting me. I made a weekly pilgrimage to the one in my bathroom for some brutal home truths. Inch by inch, I'd pull on loose skin from the stone I'd lost since Simon had gone, prod rogue folds and carefully examine my body and face for any obvious signs of collapse. I'd sigh as I charted the progression of an army of silver silkworms weaving their way across my crown. I could have lost a finger in the crevices around my eyes that had once been subtle laughter lines. Ironically, they'd only grown when the laughter died.

Neither Simon nor youth were on my side any longer. While I was still more Jane Fonda than Henry Fonda, the gap between the two was growing closer. But, whatever the direction my new life was going to take, I was going to give it my all.

Most of the checkout girls seemed decades younger than me. In reality, there were only a few years between us. But a missing husband and raising a family on your own ages you in a hurry.

Working kept me busy and stopped me from feeling sorry for myself. The mums swapped parenting stories and gave each other knowing smiles when the student part-timers swapped drunken tales and complained of exam stress like they were pioneers in the field of drinking and homework. Secretly I envied them, and tried to remember what it felt like to have so few worries or battle scars.

Sometimes I'd listen to the housewives moan about their lazy, selfish husbands, and I'd want to shout, 'At least you still have yours!' But I'd smile and nod along with the rest of the sisterhood instead.

My husband's disappearance still had a curiosity factor attached to it, like the village had its own Bermuda Triangle. It was usually the older customers coming in for their weekly shop who seemed eager to share their opinions, like only elderly people can.

'Do you think he's dead?' 'Did he have a bit on the side?' 'It'll be hard to find another man willing to take on a girl with three little 'uns, won't it?' My skin grew thicker by the day, and I learned to let insensitive comments fly over my head.

It was my supervisor Selena I had the most in common with, despite our obvious differences. She was a well-spoken, educated, bleached-blonde slip of a girl who didn't really belong there. At twenty, she was the only young single parent in the shop, and proud of it. The father of her four-year-old had abandoned her as soon as she told him she was in the family way. But it hadn't put her off going it alone.

She'd turned down a place studying economics at Cambridge University and was working like a trooper to feed and clothe her boy, something I related to. So I spent more time with her than the others. And I didn't care if it was favouritism or because she thought there was more to me than checkout number seven's chief resident, but she spoke to our deputy manager, who soon promoted me to organising float changes and working out staff rotas.

More money and longer hours meant I had to rearrange our family life. A bossy but coordinated Paula made sure that she and Baishali took it in turns to babysit Emily during the day, and pick up the boys from school in the afternoon.

'We're going to do everything it takes to help get you back on track,' said Paula. 'Aren't we, Baish?'

Baishali nodded. When Paula was in 'organise everyone' mode, nobody disagreed with her, least of all Baishali.

And when I finished work, I'd take over and finish the nightly routine, until they were bathed and in bed.

Then, when the house fell silent, I'd open a bottle of red and begin my second and third jobs.

30 October

By the time summer had given way to autumn, Simon dominated my thoughts that little bit less.

I began an ironing service for my busy neighbours who didn't have the time to work, look after a family and make sure their clothes weren't creased. I charged by the basket-load and spent a good couple of hours a night surrounded by other people's shirts and blouses on hangers around the kitchen.

I made savings where I could, buying own-brand supermarket food and the kids' toys and games from charity shops, cutting my own hair and walking or catching the bus. I'd cinched my financial belt so tightly that it pinched like a corset. New clothes were a necessity but bloody pricey for a one-parent family, especially when they grew out of them so quickly. I decided it would be much cheaper if I made them myself.

But the idea of picking up a needle and thread again scared me to death.

For much of my married life, I'd earned a little extra money doing alterations to clothes for our friends. A turned-up hem here or a zipper replacement there had progressed into making clothes for the kids to play in, a few skirts for myself, and then bridesmaids' dresses for my friend's wedding.

It was impossible not to think about those dresses without images of Billy flooding my mind. Of course, I knew that my sewing hadn't been to blame for that day's horror – I alone was to blame for that, no matter how Simon or Paula had tried to persuade me it was an accident and no one's fault – but I'd packed away my sewing machine and materials as though they were cursed. Now, though, I had to face it: making clothes was the only practical skill I had and I needed to put food on our table. My supermarket wage was enough to cover the bills and the mortgage, but left very little else.

I downed half a bottle of red for Dutch courage before I grabbed the material I'd bought from the market. Then I picked up my pinking shears and rustled up school shirts and trousers for James and Robbie.

Each bouncing bobbin, each foot on the pedal and each rattle of the machine's engine brought that day back to me. Since Simon had vanished, I'd tried my best to put it out of my mind.

And my children needed me in the world more than I did. So I held my pain deep down and ploughed on. By the time I finished I was three sheets to the wind, but I'd done it. And if I did say so, the results were indistinguishable from – all right: superior to – the store-bought garments we could in no way afford.

Word of mouth soon spread amongst the school-gate mums that I could save them a small fortune by making their kids' clothes too. And soon, half the children running around the village seemed like they were dressed in something I'd sewn.

When my friends asked if I'd make clothes for them too, a lightbulb switched on in my head. It could be the answer to my financial woes, so I gave it a bash. They arrived on my doorstep with armfuls of fabrics and torn-out cuttings of outfits they'd seen in magazines and hoped I could copy. On instinct I found I could replicate even really tricky designs without much of a problem. And it gave me the confidence to suggest my own twists and ideas.

The supermarket students, who didn't earn enough to buy what they saw pop stars wearing, began spending some of their wages on things I'd create for them for their favourite nightclubs. Even Selena, whose circumstances precluded anything like a social life until her son Daniel was older, took advantage of having a friend who could whip up a shoulder-padded jacket in an evening.

It wasn't long before all my nights found me holed up in the dining room and hunched over a sewing machine with only a bottle of wine to keep me company. I didn't have time to stop and think how my eighteen-hour days might be affecting my health.

28 October

It hurt like someone was kicking me in the stomach over and over again. Even lifting my arm to stack the last box of cornflakes on the supermarket shelf winded me.

My stomach had ached on and off for most of the day. But I had painful cramps and I knew it wasn't my usual time of the month. Eventually I had to admit something was wrong. I struggled to catch my breath as I left the pallet of boxes in the aisle, headed to a toilet cubicle to unbutton my dungarees and examined what was making my groin feel damp. I panicked when I saw lots of blood in the front of my knickers.

I clocked off and slipped out of the warehouse doors clenching my tummy, and half-walked, half-stumbled a mile and a half to the doctor's surgery. The cramps were getting worse as I waited for Dr Willows, and almost as soon as I lay on the bed, I felt a popping inside me. Then I leaked more blood as she helped me to the toilet. And when the pain became too intense, I fainted.

'You're having a miscarriage, Catherine,' Dr Willows explained slowly when I woke up. 'The pains you're feeling are contractions in the uterus. They're dilating your cervix to get the foetus out. There's nothing we can do but let your body do what it has to do.'

I struggled to get a grip on what she was saying. How could I be pregnant? Was my motherly instinct now so rotten that the only time I felt my baby inside me was when it was dying?

'But I've been having my periods,' I argued.

'It can still happen, I'm afraid.'

'How far gone am I?'

'I can only hazard a guess, but probably about five months.'

I remembered the night Simon and I last made love. It was the weekend before he disappeared and, once again, I'd instigated it. Neither of us had said it, but we both knew we were still going through the motions. I'd convinced myself that if we both kept trying to make an effort, we would, in time, feel like us again. It never crossed my mind it would be the last time, or that it'd leave me pregnant.

Dr Willows led me to the nurse's room and I lay on my side until the pain eased. She gave me a handful of sanitary towels, a bottle of painkillers and offered me a lift home. I turned it down.

It's hard to explain, but instead of feeling emotional like any ordinary mother would after miscarrying, an eerie feeling of detachment came across me. It was like the trauma of what had just happened belonged to someone else, not me.

So I calmly lifted myself up and left the surgery. I made my slow way back to the supermarket and clocked back in, and continued where I'd left off. And as I priced up a new pallet of lemonade bottles, my colleagues had no idea I'd left the aisle as two people and come back as one. Or that I'd just killed my second child in less than two years.

That night I put Emily to bed and asked James and Robbie to fend for themselves, blaming a tummy ache on my need to hide myself away in the bedroom.

I was still yet to shed one single, solitary tear. I shut my eyes tight and dug my fingernails deep into my palm to force them out, but still I felt nothing. I thought of a life without Billy and without Simon but that didn't work either. I was numb. I wondered if I'd shed so many tears in my lifetime that I'd now run out.

I rubbed my belly where my child had been hiding and wondered how I could have lost so much control of my life. I blamed losing it on the stress of worrying about Simon, the kids, my finances . . . and maybe even the bottle of wine that lay under the blanket next to me. I decided I was hopeless and defective and that my baby had had a narrow escape with me as its mother. No wonder it wanted to die – it probably had an inkling of what was to come.

My head throbbed, so I reached over to the bedside table, took a third painkiller from Dr Willows's packet and washed it down with a swig of wine, straight from the bottle. I hesitated, and then took a fourth pill. And a fifth. Then a sixth, seventh, eighth and ninth. But before I swallowed my tenth, I retched and vomited across the floor.

Resting in a puddle of alcohol and bile lay all nine tablets. I couldn't even kill myself properly.

7 December

'Bloody thing!' I shouted as I caught my finger in the sewing machine needle for the second time in as many minutes. It was either exhaustion or one too many drinks that blurred my vision. Regardless, I sucked my finger to stem the bleeding and headed for the kitchen to find another sticking plaster.

'Sod you,' I muttered to Mrs Kelly's unfinished skirt on the dining room table. I'd go back to it later when it had learned its lesson. I wrapped the Band-Aid around my finger and thought back to when I was a child and I'd lose myself in my mum's fashion magazines and a world of women draped in beautiful fabrics.

She had been an unappreciated seamstress with delusions of grandeur. I'd sit transfixed as she assembled beautiful dresses and coats from nothing. She'd get lost in a place a long way from the one she found herself stuck in with my dad and me. She once admitted her teenage dream had been to work for one of the great Parisian fashion houses, hand-stitching stunning haute couture creations until her fingers numbed.

'That would have given me greater pleasure than anything else life has thrown my way,' she said wistfully, then gave me a disappointed sideways glance to emphasise her point. She needn't have.

My mother was fascinated by the work of couture aristocrat Hubert de Givenchy and his muse Audrey Hepburn. She would copy his refined, immaculate designs in her own way. I shared her passion, but unfortunately she had little interest in sharing any of her skills with me.

I begged her to teach me what she knew, but she'd ignore me. It was like she was afraid she'd lose her gift if she passed it on to someone else – even her only child. But as long as I kept quiet and didn't ask questions, I was allowed to watch her work from the other side of the room.

Even as a little girl, I never quite understood why my parents had bothered to start a family – whether it was just the done thing in those days, or because I was an unfortunate accident. Either way, they didn't really need me. I was never physically neglected, but my mum wasn't shy in reminding me of my place in her pecking order.

'You're a guest in this family,' she once barked without provocation, 'and don't forget it.'

Despite being aware of her many faults, it was calming watching beautiful clothes come from a cold heart. Sometimes I'd wait until she'd left the house, then sneak into her wardrobe and shut the doors so I could have them all to myself. I'd close my eyes and smell them or try to identify the materials by the muffled sounds they made when I rubbed them between my fingers.

I remembered a gift I made for her when I was nine. I'd saved up my pocket money to buy four yards of ivory-cream polyester fabric, and every night after school, I ran to my room and hand-sewed a blouse ready for her birthday. Even then I knew it was crude, but I hoped she'd be proud of what I'd learned and add her own spit and polish to it. As she unwrapped the string and paper, she gave me a half-baked 'thank you' but never tried it on for size, even to be polite.

A few days later, she asked me to polish the fireguard, so I went to the cupboard under the kitchen sink for a tin of Brasso. Inside lay the tatters of my blouse, cut into strips to use as dusters. It was a cruel lesson. You can either learn from your parents' mistakes, or repeat them and use them as an excuse for your own behaviour. I vowed never to blame her for my failings. And from then on, everything I made was in spite of her, and without the need of her approval.

My mum's dresses led long but lonely lives. Once complete, they wouldn't be shown off at parties or to her friends; instead, they would hang in protective bags for only her to enjoy.

Dad worshipped the ground she laid fabric on. And his obsession with keeping her happy overshadowed everything else in his life, including me. I envied my friends when they admitted they were daddy's girls. I was nobody's girl until I met Simon. But Dad knew my mum's calling gave her a happiness he couldn't match.

'Mummy!' Emily's panicked voice brought me out of my recollections. She was standing by the door, her face scrunched up, and I could see that she'd wet her pyjama bottoms.

'It's okay,' I said. 'Let's get you cleaned up and back to bed.' I took her hand and as we walked up the stairs I racked my brains, but for the life of me, I couldn't ever remember a time I'd felt my mother's skin held so close against my own.

Christmas Day

Our house had never been so silent on a Christmas morning. In past years, I'd watch as wrapping paper spun through the air like stray fireworks on Bonfire Night. And I'd cover my ears at the deafening squeals of the kids.

They'd normally wake Simon and I up around four o'clock in the morning, prodding our arms and anxiously whispering, 'Has he been yet?' And with no hope of settling them back to sleep, we'd give in to the inevitable and follow them downstairs. We'd switch on the Christmas tree lights, and take as much pleasure watching them tear open their presents as we'd had in buying them.

But that year, eight o'clock arrived and the house was firework-free. I dreaded the moment they'd wake up – not just because their dad wasn't there, but because I was ashamed of how pitiful the gifts waiting for them were. I knew it, and soon they would too.

It was the best I could do, as my choice was simple but bloody unfair – piles of presents, or an empty dinner table for most of January. Nevertheless, I got them up one by one myself and tried to spur them into action.

'Have we been naughty?' asked James, when he saw there were only two boxes waiting for him to open.

I sighed. But without admitting Father Christmas was a big fat fib and what lay before them was all Mummy could afford, there wasn't much I could say to convince them they weren't being punished.

'Of course not, darling,' I replied. 'Santa just didn't have much room on his sleigh this year.'

It fell on deaf ears.

All day I tried my hardest to encourage them to wear those flimsy, colourful Christmas cracker hats and play with the crappy plastic toys inside. I even delayed dinner so James could watch the *Top of the Pops* Christmas special. Robbie said very little, and lay on his bed in his room stroking Oscar instead. Nothing I did lifted their spirits.

What should have been a day of celebration was missing its heart. Instead of the beautiful madness of six, it had withered to one drunken grown-up desperately pretending the Christmas chicken was really a small turkey. I knew what James was asking for when we pulled the wishbone together. Even a bottle of wine failed to bring me festive cheer.

I kept the house phone in my apron pocket for most of the day in the hope that if Simon was still alive, by some miraculous turn of events, he'd call. But, of course, he didn't.

Suddenly there came a knock at the door and my heart jumped. Before I could say a word, the children leaped from their chairs and ran towards it.

'Daddy!' squealed Emily as her little legs buckled beneath her in the scramble. For a second, I thought they were right and chased after them, praying for the kind of miracle you see in Christmas films. But as the door opened, Roger, Steven, Paula and Baishali stood there, not him.

Their arms were full of gifts, but not even Santa could give us the only thing we all really wanted.

◆ ◆ ◆

SIMON

Saint-Jean-de-Luz, twenty-five years earlier

10 September

I squatted on an upturned wooden box outside the hotel on the Rue du Jean. I placed my plastic hard hat on the pavement and lit my seventh Gauloise of the morning. Catherine had only ever allowed me to smoke socially or on special occasions. So with nobody to complain that my breath reeked of stale tobacco, my occasional habit had become a full-time addiction.

I stretched my legs out and winced as my knee joints cracked. Climbing up and down scaffolding twenty times a day with my hostel workforce was exhausting and took its toll on my body, but the results had been worth every second.

While the capital investment from the Routard's owner wasn't enough to restore it to its former glory, I'd thrown myself into my work to recreate something of worth as best I could.

I allowed myself to think back to my first project, a ramshackle collection of bricks and mortar that eventually became our first home. Before she and I could afford a car, we'd passed the cottage dozens of times on our way to and from the bus stop. It was in desperate need of restoration, yet it always caught our eye.

Ivy had crept up its faded whitewashed walls, along the patchy tiled roof, and clasped the chimney pot in its fingers. The wooden window frames had bowed and the garden hadn't seen a tool in a lifetime. Weeds competed with trees to see which could grow taller.

But I liked that Catherine could see what I saw, a shared vision of its potential: somewhere we could raise a family, our own perfect family. We were living in a tiny apartment above a fish and chip shop when we heard that a gas-meter reader had discovered the body of the cottage's elderly owner. Her withered shell had remained slumped face down on her kitchen table for up to a month.

Her estranged son put her house up for sale for a snip, like he wanted rid of both it and her memory as quickly as possible. Money wasn't abundant, what with me freshly qualified with a university BA in architecture and employed at my first job with a small firm. Meanwhile, she was window-dressing at a department store in town. But we calculated we could afford the mortgage repayments if we scrimped. There'd be years of work ahead of us before it matched the image we'd painted of it in our heads. That didn't matter – in fact, nothing mattered but buying the house.

Once our solicitor had handed us the keys, not even the stench left by a decomposing carcass put us off. We simply covered our noses and mouths with tea towels and toasted our first house with a bottle of Babycham in the hallway. We had something to build on of our own, which neither of us had experienced before.

As I stared at the progress I'd made in restoring the Routard, those same feelings of accomplishment and excitement rushed through me – the knowledge you are on your way to creating something flawless. Suddenly the voice I'd first heard in the woods the day I left Catherine made itself known: 'Do I need to remind you of what happens to all perfect things?'

I shook my head, my euphoria evaporating in an instant.

'It's only a matter of time before they stop being perfect and destroy you.'

October 18

I lifted the sledgehammer over my head, swung it towards the door handle and smashed through the lock.

Bets had been placed on what secrets lay behind the keyless door in the Routard's mysterious storeroom. Skeletal remains, valuable artwork concealed from the Nazis, an extensive wine cellar or perhaps a parallel universe were all jokingly considered.

With two well-placed whacks, the door sprang back on its hinges to reveal what not even the Dutch owner knew it contained – a six-feet-by-eight-feet, pitch-black room. When Bradley shone his torch inside, the spectators behind us gave a collective deflated sigh at the sight of crate after crate crammed with paperwork, receipts and invoices.

It wasn't until later in the day, when I'd consigned the splintered door to the rubbish, that I caught a glimpse of a photograph poking out from one of the crates I'd dropped into the garbage earlier. I leaned over the edge and pulled it out for closer inspection.

A family, possibly the original owners, stood dressed to the nines, beaming proudly before the camera outside the pristine-looking Hôtel Près de la Côte. I instantly recognised the chubby-faced man standing at their side. It was Pierre Chareau, a classic modernist and art deco designer I'd studied extensively at university. I had long admired his maverick vision. Like me, he'd trained as an architect, but he'd added extra strings to his bow by branching out into design and decoration. The pinnacle of his work was the Maison de Verre – the first house in France to be constructed of steel and glass.

I grabbed the crate and hauled it back into the hostel courtyard. I lit up the first of many cigarettes as I ploughed through hundreds of pages of designs, photographs, blueprints and illustrations. There were sheets of handwritten notes and orders – all signed by Chareau. And they weren't all related to the hotel. There were sketches of buildings that had never been, and designs of furniture that had.

When placed in chronological order, they offered a fascinating insight into the creative mind of a genius and the projects he'd never publicly acknowledged. Forty years after his death and I was residing in what had once been just his vision. I'd been charged with returning it to the glory he'd been responsible for. But with these papers, I'd also found my holy grail, and my way out.

5 December

I'd thrown myself into the final stages of the hotel's renovation. I'd become obsessive, working all the hours God sent, day and night, only napping for a handful of hours at a time. And it was starting to take its toll on me.

I was crouched in a bath, sealing its rim with adhesive against the tiled walls, when the quite dry, very French tub before me was all at once replaced by the bath in my old house in Northampton, complete with water inside and bubbles, and a toy boat floating from one end to the other. I blinked hard, and when I opened my eyes again, the image had vanished as quickly as it appeared. I felt chills across my body so I climbed out and started work on a staircase instead. Thank God that bit of madness was not repeated, but the memory of it left a stain that took some weeks to wash out.

As the countdown to the festive period began, it became a challenge not to think of the family I'd shared so many Christmases with. But when I thought about Catherine, I kept reminding myself I was no longer a father or a husband.

We'd both agreed we wanted to be young parents, and being a parent was the greatest gift she ever gave me. Nothing she nor I subsequently did to each other ever took away the feeling of utter elation in holding those tiny, hope-filled hands for the first time in the house they'd been born into. Over the years, as each midwife passed each baby to me, I'd gently slip my finger between their tightly balled fists, plant a kiss on the centre of their foreheads and whisper 'I will never let you down' into their ears. It saddened me to think the first words they'd ever heard were lies.

'Si, you need some sleep, man,' yelled Bradley, bringing me back to the present. 'Look.'

He pointed to the banister I'd just sanded down to the grain – I'd only painted and varnished it a night earlier.

I yawned and closed the lid on Catherine once again, and moved on to the wooden arc of the entrance hall. It felt smooth to the touch, but it could be better. I couldn't bring myself to stop sanding it until it was beyond compare.

Christmas Eve

I'd never spent the holidays in the company of strangers before, which was probably why I'd been reluctant to embrace the forthcoming festivities. But my apathy evaporated when I turned the corner into Christmas Eve.

Diminishing numbers wasn't going to prevent us from indulging in good food and all-round merriment. But it took queuing with crowds of locals outside the *boulangeries* and *patisseries* to collect orders for fine meats and cheeses to spark the kindling inside me. I fed off their gaiety until I found myself grinning without reason.

In keeping with French tradition, the seven of us left at the Routard International enjoyed an appetising midnight meal together before we welcomed Christmas Day. We covered the dining room table in a clean white bedsheet, treated our palates with the rich textures of foie gras on sliced brioche and smoked salmon on blinis.

My bloated stomach was already close to bursting point when the chef, who the Routard's owner had hired as a reward for my renovation work, brought out a platter of cooked meats. I was completely spoiled.

'How did you used to spend Christmas?' asked Bradley as we smoked two plump cigars on the mild seafront.

I recalled a time two years earlier, sitting in the corner of our living room watching all six of them caught up in the moment. My relationship with Catherine was completely distorted by then, and I didn't belong there. *He* had made sure of that. I was like a coiled spring that longed to unravel but didn't know how or when to.

'Not much,' I replied ambiguously.

'Thought you'd say that,' said Bradley before we puffed away and watched a trail of shooting stars blast their way across the sky.

Christmas Day

With only a handful of guests remaining under my retiled roof, the hostel had been as restful as I'd known it.

'Do you wanna call anyone?' asked Bradley when he finished with the phone, handing me the receiver. I paused. 'Do you want to call any of your family back in England or something? You know it's Christmas Day, right?'

For the first time since I'd left Catherine, something unexpected in me was curious to hear her voice. I took the receiver and, without giving myself time to debate it, held it to my ear. I dialled the country code, then the area code, and finally all but the last digit of our phone number.

My finger hovered over the last number, unable to press it. Because even hearing her just say the word 'hello' as she picked up the phone, or the voices of the children as they played with toys in the background, would do me no good. The time of year for family and togetherness was weakening my resolve, but I had to come to my senses or undo all my good work.

'No, it's okay,' I told Bradley, passing the phone back to him. I had to remain in the present, not the past.

◆ ◆ ◆

Northampton, today

11.10 a.m.

He'd spent years holding himself back from allowing her sympathy. But even he couldn't ignore how traumatic it must have been to miscarry and face it alone.

But as sorry as he felt for her, ultimately she had brought it on herself. *All of it.* And she'd been right: the baby had had a narrow escape.

He was surprised by her tenacity when it came to working three jobs, but he didn't mention it, so as not to appear patronising. He'd expected her to have quickly found a replacement for him, if only to provide financial stability for the children. But he'd seen to it that one man in particular could never have been an option for her.

So far, she'd not mentioned anyone else; it appeared she'd muddled along alone. He admired that, as he did her return to dressmaking. He recalled how she'd believed that hobby had destroyed their family. But secretly he knew it wasn't to blame. Not at all. And he understood how financially destitute she must have been to have picked up a needle and thread again.

For every story he'd recounted of his adventures without his boring wife and children, she was torn between bringing him back to the brutal reality he'd left behind and making sure he was aware of what she'd accomplished.

No one could ever really appreciate her lows unless they'd lived through them with her. She knew he understood grief, as they'd walked that path together. But he couldn't comprehend the pain of losing someone without ever knowing if they were truly lost.

She wanted him to feel the same misery he'd inflicted upon them, but she didn't need his pity. Besides, with his golden tan and tailor-made suit, he hardly resembled a man wracked with remorse or who had faced hard times.

She just desperately needed to witness some human emotion in his steely exterior, or proof that she'd not been completely blind to him throughout their relationship. That inside him, some compassion remained.

She thought she'd spotted it briefly when she told him about their Christmas without him. She noticed the uncomfortable twitch of his middle finger against the print of his thumb. It meant he didn't like what he was hearing. She would use that to her advantage, she decided.

If he was going to play games by making her wait before he told his truth, then she'd use that time to make him feel as awkward as possible. And her children would be her weapons.

But, most importantly, she would try her hardest to show him she was not the same naive fool he'd left behind.

CHAPTER SEVEN
CATHERINE

Northampton, twenty-five years earlier

New Year's Eve

'You're drunk, Mummy,' whined James.

'Don't be silly,' I snapped, yanking the hem of his costume down further still. 'And for God's sake, stop fidgeting.'

'Ow! You're hurting me!'

I was trying to finish his Batman outfit for the New Year's Eve fancy-dress party at the village hall. I'd accidentally jabbed a pin into his ankle and wasn't in the mood for his whingeing.

It'd been a relentless week. I'd had all our costumes to make from scratch for an event I couldn't give two hoots about. I'd worked an extra fifteen hours of overtime at the supermarket over two days and had a list of sewing requests as long as my arm. And I hadn't even begun to tackle the baskets of unironed clothes stacked up in the hallway. There just weren't enough hours in my day. So who could blame me for having a glass of wine here and there to help me through it?

Well, James, for starters.

Habitually, I'd uncorked the first by breakfast. And by early evening, one more empty bottle was lying on its side by the kitchen bin. But I certainly wasn't drunk, I told myself, and it annoyed me my son had the nerve to presume I was.

'Shut up, it's only a little prick,' I barked. James's eyes filled up, which irritated me even more because he was only going to slow me down. I raised my voice and dug my fingernails into his wrists until he squirmed. 'Right, you can either stop your sniffling and let me get on with this, or you can go to the party looking like a fool and have your friends laugh at you. Which one are you going to choose?'

Even as the words tripped off my tongue, I knew I was sounding like my mother. I heard a lot of her in myself these days and I didn't like it. But the colder I became, the more frequently she reared her head.

It wasn't James's fault I was in such a foul mood. I'd missed Simon more than ever over Christmas. The new year was about to begin and I couldn't see how things were going to get any easier.

It wasn't helping that it was also my thirty-fourth birthday – my first birthday without him since we were eleven years old. I wanted to throw myself under the quilt in an alcohol-induced coma and wake up seven months earlier. Then I'd never let him out of my sight for the rest of our lives. Instead, I was going to a party filled with couples who'd remind me of what I was missing.

I also resented the kids for not remembering my birthday, even while I was trying to forget it. Four unopened cards and gifts from friends lay on the kitchen table, but there'd been no special kisses or cuddles from my own family – just relentless demands for food, costumes and attention. I longed to be the centre of someone else's attention again.

'There, it's done, now take it off or you'll get it creased,' I grumbled as James stomped out of the room.

I sat on the living room floor alone, staring at the last drop of wine in both the glass and the house. I cursed the kids for taking up so much of my time that I hadn't got the chance to stock up at the off-licence before it closed early. When everything else around me went wrong, wine was my safety net, and it made me angry if there wasn't a bottle to hand if I needed it. I dreaded waiting another three hours for the party to begin before I could have another drink.

A loud crash in the kitchen was the final straw. My mother and I roared together. 'Bloody shut up now, or there'll be no party and you'll all go to bed early!' I screamed, hoping the kids would give me an excuse to be a hermit.

Their voices quietened to whispers, then giggles, then squeals.

'Right,' I bellowed and stood up, steadying my jelly legs against the arm of the sofa and going to confront them. Their backs were towards me but Robbie couldn't hide the glue and scissors in his hands or the torn newspapers scattered across the worktops and floor.

'What the hell are you doing? Look at the mess in here! And you know you're not allowed to play with scissors. Get upstairs, now!'

My words were a little blurred but my outburst dazed them. As they separated, a homemade birthday card with a drawing of our cottage and family lay on the table. They'd framed it with dried pasta tubes and gold Christmas glitter.

'Happy birthday, Mummy,' they mumbled together as Emily handed it to me. Inside, it read: *To the best Mummy in the world. We love you very much.* They'd all signed their names in different-coloured crayons and wrapped up their favourite things for birthday gifts – a seashell, a dinosaur and Flopsy.

'They make us happy so we thought they'd make you happy too,' added James, unable to look me in the eye.

I felt nothing but shame. I closed the card and noticed Simon wasn't in their drawing. They'd understood it was just the four of us now, and the only person who hadn't was me.

It was like someone had let the air out of me. My body deflated and my mouth fell open as for the very first time, I began to cry in front of them. My tears were so heavy they pushed my head forwards, then bent me over double. The kids responded by gathering around me with the force of a rugby scrum.

'Don't cry, Mummy,' said Robbie. 'We're sorry we made you sad.'

'You haven't,' I sobbed. 'They're happy tears.' And some of them were. Not all of them, mind you, but some of them. In an instant, I recognised everything that had been wrong with me since Simon disappeared.

I'd known deep down I'd been relying on alcohol to keep me sane. James had been right: I was drunk and I couldn't remember a day since Simon went when I hadn't knocked back at least a couple of glasses.

I'd used wine to replace him. And gradually it had become my crutch and the only glimmer of light in my dark corner of the world. It was the only thing that sandpapered the rough edges away and made everything bearable again. It prevented a night of tossing and turning by easing me to sleep. It comforted me when I imagined all the bad things that might've happened to him. It was my reward for getting through another day after my miscarriage without falling apart.

But when too much of it flowed through me, it made me bitter. I hated myself for it, but I blamed Simon for throwing me into a life I'd never asked for. And worse than that, he made me take out my frustrations on my babies. Of course, it wasn't his fault – it was mine.

All four of us decided against the party at the village hall, and packed the fancy-dress costumes into a bag and stuffed it into the cupboard under the stairs. Then we stayed up until midnight to see the new year in together, watching it on the TV. And the three pairs of arms that had held me up for so long without me noticing gave me more strength and support than a bottle of wine ever could – or would – again.

◆ ◆ ◆

SIMON

Saint-Jean-de-Luz, twenty-four years earlier

New Year's Day

Champagne corks flew through the air as a chorus of a thousand voices cheered across the town square. Church bells in Saint-Jean-de-Luz chimed to announce the arrival of the new year, while the townsfolk celebrated with backslapping and cheek-pecking.

My first *réveillon de la Saint-Sylvestre* had begun earlier that evening with a feast cooked, blanched and seared by the willing kitchen staff of local restaurants, cafés and bars. Crockery stacked with mouth-watering foods was piled upon every inch of available surface space at my restored Hôtel Près de la Côte for its grand reopening. Wooden tables were pushed together, draped in ivory lace and linen and decorated with plastic holly branches and white pillar candles. Flames flickered across the room and enshrouded each person in a tangerine blush, as if we were banqueting in the belly of a bonfire.

I was one of more than three hundred friends, neighbours and tradesmen sitting side by side on wooden stools, indulging in the festivities. Then, with the food still fresh in our stomachs, it was time for a traditional walk through the balmy air to the church for midnight Mass. Even though I'd misplaced my religion a lifetime ago, it was a place, somewhat hypocritically, that I needed to visit to offer gratitude for my second chance. And to prepare for a third.

As the church bells rang, I joined the extended congregation to walk en masse with blazing torches towards the square, the final destination for our celebrations. There, a uniformed brass band played traditional French folk songs as balloons floated through the breezeless air and party poppers decorated the sky.

'Happy New Year, buddy!' shouted Bradley as our glasses collided.
'And you.'

'Any resolutions?'

'Just the one,' I replied vaguely.

'And?'

'And what?'

'And what is it?'

'I can't tell you that, it's unlucky.'

'Unlucky? You Brits are weird.' He shook his head, bemused, and wandered off in the direction of a slender waitress who'd been catching his eye all day.

I remained in my place under a leafless cherry tree, taking mental pictures as the throng sang, drank and danced. I placed my half-full glass on the base of a statue, stubbed my cigarette out on the cobbles and walked slowly towards the Hôtel Près de la Côte. I stood on the opposite side of the road and dissected how my months of intense restoration had radically changed its appearance. I was thrilled with my achievement.

Unlocking the front door, I was greeted by the warm sound of silence. I headed down the corridor to my room and pulled my recently purchased green canvas rucksack from the cupboard. It held my sparse collection of worldly possessions – clothes, a couple of books, maps and money I'd kept hidden in rolled-up socks – all of which I'd packed earlier. And, of course, Darren's passport. The hotel wouldn't be the only thing to see in the new year with a fresh identity.

I closed the bedroom door and walked back towards reception, only stopping briefly to examine a photograph Bradley had pinned to a cork noticeboard. It was of a dozen of us, including Darren, sitting in the courtyard raising beer bottles towards the lens. I returned their smiles.

I'd spent the last six months of my life with people who had no idea who I really was. Nobody had judged me, challenged me or bruised me, and that suited me perfectly. I'd been safe, and I could have spent another year, two years . . . maybe five years in this town. But I knew eventually it would fail me. Everything that makes you happy eventually disappoints.

And it was pointless creating a new life for myself if I wasn't going to live it. It would all be for nothing. It was in my best interest to escape on my own terms, while I had nothing but fond memories. So, with a heavy heart, yet motivated by the thrill of expectation, I prepared to take flight.

I lit a candle for each of the three children I'd left behind and one more for myself, and placed them in the dining room, the reception area, my bedroom and by the rear door. It only took a minute before their inch-high flames licked the curtain hems, then climbed towards the sky, destroying everything in their paths.

I locked the front door behind me, strapped my rucksack to my back and made my way up the long, steep road to the railway station. I paused halfway for a final sentimental glance at the building responsible for helping to rebuild me. A red glow had already illuminated a couple of rooms, and it wouldn't be long before more followed.

Like I had with my family, I'd created something almost perfect. But perfection fades. Catherine's had, and the Hôtel Près de la Côte would follow suit. Nobody would feel the love for it I'd felt. No one would hear its cry for help like I did, or restore it like it deserved. I would not let others ruin it like they had done before. I would be the one to choose how it got the finale it deserved.

Fifteen minutes later, I perched on the pavement outside a lifeless station and drew the faint sea air into my lungs one last time. I placed my rucksack behind my head, lay on the pavement and drifted off to the sounds of pops, shouts and small explosions.

◆ ◆ ◆

Northampton, today

12.30 p.m.

'I don't understand,' she began, utterly confused. 'You put your heart and soul into renovating that building, and then you set fire to it?'

He nodded slowly and tapped his foot on the floor.

'So is that what you do?' she continued. 'You work hard to create something amazing and then destroy it because of something you think I did to you twenty-five years ago?'

This time his head remained still, but she persisted.

'Is that what the problem was with us? We were the perfect family you'd always wanted, but once you got it, you realised you didn't need us after all?'

'No,' he replied with certainty. They were far from perfect, she had seen to that. But he'd save that part for later.

Her initial anger was giving way to frustration. He appeared quite determined to regale her with select stories from his past, but because there were so many gaps open to interpretation, she naturally wanted to know more. Then he'd clam up as tight as an oyster shell or change the subject. She hated herself for letting him draw her in. Nevertheless, she wasn't prepared to end her line of questioning just because of his reluctance.

'But you'd made friends there – while I was working like a slave and selling off everything we owned, you didn't have a bloody care in the world!'

'Nothing that satisfying ever lasts, Catherine,' he replied. He was smiling, but she could see it was underpinned by sadness. 'Not the hotel, not the people, not my life here or my life there. So it's far better to leave on your own terms than on someone else's.'

'Then you were depressed? I understand depression – you knew what I went through before you went. But you could have talked to me about it, let me be there for you like you were there for me. You didn't have to run away.'

'I didn't say I was depressed, Catherine. You're making assumptions.'

She was exasperated. 'Then, once again, I don't understand! Why did you leave? All these bloody riddles and you still haven't told me the one thing I want to know. What did I do that was so bad it made you run away?'

Like the slow burning of a cigarette, he kept her waiting. She didn't know what game he was playing, but he was better practised than a politician when it came to avoiding the answers that mattered.

As much as she hated being controlled by a puppetmaster, she got the feeling she'd have to play along a lot longer before she could cut the strings herself.

CHAPTER EIGHT
CATHERINE

Northampton, twenty-four years earlier

4 January

I couldn't have felt more out of place had I been dressed in a clown suit and wearing deely boppers.

The bell above the door tinkled when I walked through the doors of Fabien's boutique. It was like stepping into the pages of *Vogue* magazine – orange, rust and gold wallpaper covered the walls, and mahogany rails of clothing were placed near display tables draped with select pieces. A crystal chandelier hung from the centre of the ceiling. The whole shop was like Joan Collins's walk-in wardrobe.

I checked the designer labels on hangers but there wasn't a price tag in sight. A little matter of cost didn't concern the kind of women lucky enough to afford to shop there. Like my mum's dresses, the clothes in Fabien's were always supposed to hang in someone else's closet, not mine.

'Stunning, aren't they?' a smoky voice crackled behind me. I turned around, startled, and yanked back my hand like I'd been caught shoplifting.

Selena had asked if I could visit her mother after the Christmas holidays. I'd presumed she'd wanted some alterations doing, but when she revealed her mother owned Fabien's, you could have knocked me down with a feather. It was one of only a handful of independent clothes shops in town selling high-end fashion imported from places like Italy and France. I'd never had the guts to go inside: my experience of Fabien's was limited to lingering glances as I walked past the window to C&A.

'I'm Selena's mother, Margaret. You must be Catherine,' she began, extending a manicured hand towards mine. Her long, ruby-red fingernails drew my eye to clusters of diamonds in her gold rings.

'Yes, nice to meet you,' I replied, ashamed of my own hands which resembled pincushions.

Margaret was every inch the boutique she owned, and precisely the reason I'd never set foot in it. Hovering somewhere around her mid-fifties, she was the epitome of old-school glamour – part Joan Crawford, part Rita Hayworth. Her chestnut-brown hair was tied into a neat bun. Lines running vertically down her cheeks and above her lips gave away her fondness for the sun and a cigarette. I wondered why she had a daughter who could barely make ends meet.

'Nothing like Selena, am I?' she asked. 'I've tried to help her, financially I mean, but she's inherited my stubbornness and refuses to take a penny. I'm proud of her nonetheless. Anyway, please continue looking around.'

I felt even more self-conscious as Margaret's eyes bored into me to get the measure of who I was by the clothes I was drawn to. Eventually, she spoke again.

'I'll get to the point, darling. I want you to work for me.'

'Um, I don't know if I'd fit in here,' I stuttered.

'No, no,' she laughed. 'I don't need you in the shop; assistants are ten a penny. I want you to make a range of clothes for me.'

I must have looked baffled. It was too early for an April Fool.

Margaret explained how she'd seen the clothes I'd made for Selena and her friends. And while the modern fashions teenage girls desired weren't to her taste, she'd been impressed by my attention to detail and the quality of my work.

'Oh, I just copy what I see in magazines,' I said, a little flattered, a little embarrassed.

'Which is a skill in itself,' Margaret said. 'Darling, I don't offer praise lightly. I've taken a very close look at your work, to the point where I've almost picked the bloody things apart looking for faults, much to my daughter's annoyance. But your standard is quite exceptional. Obviously your choice of fabrics is – how can I put this without causing offence – a tad "high street". But you clearly have an instinct for what suits a woman. And watching you wandering around my boutique like a child in a sweet shop tells me you have greater aspirations than making school uniforms and trendy frocks for mini-Madonnas.'

'I don't know,' I said, neither used to, nor entirely comfortable with, compliments. I followed her like a puppy on a lead as she walked the shop floor with a purposeful stride, sifting through rails and draping clothes over my arm.

'You're not perfect, but none of us are, darling,' she continued. 'A few of your clothes have room for improvement, but that's something we can work on. I want you to take a few pieces away with you and examine them closely. Look at how they're pieced together – the use of appliqués, grosgrain and shirring. The devil is in the detail. These are the intricacies that separate clothes you'll find on my rails from those you'll see in a Littlewoods catalogue. Then come back to me in, let's say a month, with three of your own creations. My customers don't settle for anything less than the best, and neither do I.'

Top-quality clothes were Margaret's main income, but small, independent, affordable labels were fast becoming popular – limited-edition ranges aimed at the over-forties. However, Margaret's clientele was growing older and she needed to appeal to an equally lucrative younger market with a disposable income. And I got the feeling that what Margaret wanted, Margaret got.

'If you can prove to me you're the untapped talent I think you are, then we can do business,' she added, smiling.

One nervous handshake later and I was sitting on the top deck of the number five bus, holding on to a thousand pounds' worth of dresses for dear life.

5 January

Making clothes for children who didn't care about fashion trends and teens that wanted designer rips in their jeans was entirely different from working to meet Margaret's expectations.

For the first time in my life, I had the chance to turn my talent into something really profitable. But I was scared. What if she laughed my ideas out of the boutique? What if it wasn't in me to be original and I could only stretch to copying clothes that already existed?

I could have gone around in theoretical circles for days, but the only way to find out was to stop dithering and get on with it. The day after meeting Margaret, I sat down at the dining room table with a mug of tea, and surrounded myself with Robbie's coloured pencils, a blank sketchpad and a mental image of her breathing down my neck. Then I drew. And drew. And drew.

But nothing came close to matching what she'd asked for. My designs were, at best, bland. They lacked oomph, and if I knew it, Margaret would too.

If ever I needed a glass of wine for inspiration, it was then. But when the grandfather clock in the hallway chimed four times, I retired to bed, defeated but sober.

The following three nights were exactly the same. I'd already buckled under pressure. On day five, I tossed and turned in bed and reluctantly admitted it had all been pie in the sky. My mum was right: I'd never be as good as her. Her work was so much better than mine, yet she'd known her place, and it wasn't creating something for someone else's approval. I wondered if she was still making clothes. It had been years since my parents had moved out of the village and down to the south coast. We'd send each other Christmas cards, but that's where our contact started and finished. They'd visited once, a couple of months after I had James, but that was it. My children were bang out of luck when it came to having grandparents who wanted to play an active role in their lives.

I thought about the clothes in Mum's wardrobe – timeless pieces that would still have looked fantastic on rails now, twenty years later. Well, maybe with a raised hem here or a belt there. Or an extra couple of buttons and a zip. Actually, there were a lot of her designs that could work as they were, I told myself. Then I had an idea.

I padded down the stairs in my dressing gown and slippers, spread out the silk fabric I'd been keeping for something special, and began to work from memory, borrowing some of my mum's designs for inspiration.

And I continued like that for the next four weeks with different materials until I finished my three original pieces. Then I thanked my mum and went to bed, knackered but smiling.

4 February

Silence. Fifteen long, gut-wrenching minutes of it. I was so nervous my palms were sweating.

After presenting Margaret with a business suit, a pair of stirrup pants and a silk dress, my heart was in my throat as I watched her prod them, tug at their seams, hold them up to the light and shake them like she was trying to get the last drop of ketchup out of a bottle. Finally, she was done.

'How quickly can you make another three?' she asked. I wanted to grab her and squeeze her until her bun burst or her shoulder pads split.

With a couple of minor alterations, my outfits were on Fabien's clothes rails by the end of the week. Every time I thought about what I'd accomplished, I broke into a huge, beaming smile. I crossed my fingers and hoped at least one of them might find a buyer.

I needn't have worried. By the time I returned with more, the first three had already been snapped up. Margaret handed me a cheque for one hundred and forty pounds – the equivalent of two weeks' supermarket work. If I hadn't needed the money so badly, I'd have framed it and stuck it on the wall for the entire world to see.

28 March

Dividing my life between three jobs and three kids had worn me out.

I knew I could make so many more clothes if I had full days and not just a few snatched hours here and there. When I fell asleep at the sewing machine for the second time, I was ready to admit I wasn't Wonder Woman.

Something had to give, so I took the plunge and handed my notice in at the supermarket, but as I didn't want to put all my eggs in one basket, I kept ironing my neighbours' clothes. And I saved a little money from each of Margaret's payments to start refurnishing my home.

First I bought the children second-hand bikes. Then, gradually, I replaced the pieces of furniture I'd sold and started kitting out my sewing room. Soon, what was once the dining room became a space crammed with clothes rails, stacks of magazines, rolls of fabric, two mannequin torsos and multiple boxes containing bobbins of coloured cotton.

I thought back to a few months earlier, when I'd used that room to come up with ridiculous theories as to what could've happened to Simon. Now I was using it to leaf through borrowed library books on the modern history of clothing, from classics like Christian Dior and Guccio Gucci to newer stars.

As my ideas and inspirations flowed thick and fast, I began to realise that when Simon found his way home, I wouldn't be the Kitty he used to know. I was moving in a new direction and becoming stronger, off my own back. While I was getting to know – and like – the new me, I felt guilty for thinking not all change was a bad thing.

2 April

In my dreams, Simon was only ever an outline of a man – a quiet blur hiding in the corners of rooms, watching me.

But that night, I saw his face. I stood by my bedroom window as the sun rose, watching his motionless body in the fields peering back at me. Eventually, he smiled, and I felt myself blush like I had the first time he looked at me, in English Lit class.

When he turned his back and walked away, I panicked and shouted for him, but he ignored me. I hammered on the glass with my fists, but he slipped into a speck of dust on the horizon. I screamed louder and louder until I woke myself up, then lay there, angry with him.

Suddenly Dougie's face burst into my head with such uninvited speed, it made me jump.

For four years, I'd kept him at arm's length, but I'd be a fool to think it was that easy. I'd always believed I could read people quite well, because the only way to stop myself from being burned by my mum's acid tongue was to judge her flavour before approaching her.

Simon's friends Steven and Roger were easy to pigeonhole and they hadn't changed much as they'd grown from boys to men. But Dougie was different. When it was just the two of them, they'd been a lot more serious; with the others, Simon was one of the lads. I'd nicknamed him the Chameleon and quite liked that he'd change his colours to suit his environment without ever losing sight of who he was. Dougie, Steven, Roger and I were all just pieces of him.

But Simon had been more to Dougie than just his best friend, and he hadn't exactly welcomed me with open arms once Simon invited me into his little gang. He wasn't just a boy whose head hadn't been turned by yucky girls. He genuinely couldn't understand why his best friend had fallen for one.

And when once he caught me watching him watching Simon, while Simon remained oblivious to the both of us, his red face revealed what his words didn't say. I was a little jealous of how close they were, and Dougie and I began playing childish games of one-upmanship. If I told him something Simon had said to me, he'd antagonise me with a 'yeah, I already know'. And other times, in petty retaliation, I'd do the same. We'd compete for Simon's attention.

I'd always regretted my first kiss with Simon. Not that it happened, but how and where. I instigated it in Dougie's bedroom on purpose, aware that he was about to walk in and catch us. I kissed him because I wanted to, but I also knew that putting Dougie in his place, on his own territory, would end our rivalry.

As soon as he saw us, I wished I hadn't been such a bitch. He looked so pitiful standing there with a tray of snacks and glasses of milk. The corners of his mouth unravelled and the light in his eyes paled. I'd won Simon's heart, but trampled across Dougie's.

That marked a turning point in my relationship with Dougie. We reached an unspoken understanding that while we could share Simon, I would always have the upper hand. And eventually we became unlikely friends in our own right.

Then, one night, many years later, everything changed.

7 April

I was exhausted defending an invisible man for so many months.

I'd abandoned chanting 'Simon is not dead' in the bathroom mirror, because in my heart of hearts, I'd begun to accept it might not be true. It came down to one single fact – he couldn't have been gone for ten months without something having happened to him. And with no evidence telling me he was still alive, I reluctantly came to terms with Roger's theory he'd most likely died in an accident the day he disappeared.

In the meantime, my children had come up with their own ideas.

'Did Daddy commit soo-side?' Robbie asked out of the blue on our way home from the park.

'Who told you that?' I replied.

He looked anxious. In truth, he'd been looking more and more anxious of late and it was starting to worry me. He'd often take himself into his dad's garage-office and I'd hear him whispering to him about his day. I'd thought I was the only one who did that. I wasn't sure if leaving him to chat to a memory was the best thing or not, but if it gave him the comfort his mummy obviously couldn't, then maybe it wasn't doing any harm.

'What's soo-side?' asked Emily.

'My friend Melanie says that when people are sad and they want to go to heaven, they commit soo-side,' Robbie explained.

'It's called suicide,' James chipped in before I could explain, 'and it's when people hurt themselves on purpose because they don't want to be with their families anymore.'

'No, Daddy didn't commit suicide,' I replied, unsure of how to end the conversation.

'But how can you know that?' asked James. It was clear this wasn't the first time he'd given it thought.

'Because Daddy had no reason to. People only do that when they don't think they have any other choice. Daddy loved us too much.'

I hadn't told another living soul, but it had crossed my mind that maybe he had. I mulled over everything that had happened with Billy and wondered if I'd been too wrapped up in myself to notice how badly it had affected him too. If I'd been a better wife, maybe I'd have noticed his sadness instead of wallowing in mine.

'Well, this is what I think happened,' I began softly. 'The day that Daddy disappeared, I think he went out for one of his runs somewhere new. And I think he got lost, and then he had an accident. But because nobody knows where he went, we can't find him.'

'Shall we go and look for him again?' asked Robbie.

'I don't think that will help. I don't think he's able to come back.'

I still couldn't bring myself to say out loud that maybe he was dead.

We had arrived home, and Emily skipped over towards the swing in the garden.

'Is he in heaven?' Robbie continued.

I paused, hating myself for what I was about to say. 'Yes,' I said at last. 'I think he might be.'

'When will Daddy come back?' yelled Emily from the swing.

'I don't think he will, sweetie.'

'Oh,' she replied, and frowned. 'Push me really hard, Mummy.'

I began pushing her more gently than she'd expected, so she wriggled her legs backwards and forwards to gain more height. 'Harder, Mummy. You're not pushing hard enough!'

'Why do you want to go so high?'

'So I can kick God in the bum until he sends Daddy home.'

Good idea, I thought.

◆ ◆ ◆

SIMON

Paris, twenty-four years earlier

10 January

I raised my head to look up at the publisher's third-floor offices on Boulevard Haussmann, and fumbled nervously with the twenty thousand French francs crammed into my trouser pocket.

I felt a pang of disappointment in myself for being the man to have sold all that Pierre Chareau had written, sketched and then shipped to the Hôtel Près de la Côte for reasons unknown. But I'd done what was necessary to carry me forward.

It had taken four trains and two buses to reach Paris. My backpack contained very few personal belongings, to make room for the rarest items I'd rescued from the garbage. The rest I'd sent by post six weeks earlier to Madame Bernard, a publisher of art and historical work, to offer it for sale.

I had considered handing the collection to the Musée des Arts Décoratifs, where it could be displayed alongside other notable works of famous French visionaries. But the next part of my journey would be expensive, and I was still more charity than charitable.

On my arrival, it took Madame Bernard several days to verify the authenticity of the most recent deliveries. But once deemed genuine, I was offered a fee and a percentage of future book sales, with a guarantee of anonymity.

I congratulated myself on requesting that the royalties be forwarded to an address in England. I doubted whether Darren Glasper's family would ever know why they were receiving intermittent cheques from a Parisian publisher. But if it helped perpetuate the myth their deceased son had made a success of his all-too-brief travels, then it was worth every centime.

Darren and I had shared the desire to cast aside our past lives and start afresh on our own terms. So I knew he'd understand that, with him having no further need of his passport, I could make use of both it and his identity. If heaven existed, he'd be looking down on me with pride and egging me on.

With no permanent address or bank account, I, however, preferred to be paid in cash, and with the financial means to move forwards, my next stop was a travel agent to book a one-way flight.

New York, USA

4 February

While everyone else slept soundly around us in designated bunkbeds, the girl and I silently made love in hers.

I'd placed the palm of my hand against the breezeblock wall to stop the bed's metal frame from rocking against it. The other was held over her mouth to mask from the slumbering masses her groans while she climaxed. It wasn't long before I joined her, then allowed my limp body to flop to her side.

Her name had already escaped me, but it didn't matter as she'd made plans to leave for Chicago in the morning. I pulled on my underwear and went to give her a polite peck on the cheek, but she had already fallen into a drunken sleep.

The day after bidding adieu to Paris, my alter ego Darren Glasper had landed in New York.

The ignorant often look upon America as a modern country lacking history or culture. What I saw was a continent littered with small pockets of culture in every person, in every building and on every street. Just because no one creed, religion or class stood prouder than any other didn't mean a whole nation was lacking in essence.

And what better country in which to begin again than one at whose gateway stood a landmark with broken chains at her feet and a torch to light my way forward?

In the Lower Manhattan Youth Hostel, I lived the life of a teenager trapped in a thirty-three-year-old man's body. My days lacked routine; spontaneity was the only call I answered to. I aspired to throw myself at every new sensation I chanced upon, and that included the opposite sex. As teenagers, my friends had experimented with any girls who'd indulge them. But Catherine was the only one I'd ever been intimate with. And by marrying the first girl I'd fallen for, there was so much I'd missed out on.

The hostel's arteries constantly pumped with fresh young blood. I enjoyed the company of women, and brief dalliances and one-night stands meant there was no risk of them urging me to take things further or trying to get to know me. I needed to connect with people physically, but rarely for long and never emotionally. For just enough time to remind myself I could still connect, even if it was only expressed through empty, near-anonymous sexual acts with like-minded partners.

And it happened anywhere, from restaurant toilets to alleyways, dormitories full of sleeping people to an underpass in Central Park. I had no filter for shame and few boundaries. I had many wasted years to catch up on, and sex without emotion brought immediate gratification. New York was the city that never slept, and I had every intention of following suit.

I reached my bunkbed on the other side of the dorm, zipped myself up in my sleeping bag and thought back to my first kiss.

I'd never told Catherine it wasn't with her.

21 February

I'd already walked the length of the Brooklyn Bridge once that day. On my return, I paused and leaned against the sidewalk railings to stare across the vast expanse of the East River.

I thought back to when I was eleven, and Dougie and I spent an afternoon on a long bike ride into town, eventually reaching Abington Park. Feeling mischievous, we stuffed decaying elm tree leaves, and a stack of discarded *Mercury & Herald* newspapers dumped by a lazy paperboy, into an overflow pipe leading from an adjacent stream. Finally, when our masterpiece of modern engineering was complete, we waited patiently for a watery wrath to sweep over the town once the stream burst its banks. It was, however, an overly ambitious plan, and after an hour, Northampton was still as dry as a bone.

Bored, I'd leaned back on my elbows on the grass and closed my eyes. Suddenly, something soft gently pressed itself against my lips. It remained there momentarily as I puzzled over whether I was awake or midway between sleep and consciousness. I opened my eyes to find Dougie's lips upon mine.

He withdrew them as quickly as they'd been planted. He stared at me with eyes so wide they appeared to have developed a life of their own, beyond his control. We remained motionless, one taking in the action and the other waiting for the reaction.

'Sorry,' he finally blurted out, before picking up his bike and cycling away as fast as his gangly legs could pedal.

I remained rooted to the grass, bewildered. Boys didn't kiss boys: boys kissed girls. If a boy kissed a boy, he was queer. All I knew about homosexuality was that queers were to be feared and, if found, given a good kicking. They were dirty old men who sat alone in cinemas waiting to touch young lads if the opportunity arose. Or they ended up in prison for doing filthy things to each other that I didn't really understand.

I was at a loss as to how I should respond, so I hurried through the consequences of confiding in someone else. Should I tell my father or Roger what had happened? Or would they think I was a queer too, for not knocking his block off? I didn't want to be found guilty by association. And if others knew, I wouldn't be allowed to play with

Dougie again, to spend time at his house and be a part of his family. I didn't want to be the one to blame for sending my best friend to jail. So, because I had more to lose than him, I kept quiet.

The next morning, I stopped at Dougie's house as normal to walk with him to school.

'Come on, we're going to be late,' I said.

He looked at me – confounded, I'm sure, that I'd gone anywhere near him again. And as we walked briskly down the High Street, from the corner of my eye I kept seeing his mouth opening and words forming, before sentences evaporated into nothing. Eventually, he spoke.

'The other day . . .' he began.

'Forget about it.'

'Have you told—'

'Of course not. Now hurry up, or we'll get detention.'

It was the last time the subject was ever touched on. But it didn't mean I ever forgot.

My second first kiss was with Catherine, not long after. As we sat together on Dougie's bed reading an interview with David Bowie in *Melody Maker* magazine, she leaned over without warning, cupped her hand under my chin, pulled my face close to hers and kissed me.

It was a wonderful, warm, sweet kiss. She tasted of Parma Violets. I knew the longer it lasted, the more chance Dougie would catch us. She gradually pulled away and gave me the most beautiful grin I'd ever seen. Then a shadow caught our eye, and we turned to find Dougie standing in the doorway holding a tray of snacks.

He processed what he'd witnessed before he reanimated his blank face and placed the crisps and sweets in the centre of the bed, pretending he hadn't seen anything.

I knew I'd wounded him, but I didn't know then how long he would wait to retaliate.

20 March

I scanned the row of Brooklyn brownstones a second time, then slipped across the street to a shabby vehicle wedged in among the line of cars tightly parked by the curb. I'd watched its owner forget to lock the door as she struggled up the stairs with two bags of groceries and a whining toddler.

There was a fist-sized dent in the passenger door, and the simulated-woodgrain vinyl panels were sun-bleached and had begun to peel from its body. The rear seats bore the scratches from a large dog's claws. A sticker with the name 'Betty' had been placed in the bottom left-hand corner of the rear windscreen. She had a history, but then so had I.

I slipped casually inside the Buick Roadmaster station wagon and entwined the wires beneath the steering-wheel column like Roger had shown me when I'd lost the keys to the Volvo. Then, after trial, error, a spark and a splutter, Betty burst into life.

I could have chosen something a little grander and perhaps a little more modern. But she possessed the basic criteria required – she was practical and unremarkable to look at. She had plenty of space inside her to offer passage to other travellers, and her two rows of back seats folded forwards, enabling me to sleep inside her if I wished.

I'd grown restless after two months of exploring New York's nooks and crannies. The signs of better days ahead in the dilapidated Meatpacking District, the magnitude of Central Park, the illuminated glory of Broadway, and the bars and brothels of Soho had nothing more to offer. City life had exhausted me and it was time to explore further.

I pulled out into the street and scowled at the crucifix swinging from the rear-view mirror. I yanked it off its chain and threw it onto the back seat. It bounced off something – a child seat. Suddenly I recalled the long car journeys we'd taken to the Lake District and the Devonshire coast, with three young children in the rear of the car. I remembered listening to James and Robbie fighting over whose turn it was to use my

Walkman. Emily was still a baby and more concerned with her rattle. Catherine was asleep in the front seat, gently snoring, and as I drove I listened to the buzz of the family we'd created together and smiled.

I didn't want to miss any of that, but I did.

Now I was about to take another journey into the great wide open, although this time, I'd be alone.

◆ ◆ ◆

Northampton, today

1.20 p.m.

She'd watched him grow uncomfortable and tap his finger against his lip each time their children were mentioned by either of them. She was pleased that her plan was working. Slowly and surely, she would break him down piece by piece until he showed some remorse for what he'd done to his family.

Remember why you're here, he told himself. *Remember who's in charge.* He'd fought quite successfully at the start to convince himself that not seeing the children the morning he left had been the correct thing to do. But deep in the pit of his belly, it was his one regret. Because after forcing himself to erase their young faces from his memory, it had later proved an impossible task to bring them back to life.

He'd thought about them more and more since meeting Luciana, and had to rely on guesswork as to how they might look now. He wondered whom they'd taken after genetically, and if it was just James who'd inherited his father's smile. How did their laughter sound? What were their personalities like? He felt a little downhearted knowing his own would've had little bearing on theirs. No matter what they'd taken from him biologically, she'd shaped them, not him.

He imagined what might happen if they were to meet under other circumstances. Would they like him? Ideally they'd get to know him first as an old family friend, and decide he was a decent fellow. Then, when the truth finally came out about who he was, it would be harder for them to burn bridges with someone they liked.

While he daydreamed, Catherine stewed on his recollections of sleazy liaisons with whores and pretty young things.

'So you ran away because I couldn't satisfy you in bed? Or did you just want to sleep with girls half your age?' she asked indignantly. 'You sound like a pervert.'

'Of course I'm not.'

'Well, you'll forgive me for saying so, but all I've heard so far is that your wife was a lousy lover and your morals were no better than a dirty old man's. And while I was coming to terms with your death, you were burning down hotels and screwing your way around America!'

Heard from someone else's perspective, he conceded that's exactly how it sounded, even though it couldn't be further from the truth. He bit his lip, frustrated both by his tactlessness and by her, for being too focused on the finer details to understand the big picture. He needed to regain control of the situation, but it was proving hard to wrestle from her grip.

'At any point are you going to ask about your children, or how they managed without you?'

'Yes, of course,' he replied. 'How are they?'

'That's none of your business.'

One–nil, she marked on an imaginary scoreboard.

'Don't be childish,' he snapped. It was the first time he'd grown impatient with her.

'Don't you dare call me childish.' Her voice deepened. 'Don't you dare.'

'I'm sorry, that was wrong of me.' He began to feel a dull ache in his head. He knew what it meant.

For the first time since the ghost appeared, she felt she had the upper hand. Now he wanted something from her, and she could either pretend her kids' lives without him had been a bed of roses, or twist the knife by telling him the truth.

'For the record,' she answered finally, 'I have raised three wonderful, loving children. And none of it has been thanks to you.'

It was only then that she noticed he'd been holding his breath, waiting for confirmation they were all well. She felt her eyes narrow when he let out a barely audible, but relieved sigh. She remembered they had a father too. It had been a long time since she'd thought of him as that.

So she made a snap decision to explain their ups and not to exploit their downs. And she'd make sure he understood that, in retrospect, she wouldn't have changed a minute of their lives without him for anything.

CHAPTER NINE
CATHERINE

Northampton, twenty-four years earlier

15 April

It was my own stupid fault for not thinking it through properly. It didn't happen straight away, but cracks gradually appeared in the kids after I admitted I no longer thought Simon was alive.

Despite the birthday card they'd made me with just the four of us drawn on it, they'd quietly held on to the hope he could still be found. Then I'd opened my big mouth. They didn't know how to express their grief other than to be angry with someone. And as he wasn't around, I took the brunt of it.

Becoming a single mum was made all the harder having known what it was like to have shared the responsibilities. Now I was forced to make decisions on my own. I was good cop and bad cop; nurturer and provider; friend, parent and enemy. I permanently sat under a cloud of guilt – guilt over how I used to drink; for telling them off when they were naughty; for neglecting them when I worked; for letting their daddy vanish . . . for everything.

Of course, they were too young to recognise my limits, what buttons not to push, so reacted to not getting their own way by erupting like small volcanoes, which in turn released my changing emotions towards Simon. I was grateful he was never far from their thoughts, but I also longed for the time when he'd gradually fade from their memories. It was selfish, I knew, but it would make my life much easier.

James rebelled by upsetting others. I was called to his school several times by his headmistress because of his temper. Eventually she had no choice but to suspend him for a week after a fight that left another boy missing a tooth. I tried spending that time rationalising, sympathising and punishing him, and I thought I was getting through to him. Then Roger brought him home one night in a police car after he was seen throwing stones at cars parked outside the church. I was back to square one.

James was furious at his dad for leaving him, and I was at my wits' end. He lost interest in playing with the friends he hadn't walloped, so he took his animosity out on his battle-weary toy soldiers and Ninja Turtles, staging bloody battles to the death. He even stopped reading the Hardy Boys books Simon had bought him, or watching fat men in colourful leotards wrestle on Saturday afternoon TV.

He only seemed to find a kind of peace when he was playing his records. He spent all his pocket money on CD singles, which gave me an idea. I dragged the old acoustic guitar Simon had given him for his fifth birthday from where James had shoved it under his bed. I dusted it down, paid to get it restrung and handed it to him for a predictably underwhelmed reaction.

'I've also bought you these,' I added, passing him a *Teach Yourself Guitar* book, along with some sheet music from his new favourite group, U2.

'Do you think they got where they are by just bloodying their knuckles and getting kicked out of school?' I asked, quietly assuming that's where and how all rock stars indeed got their first taste of anarchy.

He shrugged.

'Well, they didn't. They worked at their music until they could say what they wanted with it. If you want to be like them, you can start by learning how to play this. If you enjoy it and practise every day, I'll pay for proper lessons for you. And one day, you might even make a record of your own.'

Of course, I was sure he wouldn't, but a little white lie wouldn't do him any harm. A tiny, curious glint appeared in his eyes, but he tried to hide it. And when he thought I wasn't listening, he began learning chords behind his closed bedroom door.

Over the weeks his enthusiasm came loaded with its own problems, namely the repetition of hearing 'Mysterious Ways' – strummed dreadfully – again and again until the cows came home. But if it kept his mind busy and his fists occupied, my sanity was a small price to pay.

But poor Robbie was a different kettle of fish altogether.

1 May

Convincing James he could become the next Bono was a doddle in comparison to coaxing Robbie out of himself. I'd underestimated how deep his problems lay.

As he grew from baby to toddler to little boy, I'd accepted he wasn't like his brother or our friends' children. He was a sensitive, insular child who carried the weight of the world on his young shoulders at a time when it should have been carrying him. He could make a minor problem ten times worse by dwelling on it rather than sharing it with me.

And while James and Emily were adapting to a new set of rules, Robbie retreated further into himself. I needed one of those small forks you get with a plate of escargots in a French restaurant to pull him out from his shell.

His teachers said he behaved well. He was intelligent for his age and his spelling and maths were way above his six years. But he had no interest in showing how bright he was in front of his class. Socially, he was becoming reclusive.

Robbie seemed to enjoy his siblings' company – he just didn't *need* it. They hit brick walls when they begged him to join in with conversations or to play. And, gradually, he used words less and less, until one day, he fell completely silent.

In her usual matter-of-fact way, Paula tried to convince me he was merely looking for attention, while Baishali was more sensitive to my concerns. And after a week of constant quiet, I was out of my mind with worry. So began a series of doctor's and child psychologist's appointments, until eventually we found ourselves sitting in a room with a specialist in mental welfare.

'He's not stupid,' I told Dr Phillips defensively, following a barrage of questions and profile tests. I held Robbie's hand tightly, scared of the assessment she was going to make about my son.

'I know that, Mrs Nicholson,' she said, smiling reassuringly. 'The purpose of this meeting is to ascertain what the problem might be and not to judge Robbie.'

'What do you think is wrong?'

'I believe he has what's called selective mutism. It means that he can talk if he wants to, but he's chosen not to.'

'I'm not sure I understand,' I said, frowning. 'You're saying he just doesn't want to speak to me anymore?'

'Not just to you, but to anyone. It's rare, but it happens. Children, particularly ones sensitive to a change in environment or a family unit like he's had, can feel they have little control over their lives. The one thing they can control, however, is how they react to those situations. And Robbie's reacted to his by electing not to speak.'

'So it's just a phase he's going through?'

'Maybe, maybe not. I've seen cases like Robbie's last for years. Others remain for a few weeks and then they're back to normal. There is no way of determining it.'

I turned anxiously towards Robbie, who listened intently but didn't let out a peep.

'Robbie, please say something. Tell Dr Phillips she's wrong.'

He looked at me and began to open his mouth, considered it, then closed it again. His eyes fell to the floor.

Billy, my breakdown, and then his father's disappearance had clearly had a knock-on effect I should've predicted. The world was too huge and scary for my little boy, and he was afraid for anyone to hear his voice.

'I suggest you go home and carry on as normal,' added Dr Phillips. 'There's an excellent therapist I can recommend – and, Mrs Nicholson, I've yet to see a case continue indefinitely. Just try not to worry and be patient.'

It was easy for her to say.

30 May

Making Robbie feel even more self-conscious wasn't going to help him. So while we didn't pretend something in him hadn't changed, we didn't place him under any pressure either.

I learned never to underestimate the tenderness of children. His brother and sister might not have understood his reasons, but they accepted them and treated him like they always did. His teacher even stopped asking him questions in front of the class so she wouldn't embarrass him.

But Robbie's alienation meant he spent his playtimes alone. I dropped him off one morning and hovered outside the school gates, watching the other kids play with Transformer toys and hopscotch across chalk squares.

My chest tightened at Robbie, sitting in a corner, alone. I wanted to run over, scoop him up in my arms, stroke his thick blond hair, and carry him home where I could make everything all right. But I knew that wasn't possible. I had to let him work through it in his own way. I was to blame for this, not him.

4 June

Within a year of Simon's disappearance, Emily had spent almost a quarter of her life without her daddy. He'd helped create a beautiful ball of energy, but hadn't been lucky enough to watch her grow into an astonishing little girl. And without getting to know her dad, she'd missed out on a wonderful role model. It made me sad.

She'd inherited Simon's compassion for animals. Abandoned baby starlings, snails with broken shells, worms with half a body, and a jar of tadpoles she once told me 'missed their daddy frog' had all lain on our kitchen table at one time or another.

By the time the first anniversary of her daddy's disappearance arrived, our family was very much intact. We'd been scared, lonely, battered, abandoned, confused, silenced, angered and still had our bruises. But we were not beaten.

My work was earning me a healthy, regular wage, the bills and the mortgage were paid on time and I'd learned to keep my emotions in check each time I thought of Simon. I realised I wanted him more than I needed him.

The baby steps we'd taken meant we were finally ready to say goodbye to him. We each dressed in our smartest clothes and walked hand in hand from the house to the bridge over the stream, a year to the day after he vanished. Oscar lagged behind, determined to catch one of the wild rabbits that always outsmarted him. There had been times when I'd wondered what it would feel like to wade into the water and be taken away in the current. But that was all behind me.

'I want to say that I miss you very much, Daddy, and thank you for my guitar,' began James as we sat. Then he tore the words of a song he'd written about his father from an exercise book, dropped the page between the wooden railings and let it float away.

All Robbie could muster up was a smile as he placed a drawing of Simon on a cloud sitting next to an angel into the stream. Emily, excited by our trip but unable to grasp its significance, sang 'Happy Birthday to You' instead, unsure of why the rest of her family was giggling. I gave her a hug.

I'd had a print made of the last photograph we'd ever had taken of us together, at Easter, and let it drift below.

'Thank you, Simon, for the wonderful years we had together and for the family we made. I'll love you forever.'

We sat on the bridge until well beyond teatime, reliving memories and anecdotes, from how he and I had met, to the best game of football he'd ever taken the boys to watch.

A year that had begun so miserably and so painfully had closed with warmth and with love.

SIMON

Georgia, USA, twenty-four years earlier

19 April

I felt like the luckiest man alive as my American reincarnation continued.

Hotels and motels were comfortable and offered practical amenities, but they were characterless, lonely places. I appreciated my own company, but being around like-minded others made the adventure that much more exciting. So hostels became my first choice for off-road respite.

I'd scan the noticeboards where travellers asked for lifts to one place or another. Most days, Betty was packed with new faces as we dipped in and out of the East Coast, passing through Indianapolis, Memphis, Atlanta and Savannah.

These micro-relationships were, by their very nature, only ever going to offer me short-term satisfaction. Because maps, wanderlust and free will meant sooner or later we'd each begin our separate journeys, destined never to meet again.

And from time to time, it made me think about those I'd left behind. Because of my lifestyle, I would never find anyone to replace them all, but I was beginning to wonder if, one day, I might want to.

For years Catherine had been the only constant in my life. We became inseparable the day our English teacher partnered us to study *Macbeth*. It was her brown curly hair and apple-cheeked smile that drew my eye. She wasn't like her peers – she made no attempt to make herself look older by hitching up her hemline or undoing an extra button on her shirt. Her lips lacked artificial colour and she didn't frame her eyes with mascara. Her clothes were fashionable and fitted but garnished with her own twists, like a rogue ribbon or belt. I liked that she was different because so was I.

My love wasn't powerful enough to make my mother want to stay, so I was constantly amazed Catherine chose to remain by my side.

Many things tied us together, but I was especially struck by the way our home lives mirrored each other's. Doreen destroyed my family, and Catherine's was slowly disintegrating all by itself but without such drama. However, she never allowed her great sadness to define her. Somehow, she steered clear of the dark place where I dwelled.

And she seemed to know that she'd get everything she wanted from life in the end if she just believed. She inspired me to do the same – but, looking back, I wondered if she'd only wanted to fix me, and once I was repaired she lost interest. Because in the end, she turned out to be the same as everyone else who tried to break me.

But back then her strength and spirit had been infectious, and just being around her made me feel I could conquer the world.

And I did – only without her.

Miami, USA

4 June

I'd ordered my second bottle of beer from the server when a newspaper on the next table caught my eye.

I'd spent much of the morning tranquilised under the aquamarine sky of the beach in Miami's Bal Harbour. Dana and Angie, two mischievous Canadian girls I'd met over a hotel breakfast, had kept me company. We'd just finished a lunchtime picnic they'd assembled at the beach. But when the still-soaring, ninety-degree sun started burning my shoulders, I swapped the sand for a shady café.

I'd avoided newspapers for much of my journey, preferring to remain oblivious to events outside my own bubble. But the date on the *Miami Herald* felt familiar. Then it struck me – I was now one year old. Exactly twelve months ago, I'd left my house and the people in it and was en route to a tatty old caravan park. If I'd known then just how magnificent life could be, I think I'd have left much sooner.

I put the newspaper down and stared at the endless ocean. My year alone had felt like a lifetime, but in a positive way. I wondered if Catherine was now feeling the same.

I recalled how, when we were just shy of twenty-three, I'd taken her to the local art-house cinema for a matinee performance of *Breakfast at Tiffany's.* We were almost a decade into our relationship, but still gravitated towards the back row like love-struck teenagers. I was in my last year at university and living with Arthur and Shirley. So until we bought the cottage together, our romance was restricted to stolen moments where and when we could find them.

'Do you think we'll get married one day?' I asked the top of her head as it rested on my shoulder.

'Of course,' she replied without hesitation, clearly surprised I'd even questioned it. She pulled another toffee from the paper bag and popped it into her mouth.

'When did you have in mind?' I continued, trying to mirror her breezy mood.

'Whenever you like. I've been waiting for ten years, but if I have to wait another ten I might run off with Dougie instead.' *I don't think that's going to happen anytime soon*, I thought.

'Okay, Kitty – will you marry me?'

'Yep,' she replied, without taking her eyes off Audrey Hepburn. Her cool facade was only belied by a squeeze of my arm.

That weekend we caught a train to London, still a place haunted by memories of my mother and biological father Kenneth, and returned with a modest gold band and tiny centred diamond that only the Hubble Telescope could locate. I was grateful I'd found a girl who didn't need material things to feel self-worth.

Later that evening, I held Catherine's hand tightly in the living room, where my father and Shirley were eating their Saturday night salad in front of *The Generation Game.*

'We've got something to tell you,' I announced. 'We're getting married.'

Our joy was greeted with silence. I hadn't expected streamers and balloons to fall from the ceiling – a simple 'congratulations' would've sufficed. Instead, they looked at each other, then us, and then back towards the show's presenter.

'I'm going to head home, Simon. Come round later,' Catherine suggested, sensing a shift in temperature. She pecked me on the cheek and left. I waited until the front door closed before I spoke.

'What was that about?' I began.

My father swallowed his food, placed his cutlery back on his tray and folded his arms.

'Simon, you're too young for marriage.'

'I'm twenty-two. You were only a couple of years older than me when you met Doreen.'

'Precisely. Catherine's a lovely girl, but she's not worldly-wise enough to settle down. The girls of today . . . they're different to my day. They're more spirited, they expect more from life. Sooner or later she'll realise she wants more than you and then it'll be too late. I promise you, she will break your heart.'

I swallowed hard.

'She isn't Doreen,' I said. 'Just because you drove my mother away doesn't mean I'll do the same.'

Both were too flabbergasted to respond, but I hadn't finished.

'I love Kitty, and I always will. There's nothing that could happen to make either of us leave each other. Ever.'

I stormed out of the house still fuming and caught up with Catherine. If only I'd paused to listen to them instead of my heart before we walked down the aisle.

'Darren, are you coming for a swim?' Dana's voice came from behind, bringing me back to the present.

'Let me finish this and I'll be with you.'

I liked answering to a different name. I swigged the final mouthful of lukewarm beer and cast a panoramic sweep of my surroundings.

'Did you know it's my birthday today?'

'No way, dude!' squealed Angie. 'Guess what? We've got the best way to celebrate!'

Thirty minutes later and the three of us were in my hotel bedroom, snorting the first of many lines of a bitter white powder that allowed me to make love to them until late afternoon.

If my second year was to be as rewarding as the first, I was going to be a very lucky man.

◆ ◆ ◆

Northampton, today

2.05 p.m.

She wasn't sure what bewildered her the most about him – his seeming lack of regret for any of his actions, or his complete insensitivity.

First had come his disgusting admission that he'd wiped them all from his memory. Then came the all-too-detailed account of his life of Riley on his extended holiday. And now he'd desecrated the memory of the anniversary of his disappearance – such a pivotal moment in her family's lives – by celebrating it with drugs and two tarts.

Drugs, at his age? He was a bloody idiot. And he'd hurt her once again by admitting he wished he'd listened to his know-it-all father and never married her. She detested him for making her feel like a mistake.

What she hadn't noticed was that he'd found it equally as hard listening to her. He appreciated that she'd explained how the children had grappled with his absence – he wouldn't have blamed her for keeping him in the dark. But they hadn't been on the straightforward journey of acceptance and healing he'd imagined for them. Naively, he'd presumed that, because their minds were young and malleable, they'd have muddled along and eventually forgotten about him. He hadn't envisaged how necessary he'd been. The mental picture of a faceless son isolating himself from those who loved him was a sobering thought.

While he'd suspected Robbie might prove to be a little different from the others, his lack of understanding of just how fragile the boy had been placed knots in his stomach.

And they wouldn't be the last.

CHAPTER TEN

SIMON

Key West, USA, twenty-three years earlier

1 February, 6.15 p.m.

Five miles square. Twenty-five thousand people. Fifty hotels. Twenty guesthouses. Three hostels. Four thousand five hundred miles from home.

The odds against it were almost too high to calculate. Yet fate still managed to marry my new life with my old in the shape of two familiar faces.

Key West's location at the southernmost tip of America made it an attractive destination for fishermen and scuba divers. Having acquired my basic diving skills from Bradley in France, I had promised myself that, if the opportunity arose, I'd explore the oceans where and when I could.

I'd been pushing myself further and further offshore throughout the week with a party of other semi-novice divers. The crystal clarity of the water by the outer bar and the rainbow of coral colours had been intoxicating. I swam after curtains of reef fish, envious of the surroundings they took for granted.

I pencilled in my first wreck dive for the coming weekend, to explore the remains of the *Benwood* – a three-hundred-and-sixty-foot former freighter sunk off the coast of Key Largo. But after my fifth consecutive day of diving, my muscles were strained and I welcomed a night alone at an oceanside bar and diner.

As I'd spent so much time in the company of fish, it seemed heartless to then feast on them. So I ordered a Caesar salad from the bar, sat at a brightly lit table outside, and sparked up a cigarette as I readied myself to enjoy watching the sun sink over boats bobbing along the horizon.

A couple walking hand in hand on the opposite side of the road caught my eye when they stopped and kissed outside a hotel. At first they offered nothing extraordinary or significant, but even from a distance there seemed something familiar in their body language. I wondered if we'd crossed paths at a hostel somewhere. However, when the headlights of a passing car illuminated their faces, my heart stopped.

There stood Roger and Paula.

I stared, drop-jawed, as Roger took a camera from around his neck and headed up the steps and into the hotel. Paula remained on the path, fiddling with an earring.

Idly taking in her surroundings before I had a chance to react, her gaze swept over me and continued on. But when she did a double take and our eyes met, I knew the game was up.

◆ ◆ ◆

CATHERINE

Northampton, twenty-three years earlier

1 February

They had remained on the porch floor gathering dust for so long, they'd become a part of the furniture. I used to give Simon's running shoes a quick glance each time I passed them, longing to see him fill them again. But I'd grown to accept they were always going to stay empty.

Moving them was like reaching the final page of a book I wasn't ready to put down. But fighting my way through small challenges one at a time meant the giant ones were less daunting. I picked them up and placed them with my wellies under the saucepan shelf in the pantry.

Later that day, they'd reappeared in the porch. I moved them again, but by morning they'd returned. I told myself I was being a silly cow when I imagined my husband's ghost had put them back where it thought they belonged.

I guessed Robbie was the real culprit. His speech therapist was very slowly encouraging him to find his voice and confidence again, so I didn't want to confront him and risk making him feel like he was doing something wrong. But, just to be sure, I moved them once more. A couple of days later, I was sitting quietly in the kitchen unpicking the stitching on a jacket pocket. I heard the patter of Oscar's paws making their way through the house and watched, without him noticing me, as he picked up the first shoe by its laces and carefully walked away with it. Then he returned and took the second one.

I followed him and watched as he placed them by the front door in exactly the same position as they'd sat for close to two years. He was startled when he saw me, then regained his composure and wandered off. I'd taken into account everyone's feelings in the house except those of Simon's faithful friend.

So I didn't try to move them again, until he left us too.

◆ ◆ ◆

SIMON

Key West, USA, twenty-three years earlier

1 February, 6.20 p.m.

The speed at which I turned my head forced a burning, shooting pain up my neck and into the back of my skull.

But there was no time to acknowledge it or to readjust my posture. I focused on her reflection in the smoky glass of the restaurant window instead, and prayed I'd gone unnoticed. But she remained there, squinting at a memory.

Surely Roger couldn't have tracked me down in Florida? I never knew which direction I was going to choose until I reached a crossroads. So it would take a crystal ball for anyone else to predict where to find me from one week to the next. Besides, Simon had left no trail. I was Darren Glasper.

So it must have been coincidence that had brought us to exactly the same place, on exactly the same street at exactly the same time. Fate was an unpredictable bastard.

I prayed Paula would quickly come to the conclusion her eyes had deceived her. I continued watching her reflection as, behind me, she shook her head, believing, like me, it was too far-fetched to be true. Indecision made her hover from foot to foot like she needed someone to confirm she was being ridiculous. But there was no one to help.

I began to relax slightly when she twisted her body towards the hotel steps Roger had walked up moments earlier. Then she hesitated, turned back around, and repeated her movements like she was being rewound and fast-forwarded with a remote control.

My heart palpitated, and I hoped she'd run inside to find Roger and give me the opportunity to escape. But she didn't. Instead, she edged towards the curb for closer inspection.

Self-preservation set in and, without rotating my head, I threw my blazing cigarette onto the pavement, stood up and began to walk away. I hungered to look over my shoulder to make sure I was alone, but I was terrified of what I might find. I picked up my pace.

'*Simon!*'

The sound of her voice cut me like glass. My chest became inflamed and I felt the urgent need to empty my bowels. My breath was short and my legs threatened to flop beneath me. All I could do was ignore her and continue.

'*Simon!*'

It came again, but with more authority.

The proximity of her voice told me she'd gained ground but was still on the opposite side of the road. *Just give up*, I screamed inside, and accelerated my pace to a near-run. But Paula must have jogged to keep up with me. I'd forgotten how annoyingly determined she could be when she wanted something. She was like a dog with a bone. Much of the time I'd only tolerated her because she was Catherine's best friend and Roger's girlfriend. I much preferred Baishali, a passive soul who didn't like to rock the boat. Why couldn't it have been her who'd seen me?

My frustration became impossible to suppress, so I went against my better judgement and turned to see her struggling to find a break between moving cars to cross. I used it to my advantage and ran, the prey desperate to avoid the hunter.

'It's you, isn't it!' she shouted above the noise of the vehicles. Red traffic lights gave her the opportunity she needed and she flew across the road with the speed of a tornado.

'Stop running, you coward!' she shrieked. 'I know it's you!'

My body already ached from my ocean dives and my increased anxiety. My daily cigarette intake left me breathless. Short of a miracle, I knew I would have to face the inevitable. So I stopped.

Within seconds, her fingers dug into my shoulder and she spun me around. Even though she'd been so confident it was me, disbelief in the actual confirmation spread across her face. We glared at each other in silence before she unleashed her fury.

'You selfish fucking idiot! How could you do that to them?' she shouted, jabbing me in the chest.

I remained poker-faced and silent.

'Your family has gone through hell without you,' she continued. 'Do you know that?'

I didn't want to know.

'Well, what have you got to say for yourself?'

Nothing, actually.

'What's wrong with you?' she yelled, growing increasingly frustrated by my blank expression.

Everything had been very much right with me until a few minutes earlier.

She slapped me across the cheek. It smarted. She slapped me again. It became numb. Another slap. I felt nothing.

'Jesus Christ, Simon. Do you have any idea what you've put everyone through?'

I wasn't interested.

'Say something, you coward! You owe me an explanation!'

I didn't. In fact, I felt no urge to justify myself or my actions to Paula, or to anyone else for that matter. I owed the world nothing and it pissed me off that she was arrogant enough to assume I did.

'Well? Are you just going to stand there?'

No, I wasn't.

Using all the strength I could muster, with the force of everything that drove me forwards, I clamped both my hands around her cheeks, forced her backwards off the curb and then pushed her into the road and into the path of oncoming traffic.

She didn't even have time to scream.

Neither the crunching of her bones under the van's wheels nor the screeching of its brakes persuaded me to stop walking and to turn around.

◆ ◆ ◆

Northampton, today

2.40 p.m.

Catherine remained motionless as she processed the horror of his confession. Her husband was a killer.

She didn't want to believe it, because what he'd just admitted made no sense at all. She had never met anyone who had murdered another human being. Certainly not someone who she'd allowed into her home. And not one she had loved. She had no idea how to respond.

What seemed to him like an age passed by, while neither of them spoke. He focused his eyes on the rug; hers burrowed right through him. He didn't think it fitting to interrupt.

'You . . . you killed Paula?' she stuttered slowly.

'Yes, Catherine, I did,' came his reply, reticent but showing little remorse.

'She was pregnant,' she said quietly.

He inhaled deeply. 'I did not know that.'

The colour drained from her face and she felt sick. Actually, she more than just felt sick: she knew she was going to vomit. She leaped up from her chair and winced as her weight took her weak ankle by surprise. She faltered upstairs to the bathroom, slamming the door behind her. She didn't have time to lift the toilet seat before the first wave struck and she made a mess on the floor. But the second time, she was prepared and it reached the pan.

He remained downstairs, saddened to hear two lives had been lost that day, and not just one like he'd assumed. But he had done what was necessary at the time.

He stood up, paced around the room and heard her retching upstairs. He'd always known that if he was going to be completely honest with her – and that was, after all, why he was here – it was going to be unpleasant. And it was going to get worse. Much, much worse. Because Paula wasn't the first person he'd killed, and she hadn't been the last. But Catherine didn't need to know that yet.

Upstairs, her sickness eventually passed, but she remained on the floor, her arm still clutching the cistern, her back square against the radiator.

Suddenly she became frightened of the monster below, now he'd revealed what he was capable of. Her body swivelled around and she stretched her arm to turn the lock on the handle. The doors were old and heavy but not impossible to break. A few kicks were all it might take.

She asked herself how someone she'd known so deeply – built a life and family with – could've hurt a beautiful soul like Paula. Although it had been a while since she'd thought about her old friend, she remembered the horror of first hearing she'd been knocked down and killed in a random, apparently utterly senseless attack abroad. Despite a lengthy investigation, no one had ever been arrested or charged.

She'd been devastated, of course. Just before Paula and Roger had left for their holiday, Paula had confided in her, like best friends do, that she was pregnant. Catherine was over the moon for her and bashed out three Babygros and a jumpsuit to give her when they got back. She cried into them when Paula's mother told her the news.

She recalled the day of the funeral, when the whole village turned out without exception to pay their last respects. Then, afterwards, she spent much time consoling Roger, who blamed himself for leaving Paula alone for those few crucial, fatal minutes. He'd never discovered where she'd been going when she was murdered.

Without warning, the door handle turned and she jumped.

'Leave me alone!' she croaked, her throat acidic and sore. But he had no intention of leaving yet.

'Catherine,' he said calmly. 'Please come out.'

'Why are you telling me all this? Are you going to kill me next? Is that why you've come back?'

He might have laughed under different circumstances. 'No, of course not.'

'How can I be sure? I have no idea who you are. You're a stranger.'

'As are you, but we all change, Catherine. All of us change.'

'But we don't all change into murderers and kill our friends!'

He couldn't disagree. 'Come back downstairs and let's talk.'

'About what? There's nothing you can say that can justify what you did.'

'And I'm not going to try to. What's done is done and I won't take anything back. I've come a long way to see you, Catherine. Please.'

She paused and heard him walk slowly down the stairs. She took a few deep breaths and then splashed cold water across her face. She patted herself dry with a hand towel and was surprised by her reflection in the mirror. An old woman stared at her. In the time he'd been in her house, she'd been thirty-three again. Now she was every inch her fifty-eight years.

She cleaned up the mess on the bathroom floor, then disregarded common sense and unlocked the door. As she made her way to the landing, she resolved that, if she was going to die at his hands, she was going to put up a bloody good fight first.

CHAPTER ELEVEN
SIMON

Colorado, USA, twenty-three years earlier

2 May

The faces of the others I'd killed hadn't haunted me like Paula's.

Again and again, I recalled the warmth of her soft cheeks and her hair as it brushed against the back of my fingers. I remembered thinking how surprisingly light she felt when I threw her body into the road.

I could still hear the bursting of her skin and bones as the van crushed her. I still felt the adrenaline soaring through my blood as I ran back to my hotel to grab my backpack and then vanished into the night.

But when my foot pressed hard on Betty's accelerator and Key West faded behind me, all I saw was my imaginary passenger Paula's face in the rear-view mirror.

Over the next three months, Tennessee, Kentucky, Missouri, Nebraska, Kansas and Colorado all flashed past like a wheel of photos in a red plastic View-Master. The majority of my time was spent on the road manipulating fellow runaways into helping fill my hours – new groups of friends for the days and women for the nights. And when female volunteers were sparse, I'd seek out those who required payment by the hour.

Bony or Rubenesque, dark-chocolate complexions or as pale as death – appearances never mattered when I knelt behind them as they balanced on their hands and knees. And if they could provide the chemical stimulants I'd grown to enjoy since my first time with the two girls in Miami, then even better.

I offered transportation to anyone who needed to be somewhere else, even to a state hundreds of miles from the route I'd intended. I did anything to avoid being ensnared by myself, because that's when I dissected my actions.

I didn't doubt for a moment that killing Paula had been the right thing to do. In fact, I was still galled by her for backing me into a corner. Paula had had a choice; I hadn't. By following me, she'd made the wrong one. I had made the correct one.

I'd gone to great pains to keep my past and present separate. And when she'd demanded reasons, I could predict the chain of events that would've followed my allowing her to walk away. She'd have hurried back to the hotel to inform Roger his departed friend was actually thriving under the Floridian sun. Then, on their return to England, he'd have felt duty-bound to tell Catherine that she'd been abandoned, not widowed. While I was missing, there was doubt and an assumption of death. With confirmation came certainty and I did not want to be thought of in either a negative or positive light.

Paula had paid the price of interfering with what was meant to be. And I was not responsible for that.

Utah, USA

20 July

I removed my belongings from my backpack and spread them out in a semicircle across the saline terrain. I built two heaps – the 'keep' pile and the 'toss' pile. The first contained essentials such as clothing, maps, Darren's passport, and money.

The second pile was for items I wouldn't need or use again, such as the telephone numbers of people I'd already forgotten. Souvenirs only served to remind me of experiences I'd already had. It was what was to come that interested me. And if I wanted to travel light, sentiment would only weigh me down.

I placed a faded denim shirt between the piles, repacked my backpack and stored it behind a nearby boulder. My discarded items were consigned to Betty's trunk. I cut through the denim shirtsleeve, then unscrewed the petrol cap and carefully fed it inch by inch into the hole.

Betty had been the perfect travelling companion for six thousand miles, but her time had reached an end. Her rear axle throbbed over the feeblest of bumps. She required a thirty-minute rest after every three hours of travel, or steam would burst from her radiator like Old Faithful.

I chose the Bonneville Salt Flats as her final resting place. Its fifty square miles of empty, horizontal earth was so flat and brilliantly white, it was like God had run out of time when creating the world and thrown his paint pots down in frustration. Betty could make her mark there.

I pulled a cigarette lighter from my jeans, and after several flicks of its flint, the shirt's cuff caught light. I stepped back and stared hard into her windows, desperate to find the memories of those I'd been forced to sacrifice, slowly cremating in the flames inside the car. But the only thing to burn was my reflection.

I lit a cigarette, walked away from Betty and awaited a climactic explosion. Instead of a giant fireball came a belly rumble. Flames slowly lapped from under her doors and scorched her windows. One by one, her tyres burst, then her windows popped and shattered.

'You okay there, sir?' a man shouted from inside his truck as he pulled over to the side of the road. 'What happened to your wagon?'

'She overheated and caught fire.'

'Shit, man. You're lucky you got clear, I guess. Can I give you a ride?'

'That would be great.'

'Where to? The nearest town?'

'Anywhere you're headed, actually. There's nothing to salvage here and I can't afford to pay to deal with it.'

The man considered Betty's blazing remains, then looked me up and down, as if asking what kind of person wasn't more bothered that their only mode of transport had just gone up in flames. Then he shrugged. 'I'm heading to Nevada. That okay?'

I accepted his offer, and as we drove off into the distance, I watched through the wing mirror as my girl smouldered, then bid farewell by finally exploding into the sky like a comet.

◆ ◆ ◆

CATHERINE

Northampton, twenty-three years earlier

17 July

'I'm retiring, Catherine,' began Margaret. I nearly spat my tea across the kitchen table.

'Jim and I are moving to Spain,' she continued, oblivious to my dismay. 'We've bought a nice little villa on the coast in Andalusia. I plan to start scaling down next summer, and all being well, we should be there by New Year.'

'Oh,' I replied. She might as well have slapped me across the face.

I'd thrown myself into making clothes for Fabien's and had even given up ironing for others so I'd have the time to plough through well over a hundred outfits in a year and a half. It was also a therapeutic way of keeping my mind off poor Paula. Baishali and I missed her so much. It was almost too much to bear, and we took comfort in each other and tried our best to help Paula's parents cope with their loss.

Now, with Margaret's news, all I saw was my future behind checkout number seven at the supermarket again.

'Do you have a buyer?' I enquired, hoping my new boss would be just as keen on my work.

'That depends on you, darling,' she replied, screwing a cigarette into a plastic holder. 'I'm giving you the first option to buy me out.'

I laughed out loud. Clearly the prospect of spending the rest of her life under the Spanish sun, drunk on sangrias served by hunky waiters, had sent her a little doolally.

'You know I don't have that kind of money!' I answered. 'Look around you. Everything in this house is second- or third-hand, or broken and held together with Blu-Tack. How on earth could I afford to buy your shop?'

'Oh, you should never let money get in the way of a good idea,' she tutted. 'As far as I can see, you have three options – either get yourself a bank loan, remortgage your house, or you and I can come to a financial agreement until the balance is paid off.'

'But I know nothing about business!'

'You're full of excuses, aren't you? I didn't have a bloody clue about it either when I started, but did that stop me? Did it hell. So what's stopping you?'

'Margaret, I'm not like you,' I sighed, reminding her of the obvious. 'You have the confidence to do anything you put your mind to – and the money. I've got the kids and keeping a roof over our heads to worry about. It's impossible.'

She took a long drag from her cigarette and poured herself a third cup of tea from the pot.

'Do you remember when you told me about your mother, and what a bitch she was to you?'

'I didn't call her a bitch,' I interrupted, a little surprised.

'Well, she was, so learn to live with it. You took everything negative she ever threw at you and turned it into something positive. What did you do after Billy? You picked yourself up and got on with life. And what about when Simon disappeared? I bet you felt sorry for yourself, licked your wounds then put your children first, didn't you?'

I nodded.

'See? You're a survivor, darling. You always find a way, that's what you *do*. You're a much stronger person than I am. An opportunity like this doesn't come knocking at your door every day, so I implore you to grab it with both hands.'

I kept quiet for a moment and mulled over her suggestion. On the surface, pole-vaulting across the Grand Canyon looked easier.

'Be honest, do you really think I can do it?'

'When have I ever been anything but honest with you, Catherine? If I didn't think you were capable, I'd have never put the offer on the table. Now, what do you say?'

26 November

The months went by like a whirlwind.

Since Margaret had made her offer, it'd been all I could think about. The old me would have dismissed it as a pretty ridiculous suggestion. But times had changed, and so had I. Now I owed it to myself to at least think about it.

I'd calculated I had enough savings to pay the mortgage for five months, and I could show my bank manager my accounts to prove I was now loan-worthy. But that wouldn't cover all of Margaret's asking price. And it wasn't my only problem.

'The college has a night school,' she'd explained back in the summer, pre-empting another excuse. 'Two evenings a week in business, bookkeeping and accounts.'

'But what about my clothes? I won't have time to make them and run a shop.'

'That's what staff are for, dear. Ask some of the girls at the local fashion college to help – they'll bite your hand off for the experience. And while Selena's reluctant to accept my offer of employment, I'm sure she'd be more than willing to step up for you.'

For every argument I had to oppose her, Margaret found reasons why I could do it. And it lit a fire in my belly that I'd never felt before. I was like Dorothy caught up in a cyclone; only no matter how many times I clicked my ruby-red slippers, I was still in Oz. I had to give it a shot.

But in doing so, I needed to lead two separate lives. At home I'd have to continue being Mum to my brood, while at the boutique I'd be a budding businesswoman learning the ropes.

Over the following months, I followed Margaret to meetings in London with designers and manufacturers, and she even paid for my flights to Paris, Milan and Madrid for catwalk shows. It was a different world, one that scared and fascinated me. It was like jumping into the pages of the fashion magazines I read. And, if I'm honest, at times I didn't think I deserved to be in places like the third row of the runway as Thierry Mugler launched his spring collection.

My mother's voice told me I was a fraud and Margaret's charity case. So to spite her, I stuck with it to see how far I could go.

I doubted whether I'd have had the courage or confidence to do it if Simon had still been alive. I'd got all the fulfilment I'd needed in being his wife and the mother to his children. But I'd been a different woman two years ago. With each new challenge, I discovered I had passions, ambitions and a desire to be my own person.

And I was about to find something else I'd never expected to see again.

◆ ◆ ◆

Northampton, today

3.30 p.m.

She'd listened intently to every word he'd said, hanging on to a glimmer of hope that he might show some regret over killing Paula. But when he blamed Paula for her own death, it merely revealed the true character of the man. In fact, he was no man, she thought.

He was a shade: a lifeless, colourless shade.

Try as she might, she couldn't understand why he'd come back after all this time to confess to something he knew would disgust her. He could have taken his secret to the grave and she'd have been none the wiser. So why did he want to hurt her? And surely only someone who realises he has nothing to lose would so readily admit to such evil deeds? What had he already lost that had made him so unafraid?

His mind was elsewhere. To hear how far she'd come bolstered his belief that leaving had been the best thing for her. But for the children? He was still undecided and his head hurt the more he thought about it.

'Is that what you do when something stops being useful to you or gets in your way?' she asked.

'I'm not sure what you mean.'

'Paula. The car you set fire to. The hotel you burned down. Me. The children. If it becomes an inconvenience or interferes with your plans, you destroy it.'

'No, no,' he replied, unsure how she'd failed to grasp the significance of incinerating Betty or the hotel. He'd thought she'd understand they had been selfless acts, and the closing of chapters. But it wasn't an argument worth pursuing. Maybe later she might realise it was just those who'd sought to ruin him who'd fallen foul of his sourness.

'If you're not here to hurt me, then give me one good reason why I shouldn't call the police and tell them what you did to Paula?'

'I don't have one, and you have every right to. But if you're going to call them, at least wait until you've heard everything first.'

'And when will that be?' she asked, as the sick feeling in her stomach made itself known again.

Soon, he thought. *Soon.*

CHAPTER TWELVE
CATHERINE

Northampton, twenty-two years earlier

7 January

I can honestly admit, with my hand on my heart, that I hadn't given another man a second glance in the two and a half years Simon had been gone.

Sometimes I'd daydream about how it might feel to fall in love again, but there'd never been a face attached to the strapping hunk who swept me off my imaginary feet. Besides, falling in love scared me – it meant running the risk of once again losing someone. I was terrified of feeling that all over again. So I vowed to keep potential aggravation at arm's length for the time being.

Instead, I threw all my attention towards my dressmaking – and, more urgently, trying to find the money to buy Fabien's from Margaret. Steven had done a wonderful job making a success of his and Simon's business, and he now employed a staff of five. I still owned Simon's half, and when I told Steven about Margaret's offer, he thought I'd be mad to turn her down. I suggested he could give me the extra capital I needed if he bought me out.

In theory, it was the perfect solution, but before I asked him, I had to give it a lot of thought. Simon had invested so many hours in building it from scratch that giving up his share was another way I'd be letting him go. But I had to put myself first, and although I'd be waving goodbye to his dreams, he'd be helping me to reach mine. So with Steven's money and a small bank loan, I was soon to have a business of my very own.

But just when I had everything mapped out for the year ahead, something – or more accurately someone – came along to throw a spanner in the works.

Tom caught my eye the first night I began the bookkeeping course Margaret had suggested. He was the only person who smiled when I walked nervously through the classroom door. He was classically handsome, with dark, wavy hair and greying temples, and his few laughter lines drew me to his chestnut-brown eyes.

I was stacked from waist to chest with textbooks when Emily's Barbie pencil case toppled from the top to the floor. Tom's hand shot out and caught it, and he chuckled at the doll's smiling, plastic face and impossibly thin waistline. I blushed.

'I don't think you'll be needing all of them tonight,' he began as we queued for a vending-machine coffee during the first lesson break.

'I'm sorry?'

'All your textbooks, they're for the entire course,' he said, pointing to my desk. 'Unless you're planning to condense six months into one night?'

My nervous laugh came out like a pig's snort and I died a little inside.

Tom introduced himself and explained how he was about to start his own business in wood sculpture and furniture design. He'd recently quit a successful career as a solicitor to follow his dreams – a brave decision for a man in his late thirties. And, like me, he didn't know the first thing about accounts. Already we had something in common.

'Are you busy later?' he asked as we returned to our seats. 'Do you fancy a drink after school?'

'Me?' I asked, taken aback. 'Oh, um, well, I've got to get home.'

'How about the weekend then . . . Saturday night? Dinner? That's if you're free. Or if you want to.'

'I barely know you,' I replied, sounding like an uptight virgin from a Brontë sisters novel.

He grinned. 'That's what dinner's for.'

I stared at him blankly. Then my mouth stepped in before my brain had a chance to.

'I've got three kids and my husband's disappeared and he's probably dead but I can't be sure because we haven't seen him in years and I've not been on a date since ABBA won Eurovision,' I blurted out in a babbling stream.

He responded with a silent smile until he was sure the onslaught of information had peaked.

'I'm sorry, I don't know where that came from,' I mumbled.

'Well, I'm divorced with a money-grabbing ex-wife who's sadly very much alive and I'd love to go on a date with you.' He smiled at me. 'So how's about it?'

11 January

I wasn't sure how I'd found myself in a Chinese restaurant sharing a chicken chow mein with a single, drop-dead-gorgeous man.

Dating in my thirties was not such a different experience to dating as a teenager. As a sixteen-year-old, I'd been embarrassed by my growing boobs and pimply skin. As a thirty-six-year-old, I was embarrassed by my sagging boobs and stretch-marked skin.

When I started putting my make-up on for my 'date' – a word that seemed ridiculous for a woman of my age to use – I glared into that unforgiving bathroom mirror. I remembered how naturally Simon and I had fitted together, how from the start I didn't want to be chatted up by anyone else. Other boys had asked me out, but there'd been a vulnerability that came with him that they didn't have. And the Simon I remembered was funny and spontaneous, able to make me laugh with his uncanny impressions of teachers. He'd sketch beautifully detailed pictures of me and hide them in my exercise books for me to find. He made me feel like I was his all.

Now I asked myself what Tom thought he saw in me. I had more baggage than an airport check-in, my once-sparkling blue eyes had been dulled by circumstances beyond my control and my confidence with the opposite sex was at rock bottom. Actually, it was lower than that. I was not what you'd call 'a catch'.

Twice I almost phoned him to cancel, blaming a sick child, before I reminded myself dating was just another mountain waiting to be conquered. In the end, I had nothing to worry about. Once the butterflies stopped circling my stomach, I was drawn in by his sense of humour, his self-confidence and honesty.

Tom recalled how his ex-wife had walked out on him to live with a much younger man. He'd distracted himself from his divorce and high-pressured job by wood carving and creating incredible sculptures and furniture.

'I don't know if I can explain it properly without sounding like an idealist or a hippy,' he began, 'but one day it was like I had an epiphany. I realised that I was actually capable of doing anything I wanted to if I put my heart and soul into it. And being creative with wood gives me more fulfilment than the path I'd mapped out for myself in law. The other lawyers in the firm thought I was mad when I resigned, but I had to give it my best shot even if the odds were stacked against me. Do you understand what I mean?'

I identified with every word he said. And, like me, Tom was new to the dating scene.

'I quickly learned that a man who'd quit being a lawyer to follow his heart into the unknown isn't as attractive to women as one who knows where he belongs,' he continued. 'That's what I like about you. You didn't look at me like I was barking mad.'

Likewise, I examined his reactions to my story when I went into more detail than my blurted summary at our first meeting: one morning, my husband simply fell off the face of the earth.

'Do you think he's still alive?' Tom asked.

'No, I don't think he is,' I replied. 'I've been through every scenario of what might have happened, but I don't think I'll ever really know. So the kids and I have accepted we've lost him.'

'And you're ready to move on?'

'Yes,' I replied with certainty. 'Yes, I am.'

'Good.' He smiled, and reached out to hold my hand.

12 June

Tom knew without me ever having to explain that I was a repair in progress.

I took our relationship slowly and cautiously, with post-lesson drinks, pub lunches, coffees and then finally a kiss. Although the front seat of his car outside a DIY store wasn't quite straight from the pages of a Jackie Collins novel, it didn't matter. He'd given my life a much-needed thrill.

And with that came guilt. Was I cheating on Simon's memory? It was all very well promising till death do us part, but there was no clause in our wedding vows to cover an unexpected disappearance.

I asked myself what he'd do if the roles were reversed, and I wasn't convinced he'd have moved on. But after all I'd been through, I felt I deserved a spring in my step.

That said, I still made Tom wait nearly four months before I was ready to make love. I'd become used to my body as a solitary vessel navigated by a crew of one. And Tom was someone who wanted to steer her into fresh waters. With each touch, each stroke and each kiss, I found it hard to concentrate on pleasuring him or feeling him pleasuring me, as I was too focused on stopping my body from involuntarily shaking. But when the second time came around, I was much more relaxed, and by the third, I couldn't wait for more. And there was a lot more.

I still had inhibitions over what my body had to offer to Tom or any man, so lights-on lovemaking was a strict no-no. The war wounds of five pregnancies gave me as many hang-ups as hang-downs. But Tom didn't appear bothered. He was no Kevin Costner, but I didn't need a six-pack, tree-trunk thighs or the libido of an eighteen-year-old to satisfy me.

I enjoyed doing couply things like visiting the cinema and the theatre, taking long walks by the canal with Oscar or visiting woodwork and textile museums. We each took an interest in what the other liked, and slowly I began to develop real feelings for Tom, so much more than just a crush on the first boy who'd shown me a glimmer of attention.

The kids were the only part of my life I wasn't ready to share. My relationship with them was as honest as it could possibly be, so I didn't want to lie by keeping him hidden like a dirty little secret. But I didn't want to rock the boat either.

James's temper no longer had me on tenterhooks, as he focused all his energies on his guitar. I was so proud the first time I saw him on stage playing in the school orchestra, and I embarrassed him by standing up and cheering when he finished his first public solo. Robbie's conversational skills were also gradually improving. I'd resigned myself to the fact he was never going to be a chatterbox like Emily. But when he started accepting invitations to school friends' birthday parties, I knew we'd turned a corner.

So I began by slipping Tom's name into conversations here and there, explaining he was a friend of Mummy's from night school. As our dates became more frequent, Emily was the first to cotton on that there might be more to him than just the man who helped Mummy with her maths homework.

'Can we meet your friend, please?' she asked as we fed stale bread to the ducks in the park.

'Which friend?'

'The one who makes you smile. Tom.'

'Why do you say he makes me smile?' I asked, and felt my face go bright red.

'Whenever you tell us you're seeing him, the corners of your mouth go up like this,' she replied, giving me a huge, cheeky grin. 'You love him!'

'Yes, Mummy, why can't we meet him?' chirped James.

So, to my delight and terror, the decision had been made for me.

9 July

I'd both looked forward to and dreaded Tom meeting the children in equal measure. It'd just been the four of us for so long that I'd forgotten what it felt like to be five.

The day before he came, I had a sit-down chat with the kids to explain that Tom wasn't going to replace their daddy, and if they didn't like him, they should tell me. I'd always put their feelings before mine, so if it meant Tom and I were going to be prematurely nipped in the bud, then so be it.

By the time he knocked at the door, I was fully prepared for them to charge through the full gamut of childhood emotions like tantrums, awkward silences, hostility and general boundary-pushing. How wrong could I have been? They were so inquisitive, well mannered and polite that I thought I might have to reassure Tom I hadn't kidnapped them from Stepford. I also felt bad for not giving them more credit.

Tom was relaxed and had a natural chemistry with them, despite not being a father himself. He paid each one equal attention, and they couldn't wait to show him their bedrooms and toys. Even Robbie spoke a little to him – a huge sign of his approval.

As I stood at the kitchen sink washing up the dishes after dinner, I closed my eyes and took a moment to listen to my children's laughter and a man's voice echoing around the house.

I'd not expected to hear either of those things under this roof again.

24 November

Introducing another ball into my juggling act was tricky, but I found a way to make it work.

I was winning in my battle with basic bookkeeping, and Margaret was winding down and dreaming of sunnier climes. Tom knew he was going to come third in line for my attention, after the kids and the boutique. And although we weren't able to see each other as often as we'd have liked, he understood.

Twice a week he slept at our house, and once a week when Selena babysat, I'd stay at his. Most evenings he joined us for dinner and would end his day being pulled in three different directions by six hands for bedtime stories and baths.

Tom had been in a rock group during his university days but his attempts to seduce me away from my George Michael and Phil Collins CDs and towards his Led Zeppelin collection were wasted. But James was more than willing to soak up different sounds, so Tom took him to see bands I'd never heard of at music arenas in Birmingham and London, and they'd arrive home singing at the top of their voices and holding armfuls of tour merchandise.

I let him move his tools and wood into Simon's garage-workspace, and soon the smell of fresh sawdust wafted regularly around the garden.

Tom was aware Simon was a presence that would remain in the cottage for as long as his family did. But if it bothered him, he never showed it. I grew used to having a man around the house, and he reminded me of how much I'd enjoyed it with my husband.

And then, from beyond the grave, Simon destroyed it all.

◆ ◆ ◆

SIMON

San Francisco, USA, twenty-two years earlier

7 January

With Betty transmuted to a smelted shell wedged into the desert floor, I had been relying on railways and Greyhound coaches to ferry me around.

They carried me up to Canada, then back down into America and towards middle states like Colorado and Nevada. My surroundings were unimportant, as long as I kept active. Solitude posed the greatest threat to my state of mind because it allowed me time to think.

On my arrival in France, I'd had a firm understanding of how my thought process operated and I'd manipulated it accordingly. If I didn't want to think about something, it was consigned to a box and then closed tight. But I couldn't shut Paula away with such ease. And her death began to eat at me like a slowly growing cancer. No matter how hard I tried, I couldn't make the lid fit. Flashbacks of her last, fateful moments haunted me so often that I began to question whether I'd dealt with our confrontation correctly. Because if I had, then why was she playing so heavy on my mind? Why could I not stop hearing her voice as it screamed my name? Why did my cheek still sting from her slaps? Why couldn't I blank out the confusion in her eyes when I'd pushed her?

I reminded myself countless times it was Paula who'd forced my hand, and not the other way round. But it wasn't enough.

Every town and city housed an area of dodgy repute, making narcotics easy to source once you spotted the familiar signs of decay in its residents. Cocaine became the only thing that kept my thoughts of Paula sedated.

I still enjoyed cannabis, but only as my night-time buttress. I'd smoke a few joints and delay retiring to bed for as long as possible, so the moment I slipped into my sleeping bag I was too exhausted and relaxed to analyse anything.

I constantly kept moving, and crammed as many activities as I could into my weeks. I'd visit notable landmarks, seek adrenaline thrills like white-water rafting and rock climbing, or spend time with other travellers discussing the next place to visit. The more unmarked paths I explored, the less opportunity there was to revisit those I knew too well.

The prospect of being more than a few days in one location and risking further muddling scared me. But I couldn't spend the rest of my life running. Eventually, something had to give.

Two years in perpetual motion had left my bones begging for rest and my mind longing for unclouded breathing space. And so, on the recommendation of others, I settled on San Francisco as a bolthole.

I stood at the summit of one of the city's twin peaks on my arrival, and understood why so many out-of-towners had left their hearts there. Its magnificent panoramic views, adorable Victorian-style houses and misty skies were as beguiling as they were calming.

I stayed at the Haight-Ashbury Hostel, which nestled quietly in the centre of what, twenty-five years earlier, had been the heart of the hippy insurgence. Many of the peace-and-love generation had remained, and weren't hard to spot by clothing alone.

San Francisco's compact nature enabled me to work my way around it by foot and cable car. It was a world away from the sprawling landscapes I'd scoped from train and bus windows. And as my body slowed down, gradually my brain followed suit.

There were plenty of parks, museums, galleries and coffee houses for me to relax in and gawk at the absurd walking shoulder to shoulder with the elegant. I was at home in a city of misfits.

The hostel's vibe reflected its surroundings, reminding me of the temporary safety I'd found at the Routard International. Like its predecessor, it too was a former hotel that had seen better days.

However, the only restoration project I had a vested interest in was me. Until someone made me an offer I couldn't refuse.

20 April

My exposure to dozens of hostels of varying standards qualified me to advise Mike, the relatively inexperienced proprietor of the Haight-Ashbury Hostel. I'd become an expert in the minimal requirements a budget traveller expected, and he lent a willing ear to my suggestions. What began as a casual proffering of opinions over a pitcher of Budweiser escalated to an offer of employment as manager.

I had drifted towards the city to gather myself, and three and a half months of self-medication in a fresh environment brought me closer to who I'd been when I first embarked on my adventure.

And my old self appreciated a challenge. So a free rein to build a business from scraps was too interesting an opportunity to reject. It would also help my ever-active mind to remain focused with constructive ideas. I hadn't felt such purpose since I'd walked along Rue du Jean as flames from a burning hotel nipped at my heels.

I held court at twice-weekly travel workshops in which I'd advise guests of off-the-beaten-track destinations, where to find work without a green card and how to stretch their dollars. I liaised with hostels cross-country to set up discounts for mutual recommendations. And having briefly once been the guest of a homeless shelter myself in London, I encouraged our patrons to spare a few hours to serve lunches in a downtown soup kitchen.

But away from my distractions, sleep still proved elusive. So when I wasn't inducing a nocturnal cannabis coma, I was leading guests out on bar and club crawls around the Mission District. Darren Glasper was a decade my junior, and I found it physically challenging to keep up with the partying of those even younger than him. The only way to gain stamina for those interminably energetic nights was to up my cocaine intake. And when crippling hangovers ate too far into the following morning or my nostrils felt too numb to snort any more, I introduced powdered amphetamines into my daily routine via my gums, to remain conscious and functioning. It seemed a sensible solution to the internal chaos of burning my candle at both ends.

It was much more rewarding to be Darren's caricature than it was to be Simon Nicholson. I threw myself into the role with such gusto that I often struggled to distinguish where he ended and I began.

3 July

My lips tingled as gusts of cold salty wind and water splashed against my face and ruffled my hair.

As the ferry made its wavering return from Alcatraz towards its dock at Pier 33, I couldn't stop thinking about the five-by-eight-foot cells I'd just visited. Although it had been decommissioned as a prison back in 1963 and transformed into a major tourist attraction, it was still a haunting presence.

I sympathised with the thirty-six former inmates who'd attempted to escape its claustrophobia. Many had chosen death within the bay's currents over spending the rest of their lives locked behind bars. I knew the anxiety of being trapped better than most, but so had my old friend Dougie, albeit for very different reasons.

More than twenty-five years had passed, but I'd never forgotten Dougie's kiss or spoken of it with anyone else, not even Catherine. As we got older, his disguise had occasionally become transparent and I knew he'd retained feelings for me that went beyond friendship. It was small things, like his lingering glances when I spoke, or when he'd focus his attention on me at the pub instead of trying to woo girls like Roger and Steven did.

Yet his attention neither bothered me nor made me uncomfortable. Quite the opposite, in fact. I felt privileged to have two people in my life who helped to make up for my fractured family.

However, I worried for Dougie. Whether it was with a girl or a boy, I hoped he'd eventually find the happiness I had. I didn't want to see him pained, or be the one to inflict it upon him. But our opposing natures meant it was inevitable.

'I'm getting married,' I blurted out on our way to meet Catherine and Paula at a disco in town. 'I asked her last week.'

Dougie stared at me momentarily, then formed an instant, forced smile. 'That's brilliant!' he shouted, leaning over to embrace me. 'I'm really pleased for you both. She's a smashing girl.'

'I'd like you to be my best man,' I replied, aware I might be adding insult to injury.

'It'd be an honour, thank you. I'll get the drinks in to celebrate.' He sprinted to the bar, where mirrored tiles reflected him biting hard on his bottom lip. Then, quick as lightning, he flashed the same grin to the barmaid as he had to me.

Within three months, Dougie had proposed to Beth, a schoolteacher he met later that night, and the two became husband and wife a year after Catherine and I married.

Suddenly, the ferry's engines began to labour and churn the bay's water before docking.

As I navigated the wooden gangway back towards Fisherman's Wharf, I wondered what had become of Beth. I hoped she'd found happiness with a man who truly loved her, and hadn't been ruined by the man Dougie became.

11 November

Chemicals ricocheted around my artery walls as I wrung every last morsel of pleasure from my hedonistic lifestyle. But when I randomly caught sight of my reflection in the glass panel of a bookshop door, I did a double take, repulsed by a face and body that resembled mine, but which were more haunted and dishevelled than I remembered.

Now I finally accepted there'd been a correlation between Paula's death more than eighteen months earlier and my hollowed cheeks and the dark crescents that circled my dimmed eyes. The gums above my top teeth were red raw, and my left cheek had developed a tiny, visible twitch that only pulsated when my engine was running low on stimulants.

I looked so much more than my thirty-six years, and double Darren's twenty-seven. I had lost myself in the place where I'd gone to find me. The identity I'd assumed was consuming me. Yet that wasn't enough to shame or coax me into re-evaluating my lifestyle choices. Instead, I walked away vowing to repair myself by eating more fruit and vegetables.

Besides, I had more pressing matters on my mind. In less than a year, since my arrival in San Francisco, I'd snorted and drunk my way through the remainder of the French publisher's money, and was stealing from Mike the hostel owner to boost my reserves. There were plenty of rooms for me to check guests in and out of without including their names in the register. They remained anonymous to all but me and I'd pocket the cash.

Grateful contributions from a drug dealer I'd permitted to ply her trade with discretion around the building also helped to swell my coffers. Only she and I knew that the broken dispenser in the ladies' toilets contained more than a hundred plastic tampon applicators packing half a gram of cocaine each.

Darren took gratification in being the centre of attention. He was boisterous; he was unpredictable; he inspired others to push themselves to explore; he was an expert purveyor of anecdotes, even if most of them were lies. He was the protagonist to my reactionary. And, most importantly, Darren was impervious to Simon's darkness.

But what eventually demolished my prison of fakery was a man I'd never met, who'd come to find me.

2 December

Once a month, I led excursions down the Californian coast in a modified Greyhound bus that Mike had bought at an auction on a whim. For fifty dollars a time, hostellers climbed on-board the 'Purple Turtle' for a sightseeing tour through Santa Cruz, Santa Barbara, Los Angeles and San Diego, eventually stopping over the Mexican border, in Tijuana.

Mike had removed most of the bus's seats and replaced them with mattresses, creating a portable hostel where guests could explore, sleep, and feel part of a mini-community on wheels.

With my bag packed, my only requirement was a hearty breakfast before I set off on my next guided tour.

'Is anyone sitting there, mate?' a British voice asked as I attacked a mountain of pancakes in the hostel's busy dining area.

'Help yourself,' I replied, and looked up to find a shaggy-haired man in his late twenties I hadn't checked in myself. His smile reminded me of someone. 'Have you just arrived?'

He was ravenous as he tucked into his scrambled eggs and hash browns. 'Yeah, about an hour ago. I'm bloody knackered. I landed in New York four weeks ago and have zigzagged my way across ever since.'

'That's good going. Why such a whistle-stop tour?'

'I'm trying to find someone. You might be able to help, actually. Have you ever come across a bloke who calls himself Darren Glasper?'

A chill ran through me.

'Darren Glasper?' I repeated, making sure the amphetamines I'd just washed down with a pot of coffee weren't making me hallucinate.

'Yeah. It's not his real name. He's been pretending to be my brother.'

Suddenly I recognised him from the family photographs that had been pinned to the wall around Darren's bed at the Routard in France. My first response was to want to throw my plate to one side and bolt, but his lack of hostility meant he didn't know I was his man.

'No, the name doesn't ring any bells,' I lied. 'Why's he been doing that?'

'That's what I've come to find out.'

Richard Glasper introduced himself and explained how French police had informed his family of Darren's untimely death from a weak heart five months after Bradley and I discovered his body. We'd confirmed to them his nationality, but Bradley was ignorant of his surname and I'd kept it quiet to buy myself time.

An impression of Darren's teeth was sent across the English Channel, and only after his family reported him missing were both sets of dental records cross-checked and matched.

But it was already too late to bring his body home. A clerical error meant Darren had been logged as a vagrant, and cremated as such. His family was presented with a plastic tub of ashes and nothing else.

'It broke my mam's heart,' Richard continued. 'Months later we started getting these weird cheques from some French book publisher, and then the police told us my brother's name had been flagged up in New York for overstaying his American visa. The address he gave of where he was staying was a youth hostel. The manager checked his photocopied records, and someone using Darren's passport had been staying there.'

I nodded along as he spoke, but inside I was furious with myself for not having the foresight to cover my tracks. What the hell had I been thinking in donating the book royalties to his family? I might as well have left them a trail of breadcrumbs to follow, right to my front door. Not for a second had I ever considered my deception would come back to haunt me like this – I'd been too busy congratulating myself on my philanthropy.

I moved my hands under the table so Richard wouldn't notice them shake.

'My mam was convinced there'd been a mistake and Darren was alive,' he continued. 'But the police investigated and were adamant he wasn't. She didn't believe them. We contacted the Youth Hostel Association, and city by city found out this fella had been travelling and using my brother's name for the best part of three years. And the manager of the Seattle hostel reckons he speaks to Darren regularly here. They have some kind of recommendation deal between them.'

I cleared my dry throat. 'What are you going to say if you find him?'

'It's not what I'm going to say, it's what I'm going to do,' replied Richard, his eyes narrowing. 'That bastard destroyed me mam. She went to her grave with a broken heart believing her youngest didn't want anything to do with us. If it's the last thing I do, I'll put an end to this.'

'Well, the best of luck,' I replied as I rose. 'I don't mean to be rude, but I have an excursion to organise.'

'No worries mate, nice to meet you. If you hear anything, you'll let me know, yeah? I'm in room 401.'

'Of course.'

I left my half-eaten breakfast where it lay, and forced myself not to run to reach my bedroom. I crammed my meagre belongings into my rucksack and headed to the ladies bathroom, and then to Richard's room to ensure he would never bother me again.

3 December

As the Purple Turtle trundled down the Pacific Coast Highway, I knew that living vicariously through a person who no longer existed had left me exposed. I'd thought I had created a new life for myself by erasing my identity. But it wasn't my life to build upon; it had belonged to somebody else.

And there was another person's life I'd changed too. As we'd made our first stop in Santa Cruz, I'd phoned the San Francisco Police Department and informed them of a British man who was working his way around the country's hostels dealing drugs. His name was Richard Glasper and they'd find him in room 401 of the Haight-Ashbury Hostel with a dozen cocaine-filled tampon applicators hidden in his suitcase pockets.

It was in Richard's best interests for it to happen this way. I wasn't alarmed by his threats of what he'd do to the person posing as his brother. I was afraid of what I might do to him if he confronted me. And it would certainly have happened if I'd stayed.

I had sucked so much marrow out of America that there was no bone left to feast on. The halfway mark of our trip was almost complete, and I knew I couldn't show my face in San Francisco again without being unmasked.

Tijuana, Mexico

4 December

I had no qualms about leaving my party of hostellers to fend for themselves without a driver or navigator once we reached Tijuana. If I'd taught them anything in my workshops, it was that the most successful travellers were the most resourceful ones.

With my dollars converted to pesos, my rucksack strapped to my back and my passengers distracted in a tequila bar, I slipped away to Highway 1D in search of the Baja coast.

Within minutes, I'd resuscitated Simon Nicholson and he was sharing the back of a pickup truck with a dozen wooden crates of watermelons.

◆　◆　◆

Northampton, today

4.15 p.m.

He wasn't stupid. He'd presumed, if not expected, her to have found love at some point. In fact, it would've been peculiar if she hadn't.

But now his replacement had an identity and it didn't sit comfortably with him. To hear her talk of this 'Tom' with such fondness; for him to have slipped so easily into his shoes, his house and his bed . . . He couldn't help but resent the man. He'd stopped loving her long before he left, so he was surprised by how it made him feel. Almost jealous, he conceded. His temples began to throb.

He knew he had no right to judge what she did with her life or who with. But allowing a stranger to play father to his children irritated him.

'Would you have preferred it if I'd stayed alone forever?' she asked suddenly, as his expression betrayed his thoughts.

'No, no,' he stuttered, 'of course not.'

The aching in his head grew more impatient and demanded attention. But her unrelenting stare that analysed his every gesture meant he couldn't check his watch to see how late he was in taking his tablets, not without her asking why.

She'd taken discreet pleasure in watching him recoil as she'd spoken of Tom. Even adulterous, gutless murderers can feel envy when hearing how replaceable they are, she'd learned, and she smiled to herself.

However, she remained alert to the potential danger of the man in front of her, even if she was no longer as scared as she had been. Though she did feel a slight sense of relief when he admitted how Paula's death had eventually plagued his conscience. Maybe there was a smattering of hope for him yet. She understood why he'd used drugs to deal with his conscience; she'd used alcohol to cope with his loss.

'Are you and – I forget his name – still together?' he asked.

'No, Tom and I are not. Although we're still good friends,' she replied, proud of that rare feat.

'What did you mean when you said I destroyed it all?'

She glared at him. 'Things began to break down between Tom and me when I discovered you were still alive.'

CHAPTER THIRTEEN
CATHERINE

Northampton, twenty-one years earlier

16 February

My eyes darted back and forth, examining every red brick and lick of mortar of Fabien's shopfront.

Even when Margaret and I signed the contracts, it still took a while to sink in that the boutique now belonged to me. Somewhere along the line, I'd become the owner of a shop I was once too frightened to step inside.

'Well done, girl,' came Margaret's voice from behind me. 'You have no idea how proud I am of you.'

I did, actually, because I was so chuffed with myself that I couldn't stop grinning. But I wasn't daft. It was all very well taking over a business with a proven track record, but it was going to take gumption and elbow grease to keep it a success.

I continued making a range of my own clothes, either at home or in the back room of the shop while my old supermarket co-worker Selena worked front of house, dealing with the day-to-day running and charming the clientele.

Emily started showing an interest in my work like I'd done with my mum's. But even when she got under my feet or slowed me down, I refused to follow the example I'd been set. She wasn't even eight, but I was already teaching her to sew on buttons and chalk up hemlines. And I'd encourage her to help me pore through fashion magazines looking for inspiration and to keep up with current trends.

While Robbie found a new interest in computer games and Tom taught James new songs on his guitar, I cherished the time Emily and I spent together. But at the same time, I pitied Simon for what he'd lost.

1 August

Silence didn't come to the cottage very often, but when it did, I welcomed it like an old friend.

Tom enjoyed taking the kids out on his own every now and again, and it gave me a few rare hours without the TV blaring or the sound of a football banging against the garage door. So while the rabble was at the park, I fulfilled a long-delayed promise to myself to clear Simon's clothes from our wardrobe.

I'd thought about it several times over the past few months with Tom now in our lives. But it always seemed such a daunting prospect, like throwing another part of him away. And even if he were to miraculously reappear on our doorstep, I didn't think it would be for a change of shirt.

So I closed my eyes and opened the wardrobe door. Then, one by one, I carefully removed Simon's things from the wooden hangers, folded them up neatly and placed them into plastic bags I'd earmarked for the charity shop.

Each item brought with it a forgotten memory, like watching him unwrap a new jumper I'd bought for his birthday, or a shirt he'd worn to a party. I lifted the lapels of his brown corduroy jacket to my nose and found a vague trace of his Blue Stratos aftershave. Around my hand I wound the blue-striped tie he'd had on for his first appointment with the bank manager to ask for a business loan. I'd tied him a Windsor knot because his hands were shaking too much to do it himself.

I'd expected to break down in tears, but I felt warmth, not sadness. I was giving his clothes away, not him. The bags were spreading across the floor when the telephone rang.

'Could I speak to Mr Simon Nicholson, please?' a gruff male voice asked.

'I'm afraid my husband has passed away,' I said. 'Who's calling, please?'

'My name is Jeff Yaxley. I'm a warden at Wormwood Scrubs prison in London.' That piqued my curiosity.

'Mr Nicholson's father died a few months back and I have one of his possessions he asked us to send his son,' he continued.

'Arthur's dead?' I asked, shocked. 'Sorry, did you say you were calling from a prison?'

'Arthur? No, Kenneth Jagger. When Mr Nicholson visited him, he put down your address.'

'I think you've got the wrong Simon Nicholson,' I replied. 'His dad is called Arthur and lives in the next village. And as far as I'm aware, Arthur's never been to prison.' A mental picture of the old coot behind bars made me smile.

'Oh, there must have been a mix-up,' he replied. 'Sorry to have troubled you.'

'Wait,' I said quickly before he hung up. 'So someone using my husband's name and address visited this man in prison? When was this?'

'Bear with me a minute,' he said, and I heard the rustling of papers. 'According to the visitor's book, it was June eighth, four years ago.'

199

'Well, that definitely couldn't be Simon, because he went missing on June fourth.'

'Missing?'

'Yes, my husband disappeared that day and hasn't been seen since. The case is still open but he's presumed dead.'

I mulled it over but I couldn't work out who might've pretended to be him.

'What did this man Kenneth leave for him?' I asked.

'A watch.'

Suddenly the dim glow of a lightbulb emerged in my brain. I swallowed hard.

'It's a gold Rolex,' he continued. 'It feels quite heavy. Nice-looking piece . . .' But by then I'd stopped listening. I felt a stabbing pain in my chest as his words bloomed like a drop of blood in a glass of water, staining everything.

I hung up, then raced up the stairs and back into the bedroom to face a square green box lying on a shelf at the back of the wardrobe. Inside should have been the watch from Simon's mother: the only thing she'd ever given him, yet I'd never once seen him wear it.

I held the box in the palm of my hand and then stopped myself from opening it. If his watch was inside, someone had used his identity. If it was empty, it could only mean one thing: that Simon had taken it with him and that he'd left me on purpose.

'Please, please, please,' I whispered as the gold hinges creaked open. There was nothing inside.

No, you must have put it somewhere else, I thought. So I rooted around the rest of the wardrobe, but it was almost bare. I yanked all the folded clothes from inside the bin bags and rifled through each pocket. Nothing. I felt inside each pair of shoes to see if he'd put it there, then rummaged through the drawers of his bedside table. Every time I drew a blank I thought of somewhere else to look. I searched each nook and cranny of the house, even places I'd already hunted through when he first disappeared. Then I threw my trainers on and ran to see the one person who could put my mind at ease – Arthur.

Fifteen minutes later, I was at his front door, almost breathless from running.

'Who is Kenneth Jagger?' I gasped.

I prayed for him to plead ignorance. Instead, Arthur's face immediately drained of all colour. Two things I was now sure of – that a man called Kenneth Jagger was Simon's real father, and that my husband had planned to leave me.

'You shouldn't be here,' he replied nervously and tried to close his front door. I stuck my foot out to block it.

'Who is Kenneth Jagger?' I repeated.

'I don't know who you're talking about. Now, please leave.'

'You're lying, Arthur, and I'm staying here until you tell me the truth. Or would you like me to involve Shirley in this?'

He soon surrendered when he saw my threat wasn't an empty one.

'I'll meet you behind the garage in five minutes,' he replied. He was there in two.

'How do you know his name?' Arthur demanded, keeping a deliberate distance from me.

'It doesn't matter,' I replied, unwilling to tell him it was likely Simon was still alive.

'Has Kenneth been in touch?'

'Not unless it was through a clairvoyant. He's dead.'

Arthur looked relieved.

'Well? Was he Simon's father?'

'No, I am,' he snapped, then paused. 'But Kenneth is, biologically.'

Arthur may have been a browbeaten, pathetic little man, but he wasn't a liar. He reluctantly told me the story of meeting Doreen while she was pregnant, and how during her many absences, she'd often gone back to Kenneth.

'And Simon knew all about this?' I asked, amazed I'd not known.

'Yes, but not until he went to visit her in London when he was thirteen. Kenneth was there and Simon found out who he was. It devastated him. Simon never saw him again.'

But I had proof he was wrong.

'Now, what's all this about?' he added.

I hesitated. I could tell him everything I knew: Simon had upped and left of his own free will, and four days later went to visit that Jagger man in prison. But what would be the point? If he'd planned to come back, he'd have done it long ago. So I'd only be giving Arthur false hope. And once he told his wife Shirley, she'd inform Roger and old wounds that were still healing would be reopened, all to find a man who didn't want to be found.

What on earth would I tell the kids? For four years I'd led them to believe their dad was dead – how was I supposed to explain I was wrong and that he'd left them? God only knows how much damage that could do. So all I told Arthur was that a prison warden had been trying to trace Kenneth's next of kin after his death.

'Catherine,' he asked as I began to walk away, 'how are the children?'

'You lost the right to ask about them the moment you accused me of murder,' I replied, and left him to wallow in guilt alone.

I was beyond angry and I needed to hurt Simon. I hurried home with my fists balled, furious at Simon's gut-wrenching betrayal. Once inside, I grabbed a pair of scissors and tore into his clothes. Ribbons of material from every jumper, pair of trousers, T-shirt and jacket flew through the air and scattered around the room. I didn't want anybody else to wear clothes stained by his lies.

Framed photographs of him I'd kept on the sideboard were hurled into bins. Any visible trace of my bastard husband was erased from the house there and then. Suddenly I remembered the pink rosebushes he'd planted for me by the kitchen window.

I ran to the garage, took the shears from a hook and hacked them to the ground. He'd planted them for me when I was at my lowest, and they'd become a place I'd visit when I needed comforting. He'd even ruined that.

When I finished, I sat on the lawn, too numb to blink, cry or be sick despite wanting to do all three. By the time everyone arrived home late in the afternoon, Simon was dead to me. Again.

'Where have Dad's pictures gone?' frowned James, the first to notice.

'They're in the loft,' I lied.

'Why?'

'Because I put them there,' I replied sharply.

The kids looked at each other, puzzled, but rightly sensed not to push me any further. Tom followed me upstairs to the bedroom.

'What's going on, Catherine?' he asked. When I didn't reply, he put his hand on my shoulder and tried to pull me towards him. I couldn't even look him in the eye.

'I've cleaned out the wardrobe. You can use it for your clothes if you like.'

'What happened today?'

'I woke up.'

Then I locked myself in the bathroom to try and put the roof back on my rage. It was only the second time I'd kept something from Tom – the first was something I'd never told a soul, not even Simon.

But Simon's secret was far worse than mine.

Christmas Day

Tom and the children were fast asleep while I spent the early hours of Christmas morning in the attic, tearing up my wedding photographs.

I'd been struggling to get to sleep when I suddenly remembered where they were, and I couldn't let Simon's face remain in my house for even one more night. I didn't look at any of them as I took them out of the albums and ripped them into pieces. By the time I finished, they surrounded my cold bare feet like confetti. I was too angry to go back to bed. I sat on the floorboards listening to the central heating gurgle, thinking about him again.

I was livid with myself for the time I'd wasted crying over him; worrying about him; making 'missing' posters; phoning hospitals; mourning him . . . It had all been for nothing. He'd simply run away.

While we'd left no stone unturned in our frantic search, he'd been on his way to London to visit a man he barely knew to give him his most treasured possession. His body wasn't rotting in a ditch somewhere – it was very much alive and out there, away from us.

I wished he were dead.

I clenched my fists every time I thought what an idiot and a liar he'd made of me. I was embarrassed and humiliated. The only person who I might've possibly confided in was Paula, but I'd lost her too. And even then I don't think she could've taken on that burden without telling Roger.

It was like someone had attached a valve to my heart, and any love I'd ever felt for Simon was leaking into the air like a foul-smelling gas. And, all the time, I kept returning to the same three-letter word: *Why?*

I knew one place on earth he'd gone after leaving us, to see his biological father in prison, but it threw up so many new questions, each more impossible to answer than the last. Where did he go after he saw Kenneth? Who else knew he wasn't dead? How long had he dreamed of running away? Was it a spur-of-the-moment decision or part of a twisted plan to marry me, play the doting dad and then move on? Why had I never felt him slipping away?

Was he more like his mother than he'd let on? Like her, did he have other lovers scattered around the country? Where does someone go when they have no friends and no money? Did he regret it, but didn't know how to come home?

Why, Simon? Why?

My frustration rang louder than the church bells would later that day. But the only thing I prayed for was that he was roaming the earth in an eternal state of wretched misery.

Because that's exactly how he'd left me.

Northampton, twenty years earlier

11 April

There was nothing wrong with Tom: he was what most women would describe as Mr Right. But Simon had taught me even the right people can wrong you when you least expect it.

I hadn't jumped into our marriage wearing rose-tinted glasses. I'd known, given our history with both sets of dysfunctional parents, that we'd be lucky to get through life without a bump or two in the road. And when we bickered, or when screaming kids made the house feel like a prison, it was normal to fantasise about running away.

But that's precisely what it should have remained – a fantasy. Only he'd made it his reality. And my logic reasoned that if he, the man I'd loved and trusted since forever, could do that to me, then Tom, someone I'd only known five minutes in comparison, was going to do the same.

After finding out about Simon's deceit, I took out my rage towards him on that poor innocent heart, without Tom ever understanding why. I'd watch him over dinner and wonder why someone so attractive, funny and caring would ever want to be saddled with a family that wasn't his. Instead of feeling lucky or grateful and that I deserved him, I didn't trust him.

I asked myself if I was just a stopgap until he found a younger, better-looking model who could give him kids of his own. Then I gave serious thought to having his baby. It was a man's basic instinct to reproduce, and I was stopping him from doing that, even though he'd shown no inkling of wanting his own children. But having ours hadn't stopped my husband from running away.

Besides, I had a business to run, and I knew I couldn't deal with all the craziness and upheaval another child would bring. And that meant it was a given Tom would leave me. That's what people I loved did. They left me. Mum, Dad, Billy, Simon, Paula . . .

So, before he had the chance to run, I spent months trying to drive him away. I had to be aware of his every move, winding myself up a treat over what he was doing if he wasn't doing it with me. I rifled through the glovebox of his car hoping to find a pair of some other woman's knickers. I flicked through his wallet for receipts from places he hadn't told me he'd visited. I checked the suitcases he stored in his garage to see if they were packed in case he wanted to do a moonlight flit. One night, I even left the kids to sleep home alone while I stood behind a conifer outside his house waiting for female visitors.

But despite every sneaky, stupid way I tried to prove myself right, there was no evidence to suggest he was anything other than a decent, honest man. And that frustrated the hell out of me – if I'd missed traces of Simon's unhappiness, I probably couldn't see Tom's either.

So I created arguments over nothing – missing groceries he'd forgotten to buy; not putting the bins out before they were collected; even how he wasn't satisfying me in bed.

All the time I knew exactly what I was doing. I just couldn't stop myself from tarring all men with Simon's filthy brush. They say the quickest way to drive a dog mad is to stroke it then smack it.

But my dog just kept running back for more.

12 May

'Let me move in,' Tom asked suddenly.

'What – why?' I replied, confused that after all my goading, he'd still not cracked. Quite the opposite, it seemed.

'I'm not stupid, Catherine. Something happened the day you threw Simon's clothes away. And while you're obviously not ready to tell me about it, I know you need to feel more secure about us. So let me prove to you I'm serious. I love you; I love the children. We've been together more than two years now, so let's see where this takes us. Let me move in.'

I looked him in the eye, pushed him onto the bed and made love to him there and then, all the time knowing we were never going to last. All it did was extend the inevitable.

I went through the motions of pretending we were a family – trying to convince myself we might just work. But eventually my resentment towards Simon reared its ugly head again. I'd wake up in the night and stretch my arm across the bed to check Tom was still there. Once I shouted at him for not being next to me when all he'd done was go to the bathroom.

I gave him the silent treatment for the best part of a week when he came home from the pub later than usual. And when I found two phone numbers I didn't recognise on my itemised bill, I refused to believe he wasn't having an affair.

No matter how often Tom assured me he understood my unforgivable behaviour, Simon had already ruined any future we could've had together.

And six weeks after he came to live with us, I asked him to leave.

◆ ◆ ◆

SIMON

Los Telaros, Mexico, twenty-one years earlier

13 April

The pool cue snapped in half as effortlessly as a toothpick when it made contact with the old man's shoulders. He grunted as it thrust him forwards and he sprawled across the table.

His attacker, equally as drunk and elderly as his victim, swung one hundred and eighty degrees with the remaining half of the cue in his hand, and collapsed into a disorientated heap. His counterpart fumbled around the table for a ball to smack against his assailant's head, but when he heaved it, one too many bourbons made him lose his grip and the ball nosedived a few feet across the room instead, barely nudging the skirting board.

Trying our best not to laugh at the clumsy fight before us, Miguel and I stepped in to lift the two drunken pensioners to their feet. Their arms spun aimlessly, like hurricane-damaged windmill sails, only making contact with the smoky air around them as they fought for the attention of the same prostitute.

'They're like this every time,' explained Miguel as he pulled the frailer-looking of the two up from the floor where he'd just landed.

'Aren't they friends? I saw them arrive together,' I asked, safely concealing the other behind me.

'Friends? They're father and son!' he laughed. 'They share the same taste in women. By the time you leave this whorehouse, there won't be much of life you ain't seen.'

I'd been drug-free and hitchhiking around Mexico for the best part of four months when I'd walked through the bordello's doors for the first time. Many towns I'd blown through had their own *whiskerias* – brothels that sold much more than Wild Turkey in their back rooms. Their neon signs targeted long-haul truck drivers who wanted to take their minds off the endless roads ahead with female company.

But with its orange-tiled roof and black wrought-iron balconies scattered across the first-floor facade, this bordello in Los Telaros resembled a hotel. There was no signage or indication it was anything else. I hadn't intended to look for work, and sex had been the last thing on my mind. All I'd required was something alcohol-based to quench my thirst and a place to rest my blistered feet.

Inside, porcelain lamps on smoked-glass tables discreetly illuminated purple walls. Glass chandeliers hung from wooden rafters above white leather sofas and a solitary reception desk. Scented candles masked cigar smoke with hints of sandalwood and vanilla. The crushed velvet curtains remained closed to prying eyes.

Its true purpose was revealed at the bar, where men of all ages were fussed over by attentive girls in varying states of undress.

I'd sat at the counter, swirling ice cubes around my glass of Jim Beam, amused by the show. The girls' acting abilities were faultless as they pretended to desire the customers and not the pesos in their pockets.

'Can I introduce you to a young lady, *señor*?' said the barman.

'No, I'm just here for a drink,' I replied.

'That's what all first-timers say,' he laughed as he refilled my glass. 'Are you European?'

'Yes, British.'

'You're a long way from home. What brings you here?'

'I'm seeing the world, and picking up a bit of work here and there.'

'What kind of work?' he asked, carefully stroking his goatee.

'Carpentry, repairs, building work, decorating . . . that kind of thing.'

'You ever hit a woman?'

'Of course not!'

'Do you do drugs?'

'No.' Well, not since I'd left San Francisco.

'Do you like to fuck pretty girls?'

'What?' I laughed, stopping just short of snorting whiskey through my nostrils.

'Do you like to fuck pretty girls?'

'Sometimes! But like I said, I'm only in here for a drink.'

He turned his head and shouted towards a room. '*Madama! Oiga, madama!*' A middle-aged niblet of a woman, with grey hair swept back into a ponytail, limped quickly towards us.

'*Cuál es el problema*, Miguel?'

'I've found your man. What's your name, *hombre?*'

'Simon,' I replied.

The woman scowled as she looked me up and down, muttering something under her breath. Then she grabbed my hand and bent my fingers backwards.

'Ow!' I winced and tried to pull them back. But her grip was remarkably strong.

'Don't drink my spirits, do the jobs you're given properly and make sure the men don't hurt the girls,' she spat in an unidentifiable accent. 'And don't fuck the pretty ones.'

'Okay, okay,' I replied, snatching my hand back and nursing my throbbing fingers. She disappeared into a back room and I stared at Miguel, puzzled.

'What just happened there?' I asked.

'Welcome to Madame Lola's.' He smiled, raising a shot glass. 'You got yourself a job!'

1 August

I was accorded a peculiar mixture of respect and envy from the male townsfolk for working in a bordello. A walk into town to pick up supplies saw me ignored by patrons if accompanied by their wives, but I was acknowledged with a nod or a knowing smile when they were alone.

I'd acclimatised quickly to my unusual surroundings. It became the norm to hear a leather riding crop beating the skin of a repressed businessman from behind a closed bedroom door. I didn't think twice when a misplaced key meant I had to cut a naked police officer from a bedpost he'd handcuffed himself to. And I barely noticed the priest in women's underwear being chased through the corridors by girls in French maid outfits, like a Mexican Benny Hill.

The brothel had been standing there for as long as the village, a forty-five-minute drive away from Guadalajara, Mexico's second-biggest city. While some men travelled miles for its courteous and discreet reputation and highly desirable girls, at least a quarter of the bordello's clientele came from within a mile or two of its own doorstep. Some even slipped out of their marital beds once their wives were deep in sleep, and crept back home a couple of hours later with a smile on their face and a non-the-wiser partner.

For me, it was a place of work and not play. Of course, I had urges, but the purpose of exiting San Francisco was to leave behind all that had been faulty in Darren and myself.

However, the course of my life was to change yet again when I fell in love with a whore.

23 October

'You got it bad for her, don't you, *hombre?*'

I almost fell off my stepladder when Miguel crept up behind me.

'She's going to break your heart,' he laughed. '*Chicas* like that always do.'

'I don't know what you mean,' I replied, lying to the both of us. I replaced the lightbulb, folded my ladder up, returned it to the storeroom and left the girl alone.

I headed towards the pickup truck to drive into town and buy new electrical cables. As I looked towards her bedroom window, her closed curtain moved ever so slightly. I longed to be behind them with her. The truth was, I was smitten.

I decided as I drove that those who worked for Madame Lola believed themselves to be the fortunate ones. Skinny women, Oriental women, ageing women, tattooed women, European women, redheads, shaven heads, and one who tipped the scales at a quarter of a ton . . . all flavours and tastes were catered to on secure, clean premises.

Other prostitutes weren't so lucky. As I approached town I spotted them, barely clothed and standing by roadsides, or sitting on broken plastic chairs with their knees pulled apart to attract passing trade. Others hovered in fields like worn-out scarecrows.

Most men visiting Madame Lola's brothel behaved respectfully towards the girls, but the exceptions believed they'd also paid for the right to be heavy-handed if it heightened their sexual pleasure. And that's when Miguel and I stepped in.

I'd always deplored violence, especially towards women. My mother, Dougie's mother . . . both of their lives had been destroyed by the unwarranted rage of a man.

Beth had walked out on Dougie five years into their marriage. I'd arrived home to find him sharing dinner with my family, desperate to avoid returning to an empty house. When I wasn't there to offer support, he'd bent Catherine's ear instead. But I'm sure there was much he hadn't told her.

'I'll never have what you have,' he slurred one evening after she left him. He misjudged the distance between his empty can of lager and the kitchen table. Catherine was upstairs asleep and I longed to join her.

'What do I have then?' I sighed, opening myself up for a fresh wave of self-pity.

'Someone who loves you. A family.'

'You'll find that. You just need to meet the right person.'

'No, I won't, because I'm just like my father. Sooner or later we all end up like our parents, no matter how hard we try and fight it. You will too.'

'That's rubbish. I'm nothing like Doreen and you're nothing like your dad.'

'Yes, I am.' He stopped and rubbed his eyes before he whispered, 'I hit her.'

'Who? Your mum?'

'No, Beth.'

'What?' I hoped I'd misheard him. 'Do you mean "hit her" as in you did it by accident, or as in on purpose?'

'A lot.' He hung his head in shame.

I leaned against the back of my chair, astounded and disappointed. After witnessing all his mother had been subjected to, he'd still been inclined to repeat history. 'Why would you do that?' I asked, baffled.

'I don't know. I just get angry and frustrated all the time and then I lash out. I can't help it.'

'Of course you can help it! You don't just hit your wife for no reason. Why?'

He looked up at me slowly, his eyes channelling deep into mine. 'If anyone should know, it's you . . .' His voice trailed off, and he picked up his jacket and stumbled out of the house.

I had reluctantly followed him, propping him up with my arm around his waist, ready for a long walk on a short journey.

Memories of that night left my head as I pulled the pickup truck over to the side of the road by the storefront. I wondered what the girl behind the curtain was doing right now. Did she ever notice me like I noticed her? I could only hope.

11 February

For months, I'd watched her lose herself in different books each day. She was loyal to the authors she chose – always works by Dickens, Huxley, Shakespeare and Hemingway. I presumed they offered her an escape to somewhere far from the whorehouse she'd made her home.

Wherever I was carrying out maintenance work around the bordello, she would stop me in my tracks through proximity alone. Of the thirty or so women who lived or worked in the brothel, she was the only one who ground my world to a halt just by *being*.

It wasn't the delicate shine of her shoulder-length auburn hair, her olive skin or her plump, rose-pink lips. It wasn't the silk camisoles that clung to her hips and breasts, or the brown abyss of her eyes that intoxicated me.

It was her air of complete indifference towards the world she found herself in. While other girls competed for a customer's attention, she was aloof. And that made her an all-the-more-attractive purchase for those with deep pockets.

Her colleagues took as many men as were willing, but she was discerning – accepting just one per day, and never at weekends. And her self-rationing put her in great demand. Her time between clients was spent in Madame Lola's office or making herself invisible in her bedroom at the back of the building.

We never spoke; we never made eye contact; and as far as she was aware, I did not exist. But it didn't matter. I was obsessed with Luciana.

◆ ◆ ◆

Northampton, today

5.05 p.m.

'Why didn't you tell me about Kenneth Jagger?' she began.

He paused to reflect on his teenaged self's decision to keep his biological father to himself. Then she listened closely as he revealed things about his life he'd kept hidden when they were a partnership.

He explained why London had been his first destination after fleeing, and how he'd discovered the circumstances surrounding Doreen's

214

death. He spoke of meeting Kenneth, but neglected to mention what he'd whispered into his ear or why his biological father had branded his only son a monster.

She'd never met Doreen and had only heard bits and bobs about her through the years. Naturally, she'd been curious about the mother of the man she loved and wanted to know more. But it was obvious he'd been hurt by his mother more than he'd ever admitted. She'd never even seen a photograph of Doreen, so she'd built a mental picture instead. To her, she looked like Dusty Springfield. She'd told him that once and he'd laughed.

When he spoke of spending time by Doreen's grave so she wouldn't be alone, it reminded her of the sensitivity he was capable of. She would always be grateful to him for the four children he'd given her, but his subsequent actions had all but erased any of the good he'd done in the past.

'I didn't tell you about Kenneth because I didn't want to acknowledge him as my father,' he admitted. 'I hated the man from the moment we met, and I didn't want you to see in me what I saw in him.'

'Yet he was exactly what you've become, if not worse.' She knew it was a callous thing to say, but he hadn't spared her feelings so she wasn't going to pull her punches either.

'Not now,' he corrected, 'but for a while, maybe, yes.'

'So if you hated him that much, why go to the trouble of trying to find him?'

'Closure.'

'But it took you twenty-five years to offer me the same courtesy, didn't it?'

He said nothing.

She was hurt that he hadn't trusted her with such an important secret, but she was angry he hadn't mentioned Dougie's violent streak towards poor Beth. Although she and Beth hadn't been as close as she,

Paula and Baishali were, she was sure the three of them could have helped Beth. And that might have changed so much that followed.

Meanwhile, he was glad it hadn't worked out with her fancy man. He didn't like the sound of him. No one was that perfect; she'd have found that out eventually. She should thank him for saving her the heartache.

'Are you aware you're dead?' she asked out of the blue. 'I mean, legally dead. You have to wait seven years before you can declare a missing person deceased. So on your seventh anniversary, I hired a solicitor, and a few months later I held your death certificate in my hand.'

'But you knew I was alive?' he replied, unsettled by her sudden deceit.

'That's true. But if you didn't value your life with us, then why should it have mattered to me?'

He understood her motives, yet her nonchalance made him uncomfortable. She enjoyed playing with him.

'It wasn't easy, either legally or morally,' she continued, 'and I had to keep up the pretence you were dead to the children and the authorities. Then I had to prove I'd exhausted all avenues in looking for you. But that was the easy part, because as Roger and our friends testified, I'd been very thorough. After a high court hearing, you weren't just dead to us, but in the eyes of the law as well.'

'Why go to all that effort? It sounds a little pointless.'

'I don't care what it sounds like to you. I did it because had you decided to rise like Lazarus – which you have – and I wasn't going to make it easy for you. Plus, your insurance money helped to put Emily and Robbie through university, so the legalities of your death benefited us all.'

She'd knocked a little of the wind from his sails, as he realised once again he'd underestimated her strength of character. And he wasn't sure how her course of action made him feel.

'Did I have a funeral?' he asked hopefully.

'Yes, but only for the kids' sake. In fact, they were delighted to draw a line under you, because having a dad who vanished into thin air was a millstone around their necks. So it helped them move on. They rarely spoke about you as they got older, anyway.'

That last part was untrue, but he didn't need to know that. She'd actually learned to bite her tongue when they brought his name up, and particularly when they talked of him with longing.

He also knew it was a lie, and remembered word for word what James had told that website.

'Could you tell me a little about my funeral?' he asked, still wounded by her frosty relish.

'What else is there to say? You have an empty grave and a headstone in the village cemetery. I don't really remember much about it other than it came as a relief.'

Again, she was not being honest, and he saw through her inconsistencies.

'You buried your husband and you don't remember much about it? I don't believe you.'

'And what makes you think I care what you believe?' She laughed as people do when talking about something that's not actually funny.

'Because if you cared so little, why did you bother with a gravestone?'

'Like I said, for the kids' sake.'

'But you said they never spoke about me, so why would they want me to have a grave?'

She looked away and didn't reply. Every few months, one of the children still took flowers to the churchyard, and arranged them in a vase Emily had made in pottery class when she was eight. At Christmas, they all still made an annual pilgrimage there together – even her, to keep up appearances. It was the only time of year she allowed herself to think about him.

He pleaded to her better nature. 'Catherine, I promise you, after today, this will be the last you'll see of me. So please. Let's be honest with each other.'

'What do you know about honesty, Simon?' she replied flatly.

'I've learned it's what people need before they can move on. There is so much we should have said to each other back then. But I'm here to explain everything, even though a lot of it will hurt you.'

You're right there, she thought. He had hurt her many times already in the past few hours, and she had a gut feeling it might only be the tip of the iceberg. She inhaled sharply.

'The kids begged me to organise a funeral because they felt robbed of a proper goodbye, as there was no body to bury,' she explained reluctantly. 'Is that what you want to hear? Everyone you'd ever known turned up for it. I even ordered a maple coffin – your favourite wood – for people to place reminders of you inside, like your pub beer tankard and football medals. And after the service, we had a party at the house where they celebrated your life.'

He listened intently and smiled, touched by the effort she'd gone to despite what she knew.

'I didn't do it for you,' she added sharply. 'I felt sick every second you forced me to play the grieving widow. You made me complicit in your lie, and I hated you for that. Still do. Had it been my choice, I'd have cremated everything you'd ever touched.'

His eyes sank to the floor like a scolded dog's.

CHAPTER FOURTEEN
SIMON

Los Telaros, Mexico, twenty years earlier

13 May

No matter where in the world I went, death was sure to follow.

It was commonplace for the sounds of grown men, bawling and shrieking from ecstasy and pain, to seep under bedroom doors and echo around the corridors of the bordello.

But the screams I was hearing that afternoon were female and born out of distress, not pleasure. And noises rarely carried from Luciana's room. I dropped my paint pot and brush and bolted up the staircase, across the corridor, and banged on her door with my fists.

'Are you all right?' I yelled anxiously. 'Luciana!'

Inside, a male voice shouted something as he suppressed her muffled cries. I turned the handle but it didn't budge, so I panicked, raised my leg, and kicked and kicked at the door as the scuffle inside continued.

Finally the door split from its frame and I ran inside, but before I could focus on anything or anyone, something weighty collided with the side of my head. My body hit the wall and I dropped to the floor like a bag of rocks. Disorientated, I began to lift myself up until the second blow stopped me in my tracks.

This time my reaction was instinctive and I grabbed the bare ankle of my assailant and twisted it hard. Its owner was felled like a tree in a storm, but then he climbed atop me and unleashed a flurry of fists upon my head and neck. I tried to shelter myself as they rained down on me in a pounding, furious barrage, my head becoming increasingly numb to the pain. A lucky jab to his bare genitals left him curled to one side and temporarily disabled, and I almost reached my feet but he beat me to it and his fist broke my nose.

As his face moved towards mine, I grabbed both sides of his head, but he took advantage of my exposed torso and hit me in both kidneys. Dazed and winded, I landed two clumsy whacks somewhere around his ears but they only riled him further.

For the first time, I took in his appearance. At six foot five and at least sixteen stone of sculpted muscle, I questioned whether the naked, hairy creature before me was man or beast. I erred towards the latter.

Then he picked up an ornament, raised it above his head and spat as he laughed. I expected his black, widened pupils and salivating mouth to be the last things I'd ever see and had accepted the inevitable when, suddenly, a metal table lamp appeared from nowhere and smashed against his crown. He fell to his knees, his face contorted by shock and incomprehension. The lamp swung backwards, then crashed into him over and over again. The man's eyes rolled to the back of his head, leaving shiny white ovals, before he slumped face down onto the wet carpet, convulsing.

It was only then I noticed Luciana, her face – smeared in murky redness – hiding behind matted hair. Her underwear was in shreds, and the lamp shook in her trembling hands.

I crawled towards the floored titan and rolled him over, face up, to steady his spasming body.

The first words she ever spoke to me were devoid of all emotion.

'Leave him.'

'We should call an ambulance.'

'We do nothing. When I refused to let him force objects inside me, he said his daughter bites her lip and stays quiet when he does it to her. Let the animal die in the way he deserves.'

I had no case to offer for the defence. Instead, I fixated on the pulp of a man biting deeply into his own tongue. Together we watched as his mouth effervesced with delicate pink bubbles, until the convulsions petered out into nothing. Finally, his brain stopped fighting and his soul began its journey from whence it came, back into the arms of the devil.

From the moment I limped downstairs and alerted Madam Lola to the battle in Luciana's room, she responded with military precision to remove any trace of the man or his rage. She gave every impression it wasn't the first time she'd been forced to clean up an unexpected mess.

She slipped into autopilot as she relayed orders to a crowd of horrified girls, gawping at the remains by the door. They scuttled in numerous directions like stray fireworks.

'Miguel – is there enough gasoline in the truck to reach the ravines?'

'Yes.'

'*Bueno*. Take it around the back. The rest of you, go back downstairs and see to your guests.'

She looked directly at Luciana. 'Who did this to him?' she asked.

'I did,' I replied, and Madam Lola nodded her head approvingly.

'Good. No man here would touch her again if they ever learned of this. So you will make sure they don't.'

An hour later, and Luciana's face had been occupied by an observant silence for much of the journey, the hush only peppered by her directions.

She gazed at the passing fields from the passenger window. I longed to talk to her but the circumstances were hardly appropriate considering the body of the man she'd just killed lay wrapped up behind us in the back of the truck.

I drove along dirt-track lanes away from the main roads, and wondered how much rage must have been bottled up inside her to watch without pity as the man dissolved into nothing. I understood it completely. I had once been where she was now.

'Over there.' She pointed with a torn fingernail.

I pulled the truck over to the side of the road between fields of scorched corn. We removed two shovels and began to dig a grave. The ground was arid and stubborn, so it took us an age to burrow a ditch deep enough for spring's flash floods not to send his body sailing down the valley like a polythene raft.

The man's features were indistinguishable under the tightly wound plastic. I used all my strength to pull his hulking frame by his ankles from the truck to the ground below. Then I dragged him along the rough terrain before I rolled him into his hole.

Luciana kneeled down to unwind the plastic covering his head. Then suddenly she pulled out a silver pistol from the back of her jeans. I froze as without hesitation she pulled the trigger twice, shooting him first in the left eye and then in the right. I stumbled backwards as my ears rang.

'It's a calling card of the gangs,' she explained. 'A bullet in each eye means he's seen something he shouldn't have and has been punished. If his body is ever found, the police will think he was executed by one of his own.'

I gave an agitated nod as she wound the plastic back around his head and we shovelled dirt upon him. We threw the shovels back in the truck, but when I turned around, she was standing inches away from me. Then she pushed my aching shoulders against the door, pulled my mouth towards hers and kissed me with a passion my body had never experienced. The pain from her nose brushing against my broken one was excruciating and spread across my face, but it was worth the sacrifice to be so close to her.

She loosened my belt buckle, I removed her T-shirt and we winced as our cuts, swelling skin and emerging kaleidoscopes of blue, yellow and purple bruises collided against each other. And when we had finished, we drove back to the bordello as silently as we'd left.

23 July

Each night she crept into my bed, and we'd make love silently. It was always a slow and sensual experience, unlike our first time with the bitter taste of death and lust in our throats. Then, when she'd decided we were done, she'd slip back into her clothes and vanish like nothing had happened.

Luciana and I never spoke of the day she'd killed a man. In fact, we never spoke at all. I wondered if she made love to me out of gratitude, or whether it was a way of controlling me. Her profession meant surrendering herself to men for their money, so by dictating to me when we had sex, there was no doubt who was in charge.

Her reasoning didn't matter. If sex was the only means by which I could breathe her air and feel her skin against mine, then I was grateful for anything she offered. And as the days progressed to weeks and then to months, she remained in my room a little longer with each visit.

My deepest fear had always been discovering the one I loved was finding love with another. But because Luciana's profession was to have sex with other men for money, it wasn't adultery. It was business. I didn't doubt for a moment that I was her only extracurricular activity. It was the perfect partnership, and the most mutually monogamous relationship I'd ever had.

14 November

I rolled onto my side and faced the door when I heard the handle turn. I smiled and pulled back the bedsheet to invite her in, but she chose to sit in an armchair by the window opposite my bed. She lit a cigarette and began to blow smoke rings.

Finally, following six months of nocturnal liaisons, Luciana cast her die and waited cautiously to see where it might land.

'My name is Luciana Fiorentino Marcanio,' she began carefully, 'and I was born and raised in Italy.'

I propped myself up against the headboard and listened closely.

'I came to Mexico with my mother after my father tried to have us killed. He was a wealthy but vicious man who abused her, convinced she was having affairs with anyone who paid her attention. He was her only love, but his paranoia and insecurities wouldn't allow him to believe that. My mother was not strong enough to leave him. She tried her best to please him and win his trust, but when you accuse someone so often, eventually they will give in and prove you right. He drove her into the arms of one of his business colleagues. And eventually my father found out. He paid for her lover to be killed, but not until he'd had him castrated. The first my mother knew of this was when she found his genitals in a gift-wrapped box on her dressing room table.'

I lit up a cigarette of my own and took a long drag. I was captivated by her story.

'As my sister Caterina and I grew up, he told himself we too would become whores like my mother,' she continued. 'He was suspicious of our every move and hired guards to escort us to and from school so we would not mix with boys. But Caterina and our gardener's son Federico became close – he was probably her only friend apart from me. And when my father saw them talking together, he had Federico beaten so badly the poor boy could never work again. Caterina was inconsolable and blamed herself. When she looked to the future, all she saw was more of the same and she could not live like that. She waited until my father's birthday before she cut her wrists and died in one of his vineyards. I found her body.'

She paused and glanced down at her feet.

'Naturally my mother and I were devastated. But it was like someone flicked a switch in her head. She'd already failed one daughter and she wasn't going to make the same mistake again. So with only our passports and some money our housekeeper gave us from her savings, we ran away and never saw him again.'

Luciana closed her eyes.

'The man I killed who attacked me . . . he was not the first to have died at my hands. My mother and I fled to London to stay with cousins, and finally life was good. It wasn't like Italy where we lived in a gilded cage – we had nothing of material value, but we had our freedom. Then my father's people tracked us down. A man appeared at our apartment and shot my mother's cousin and her son through their heads. He was going to kill her too, but he didn't see me in the kitchen behind him. I took a knife and stabbed him in the neck, but not before he pulled the trigger and hit my mother in the leg. I patched her up and we fled, eventually making our way to Mexico, where my father would never think to find us. We began working here, selling our bodies to survive, and over time, it became like any other job.'

'The man we buried,' I interrupted, 'did your father send him too?'

'No, he was just a monster who couldn't recognise the monster in me. I have killed twice, and I know you have killed too.'

She paused again and watched as I froze.

'I saw the way you looked at me in my room that day. Most men would have run for the hills, but you stayed. You had fallen in love with me because you thought you had found a kindred spirit. I knew then that, for whatever reason, you had done something awful but necessary to protect yourself. And there is nothing more awful than taking a life. You knew me.'

I considered telling her there and then about my past, but it was her moment, not mine.

'What happened to your mother?' I asked. 'Is she still in Mexico?'

'Yes,' she smiled. 'She's downstairs. And her name is Lola Marcanio.'

'Your mother is Madame Lola?' I asked, taken aback.

She nodded. 'I know what you're thinking – how could she allow her daughter to keep working as a whore? Well, she has no choice! When we eventually saved enough money to buy out the previous madam, Mama tried to persuade me to give it up and help her manage the place instead. But it's not what I wanted. I assist her with the bookkeeping but I continue to prostitute myself. Maybe I do it to spite my father; maybe I just like being in control of something when I grew up controlling nothing . . . I don't know. But, right or wrong, I make my own choices and my own living, and this job is what I choose to do.'

Luciana stubbed her cigarette out in an ashtray and stared outside at the rooftops of the dimly lit town.

'Why are you telling me this now?' I asked.

'Only our old housekeeper knew where we were and she didn't tell a soul. I received a letter from her this morning informing me my father was dead. So now I'm ready to go home to Italy. And you are coming with me.'

◆ ◆ ◆

CATHERINE

Northampton, twenty years earlier

22 October

The swirling 's' in Nicholson gave away the name of its author before I opened the envelope.

I wondered why Simon's stepmother Shirley had written to me after five years of mutual silence.

A white card lay inside with a photograph of Arthur attached. An added Post-it note read: *I would really appreciate it if you all could come.*

I gazed out of the window and into the garden. Arthur's and my paths hadn't crossed since I'd barged back into his life demanding to know who Kenneth Jagger was. And it had been a long time since I'd given either of them any thought.

And now I held an order of service for his funeral in my hand.

25 October

'I'm convinced he died of a broken heart,' Shirley admitted quietly after Arthur's cremation. 'Please don't misunderstand me, I'm not blaming you. But after your visit, he was never the same again.'

The children, unamused at being dragged to the funeral of a grandparent they barely remembered, sat in the corner of Shirley's living room huddled around a game on a mobile phone. Meanwhile, she'd ushered me into the kitchen, away from the small number of mourners.

'He's alive, isn't he?' she asked solemnly, looking me straight in the eye. 'I mean Simon: he's alive.'

I hesitated, reluctant to reopen a can of worms I'd struggled to keep a lid on. But secretly, I longed to tell someone. She poured herself a glass of wine and offered me one, but I shook my head.

'A few days after you last saw Arthur,' she continued, 'he told me you'd been to the house to ask about Kenneth. Then he told me the story about Kenneth being Simon's real dad. Well, I hadn't had a clue but I could understand why he'd not said anything, because he loved Simon like he was his own. It hurt him having to rake it all up.'

'I'm sorry, but I had no one else to ask,' I replied, now wondering if I'd done the right thing in dragging up his painful past.

'He knew you must have asked for a reason, so he contacted Roger for help in finding Kenneth. I think Arthur told him Kenneth was an old schoolfriend or some fib like that. To cut a long story short, Roger put Arthur in touch with the prison and they told Arthur what they'd told you – that after Simon went missing he'd turned up there.'

'I haven't said anything to the kids,' I replied defensively. 'I don't think they should know.'

'I wouldn't have either,' said Shirley firmly. 'It would only cause more damage. I saw what it did to Arthur. He couldn't understand what he'd done to make Doreen and his only child abandon him. Try as I might, I couldn't convince him it wasn't his fault. He did his best to put a brave face on it, but he became very depressed. He knew deep down Simon wouldn't be coming home, and eventually his heart became too heavy for him. He just gave up.'

No matter what I'd thought of Arthur in the past, he'd always tried to do his best by his son, but it wasn't enough.

'Do you still not have any idea why he left?'

'I don't know, Shirley. I just don't know.'

'This is long overdue, but I'm sorry,' she added, grasping both my hands. 'On behalf of both of us, I'm sorry we didn't give you the support we should have, and I'm sorry for the accusations. We were awful to you – and I, like Arthur, will go to my grave regretting that.'

'Thank you,' I replied. I knew she meant it. And now that I realised she and Arthur were two more of Simon's casualties, all those years of bitterness between us began to drain away. I would not let him destroy anyone else.

Shirley smiled appreciatively, took her glass and made her way back into the living room.

'Do you have any plans for Saturday night?' I asked. She shook her head. 'Come to ours around six for something to eat so you can meet your grandchildren properly.'

She gave a grateful nod, and a new chapter in our relationship began.

◆ ◆ ◆

Northampton, today

5.50 p.m.

It began as a smirk, but it wasn't long before she was unable to mask it, even by pretending to cough.

'I'm sorry,' she said, placing a hand over her mouth to stem a fit of giggles. He glared at her, spooked by her reaction. He'd witnessed a range of them throughout the day, but none that resembled amusement.

'I don't mean to be rude,' she continued, 'I really don't. But how am I supposed to react when you tell me you fell in love with a prostitute?'

She removed a tissue from her sleeve and dabbed her eyes, still chuckling at the absurdity of it. She wouldn't have believed it if someone had told her yesterday that her missing husband was about to reappear and explain how he'd been on a twenty-five-year, round-the-world jaunt. Oh, and along the way he'd murdered one of her best friends and given his heart to a whore, who, like him, had no qualms about killing people.

As her laughter faded, she wondered if she'd ever be able to completely get to grips with all he'd said and done. Every time she tried to get her head around a new revelation, along came another that dwarfed the last. She needed a moment to collect her thoughts, alone.

She said nothing when she left the room and headed for the garden. Once outside, she didn't know what to do with herself, so she unpegged

229

the clothes from the washing line and put to good use the breathing techniques she'd learned in her Pilates classes.

He remained in the living room, thinking about Arthur. For so long, memories of his father had been attached to unhappy ones of Doreen. He'd failed to appreciate the man behind the mother, the man who'd loved him as his own.

Neither of his parents had gone to their graves knowing what had happened to their son. Only Kenneth had had matters resolved, and he'd been the one who least deserved it.

'Sorry, Dad,' he whispered, and wiped the corners of his eyes with his hand.

6.00 p.m.

'If it's any consolation, I didn't plan to fall in love again,' came his voice from behind, startling her.

She stood in the kitchen with a red tea towel in her hands, like a matador in a bullring. The more she'd asked herself how a whore could give him a better life than she had, the more she wound herself up.

'How much did she charge you?' she snapped. 'Fifty pounds? A hundred? Or did you get a discount for being a regular customer?'

He didn't respond because it was clear that anger was bringing out a petty side to her. He weighed up whether it was worth trying to explain it to her again, or if she was only going to hear what she wanted to hear.

'Well, you sound like a perfect match,' she continued. 'I mean, you're both able to murder at the drop of a hat. At least you buried that body and didn't just leave it in the middle of the street like you did with Paula. Actually, is that why you're here? Is the tart back on the game, so now you've come home?'

'No, Catherine,' he replied wearily. 'I promised Luciana I'd put things right with you before it was too late.'

'You can never put right what you did to me. And I don't need a prostitute's pity.'

A wall next to the pantry, covered with ornately carved wooden picture frames she'd bought in Bali, distracted him. He got distracted a lot these days.

They contained photographs of their children. The snapshots of life without him spanned two decades, and he couldn't help but wonder what might have been.

'Is this Robbie?' he asked, pointing to a boy standing by a blue Ford Fiesta. She nodded. 'He looks so much like Luca.'

'Who's that?'

'My son,' he replied. 'I have a daughter too.'

Her jaw dropped. But before she had the chance to fly off the handle again, they were stopped in their tracks by the sound of the front door opening. Time froze until Emily breezed into the kitchen.

'Mum, did I leave my purse in—' she began, before noticing her mother had company. 'Oh, sorry,' she said, oblivious to the panic spreading across her mother's face. Her parents glared at each other like a clandestine affair had been interrupted.

Mum, he silently repeated to himself. He recognised her as the girl who'd passed him when he arrived at the cottage that morning and he lost himself in the daughter he'd last seen as a toddler. *How much have I missed out on?* he thought. *Just how much?*

Catherine's brain went into slow motion, unable to muster a word of explanation to her daughter as to the identity of the stranger before them. She was petrified when he opened his mouth to speak.

'Hello,' he said, 'I'm Darren.' He smiled politely and held his hand out towards Emily. It was the first name that sprang to mind. Old habits die hard.

'Hi,' she replied, shaking it but still unsure who the dapper gentleman with such warm hands was.

'I'm an old schoolfriend of your mother's,' he said.

'Really?' asked Emily, enthusiastically. 'It's nice to meet you.'

'Yes, and you. I've not seen Catherine for many years and I was passing through, so I thought I'd drop in on the off-chance she still lived here.'

He was a convincing liar, Catherine conceded, but then he'd had so much practice. She felt like a rabbit caught in the headlights as father and daughter conversed, not knowing how to bring herself out of their glare.

'I'm her daughter, Emily,' she offered. 'So what was my mum like at school then? I bet she was a real goody two shoes.'

He laughed. 'You could say that. She was a bright thing, always destined to do well.'

'Has she told you about her shops?' Emily asked, clearly proud of her mother's achievements. 'She's got eight now . . . even one on the King's Road in London.'

He smiled. 'Yes, she's done very well for herself.'

'Anyway, Mum, did I leave my purse here?'

'I'm . . . I'm not sure,' she stuttered.

'I'll have a look,' replied Emily as she headed towards the living room. In her absence, Emily's mother and father stared at each other – he delighted to have met Emily, and her grateful he'd not revealed his identity. They remained silent until she returned with her purse.

'Found it. Do you still want to come round for dinner tonight, Mum? Olivia's been asking to see her granny, but if you're busy with your friend, we can do it another night?'

She saw him react when Emily said the word 'granny', and became irritated he was learning things about her family he had no right to know. 'Can I come tomorrow instead?' she asked, her voice close to breaking. She willed her daughter to leave.

'Of course,' Emily replied, and reached the door, then turned around. 'Darren, if you went to school with my mum, you must have known my dad, Simon?'

He dug his fingernails into his palm. 'I recall him, but didn't know him very well, I'm afraid.'

'Oh,' said Emily, clearly disappointed. 'Well, it was nice to meet you. See you tomorrow, Mum.'

The door closed and they gradually made their descent back to earth, remaining in a relieved but awkward silence.

'She looks like you . . .' he began eventually, but she wasn't interested.

'Don't,' she replied. 'Just don't.'

CHAPTER FIFTEEN
CATHERINE

Northampton, ten years earlier

14 August

We sat huddled together staring at a television hanging on the wall of the Fox & Hounds' function room. I switched between tapping my nails on a tabletop with nervous excitement, and fiddling with a damp beer mat, waiting.

Ten minutes felt like an eternity before the chirpy young presenter announced what we'd gathered to see. The landlord turned the volume up and an instant hush fell across the packed room.

'Next up, it's a band making their debut *Top of The Pops* performance. In at this week's number four, it's Driver, with "Find Your Way Home".'

A jubilant pub clapped and cheered as the camera cut to a close-up of the guitarist strumming the opening bars of the song.

'That's him! That's him!' I yelled, unable to stop myself. There for all to see was my son James, on the TV, playing with his band.

James had never given university a first, let alone second thought, especially after forming a group with three other music-minded friends at his upper school. They'd spent hours every night rehearsing in Simon's old garage-office, and I made them cover the walls with empty egg boxes from the local poultry farm to stop the neighbours complaining about their racket.

When James turned sixteen, my little boy became a free man, and his first act of rebellion was to leave school with a handful of average GCSE results and all the time in the world to follow his heart. It wasn't what I'd have chosen for him. I'd read enough over the years about showbiz casualties to know it was a notoriously unpredictable and unforgiving industry. But like I had done with my dreams and the boutique, I encouraged my son to follow his even if they'd only lead him to the unemployment office.

It took his band six long years of playing spit-and-sawdust venues before their determination paid off. A record company A & R man watched them on the bill at a small rock festival in Cornwall and spotted their potential.

Eventually, their third single, 'Find Your Way Home', was picked up by Radio 1, and before long their youthful good looks propelled them into the pages of magazines, gossip columns and the charts. And *Top of the Pops* was their first major TV exposure.

Robbie handed his grandmother Shirley and Emily tissues to dab their eyes, and they weren't the only ones who needed them. Tom had remained in the kids' lives even though we were no longer together and had joined us at the pub with his lovely fiancée Amanda. He'd often been to Driver's gigs, and by the time their three and a half minutes of TV fame had ended, he and I were both in tears. Everyone in the local pub had known James his whole life and shared my sense of pride.

But I was proud of all my children, of course. Robbie had remained the quietest of the bunch, even into his teenage years. But he'd overcome his self-imposed exile and surprised us all by moving as far away as Sunderland University to study things I didn't really understand involving computers, hard drives and mega-somethings. And with his graduation still some time away, he'd already been offered and accepted a job in South London designing graphics for games.

Emily took her mother's and grandmother's interest in clothing and design one step further and couldn't wait to start her first year at the London College of Fashion. And while there was probably no easier way of attracting boys than to tell them your brother's been on *Top of the Pops*, she only had eyes for Daniel, Selena's son.

They'd been sweethearts forever, and watching them together making each other laugh reminded me of Simon and I at their age. I prayed to God Daniel would never hurt her like Simon had hurt me.

I glanced around the pub at my family and friends, happy with my lot. There was no significant other in my life, but I had three children I adored and a business that had expanded to five boutiques across the county. And with plans for three more, including one in London, my life was as close to perfect as it was ever going to be. But the greatest moments of your life are exactly that – just moments.

And by their design, moments don't last.

SIMON

Montefalco, Italy, ten years earlier

3 July

'That's my lot. You win, my friend,' I gasped, and dragged my leaden legs across the red clay and towards the iced water under the pagoda's shade.

Stefan, my coach, smiled and gave me a thumbs-up sign while I downed the entire bottle's contents to quench my thirst. I waved him goodbye, mopped my sweating brow with a towel and caught my breath. I cursed myself for being both a mad dog and an Englishman to schedule a mid-afternoon tennis lesson under the searing Italian summer sun.

I was constantly in awe of my surroundings. I must have stared at our breathtaking valleys and vineyards a hundred times, but I never took for granted the warm embrace of the magnificent country around me.

When we first arrived in Italy, I'd been hesitant about the prospective life that lay ahead for Luciana and me. It had been second nature for me to live hand to mouth from limited means, but suddenly I'd found myself in love with a woman who'd inherited a wealth I'd never dared to imagine. And the potential for stability would take me worryingly far from what I'd been accustomed to. I'd known the warmth of normality once, and I knew the agony of having it torn away from me.

Luciana sensed my trepidation on our arrival and squeezed my hand reassuringly as her chauffeur drove his late *padrone's* Bentley through the open iron gates and up the brick-paved driveway.

I squinted as the sun played hide and seek behind the vast sprawling villa ahead of us that Luciana had once called home. Lavender plants in flowerbeds and terracotta pots filled the air with their scent.

We walked through its colossal wooden doors as she explained how a house had stood in that spot for three hundred years. It was deliberately constructed a mile above the town of Montefalco, as if to remind those living under its shadow of its owner's importance.

As soon as Luciana saw Marianna, her housekeeper, saviour and old friend, she collapsed into her arms and cried with gratitude for her past help. It was the first time I'd seen such vulnerability in her. Together they wandered the villa's haunted corridors, reliving lost memories of Luciana's sister and confronting the ghosts of her father.

I'd heard no positive stories about Signor Marcanio from Luciana's childhood recollections. But, quietly, I found something to admire in a man so vulgar through his home.

He had restored the building's charm with sympathetic and meticulous effort. The gaping dual-aspect living room formed the centrepiece, its walls supporting an exposed beamed ceiling some twenty feet high. The fireplace was the room's focal point, standing like a church altar ready for a congregation that would never be invited inside.

But the pristine decor lacked any personal touch and there were no family photographs or knick-knacks scattered around, only carefully selected abstract paintings, ornate glass ornaments and an exotic fish tank. Luciana had grown up within a man's design, not his heart.

We weaved our way into the gardens, where cobbled patios cut into vast, luscious lawns, some hidden from the sun's reach under wooden pagodas strewn with leafy vines. The positioning of the main terrace enabled a one-hundred-and-eighty-degree view, and a cobbled pathway sloped downwards to a tennis court and swimming pool. And what a view it was: mile after mile of vineyards and valleys painted in alternate shades of greens and browns as far as the eye could see.

'Do you think you could be happy here?' she asked me tentatively as we sat perched on a wall overlooking the canyons and lowlands.

'It'll take some getting used to, but yes, I could. More importantly, can you?'

'As long as I'm with you, I could be happy anywhere,' she replied.

Luciana's voyage into her past was relatively smooth. Signor Marcanio had left no will before his fatal stroke, so his estate and businesses were automatically awarded to a wife he'd not divorced. But Madame Lola had no desire to return permanently, and remained in

Mexico, visiting us every few months for two weeks at a time. It was Luciana who needed to be there and had something to prove.

She threw herself into her father's business interests, but it took years to wipe away his presence. His investments were wide and many, and their value far exceeded what she'd first predicted. Her own accountants unearthed an Aladdin's cave of below-the-radar dealings masquerading as reputable, so she culled each black sheep from the company portfolio until only legitimate enterprises remained.

Luciana saw to it that removal men cleansed the house of the few remaining traces of Signor Marcanio. His clothes were given away to charity and his jewellery sent to auction, and the proceeds were donated to a shelter for victims of domestic abuse. I briefly wondered what Catherine had done with my things when I'd left.

Next, she reassured the small army of browbeaten maids, cleaners, cooks and gardeners who'd scuttle past us, heads bowed, that this new regime would not mirror the last.

And while she was kept busy untangling her father's affairs, I focused on Signor Marcanio's sprawling, largely ignored vineyards. He'd treated the production of wine as a hobby, and because it was the place of Caterina's suicide, it wasn't an area Luciana was ready to be reminded of just yet.

I, however, wondered about its potential, as my desire to create and construct reared its head once again. I knew nothing about the workings of a winery, but I was a fast learner and a willing student. While the manager patiently taught me all its aspects from land irrigation to pressing harvested grapes and sourcing bottling plants, I knew it would take many years of hard work and determination before I might turn her father's pastime into a profitable product.

Never had I imagined I could live a life so perfect, but that is what Luciana and I came close to. But perfection comes at a price, and I was scared of how much I'd pay in telling her my truths. As our years together progressed, it became an increasing burden to hide the man I'd been from the woman who'd rebuilt me.

1 September

I'd held Luciana's hand while she bravely walked me through the complicated chapters of her past. But what had she known of mine?

In truth, I had given away mere morsels – snapshots of a life lived through the destruction of others. She had guessed children had once played a part in my life, by observing my paternal instinct when our daughter Sofia was born.

The first time I held her body in the crook of my arm, I whispered into her ear words I never thought I'd use again: 'I will never let you down.' And when our son Luca followed a little over a year later, I vowed never to have reason to go back on my promise, no matter how precarious my journey became.

Most people are fortunate even to be given a second chance. My family was my third chance and I no longer wanted to hide my flaws, mis-sell my adventures or conceal my truths from her. I had shown Luciana unconditional love and loyalty, but by keeping many past actions, reactions and repercussions buried deep beneath my skin, I had little integrity.

We were sitting on the lowest tier of the garden terraces watching the sun melt like ice cream over the vineyards, when she commented on my silence.

'You have the face of a troubled man,' she began.

I considered denying it, but she could see through my every mask.

'There are things I think you should know about me,' I replied, afraid to disfigure the beauty around us with my ugly words.

'Tell me because you're ready and not because you feel you should.'

'I am, really, but I'm scared of how you'll react.'

'There is nothing you can tell me that will ever make me think any less of you, Simon.'

Neither my head nor the pounding heart rattling against my ribcage was convinced. But I couldn't stop my ribbons from unspooling as I explained how I'd met Catherine, and the children we'd had together. Then I recalled in detail how it had gone so very, very wrong; about Billy; why I'd had no option but to leave her; where I'd gone; about my mother, both my fathers and then my travels.

I described how I'd relieved a dead man of his identity, why I'd muted an old friend in Key West and how my guilt had manifested in my near self-destruction. And I admitted that given the same circumstances, I'd probably do exactly the same all over again because in its own twisted way, it had been worth it. It had led me to Luciana.

I was prepared to accept any punishment or consequence she felt necessary. For the first time, I was in the presence of someone who knew almost as much about me as I did. And only when my history was complete did my fists unclench as I waited for her to break the silence.

'You did what you had to do,' she said, finally. 'Nobody can judge you but God, Simon. I won't. While I cannot lie and say the things you've done haven't been cruel and selfish, or that you haven't hurt people who might not have deserved it, you know that for yourself. And if you had to suffer all of that to become the man and the father I love now, then so be it.'

She left her seat, sat on my lap and wrapped her arms around my shoulders while the dam I'd spent fifteen years building crumbled under the weight of my tears.

'But you cannot hide from your family forever,' she whispered. 'Catherine deserves to know what happened to her husband, and your children deserve to know why their father left. You, them . . . everyone needs the chance to put the pieces together.'

My head pressed against a heart I knew would always be open to mine. But hers wasn't destined to beat for long.

◆ ◆ ◆

Northampton, today

6.15 p.m.

The picture he painted of his life in Italy was all too vivid and left her feeling bitterly cheated.

'Those were *our* dreams,' she said sorely. 'We were going to retire to Italy – you and I. They weren't yours to take away and live with somebody else.'

She moved across the kitchen, avoiding his eye, and removed a bottle of wine from the cupboard. She kept alcohol in the house only for guests, and it had been two decades since a drop had passed her lips. But if ever she'd needed a glass, it was today.

'It's a good year,' he offered inappropriately as she uncorked it.

'What is?'

'The wine. It's one of ours – 2008, if I'm not mistaken.'

She glanced at the label: *Caterina's Vineyard*, it read. She rolled her eyes, poured herself a glass regardless and took a hesitant sip, but wine didn't taste like she remembered it – or maybe it was just that anything he'd come into contact with was destined to leave a sour taste in her mouth. She poured the rest of the glass down the sink.

She mulled over Luciana's reaction to his confession and couldn't comprehend why she'd forgiven him so readily. And it irked her that it had taken a whore to set his moral compass straight when it came to facing up to his crimes.

'I suppose it says something about her, doesn't it,' she began rhetorically. 'I mean, I don't know why I'm surprised that a woman who sold her body and had two bastard children with a married man could forgive him for murder. She's hardly Mother Teresa, is she?'

'Say what you want about me, Catherine, I'm old enough and ugly enough to take it,' he began defensively, 'and a little of it I probably deserve, but do not bring Luciana and my children into this. They have done nothing to you. I'm sorry if you haven't liked what you've heard, but it's the truth, and in the great scheme of things, it doesn't matter how I got here. Because I'm here now, and I want to make my peace with you.'

'Make your peace? How generous of you! Jesus, man, you should be on your hands and knees begging for my forgiveness! You should be here because you realised all by your stupid self that what you did to us was terrible, not because you were told to by my replacement.'

'She wasn't your replacement.'

'You replaced all of us with them.'

'I didn't plan to start another family.'

'With a whore, let's not forget.'

'No, with Luciana.'

'A whore – you even called her that yourself. And a murderer.'

'Don't call her those things, please.'

'But that's what she is, isn't she? A whore who killed two people. At least you had a lot in common.'

'It doesn't matter what she did,' he shouted. 'She's the mother of my children.'

By the time he'd realised the irony of his words, it was too late.

'And what was I?' she yelled, throwing the glass into the sink, shattering it. 'A trial run? You didn't give a damn about the mother of your other children! You traded us in for a woman who'd screw any man if he had cash in his wallet! And you expect me to offer her some respect?'

'You really don't understand,' he replied, shaking his head.

Once again he was disappointed by her reaction. He thought he'd explained there was so much more to Luciana's make-up than the choices she'd made to survive. But repeatedly, she'd chosen to focus only on the negative. He began to feel tired and disappointed that even after all this time, she was still so bitter.

'I didn't leave you to run off with another woman and start another family,' he continued.

'You might not have set out to do it, but you did it all the same.'

'Could I use your bathroom, please?' he asked, his head now hurting from her ill-tempered reaction.

His ability to change the subject at the most inopportune moments frustrated her. Several times he'd cut her off in the midst of her responses. Either he was trying to defuse the situation or he'd lost his ability to focus on one subject for any length of time.

'Yes,' she replied, fatigued.

He turned to leave the kitchen and walked towards the staircase before pausing.

'I'm sorry, can you remind me where it is?'

She frowned; he'd lived in the house for almost ten years, and earlier that day he had stood on the other side of the door as she vomited after he recalled what he'd done to Paula.

'Upstairs, on the left.'

'Yes,' he replied. 'Of course it is.'

When he'd finished urinating, he rinsed his hands in the sink and stared into the mirror she'd referred to as the unforgiving one. She was right, he thought. It made his cheeks look puffy and paled his skin like an old man's.

He noticed the bathroom still had the faint odour of bile as he removed the blister pack of tablets from his jacket pocket and scowled at the enemy. He cupped a hand under the tap and swallowed two of the pink pills. He considered taking one of the antidepressants his doctor had also prescribed, but he hated the synthetic happiness it brought him.

He surveyed a room he never thought he'd be standing in again as he felt the tablets sink slowly into his belly. The layout was the same, but the suite was no longer a dowdy avocado colour; it was plain white with silver fixtures and sandstone tiles. He approved of her taste. *It wouldn't look out of place in my home.*

His eyes were drawn to the bath and the mat that lay in front of it, when a cold breeze suddenly swept through the room. The chill made the hairs on his arms reach for the heavens. He panicked and struggled to catch his breath. His eyes darted back and forth as he remembered the aroma of the bubble bath and the sound of her muffled voice in the bedroom that day. He shook his head until the thoughts disappeared, and he took a long, hard breath.

Just hang in there, he told himself, and hoped his brain was listening.

CHAPTER SIXTEEN
CATHERINE

Northampton, three years earlier

2 February

'Bloody useless,' I grumbled as I yanked off my glasses and stuffed them back into their case on the kitchen table.

I left the accounts ledger I'd been ploughing through all morning to fend for itself, rubbed my weary eyes and rummaged through a drawer for my painkillers.

Arthritis was making its way through my ankle and I didn't have the energy I'd once had to work all the hours I needed to.

I'd survived for so long without the need of a second set of eyes, and had thought of it as a minor triumph in my war against age. However, the nature of my work relied on a strong eye for detail and an even more tenacious one for flaws. Together, they'd gradually taken their toll on my vision.

So when blurriness and headaches went from occasional to daily and then to just bloody annoying, I finally gave up fighting and made an optician's appointment. My reward was a £200 bill and a pair of glasses I resented. They made me look like my mother, and to be honest, they were a fat lot of use. My eyesight had improved a little but the headaches still came. So I swallowed two tablets, and left the spreadsheets for another day.

The growling of two very loud engines above the house caught my ear, so I went out onto the lawn and squinted at the sky. Three yellow vintage biplanes flew so low overhead I could see their pilots. Then, without warning, my head exploded.

There was no noise, just a pain I'd never felt before, followed by complete disorientation. I saw nothing but blackness peppered with bright shining stars. My eyes burned and my whole head throbbed like one of James's guitar amplifiers when he turned it up loud. I dropped to my knees and steadied myself by digging my fingernails into the grass.

The pain dissolved after a few moments, but my body was trembling and I was hit by a savage migraine and sickness straight away. I slowly stood up and fumbled my way into an empty house, grasping onto windowsills and furniture to keep from keeling over. I fell onto the sofa, breathing quickly as my vision slowly returned.

Then I closed my eyes and slept for the rest of the day and night.

SIMON

Montefalco, Italy, three years earlier

11 February

It had begun as an innocuous little lump on her left index finger – nothing you'd notice without searching for it, and certainly no bigger than a small ball bearing.

It itched, Luciana told me, and the more she scratched it, the sorer it became. Two weeks passed and it continued to irritate her, so I persuaded her to make an appointment to see her doctor to check it wasn't an infected insect bite. He admitted it puzzled him, so he erred on the side of caution and took a biopsy. Within five days, we were called back to his surgery to discover that innocuous little lump we could barely see was going to make our perfect lives implode.

It was malignant.

We carried on with our lives regardless and with relative normality while we awaited the results of an urgent barrage of tests to ensure it was just a one-off, random cluster of cancerous cells. Luciana remained convinced we had nothing to fear, but inside I knew the darkness I'd eluded for two decades had found me again.

Our wealth paid for speedier results, but it couldn't pay for positive ones. Her cancer was not a rogue occurrence, but a secondary form. Its parasitic parent had already made a home in her right breast before silently creeping around her body.

'I believe it's an intrusive cancer that's already spread to a kidney and your stomach,' her doctor began solemnly, then paused as we absorbed the news.

Luciana reacted like she would towards one of her businesses failing. Without a hint of self-pity, she was collected, optimistic and sought to formulate a plan of attack. 'What are my options?' she asked without expression, staring her doctor firmly in the eye.

'It has moved far too quickly and it's incurable, Luciana,' he replied softly. 'I'm very, very sorry.'

'There are always options,' she said firmly, gripping my hand tightly.

'We can try and control it as best we can. But the best-case scenario is a year to eighteen months.'

She nodded her head slowly. 'That's good,' she replied. 'That's a good time. I can get a lot done in that time.'

We left his surgery too stunned to speak and with a schedule of medical treatments designed to slow down her cancer's rate of growth. We each had one eye on the clock. Hers was to remind herself of how much longer she had left as the centre of my universe.

Mine was to decide on the right time to leave her.

◆ ◆ ◆

CATHERINE

Northampton

14 February

The second explosion walloped me almost a fortnight after the first, as I wandered around the supermarket shopping for groceries. It followed the same course as its predecessor – unexpected, excruciating stabs to the brain, darkness, white lights and then dizziness – and it scared me to death. Not just because of how much it hurt, but because it meant the first wasn't a one-off.

I tried in vain to steady myself against a freezer chest, but I missed the lid and fell into an ungainly heap on the floor. Someone helped me to my feet and took me to the manager's office, where a kind boy asked if he should call me an ambulance. But I reassured him I'd just had a funny turn and all I needed was to sit down and compose myself.

I tried to fool myself into thinking it was nothing more than a delayed but extreme reaction to my new HRT medication. But I knew the difference between a hot flush and something that was trying to blow my scalp off. And naively keeping my fingers crossed and praying it would go away as quickly as it had appeared probably wouldn't work.

Nevertheless, I chose denial. I took a few days off and left Selena in charge of the shops so I could hide in the safety of my home. And when a week passed without incident, I almost began to stop waiting for another one. More fool me, because the next was by far the worst.

I was in my granddaughter Olivia's bedroom at Emily and Daniel's house, playing imaginary tea parties, when my words became slurred and jumbled.

'Teddy cake go and find to him,' I mumbled, unable to correct myself. In my mind, I knew what I was trying to say but when it came out, it made no sense. I tried again, then again and again, but it made no difference.

'Nana, you're being funny,' giggled Olivia, but it was only amusing to a three-year-old. I tried several more sentences but each one failed. Terrified, I lifted myself off the floor and perched on her bed.

'Mummy for Nana,' I begged. 'Mummy . . . Nana.'

Her little face fell and I could tell I was scaring her. She ran from the room yelling for Emily.

I remained frozen on her bed, and the last thing I heard were her feet scampering down the staircase before I fell unconscious.

SIMON

Montefalco

16 February

It was a myth that God is merciful. To me, he was a cruel, cold-hearted, vindictive bastard who was predominantly interested in punishing me.

From birth, he had strewn my path with a deceitful mother, cunning friends and disloyal lovers.

I'd tried so hard to live a good life since I met Luciana, and for a time, he'd fooled me into believing he'd taken notice. He'd blessed me with two incredible children and the love of a woman I didn't deserve.

I showed my gratitude by being a worthy husband, a doting father and a charitable man. A third of the profits from our winery went directly to a foundation providing aid to the children of poverty-stricken widows in the region. We sponsored five scholarships for gifted students from low-income families to attend the same private school as Sofia and Luca. We'd even donated three acres of land to a sanctuary for retired working horses.

But that wasn't enough for God. Not nearly enough. By granting us a life of privilege, he'd merely lulled me into a false sense of security before striking me with his next blow. He could have taken Luciana away from me in an instant with a sudden, fatal accident. But he decided he'd gain more pleasure in watching me suffer, watching her suffer.

I'd already experienced life with someone so utterly tortured by sorrow that they were unable to recognise night from day. I'd been the one who had hovered in the corners of rooms, watching as grief devoured Catherine.

Now history was about to repeat itself and I was going to be forced to see the love of my life slipping away. The only way I could prevent his victory was to do what I knew best – run. And when I was miles and miles from her failing body, I would remember with fondness her love – and not someone locked into a death sentence.

Our house had not been built of brick, as I'd thought, but of feathers. A wind I couldn't harness would destroy it whether I was present or not.

◆ ◆ ◆

CATHERINE

Northampton

18 February

'I'm sorry to tell you this, Mrs Nicholson, but the scans suggest you have an intracranial solid neoplasm, otherwise known as a brain tumour, on the left-hand side of your temple,' explained Dr Lewis, as sympathetically as he could.

Four days after my last attack, I had yet to leave the hospital. When Dr Lewis came to my room with the results of the MRI scans and blood tests, I wished I'd not insisted Emily leave her bedside vigil and go home to rest, so that I had somebody's hand to hold.

'We will need to operate as soon as possible to take a sample, then test if it's malignant or benign,' Dr Lewis continued. 'I'd like to arrange it for first thing tomorrow morning, if that would be convenient?'

'Is it going to kill me?' was all I could think to ask.

'Once we get the results of the biopsy we can decide which approach to take. The tumour is most likely the cause of your headaches – blood vessels in your brain bursting under the pressure as it grows.'

'You haven't answered my question,' I said. 'Is it going to kill me?'

He paused. 'We'll know its severity once we do the biopsy. Then we'll talk again.'

'Thank you,' I replied politely, and picked up Emily's iPod, put the headphones into my ears, closed my eyes and blasted her music as loud as I could to drown out my fears.

◆ ◆ ◆

SIMON

Montefalco

20 February

I walked away from Luciana with only what I'd brought with me – the clothes on my back and an uncertain future.

I knew starting afresh would be a much harder task, as my years were more advanced than when I'd last decamped. Nevertheless, my mind was made up.

I waited until she was alone at a doctor's appointment and the children were at school before I packed my old rucksack with the bare essentials and began the steep walk downhill to the town in the shadow of the villa.

I planned to make my way up to Switzerland and then through Austria, before exploring the Eastern bloc. According to the bus stop timetable, it would be another hour before my ride arrived, so I sat by the side of the road and began the process of putting the life I had cherished so much out of my mind.

Only I couldn't.

The boxes were open and waiting, but the beautiful spirits I loved so dearly were too large a presence to be contained. I had left my other children when they were too young to be affected by my absence. I'd only left Catherine when she was finally well enough to cope with it.

But Luciana, Sofia and Luca were different – and now so was I. They had made me a better man. I thought about how, through Catherine's sadness, I'd learned to tend to fragility and incite a person into believing that, against all hope, there was always hope to be found if they just kept searching.

I couldn't find that hope for Luciana, so she would need me more than Catherine ever did. I'd spent half my life running away from my responsibilities and I was an idiot for thinking I could do it again. But if I stayed, I'd need to muster up all my strength to help the three of them and the four of us.

I couldn't allow myself to shed a tear or feel an ounce of self-pity until Luciana surrendered to the inevitable. It would be *our* cancer, not just hers – we would both take ownership of it.

By the time my bus appeared, I was already half the way home. I didn't hear the car pull up next to me until its rear door opened. Inside sat Luciana. She looked at my sweating brow and my rucksack and she knew instantly what I had planned. She saw the coward in me. But her eyes softened when she understood I was walking towards our life and not from it.

She stepped out of the car, closed the door, entwined her arm through mine and we climbed the rest of the steep hill together.

◆ ◆ ◆

CATHERINE

Northampton

1 March

All of my children were sitting around my hospital bed when I came round from my operation. Even though they were normally scattered far and wide across the country and beyond, they'd always remained a close-knit bunch, phoning and texting each other to keep up to speed. I wondered if they'd have been like that had we not been forced to close ranks after their father deserted them.

Emily and Daniel's wedding four months earlier had been the last time we'd all been together in the same room. Giving my daughter away was one of the proudest moments of my life, and I pitied Simon for throwing away his chance to be in my place.

Emily had broken my news to the boys earlier that week despite my pleas not to worry them. Robbie drove up from his flat in London, and James flew back from Los Angeles where he'd been recording with his band.

I kept my eyes closed at first just to listen to their chatter. Then the urge to vomit took hold as my anaesthetic wore off. The first words they heard their post-op mother mumbling were 'I'm going to be sick' followed by the act itself, all over the bedsheets. Charming.

The morphine either knocked me out or left me barely conscious for two days. Even in sleep, my headaches were constant – but because of the operation, not the tumour, Dr Lewis explained. A few days later, he was back to remove my bandages and check on my healing.

'Can I take a look, please?' I asked tentatively.

I held my breath as he passed me my mirror from the bedside table and I slowly examined from all angles what looked like a machete wound. The hair had been shaved on the left side of my still swollen head, leaving me with a three-inch, crescent-shaped wound, pinned together with large black staples.

There was also a prominent concave dip in my head, and I wondered for a moment if it was deep enough to catch rainwater. I tried really hard to take it on the chin, but my emotions were as raw as the cut. When I was alone I couldn't help but pick up the mirror and stare at my grotesque self. All I needed was a bolt though my neck and Dr Frankenstein could have claimed me as his own creation.

Dr Lewis came to see me a few days later. But my brain, in its own infinite but damaged wisdom, decided to filter out what he was explaining. Once he'd confirmed the remains of my tumour were indeed cancerous, there was very little else I wanted to hear.

I saw him almost every morning during my hospital stay. His skilled hands had tinkered around inside my brain like it was the engine of an old jalopy. But I still didn't know a thing about the man who'd seen a part of me that no one else ever had. So instead of listening to his words – which I knew early on were going to make me unhappy – I focused on the man delivering them.

I placed him in his mid-fifties. He was blessed with a thick head of greying hair. His teeth had been capped but the wrinkles etched on his forehead from years of puzzling over cases like mine showed he wasn't vain enough to use Botox. He reminded me of a slightly less swarthy Antonio Banderas.

He didn't wear a wedding ring, so he was either eligible or just one of those men who wasn't comfortable with jewellery. And when he spoke, I couldn't decide if I was attracted to him because every girl loves a doctor, or because he was the only man I'd ever met who could really see inside a woman's head.

'Catherine?'

Suddenly I was back in the room.

'Do you need a minute, Catherine?'

'No, I'm fine, please carry on,' I replied in an exaggerated, cheerful way.

'On a positive note, we know it's not a secondary tumour, so there's no cancer elsewhere in your body. We managed to scrape much of it out, but because of its awkward positioning, we couldn't remove it all. So the next course of action will be radiotherapy to try and prevent it from destroying any other parts of the brain.'

'Okay then, well, thank you very much,' I chirped.

I don't know why, but I felt compelled to shake his hand like we'd just completed a business deal.

◆ ◆ ◆

SIMON

Montefalco

18 March

Breaking the news to Luca and Sofia that their mother wasn't immortal was the hardest illusion I'd ever shattered. I took them to lunch at a restaurant near Lake Trasimeno, a place where I'd occasionally brought them as children, to hike and to pretend to fish.

Luca at fourteen and Sofia at almost sixteen responded to the news with tears, disbelief and denial. They were angry with their father for failing to protect their mother, at her doctors for not repairing her, and at Luciana for instilling a time limit on their relationship.

But I made them promise to take their distress out on me and not her. Instead they gave her cuddles, picked her flowers from the gardens and filled her iPhone with music to listen to during her first hospital stay.

It's difficult to reconcile the knowledge there's something feeding on your body when you can't see it or swipe it away. Only when the physicality of its damage becomes visible does it make it real. In Luciana's case, the gravity of the situation hit home when she had her double mastectomy. While it wouldn't cure her, it might give us more time.

'Sometimes I feel like I'm trapped on a conveyor belt but if I try and get off it, I'll die,' Luciana muttered.

I stroked her arm as she floated on a glorious cloud of morphine above her sterile hospital bed. 'I know, darling,' I whispered, 'but if it means the kids and I get to share more time with you, then it's worth it.'

'Remind me of that after the chemotherapy begins,' she replied, before closing her eyes and setting sail for the skies again.

◆　◆　◆

CATHERINE

Northampton

18 March

Telling the children my tumour was cancerous was almost as hard as when I explained their daddy wasn't coming home and was likely dead.

Even though they were adults, I still reassured them everything was going to be okay, like mothers do, although I couldn't be sure it would. Emily responded practically, by planning care rotas and making sure I never went for treatment alone.

Robbie drove home every Friday night to stay for weekends and help out where he could around the house, and James promised to call every day no matter where in the world he was.

Shirley, Baishali, and Tom's new bride Amanda filled my freezer drawers with a never-ending supply of hot pots, pastries and casseroles. Selena was already responsible for area-managing my boutiques, so it made sense for her to take the reins and oversee the rest of the business too.

It was only when the fuss died down and I was home alone that the seriousness of my situation hit me. I wrote a card for Olivia's fourth birthday and wondered if I'd be around to see her next one, then couldn't stop myself from crying my eyes out.

I hadn't sobbed that hard since we'd found Oscar's lifeless body in his basket a decade earlier. I remembered how each one of us took it in turns to hold him, stroke him and brush his ginger and black wiry coat and tell him how much we'd miss him. Then I wrapped him in a blanket and carried him to the bottom of the garden, where Robbie had dug a hole under the crab-apple tree as deep as his arms could stretch.

We gently placed Oscar into the ground and lay Simon's running shoes by his side, before heaping soil and tears on his final resting place. I smiled when I wondered if that's what the kids would do to me, too.

At an age where I should have been thinking about taking my foot off the accelerator, I was desperately trying to stay in the car.

◆ ◆ ◆

SIMON

Montefalco

17 April

Luciana had shied away from examining her altered appearance in the hospital room, preferring to do it in the cosiness of our home.

She stood before our bedroom mirror, unbuttoned her loose-fitting blouse and carefully unravelled the zigzag of bandages that covered her torso like an Egyptian mummy. A six-inch horizontal scar lay beneath, lip-red and raised. At a glance you'd be mistaken for thinking it had been clumsily hacked off with pinking shears.

'I once kept a roof over my mother's and my head with these,' she lamented. 'Now I'm a monstrosity.'

I wrapped my arms around her waist but she tried to edge away. So I held on tighter. And looking her reflection in the eye, I tenderly traced her scar from right to left as she steadied her shaking hands on my arm.

'I hate it,' she continued.

'I don't,' I replied. 'Your loss is my gain. It's a beautiful scar because it means I get to keep you for longer.'

◆ ◆ ◆

CATHERINE

Northampton

18 April

Information and a positive mental attitude were the most powerful weapons I could have in my armoury. At least that's what the Internet told me.

I began my fight by taking the laptop to my bedroom, placing it on my knees and learning about the enemy within from the comfort of my own duvet. I searched on Google for survival statistics, then message boards and forums, asking questions and weeping at stories written in memoriam about those who'd lost the fight.

No matter how many positive things I read, it was always the negative ones that stuck in my head. And sometimes I'd have rock-bottom moments where I thought 'sod it' and wondered how much easier it'd be if I gave in and let nature take its course. But there was still so much of life I wanted to experience, so many places I hadn't travelled to and business opportunities I wanted to explore. I wasn't ready to give up.

I drank cup after cup of herbal tea and munched on snacks high in antioxidants while researching complementary treatments and holistic remedies.

When I next found myself at the hospital, with my face covered in wet plaster bandages, my scar was healing and my hair was gradually growing back from when it had been shaved for the operation. Staff at the radiotherapy unit had to make a mould of my head to create a Perspex mask before my treatment began.

Once it was complete, I sat with my mask in my lap, tracing the impression of the curves, crevices, lumps and bumps of my head. It was then attached to a table and, with my head slotted inside it, I was kept perfectly still while, five days a week for seven weeks, a machine blasted my dent with a ten-minute burst of radiation.

The sessions often left me nauseous, so I was never more than a few feet away from a bucket. But mostly I was just exhausted. And as a result, I lost interest in anything that didn't involve me.

I couldn't be bothered to read newspapers, listen to the news or Radio 4's *Desert Island Discs*. Instead I dipped in and out of *OK! Magazine* and watched *This Morning* on breakfast TV for my fix of world events.

The seventeen types of tablets I took each day controlled when I ate, what I drank, when I woke up, what time I napped and how far away I could be from the nearest toilet. I hated them, but by controlling my life, they were saving it.

But nothing I read on the Internet had warned me of how much cancer treatment could drain your femininity. Lack of regular exercise and steroids gave me a moon-face and made my weight balloon. Make-up only highlighted how ugly I'd become and made me look like a cheap drag act, so even the basics like lipstick and mascara were left to gather dust on the dressing table. In fact, my entire beauty regime was given the heave-ho.

I hadn't coloured my hair for so long, it looked like I'd taken to wearing a silver skullcap. My legs resembled the Forest of Dean, and the skin on my left cheek near the radiotherapy zone was corrugated and sore.

The pricey moisturisers I'd bought on my trips to Paris were boxed up and put into a cupboard, and replaced with E45 cream and aloe vera. I avoided my beautiful wardrobe of Gucci and Versace outfits and asked Selena to order me a selection of brightly coloured, elasticated leisure suits. I went from couture to velour.

And I all but ignored my own reflection. I wouldn't give that bloody bathroom mirror the satisfaction of seeing me in such a state.

◆ ◆ ◆

SIMON

Montefalco

27 July

Our family crammed so many memories into the time we'd been allowed.

A former colleague of Luciana's father with a shady reputation secured me a forged British passport of my own. So the four of us flew from city to city across Europe for weekend breaks and explorations.

And when the short bursts of chemotherapy on Luciana's kidney and stomach weakened her resolve, we hid indoors and watched old Jimmy Stewart and Audrey Hepburn films with subtitles instead.

A large proportion of her hospital appointments involved tests and scans. They could be fraught affairs not only because many were invasive, but because each time, her disease had advanced that little bit further.

The shame I felt over my earlier plan to abandon her and teach God a lesson pushed me to double my efforts to be there for her. I became more than just Luciana's chauffeur and helper; I was also part of her treatment team.

I never missed a single appointment again, and even when her doctors and specialists probably didn't welcome my presence, I sat by her side and irritated them with questions and suggested drug trials and treatments I'd read about on the Internet. I didn't care what they thought of my silly ideas. She was *my* soulmate, not theirs.

The side effects of Luciana's treatment were undignified when occasionally she'd soil herself. Sometimes the palms of her hands felt like ice blocks, and I'd rub them hard between mine to make her feel human again. Or she could spend days in bed poleaxed by crippling stomach pains. All I could do was fill her plastic beaker with water or rub her arm as she vomited. It was heartbreaking to witness and feel so useless.

Madame Lola frequently flew from Mexico to stay with us. Sometimes Luciana wanted both of us around her, and other times, it was just one of us. And occasionally she took herself down to the vineyards to sit alone on a blanket her sister had crocheted and watch the grape pickers come and go.

Whatever made her happy made me happy.

◆ ◆ ◆

CATHERINE

Northampton

8 October

'It's looking good, Catherine, it's looking good,' said Dr Lewis, nodding as he examined my latest X-ray against a light box.

I didn't feel it, I thought, but I kept quiet for fear of sounding like an old whingebag. My check-ups with him were the only highlight of my miserable weeks. Sometimes, the dishy doctor dropped by on treatment days to say hello and offer words of encouragement. He'd pat me on the shoulder each time he left and I'd always get goosebumps.

I'd had no significant other in my life since Tom. I holidayed alone; I shopped alone; I went to parties alone; to Selena's wedding and Olivia's christening alone; to Emily and Robbie's graduations alone. I'd been on dinner dates with several men over the years, sometimes set up by friends and others who I'd met through the boutique. But there was nobody who'd reacquainted me with romance. Or maybe I just hadn't given them much of a chance.

I'd spent so long throwing myself into my business and my children's lives that it hadn't given me time to think about what I might be lacking. Now I was spending time at home recovering, and I began to realise what I'd been missing out on. I was lonely, and fed up with being everybody's single friend.

Dr Lewis was the first man who'd turned my head in some time. Albeit a bulbous and, in places, dented head. So I made a deal with myself: if I could make it through my treatment and get a second shot at life, I'd throw my hat in the ring, open myself up and take a gamble on love.

◆ ◆ ◆

SIMON

Montefalco

18 November

Luciana insisted on taking care of all the details of her birthday party herself. Despite my protestations, nothing was going to prevent her from leading the team of caterers and planners she'd hired to throw a lavish fortieth birthday party.

'I am bored, Simon – I need to do this,' she explained with a passion I thought her disease had extinguished. 'I need to have one day where we're all thinking about the present, not the future.'

I decided against arguing with her. Friends, our children's friends, our staff and their families, the doctors and nurses who treated her, and villagers joined us as we threw open the doors to our home.

Waiters served drinks as ice sculptures slowly melted into lawns; a casino in the dining room made temporary millionaires out of some, while others danced to a twenty-five-piece swing band playing Rat Pack classics on the terrace. It had been many months since I'd last heard laughter echoing through the corridors.

Mid-evening, I searched high and low for Luciana until I found her perched on a stone wall, her bare feet resting in the infinity pool that overlooked the valley. I placed my arm around her shoulder and she rested her head on it as we stared into a distance we could never reach.

'It's not working,' she whispered.

'Of course it is. There are two hundred people behind us having the time of their lives.'

'No. The treatment. Sometimes at night when I'm trying to sleep, I can feel the disease finding new bones to dine on.'

I shivered. 'No, it's your imagination. I've read about it, plenty of people with cancer think they can hear the cells growing but—'

She gave me a gentle look that asked me not to doubt her. 'You know this party isn't just to celebrate my birthday, don't you? It's my way of saying—'

'Please don't,' I interrupted, my throat tightening.

'I'm ready, Simon.'

'I'm not. Please don't go without me.'

'I have to. And we have two wonderful children who need you.'

'But I need you.'

'And one day, by God's good grace, we will find each other again. But for now, let's enjoy the time we have together, shall we?'

She rose to her feet and moved her hand towards mine. We linked fingers and I wrapped my other arm around her skeletal waist as we swayed together for the last time. And, as if on cue, the band began to play the opening bars of 'Let's Face the Music and Dance'.

◆ ◆ ◆

CATHERINE

Northampton, two years earlier

9 April

Radiotherapy and chemotherapy had ravaged my looks, sapped my strength and ruined my wardrobe, but thirteen months after my diagnosis, they gave me back my life.

'The tumorous cells have entered a phase where they've stopped growing or multiplying,' explained Dr Lewis, with a broad smile on his face. He looked like the news was going to change his life, not mine. 'I'm really pleased, Catherine.'

I slumped down in my chair and nearly screamed with relief. He might have delivered news like that to a thousand patients over the years, but Dr Lewis couldn't possibly have known just how much it meant for me to hear I was going to live. It meant God had listened when I'd asked him for more time: that now I'd have the chance to see my granddaughter grow up, watch my children get older, and to do all the things I'd never made time to do on my wish list.

'It doesn't mean the cells will never appear again,' he warned, 'but it could mean the tumour has been destroyed and the area it occupied in the brain is composed of only dead tissue.'

'So what you're telling me is I'm brain-dead.'

'In a manner of speaking, yes. Now you won't need to come back to see me for another three months.'

I stood up to leave, and was about to thank him for all he had done when I remembered the promise I'd made to myself about taking a gamble.

So instead I asked: 'Does it have to be that long until I see you again?'

◆ ◆ ◆

SIMON

Montefalco

9 April

The end came too close to our beginning.

The most gifted Italian specialists money could hire were unable to prevent the cancer from wreaking havoc on her body. The tumours wouldn't shrink, only the eighteen months we'd hoped for. Once they infected Luciana's lungs and seeped into her bones, there was very little any clinic could do but send her home so we could make her remaining weeks comfortable. Drugs eased her pain considerably but transformed her into a vacant, slumbering shell.

Our children had already bid farewell to the mother they'd known when a diseased impostor took her place. Hearing and observing her obvious discomfort began to scar them, so I encouraged them to embrace their youth with their friends and shun death's waiting room. Only when she slept would I allow them into our bedroom to visit.

I employed a round-the-clock staff of nurses to attend to Luciana's needs, but for the most part, I took care of her myself as best I could. I had not wanted to admit how vulnerable she was, but begrudgingly I accepted that was exactly what she'd become. The emaciated frame that barely dented our bedsheets bore little resemblance to the enigma I'd loved. Her angular bones jutted out of her paper-thin flesh. Her olive skin had greyed and her eyes remained glued tight.

I felt her pain as much as anyone watching a loved one in physical distress could. It didn't matter what dose of anaesthetic the syringe driver regulated her body with – it simply wasn't enough.

After one awful night in our crepuscular hole, she clasped my fingers tightly as lucidity made its slight return.

'You know what to do, Simon,' she groaned, opening her eyelids to reveal whites pricked with brown flecks. She referred to a conversation we'd never had, yet both understood.

Please don't ask me to do this, I yearned to reply. But if you truly love someone with every ounce of your being, you'll die for them, or you'll help them to die if waiting for the inevitable is too much for them to bear.

'You're sure?' I hardly needed to ask.

She nodded slowly. 'Tell our children I love them. And promise me that before you join me, you will make things right with God and with Catherine. She must know what you did and that you are sorry.'

She felt my hesitancy and squeezed my fingers again. 'I hurt too much to live,' she continued, 'but I'm terrified to leave in case I never see you again. You must give me your word.'

She stared at me with such expectation that I knew I couldn't make my last promise to her a lie.

'You have my word,' I replied.

The corners of her darkened lips rose very slightly before her eyes closed one last time.

My legs were heavy as I walked from her bed towards the medicine trolley in the bathroom. My hands shook as I followed her nurse's instructions on how to prep a syringe.

I drew triple the required amount of morphine from the vial and went back to her. It took all the courage left in my heart to place the needle tip into a near-invisible vein in her forearm. Then I reluctantly pushed the plunger until the glass barrel drained.

In less than a minute, her agony made way for sweet relief.

As she lay before me, I climbed onto our bed, placed my head on her chest and listened to the ever-quieting sound of her heartbeat. Its gentle, diminishing rhythm eased me to sleep where I dreamed of the day my own would do the same.

When I awoke, I was alone in the world again.

◆ ◆ ◆

Northampton, today

6.40 p.m.

It was the first time in twenty-five years either of them had a true understanding of the other's suffering.

Being with Luciana at her worst allowed him a much clearer impression of what Catherine had been through when she was sick. Maybe God's wrath hadn't only been directed at him, but at all those he'd touched, too. He regretted she'd not had a soulmate to take care of her. She'd had the support of their children, but if he and she were anything alike, she would have shielded them from the worst of it and carried her pain alone as best she could.

There had been little about him she could identify with that day. From the gutlessness of his escape to the lives he'd ruined and taken away, sometimes she felt like he was reading extracts from a stranger's diary.

But his tender description of their relationship during Luciana's final months reminded her of who he'd been. And it made her envious because she remembered what his undivided attention had felt like; she had benefited from it when she'd needed it most. When all she'd wanted to do was run outside and scream at the thunder, he'd been the one to hold her back until the storm passed. But when she'd needed to be held like that again, he was holding someone else.

She knew it was pointless begrudging a dead woman. Luciana hadn't fallen in love with the wrong man; it was she who had. And remarkably, she respected him for having the courage to end the life of the only thing he'd wanted to live. Maybe he knew what love was, after all.

Eventually he broke their contemplative lull.

'Are you well now?' he asked, genuinely concerned.

'Yes,' she replied quietly. 'I still have check-ups every six months, but so far, so good. Touch wood.' She tapped the dent in her head.

'Good,' he replied, 'good.' He paused. 'And was James a big help, what with him being away so much?'

She wondered why he'd singled out the eldest of all their children. 'Yes, he was. He often texted and phoned, and came home when he could.'

However, he didn't appear to be listening to her reply and it wasn't the first time she'd noticed it. She couldn't put her finger on exactly what it was, but chinks were appearing in the armour he'd arrived wearing.

Granted, it had been a mentally exhausting day for both of them, but something about his ever-increasing vacantness perturbed her. The room went silent again as he stared out of the window and into the garden.

'Simon?' she asked, baffled by his stillness.

'Yes?' he said with a start.

'Are you all right? You look a little dazed.'

'Would you mind if I had a glass of water?'

She nodded and went to the kitchen, removed a filter jug from the fridge and poured some water into a glass. When she returned, he was examining a framed platinum disc hanging on the wall that James had given her.

'James looks a lot like you,' she said, handing him the glass. 'He has your eyes and your skinny legs. Sometimes I find myself staring at him because he looks like your double.'

'I know,' he replied. 'I've met him, Catherine.'

CHAPTER SEVENTEEN

SIMON

Montefalco, Italy, one year earlier

26 January

I sat under the shade of a plump, lemon-yellow umbrella and watched the locals go about their business from the cobbled village square.

Since Luciana's passing, there was just too much time. My capable staff ensured the winery ran smoothly, and the management structure she'd put into place before her death took care of our business interests. Everything had been plotted, planned for and preserved, with the sole exception of me. I took pleasure in seeing glimpses of Luciana in both Sofia and Luca, but glimpses were not enough. I ached for her.

My life and our home were stark without her. I moved into a different bedroom when her citrusy perfumes that lingered on the fabrics in our own became too much to bear. I craved her presence with such force that it disorientated me. I'd talk myself into believing her death had been an awful dream and that when I awoke I'd find her out in the garden, lost in a novel or chatting to our grape pickers. It never happened, of course; I was alone in my coma.

I found it impossible to concentrate on anything for long, and I'd have to write down my 'to do' lists, otherwise I'd forget my chores from one hour to the next. Grief's malevolence crippled me.

When Luca and Sofia were out of the house, I'd pass the time by walking down to the town, installing myself outside Senatori's café and nursing a latte with cinnamon sprinkles. People-watching eased the loneliness a little. I'd appraise the tourists as they passed me by and try to spot obvious signs of Britishness – milky-white or sunburned skin; trainers worn for every occasion.

Every so often I pondered whether I'd recognise one of my other offspring if they stood in front of me. More than likely, neither of us would ever know we'd been in touching distance of faded flesh and blood. I remembered parts of them all, like eye shapes, hair colours and bone structures, but I couldn't put enough pieces together to make them anything other than excerpts of children.

Luca reminded me of James, in the way the corners of his mouth hid under his cheeks when he giggled, or how his ankle rested on the shin of the opposing leg as he slept.

Sofia was an amalgamation of the best aspects of Luciana and the worst of Doreen, and that frightened me. As she grew older, she became more listless. I had admired her mother's independent spirit but I prayed she wouldn't follow her grandmother's path. I wanted her to take time to smell the flowers growing beneath her feet before she trampled over them. I loved Sofia like any father loves his daughter, but slowly I began to pull away from her, knowing I'd never be able to harness her true nature.

Luca was her opposite and I admit I put more into our relationship than I did with his sister. Perhaps I tried to replicate what I'd had with my first-born with my second from a third life. I even bought him an acoustic guitar for his birthday like I had with James – only he didn't abandon it like his brother had. I smiled as I recalled how painful it was trying to teach James the three chords to 'Mull of Kintyre'.

As he grew older, Luca discovered rock music, and in particular, a British band having worldwide success called Driver. I couldn't escape his obsession with them, and if their music wasn't thundering from his bedroom stereo, then it was booming from the speakers of my car.

About a month ago, he'd been devastated when his alarm clock failed to go off the morning tickets went on sale for their Italian tour. Ever since, I'd watched him mope around the villa, cursing it.

Suddenly a motorcycle engine interrupted my coffee break as it pulled up in front of the café. A courier removed his black crash helmet and spoke to me.

'Signor Marcanio?' he asked. I nodded and he handed me a brown padded envelope. I thanked him, picked myself up off the chair and began the slow walk back uphill to the house.

I hoped at least one of the children would be there to fill its hollow corridors with the life that had been sucked out of it.

2 April

Luca beamed up at me after opening the envelope to find two tickets for Driver's concert. 'How, Papa?'

'I have my ways,' I replied with the mysterious smile fathers only give when they want to prove they're still of some value to their growing offspring. I'd pulled a few strings with the venue's bar manager, who I supplied wine to, and then kept it a secret until a few days before we were due to fly.

'Who are these scruffy devils then?' I asked, pointing to a photograph of the group on his computer screen.

'That's Kevin Butler, the singer and bass guitarist,' he began excitedly, 'and on drums Paul Goodman, on keyboards David Webb, and James Nicholson on lead guitar.'

Two seconds passed before the latter's name sank in. 'James Nicholson?' I repeated.

With a click of his mouse, Luca blew up a thumbnail-sized picture. Immediately I was certain I was staring at a man I'd only known as a boy. His dark-brown hair was shoulder-length. Stubble had sprouted from his cheeks and chin, and his shoulders were broad. But there was no mistaking his smile or the sparkle in his green eyes.

No, I told myself. *Your head's playing tricks on you again.*

'Can you get me a bottle of water while I read up on them?' I asked Luca, trying to get a grip on my nerves.

As he bounced downstairs to the kitchen, I typed 'James Nicholson' into a search engine and thousands of threads appeared. I refined my search, trying 'James Nicholson' and 'Northampton', and there were plenty of mentions of the two together. I clicked on his Wikipedia page and it confirmed his date of birth as October 8.

I leaned back and felt the blood drain from my face. It was James. It was my James. I was staring at a picture of the son I had abandoned. I scrolled through online newspaper features and found an interview.

> The eldest of three siblings, James was raised single-handedly by his mother after his father suddenly disappeared. 'I don't remember a whole lot about him,' James tells me, clearly uncomfortable with the topic. 'I do know that he loved us all, but when he disappeared, our lives changed forever.'

I stopped and closed my eyes. The ghosts in the machine had found me.

> 'Nobody knows what happened to him. It was
> hardest on my mum, though . . . Everyone who
> knew Dad says it wasn't like him to just vanish and
> that something must have happened. And it hurts
> that we'll probably never know what. Do I still think
> about him? Yeah, of course. Not every day, maybe
> not even every week. But he's always in the back
> of my mind, somewhere.'

I was a naive idiot for not predicting how much the uncertainty might have haunted him. I glanced up at the wall in front of me to see a poster of Driver staring back. I'd walked past it dozens of times, never knowing my son was in my house.

'He's an amazing guitarist,' said Luca when he reappeared with my drink, oblivious to the earthquake rocking his father. 'He's been giving me advice.'

'You've spoken to him?' My heart beat faster than I ever thought possible. 'How?'

'On Twitter. I messaged him to say how I think he's really good and how I play the guitar too. I don't know why I did, but I told him about having trouble with this one chord. He wrote back with advice and we've been direct messaging for a few weeks. Can you imagine how many kids write to him? But he makes time for me. He's really cool.'

My two sons had been corresponding from opposite sides of Europe, neither of them knowing who the other really was.

'That's great,' I replied before making an excuse to retreat to my bedroom balcony for air.

In organising Luca's tickets, I had unwittingly unlocked Pandora's box. But what scared me the most wasn't that I was being forced to confront my past.

It was that maybe I was actually ready to.

Rome, Italy

7 April

I barely noticed the moisture pouring down the walls or the ringing in my ears as my son James played an energetic guitar solo on the colossal stage in front of me. As everyone around us cheered and sang, I stood motionless in the PalaLottomatica arena, gazing at him in awe. Luca was doing the same, but for very different reasons.

Goosebumps spread across my skin and made me itch, but I was unable to tear my eyes away from the boy I'd once tried to forget. I wondered how that scrawny, anxious little lad who'd urinated in his shepherd's costume during the school nativity play had gained the mastery and confidence to enthral ten thousand strangers. I don't think I absorbed a single lyric or was aware of how long Driver had remained on stage by the time the house lights illuminated the room.

'Come on, Papa,' yelled Luca, tugging my arm. But instead of heading for an exit sign, he dragged me against the flow of human traffic and towards the metal barriers at the side of the stage.

'This isn't the way out,' I protested as discarded food cartons and plastic bottles crunched under our feet.

'I know – we're going to meet the band!' He grinned. 'I tweeted James and told him you got us tickets, so he put us on the guest list for the after-show party.'

My unprepared mind raced through a list of excuses. 'We can't, you're too young,' was all I could offer on such short notice.

'I'm sixteen,' he chirped, dragging me ever closer. 'It's cool.'

'Luca, no. It's late. I'm tired. Let's go back to the hotel.'

He stopped in his tracks and shot me the most wounded of glances. 'Papa! Please,' he begged.

I desperately wanted to explain that we couldn't meet his hero because, against all odds, they shared the same blood. Watching James perform at arm's length was one thing, but being in the same room when he met his half-brother wasn't something I was prepared for.

I'd promised Luciana I'd make things right with my past, but it was not the right time. I cursed God for playing more of his cruel games with me.

'Luca Marcanio,' shouted my son to a balding hulk wielding a clipboard and a headset. 'We're on the list.'

The man eyed us suspiciously, checked his list, crossed our names off and directed us backstage with a grunt. My breathing was shallow as we stepped into a sterile, whitewashed corridor and followed the sound of distant music. Eventually, we turned a corner to find a bar and a group of young people drinking and eating exotic canapés from waitresses' trays.

Luca grabbed two glass bottles of cola from an ice bucket and passed one to me. I clenched mine to my wrist, hoping it would cool down my growing fever. He pointed out the other band members one by one as he scanned the room, desperate to see James.

Eventually his hero entered, clad in black jeans, a belt with a silver ram's head buckle, and a white shirt. Quick as lightning, Luca scampered towards him.

I watched intently as, out of earshot, they shook hands. They shared the same dark, wavy hair, dimpled chins and my green eyes. I wondered if I alone was struck by their similarities.

I assumed James would be polite but brief with him. Instead, he reacted like they were old friends. I attempted to blend into the background until both pairs of the same eyes reached mine.

'Papa!' I looked down, pretending not to hear as my stomach dropped. 'Papa!' Luca repeated, a little louder. There was nothing for it but to look up. He beckoned me over. My legs threatened to give way as I joined them.

'This is James.'

He smiled and held out his hand to shake mine. His fingernails were painted black and they drew me towards his cufflinks. They were ruby-red with small black squares in the centre. Catherine had bought them for my thirtieth birthday, the day everything changed.

'Nice to meet you, Mr Marcanio,' he began. 'You have a good kid here.'

'Thanks for inviting us,' was all I could think to say.

'Hey, a fellow Brit!' said James, engaging me in a conversation I didn't know how to behave. I just wanted to throw my arms around him without explanation and then leave. 'Where are you from?' he continued.

'I travelled around a lot.'

'He comes from the same place as you,' Luca chipped in. I instantly regretted offering him scant details of his father's origins.

'Northampton? No way! Small world,' replied James. 'How long have you been in Italy?'

'Eighteen years or so.'

'Papa gave me my first guitar,' Luca said proudly, smiling at me.

'That's how I got introduced to music – my dad did the same for me,' said James. 'I still have it, although it's kind of battered now. He taught me how to play "Mull of Kintyre" on it, but I was pretty bad to start off.'

I swallowed hard. I hadn't been in his life for so many years, but he had remembered that. I still had a place in his memories.

'It's at my mum's house now. She keeps threatening to put it on eBay.' He laughed. I fixated on the words 'she keeps'. He'd used the present tense. It meant Catherine was still alive.

'Does she still live in Northampton?' I asked without thinking.

'Yes, all her life. I don't get the chance to go back much, but when I do I always stay at hers. Do you go home very often?'

'No, not for a long time.'

Suddenly a young woman appeared behind James and passed him a deep-red Gibson Les Paul electric guitar.

'This is for you, Luca.' He handed it to his brother, who was too lost for words to respond. 'If you keep practising hard, there's no reason why you can't be doing what I'm doing in a few years.'

'*Grazie, grazie,*' Luca replied breathlessly. 'I . . . I promise I will look after it.'

'Don't look after it – use it. Play it until you wear it out!'

Luca accepted the gift like Jesus had offered him a blessing, and held it close to his chest. A hand tapped James on the shoulder and a man whispered in his ear.

'Luca, it was great to meet you, but I've gotta shoot. Email me an MP3 when you've mastered the break in "Find Your Way Home".'

'I will, I will.'

James turned to me. 'Nice to meet you too . . . Sorry, I didn't catch your first name?'

'It's Simon,' said Luca before I could reply.

Suddenly something happened. Something so infinitesimally small, that if you freeze-framed it on a television screen, nobody but James or I would have noticed it.

It was *recognition*.

As he shook my hand, for a fraction of a second James's irises expanded and his handshake lost its brawn. I knew exactly what he was thinking. At first he'd asked himself if we'd met before. Then my name and place of origin had made him think of his father. Now he was allowing himself to consider that maybe he wasn't dead after all and was standing right there before him.

He'd be trying to recall from his youth his dad's voice and appearance – the scent of his aftershave, the direction he parted his hair, his posture, the sound of his laugh and shape of his smile – and comparing them all to the stranger before him. Then his rational side took charge and he realised his imagination had got the better of him. Fate didn't work that way, and he'd be feeling foolish for even considering it.

He regained his composure, his irises shrank and the strength reappeared in his grip.

'See you guys again,' he smiled, and followed his assistant.

An animated Luca jumped up and down, gabbling in his excitement, but I couldn't hear him. Instead I watched my James walk away, turn around to give me a final glance, and then disappear from my life as quickly as he'd arrived.

Montefalco, Italy

19 December

My driver parked the Bentley in front of the villa and opened the rear door for me. I smiled at a housemaid whose name eluded me as she flirted with a handsome young handyman. I made my way to a patio that overlooked our valley of vineyards.

I searched the sky for an invisible crop duster, which was giving off a gentle buzz. The midday crickets chirped as they rubbed their wings together in the hope of finding a mate. The horizon I'd stared into so often with crystal clarity now mimicked a melted oil painting as the sun blended sky, field and lake into one.

'This is your life, Simon. Not the one you walked away from,' came a long-forgotten voice. 'This is your reality.' But my reality was vacant without Luciana.

Eight months had passed since James and I had breathed the same air, and he was still all I thought about. And no matter how many times I told myself his world was a worthier place while he was ignorant of my existence, I was beginning to crumple under the pressure of keeping myself a secret and a promise I'd made.

Everyone and everything I'd stored in secure boxes had escaped since that day. I was haunted by untethered memories that disorientated me. My darling had been right when she told me I had to find peace. Maybe then I'd feel more like my old self again.

I had to learn what had become of Catherine and our other two children. She deserved to know I was still alive and what she'd done to drive me away. And there were things I also needed her to understand.

Time was running out, as fate threatened to erase a life she had never known I'd lived. I was almost ready to face her.

◆ ◆ ◆

CATHERINE

Northampton, one year earlier

3 February

I dreamed about Simon that night. I don't know what prompted his reappearance, as he hadn't visited me for years. But suddenly, there he was, every bit as youthful and as handsome as I remembered, standing in my garden, deadheading my pink rosebushes. Oscar was still a puppy and bounced excitedly around his bare feet.

'Why are you here?' I asked, neither upset nor delighted to see him. He didn't reply.

'Simon,' I repeated, firmly. 'Why are you here?'

Again, nothing, and I felt a sudden urge to slap him across the face and beat my fists against his chest like wronged women do in black-and-white films. But the moment soon passed, and instead I put my arms around his shoulders and kissed his cheek.

'Goodbye, Simon.' I smiled before turning my back on him and walking away.

Then I heard his voice for the first time since he'd left me twenty-four years ago.

'Kitty, where are you going?' he asked, but I didn't respond or turn around. I walked towards the kitchen and quietly closed the door behind me, on him and on us.

I woke up, disorientated, and just to be sure it was a dream, pulled back the curtains and glanced across an empty garden. I smiled to myself, then climbed back under the duvet, turned on my side and slid my arm across Edward's chest.

'Is everything all right?' he mumbled.

'It's perfect,' I replied. 'Go back to sleep, Doctor.'

15 April

I likened being in remission from cancer to a soldier returning home from war. You put your life on the line to fight an unseen enemy that wants to kill you. Then, if you're lucky enough to return in one piece, it can be a struggle to find your place in the world you left behind.

While I'd been at battle, everyone else had simply gotten on with their lives. Selena ran my businesses more than competently; the kids returned to work and no longer worried about me on a daily basis. In short, nothing had changed, except for me. I was restless. I'd accomplished so much and was ready to share it with someone else. And Dr Edward Lewis was the someone who wanted to come along for the ride.

The day he told me my radiotherapy had been successful, I'd asked him to join me for dinner.

'You must have received plenty of offers from single women,' I asked over our meal at a posh fish restaurant in town.

'I suppose so, and not all of them single.' He blushed. 'But I usually politely decline.'

'Should I be flattered then?'

He smiled. 'Actually, I've had no interest in meeting anyone, even platonically. I felt blessed to have had twenty-seven years married to a wonderful woman, and probably didn't deserve a second chance.'

'If I've learned anything in life, it's that we're all entitled to a second chance. Why did you change your mind?'

'Not once during your treatment did I hear you feeling sorry for yourself. You showed strength and courage and I could see what a good person you were by how much your children adored you.'

'Oh, I had my moments.'

'We all have our moments. But you and I don't give in to them for long.'

Hook, line and sinker, I fell for Edward. Our fledgling courtship went from back to front. He'd already seen me feeling my worst, looking my least attractive and knocking on death's door. Yet it hadn't put him off.

Gradually our dinner dates became more frequent, and any time we spent apart, I wanted to be near him. He was charming, attentive and had a sense of adventure and spontaneity. He made me feel like I carried no baggage and, like me, he discovered he enjoyed having a companion.

His late wife, Pamela, had died suddenly of a heart attack six years earlier, and he'd taken awkwardly to life as a widower. He was bitter they'd been robbed of an early retirement together, making up for the years they were separated by his work while she raised their sons Richard and Patrick. With one studying economics at Cambridge and the other working in finance in the Netherlands, he admitted his days were too long as an 'only'. I knew how that felt. I'd lived it for twenty-four years.

I reintroduced him to my children, but this time as Edward and not as Dr Lewis. And slowly our families integrated, as he became a regular fixture around our dining table.

He'd brought me back to life not once, but twice.

19 December

A dark-grey car with tinted windows and a lot of doors pulled up outside the cottage six days before Christmas. A firm rap at the front door made the ivy wreath shudder. Before me, a young uniformed driver with a grey peaked cap clutched tightly under his arm handed me an envelope.

Your suitcase is under the bed, a note in Edward's handwriting read. *Pack enough warm clothes for a week. You only have thirty minutes. All my love, Edward.*

'Where am I going?' I asked the driver, bemused.

'I'm not at liberty to say, madam.' He smiled. 'But I'm under strict instructions to get you there on time.'

My work and family had made me an expert in timetable juggling and forward planning, so spontaneity wasn't something I was entirely used to until Edward came along. Whether it was supper on a hired canal boat or golfing lessons at Gleneagles, he loved his little last-minute surprises. So as I scrambled around for suitable clothes, I texted Emily to warn her I was off on another of Edward's jollies.

An hour and a half later, we pulled up outside Heathrow's Terminal 4. Edward stood waiting for me with his suitcase by the revolving doors. He grinned.

'Where are we going then?' I asked.

'To see Holly,' he replied, and pointed to the destination board. When I realised where we were headed, I threw my arms around him like a child meeting Father Christmas for the first time.

I'd wanted to visit New York ever since I was a little girl. *Breakfast at Tiffany's* was the only film Mum had ever taken me to and I'd watched it a dozen times since. I grew up wishing I could have Holly Golightly's carefree life, instead of the glum one my parents had thrown at me.

My friends' bedroom walls were plastered with posters of The Beatles and Elvis, but mine were decorated with black-and-white postcards of Audrey Hepburn. I'd pretend she was my long-lost big sister, and while I followed her every move in the newspapers, Mum found inspiration in her wardrobe.

Looking back on it, I'm sure people must have laughed behind my mum's back as she sauntered through the village wearing her designer scarves and stylish hats even at the height of summer. But she didn't care, and it was one of the few things about her I actually admired. Audrey offered us both an escape.

And whether it was because *Breakfast at Tiffany's* was the only piece of herself Mum had ever given away, or the lure of a magical city across the pond that had more love to offer than my parents, New York was a place I'd fantasised about most of my life.

I'd never found the time to go, or maybe I was just scared it might not live up to my expectations as a little girl. But Edward never accepted a packed diary or the fear of disappointment as excuses for not following a dream.

After landing and checking into our hotel, we'd not even had time to unpack before Edward whisked me off to Fifth Avenue's Tiffany & Co. It was every bit as timeless as I'd imagined it. I didn't think my day could be any more perfect until I peered into glass counters and tried on sparkling bracelets and necklaces displayed in boxes as blue as a robin's egg. I grinned at a framed photograph of Audrey hanging from the wall on the second floor. I was in my element, but typically, Edward found a way of making it even better.

He ushered me into the centre of the shop floor, held both my hands and cleared his throat as the room hushed.

'What are you doing?' I asked, feeling my face redden.

'I never thought I'd ever ask this question again. But, Catherine, will you do me the honour of being my wife?'

My eyes opened so wide I thought they might pop. 'Yes, of course,' I sobbed as staff and customers began a ripple of applause around us.

'We are ready for you, Dr Lewis,' smiled a manager in a smart tailored suit, and he led us upstairs into a private viewing room. Row after row of twinkling rings had been laid before us on dark cushions like stars across our own private universe.

'I don't believe in long engagements, so why don't you choose your wedding ring instead?' suggested Edward.

I wasn't going to argue. And after much deliberation, I chose a gold cobblestone-band diamond ring that simply cried out for my finger. And once placed inside a box and Tiffany's iconic bag, I skipped out of the shop and floated back to our hotel leaving a twenty-four-carat chunk missing from the Big Apple.

Holly was right. To anyone who ever gave you confidence – you owe them a lot.

Later, and too excited to give in to jet lag, Edward and I went out for a celebratory meal at an Italian restaurant in Manhattan that a friend of his had recommended. As he opened the frosted-glass door, I nearly fell backwards when a huge roar rang out. In front of me sat my family and friends, with champagne flutes raised high in the air like Gabriel's trumpet.

Edward had paid for my children, their partners and my granddaughter to fly to New York earlier that morning. James had arrived from Mexico where he was touring, and Roger, Tom and Amanda and Selena had landed a day earlier with Edward's sons. Steven and Baishali had travelled directly from their villa in the South of France, and even Simon's stepmum Shirley had overcome her lifelong fear of aeroplanes for the first flight she'd ever taken in her eighty-seven years.

'Edward called us all one by one to ask for our blessing,' whispered Emily. 'If you'd said no, Shirley was going to say yes!'

I didn't think it was possible to love anyone as much as I loved Edward right at that moment. I would have done anything for Edward with one exception – tell him the truth about how Simon had left us. Shirley and I had kept that secret to ourselves.

'I take it that's the end of the surprises for one day?' I asked later, tucking into a delicious amaretto cheesecake dessert. 'Because I don't know how much more my nerves can take.'

He smiled. 'There's just one more small thing we need to do. But you'll have to wait till tomorrow for that.'

20 December

As the Five Boroughs Children's Choir sang 'Silent Night', I glided up the mauve carpet towards a white iron altar in Central Park.

The heavenly Vera Wang wedding dress Selena had chosen for me fitted perfectly. My bridesmaids – Emily and my granddaughter Olivia – reached the minister before I joined them, clinging to my boys' arms for dear life. The fairy lights wrapped around the plinth bounced off a light dusting of snow on the ground, then I greeted my husband-to-be and his two best men, my new stepsons.

And as I faced the love of my life I'd waited so long to find and sobbed 'I do', it was impossible to feel the freezing December temperatures when I glowed so warm inside.

◆ ◆ ◆

Today, 7.05 p.m.

She'd howled in anger, tried to gain his sympathy and reluctantly appealed to his better nature, but nothing worked. He had yet to offer a single explanation for his sudden departure.

But the mood in the room, and specifically his, had shifted. When he spoke of James, he sounded wracked with remorse. And there was more to it than being reminded of the family he'd left, or a promise to the dead.

She needed to change her tack if she was going to get her answers.

'Why now?' she coaxed calmly. 'You said time was running out? Is it because we're getting older?'

His eyes surveyed the room. He looked forwards and sideways but not directly at her. He absent-mindedly chewed the inside of his cheek until he penetrated the skin.

She couldn't decide if he was choosing to ignore the question or if he'd heard something completely different altogether. He'd become unreadable.

'What do you have to put right with me, Simon?' she said, like she was talking to a frightened child. 'What do you need me to know?'

He looked like she'd woken him from a bad dream, and that he'd been further confused by unfamiliar surroundings. He was ageing before her eyes and it alarmed her.

She broke off from analysing him to ask herself why she was feeling concern for a man who hadn't given a damn about her. But that was her nature. And he was pained.

Regardless of learning about Paula's brutal killing, she no longer feared him. Even the hatred had lessened slightly. Now she felt pity for the obviously troubled soul before her. She'd wondered during their conversation if sometimes he was even listening to what she was saying, because his expression would switch from engaged to blank in a heartbeat. His vacancy reminded her of someone else, and her mind raced through a lifetime of mugshots, trying to recall who it was.

He tasted the blood trickling from the bite mark inside his cheek. He clenched his fists once again. He knew his eyes had glazed over and his brain was sluggish, but there was nothing he could do but wait until it passed, like it always did. He dug his fingernails into his palms, hoping it might let him focus on what he needed to say.

He'd dipped in and out of her recollections of her second wedding and now was finding it difficult to respond. His words were caught up in a swirling current and the faster he swam, the more they collided.

'My brain feels like Swiss cheese,' he'd told Dr Salvatore. His physician had warned him it was one of the symptoms. A year he had lived like this, blaming his altered state of mind on grief, stress and remorse before the truth was revealed. God had had one last plan for him. He could run away from everyone else in the world, but not himself.

'You have Alzheimer's!' she gasped, startling both of them.

Suddenly it made sense to her. She'd witnessed the same behaviour with Margaret, her old mentor at Fabien's and Selena's mum. Margaret's husband had brought her back to England from Spain and placed her in a nursing home after she'd been diagnosed. Catherine had visited her many times, and when Margaret was less blurred, she chatted in minute detail about her past. It was as if she needed to get it all off her chest while she was still able to.

And Simon had been doing the same.

The resigned look he offered said more than his muddled sentences could. Soon their shared memories would only belong to her.

'Why did you leave, Simon?' she asked softly.

He stared at her while he chose the right words and tried to put them in the correct order.

'I saw you with him,' he replied. 'I know what you did.'

It was her turn to embrace confusion. 'Who?'

'Dougie. My best friend. You had an affair with my best friend.'

CHAPTER EIGHTEEN
SIMON

Northampton, twenty-eight years earlier

14 March, 11.15 p.m.

The stylus lurched backwards and forwards like a ball in a roulette wheel, until it settled into a groove it could work with.

Baishali and Paula had twice bumped into the record player as they stood back to back, imitating the girls from ABBA. 'Knowing Me, Knowing You' blasted out from speakers mounted on wall brackets, and a circle of people formed around them as they recreated the band's iconic routine.

But I paid them little attention, as I was fixated by my wife and Dougie dancing together in the corner of the living room.

By early evening, the party she'd thrown to celebrate my thirtieth birthday was in full swing. Our friends and neighbours had marched up the path like worker ants, carrying cheap French wine and trays of cling film–wrapped sandwiches.

When You Disappeared

Neither she nor Dougie were aware of anyone else's presence. They faced each other, his hands on her hips and her arms draped around his neck, as she swayed drunkenly to the music.

Dougie had spent more time of late offloading his woes onto her than onto me. And in all honesty, I'd found it arduous listening to the complaints of a man who'd been deserted by his marital punchbag, so Catherine's willing ear came as a relief.

But I hadn't thought twice about their growing closeness until tonight. Despite the many distractions, neither of them lost eye contact – not when the song skipped, when the ABBA tribute act disbanded, nor when an excited Oscar began bursting balloons with his claws.

You're reading too much into it, I rationalised, fiddling nervously with the new cufflinks she'd bought me. *They're friends*. So I dismissed my insecurities and headed into the garden for a cigarette. When I gave it more thought, I knew all I'd witnessed were two pals sharing a boozy dance.

'Happy birthday, mate!' shouted my inebriated business partner, throwing his arm around my shoulder.

'Cheers,' I replied, and held my pint out in front of me to toast the occasion.

'Baishali would never throw a party like this for me,' Steven said. 'She'd be terrified of what the house would look like afterwards. You've got a good girl there.'

'I know,' I said, smiling. 'I have.'

He was right. I'd been a fool for having doubted her, even for a minute. I would go back inside to find her, give her a cuddle and thank her for her efforts. And I'd apologise for having put my work before her in recent months. I'd lost my sense of fun and spontaneity, and I knew it had created distance between us. I'd been selfish for ignoring it.

I stubbed my cigarette out on the path and went inside, but the corner of the room they'd dominated was vacant. My eyes combed the living room but Catherine was nowhere to be seen. I scanned the dining room and the kitchen before going back through the patio doors, into the garden and towards Roger.

'Is Kitty out here?' I asked.

'No, mate,' slurred Roger. 'Do you want another beer?'

I shook my head, but as I turned to go back into the house, I was drawn to our bedroom window. I looked up to see the shadow of two figures behind the curtain before the lights went out.

I remained there for a moment, temporarily paralysed.

◆ ◆ ◆

CATHERINE

14 March, 11.15 p.m.

I enjoyed spending time with Dougie. I understood why women fancied him. He was broad-shouldered and ruggedly handsome; he knew how to dress well and he was a great listener. If I were single, he'd probably have caught my eye.

And as Simon threw all his attention into setting up his business, and Dougie adjusted to his single life after Beth walked out on him, we'd both found ourselves in the same lonely boat together.

The children took up most of my time, but Dougie had nothing to take his mind off her. I hated to think of him rattling around his house without her. So he came to ours on weeknights for dinner with the kids and me. They adored their Uncle D because he chased them around the house pretending to be a monster from the *Ghostbusters* film and gave them the attention their father used to give.

After I'd packed them off to bed, Dougie and I might sit in the garden or around the kitchen table, unscrew a bottle of wine and wait for

Simon to come home and join us. Invariably, we'd chat for a couple of hours – he'd complain about his directionless life and I'd moan about my lack of a husband. He'd always defend Simon, though, reminding me his long hours were a means to an end. I knew he was right, but occasionally I needed someone else to turn on the light at the end of our tunnel.

Despite our many conversations about Beth, Dougie never really explained why she'd left. Instead, he danced around the subject, making it clear he wasn't ready to confide all in me just yet. I wondered if he'd told Simon, because my husband hadn't said anything either.

'Was there someone else?' I'd asked him a week earlier, opening a second bottle of Lambrusco.

'No, Beth would never do that,' he replied.

'I didn't mean her.'

'I'd never have an affair,' he said, a little put out I'd suggested such a thing.

'You don't need to have an affair to want someone else.'

He knew what I was getting at. I don't know why, but something in me wanted to hear him admit it was my husband he wanted. But instead I changed the subject to Simon's impending birthday party.

We'd both begged him to take a Saturday night off for a knees-up – he'd have nothing to do but turn up to his own living room. But even that, he did reluctantly.

Making food for the buffet, blowing up balloons, organising a babysitter and rearranging the furniture by myself meant that by the time the party was in full flow, I was shattered – and drunk as a skunk by nine o'clock. But despite all my efforts to encourage Simon to let his hair down, his eighty-hour working weeks meant he found it hard to unwind. I playfully pulled at his arm to dance, but he yanked it away and chose another pint of beer instead of me.

Sod you, I thought and grabbed the next best thing, Dougie, to stamp my dance card.

I wrapped my arms around Dougie's neck to stop myself from slumping to the floor, and he propped me up around my waist. As we danced, his thoughts and eyes were fixated on me.

'You're in love with Simon, aren't you?' I blurted out so suddenly, I even let out a surprised gasp. Then I held my breath as I waited for his denial.

But Dougie's expression didn't change. And for the next few moments, we just swayed, holding each other's gaze. Without needing to put it into words, I told him I didn't mind, and I read gratitude in his eyes.

'Come with me and we'll talk properly,' he finally whispered.

◆ ◆ ◆

Northampton, today

7.25 p.m.

She remained silent as she mulled over how to proceed.

He'd brought up her mistakes and stupid decisions she had long chosen to forget. She had no idea he'd seen her with Dougie in the bedroom. Of all the reasons he could have chosen to walk away from her, she'd never thought that to be the one.

She cleared her throat. 'You think I had an affair with Dougie?'

He nodded and tapped his head. 'I may have this thing growing inside me now, erasing my memories, but I know what I saw and I know what I heard.'

She looked towards her feet and brushed her hand through her hair. Her face felt flushed and her bottom lip quivered. Going up the stairs with Dougie was still the second biggest regret of her life. She was ashamed of what had happened between them and she never thought she'd have to talk about it with anyone, let alone her husband.

Then she shot him a look of absolute contempt.

'You stupid man,' she growled. 'You stupid fucking man.'

CHAPTER NINETEEN
SIMON

Northampton, twenty-seven years earlier

14 March, 11.25 p.m.

I took two stairs at a time but I still couldn't climb them fast enough. The higher I reached, the steeper they became, and by the time I reached the top, I was nauseous. I had wanted to be wrong and for the people behind the door to be two neighbours getting a thrill from having sex in someone else's house.

I placed my hand on the bedroom doorknob and began to turn it. Inside came the stifled noise of two bodies colliding that did not belong together. I recognised the sounds of Catherine's muffled groans the moment I heard them.

I stopped, removed my hand from the doorknob and the world fell silent. I clenched my stomach as a dozen invisible fists punched me over and over again. I didn't need to open the door to know what was happening. All I'd accomplish would be to solidify a mental picture that would etch itself into my brain forever. So I left her and Dougie alone to continue my ruin.

I suppressed my tears and crept back downstairs, weaving my way through our friends, then snuck out through the front door and down the darkened lane towards the woods. I bulldozed my way through bushes and bracken before the moon's glow illuminated a clearing. I threw myself on a fallen tree trunk, buried my head in my hands and wept.

She was the one who knew the most about me. She'd accepted all my insecurities and knew how important faithfulness was to me. She was the only one who understood how much emphasis I placed on honesty. It was her who'd encouraged me to believe not everyone was like my mother.

But she'd lied. It was all lies. She'd made the ultimate betrayal – and with Dougie, of all people.

I wracked my brain to work out how long I could have been oblivious to their poisoned coupling. Had it been weeks, months or even years? I thought back to the many occasions I'd returned home late to find him in the company of my family. *My family.* Not his. And tonight they'd decided to rub their relationship in my face, under my roof and in my bedroom.

How could I have been so mistaken about him? Everything I had presumed to know about Dougie had been a figment of my own imagination. The kiss he'd given me as a lad had been a foolish, one-off impulse. The covert glances he'd thrown at us over the years had nothing to do with unrequited feelings towards me – they'd all been directed at Catherine.

His willingness to cross such a sacred boundary horrified me. His desire for what was mine had more than likely directed his anger towards Beth. She and I were collateral damage in a war we were unaware we'd been fighting.

◆ ◆ ◆

CATHERINE

14 March, 11.20 p.m.

We squeezed past everyone as I followed Dougie upstairs and into the bedroom. I closed the door and sat on the bed.

'I'm sorry, I shouldn't have said anything,' I began. 'It's the wine talking. I just wanted you to know that I understand and I'm fine with it.'

'You've always known though, haven't you?' he asked, his forehead furrowed.

'Yes, ever since school. It doesn't matter though, because Simon's lucky to have both of us who care about him so much.'

Dougie smiled and looked to the floor. Suddenly his face fell. 'Yes, he's really lucky to have someone like you, isn't he, Catherine?' His sarcastic tone took me by surprise. 'Is that why you invite me over – so you can rub my nose in it? So you can keep showing me that you won?'

'What? No! No . . .' I stuttered. 'Don't be silly. I like spending time with you. We all do.'

'Don't bullshit me – I'm your charity case,' he shouted. 'You do it to feel better about yourself. I listen to you complain about how little time Simon spends with you, while you sit in your perfect house with your perfect children as your perfect husband works all the hours God sends to keep his perfect little princess happy. Except you're not perfect, are you?'

I'd never heard Dougie speak to anyone like this and it made me nervous.

'And despite everything you have, still you moan,' he added. 'But what do I have, Catherine? What do I have? Nothing. And whose fault is that?'

'You can't blame me for Beth leaving!'

'I'm not talking about that stupid bitch. You know who I mean. You took away the only good thing I had in my life.'

'What? Dougie, this is silly,' I reasoned. 'Simon never wanted you as anything more than a friend!'

'And what makes you think you're better for him than me?'

'Because he chose me over you!'

Dougie said nothing and the room went quiet. I wanted to leave, and leave quickly. I didn't know the man Dougie had become. He wasn't my friend anymore. He was a stranger with a temper I didn't like.

He glared at me with utter distaste as I stood up and moved towards the door, but he blocked my path with his arm. My pulse raced and I swallowed hard.

'I haven't finished,' he growled. 'What's so special about you then, eh? What exactly does he see in you? 'Cos I'm fucked if I can see it.'

'What's got into you?' I replied, trying to stop my voice from cracking.

'You have. You get under my skin and you make it crawl. You deliberately hurt people, then you sit back and enjoy watching them suffer. You think you know everything about everybody, but you don't. You make me sick.'

'You're drunk and talking rubbish. Now get out of my way.'

I tried in vain to push him to one side, but he wouldn't budge. Instead, he grabbed my wrists and pulled his face close to mine.

'You aren't going anywhere, sweetheart,' he spat.

Before I could struggle, he turned me around, twisted my arm behind my back and marched me towards the bed. I opened my mouth to scream for help but, before I could make a sound, he clamped his hand over it. Then he shoved me face down onto the bed. Instinctively I twisted and sank my teeth into his hand but he retaliated by punching the back of my head, dazing me. He gripped my hair and pressed my face into the bed. I kicked my legs but they wouldn't budge under the weight of his body.

'No, Dougie, let me go,' I shouted, but my cries were muffled by the bedspread.

From behind, I felt him push up my skirt and yank down my underwear, then he pulled down his trousers before forcing himself into me. The searing, agonising pain felt as though he were tearing me in two. I shook, squirmed and fought, but eventually his brute strength pummelled me into submission.

His hot, foul, beery breath scorched the back of my neck. I wrenched my head to the side and tried to yell again but the pain made me retch, and I covered my cheek and the sheets with sick. Every part of me throbbed at the same time, struggling to eject the parasite.

Suddenly, amongst the music and voices echoing around the house, I heard footsteps running up the stairs. I begged God to guide whoever it was into the bedroom and end my hell.

Dougie was oblivious to the person outside the door. Then the footsteps stopped as quickly as they'd started. My scream came out as a muffled moan as his hand drove my head ever deeper into the mattress. I begged for the bedroom door to open but my guardian angel paused, and walked away.

I let out my last cry and then, to my eternal shame, I gave up my struggle. Everything fell quiet and all I heard was his shallow breath and the sound of his belt buckle shaking before he climaxed.

Even when he finished, he continued to lie on me, his whole wretched body suffocating me. But I was no longer in pain. I'd been swallowed by numbness. My senses shut down until his weight lifted off me.

Then he pulled his trousers up and left without saying another word.

I lay there for I don't know how long, immobilised and still partially undressed, trying to make sense of what had happened. It didn't make sense, but I needed it to.

I realised Dougie had punished me for taking Simon away from him. Somehow I'd been responsible for my husband having a mind of his own and making his own choices. I'd become the one Dougie blamed for everything that went wrong in his life, and he'd needed to force me to understand how helpless he felt by making me feel the same as him.

A voice shouted my name from the garden and it brought me back to reality. I stood up, took clean underwear from the chest of drawers and headed for the en-suite bathroom. I wiped myself and saw blood on the toilet paper. I flushed it away and then fell to my knees. I was sick in the toilet until there was nothing left to bring up. I was empty in every sense of the word.

I raised my head and glanced at myself in the mirror. I'd never noticed how unforgiving it was until then. I wiped my eyes and mouth and forced myself not to cry. I held my hands together so tightly to stop my arms from shaking that I thought my fingers might break.

Then, after a time, slowly and awkwardly, I re-joined the party. I looked around nervously, but Dougie must have left. I was relieved when I couldn't find Simon either. I had no idea how to tell him what had just happened.

So I carried on, as best I could, like nothing was out of the ordinary. I smiled, I laughed and I topped up people's glasses. But the life and soul of the party was dying inside.

You have just been raped. You have just been raped. You have just been raped. A voice inside me kept repeating the words like it desperately wanted me to understand what had just happened. But I couldn't process it, not now, not yet.

When the numbers finally dwindled in the early hours of the morning, and Simon, I presumed, was asleep in one of the kids' empty bedrooms, I remained wide awake. I washed dishes, scooped rubbish into black bin bags and cleaned the house until everything was spotless.

Except for me.

◆ ◆ ◆

Northampton, today

7.40 p.m.

The world beyond her front doorstep could have exploded into a tumbling mass of fire and brimstone but it still wouldn't have been enough to break the eye contact between them.

He knew that for twenty-five years he had got things very, very wrong. And that was by no means the end of it.

CHAPTER TWENTY
CATHERINE

Northampton, twenty-eight years earlier

18 March

I pretended I was asleep when I heard Simon get up and leave the bedroom, then quietly close the front door.

I knew he'd been having difficulties sleeping and guessed he'd probably gone to put in a few more hours in the office in the garage. He'd done that a lot lately, and secretly I was glad. What Dougie had done to me wasn't my fault, but it didn't stop me feeling like I was the most disgusting human being on the planet.

I'd never been more in control of my emotions than I'd been during these past few days after his attack. I was afraid that if I stopped running even for a minute, I'd grind to a halt and fall to the floor in a thousand shattered pieces. If I kept moving, I wouldn't have time to think. I occupied every waking moment of my day with multiple trips to the supermarket to buy groceries we didn't need, playing pirate games with children who'd rather have been with their friends, digging the garden until there was no soil left unturned.

But being in bed alone – or with Simon – scared me. It gave me time to think. I considered telling him everything, but in the end I decided I'd have been the only one it would help. Trusting those closest to him was such a huge part of his make-up that I knew the truth about his best pal would destroy him. I'd have been in even smaller pieces seeing him so unhappy.

He might also urge me to report the attack, but I'd been drunk, so who's to say I hadn't willingly consented then had an attack of conscience? There were no witnesses and I'd taken so many baths to wash him out of me, there was no physical evidence anything had ever happened. It was absolutely my word against his.

Even if there'd been enough proof for the police to charge him, a court case would have meant everyone knowing about that night. I'd have been forced to relive it to a room full of strangers judging me, and his barrister ripping me to shreds. I wasn't strong enough to be humiliated like that.

But most important to me was my marriage. I was terrified that Simon would never look at me in the same way again: that he'd think of me as damaged goods. If he'd have grasped even a small measure of how dirty I felt, I couldn't have borne seeing my pain reflected in him. When all things were considered, our family had too much to lose.

Instead I bottled up my tears, and when no one was around, I'd slip inside the garage, shut the door and uncork that bottle until they spilled across the floor. And when it was empty, I'd pull myself together and go back to pretending I wasn't on the brink of a breakdown.

22 March

The thought of ever seeing Dougie's face again petrified me and, in a small village, our paths were bound to cross eventually.

When I was outside, I stopped at each street corner and looked around in fear of coming face to face with him. And home alone, I'd lock the doors and keep the curtains closed. Anyone in their right mind wouldn't have dared to return to the house of a woman he'd raped. But someone who could so degrade and violate another person – and someone who was supposed to be their friend – wasn't in their right mind anyway.

I never brought his name up again, but strangely, neither did Simon. He just disappeared from our conversations. Simon didn't go to the pub with him again. He never asked why Dougie hadn't been round for dinner, and never invited him over to watch a football match on TV. It was like he'd suddenly ceased to exist to Simon, too. The kids were the only ones who seemed to miss him.

'Is Uncle D coming for tea tonight?' Robbie asked us over breakfast.

'No,' Simon replied quickly, without raising his head.

I can't explain how relieved I was to hear that two-letter word, but I couldn't ask why. So it was only when we were invited to Steven and Baishali's house for drinks to celebrate Simon and him winning a large county council commission that the murky waters cleared.

'Is everything all right?' Baishali asked when I joined her in the kitchen. The truth was that I was as anxious as hell and clearly I was showing it. I'd avoided Paula of late because she'd have seen straight through me and demanded I take action – or worse, started the ball rolling without my permission. But Baishali didn't like confrontation, so I'd picked her and Steven as my first social engagement since the attack to try and navigate my life back to normality.

'Yes, everything's fine,' I replied, and gave her a fixed grin.

'It's a shame about Dougie, isn't it?'

I swallowed hard. 'What about him?'

'He's gone back to Scotland, hasn't he? He popped a note through our letterbox saying goodbye. Seems very sudden, doesn't it?'

'Yes,' I replied, trying to disguise my relief.

'Simon must be disappointed.'

I had no idea what my husband was thinking anymore. I asked myself why he hadn't told me his best friend of twenty years had suddenly moved away. I was growing increasingly uneasy over how our lines of communication were becoming disconnected. But if it was true, that the animal had crawled back to Scotland, maybe I could start to try and live again.

At a time when every part of me craved normality, Simon and I were drifting apart in separate lifeboats.

Sex and intimacy were the furthest things from my mind, but when we got home from Steven and Baishali's, I was crying out to feel like a normal woman again. I desperately hoped that by making love to Simon, I could push that night from my mind.

Physically I was still sore, but I forced myself to make him want me because I didn't want to equate sex with pain and violence for the rest of my life. Even during the act, which is exactly what it was, I knew we were both only going through the motions. And if I felt it, I'm sure he did too.

But it was the start I needed to repair what someone else had almost ruined.

14 May

I hadn't guessed I was pregnant, even when I missed my period.

I presumed that while I'd been focused on blanking things out, I'd simply neglected my body by skipping meals and sleeping badly. I chalked it up as an off-kilter cycle and my body's delayed reaction to trauma.

But when the second month rolled by with no sign of its arrival, I nervously made a doctor's appointment. Three days after my test, Dr Willows rang with the results. I slumped onto the stool by the telephone, the wind knocked out of my sails. I was pregnant and I had no idea what to do.

I was already stretched to breaking point. I was a mum to three children under the age of five, I was married to a workaholic husband and I was trying to hide the mental scars Dougie had left me with. The thought of having to cope with another little one mortified me. It would be another distraction that stopped Simon and I from repairing our relationship. I'd accepted that our sex life had shifted from passionate to sporadic and unfulfilling, but at least we'd made a little effort to be intimate. And while neither of us had climaxed and so it was unlikely, biologically it didn't mean I couldn't fall pregnant.

I seriously considered an abortion. I imagined organising it while Simon was at work and the kids were at school. And by the time they'd all pour through the door at teatime, none of them would be any the wiser.

But *I'd* know. I loved motherhood and I had no right to stop a second heart beating inside me because mine was broken. Poor timing was an excuse, not a reason, and a pretty weak one at that. So I forced myself to come to terms with it. I had gotten through tougher times.

I didn't know what the future would bring for Simon and I. But I knew there was a future for the baby inside me.

◆ ◆ ◆

SIMON

Northampton, twenty-eight years earlier

18 March

'Why? Why?' I bellowed while my fists took on lives of their own, raining blow after blow upon Dougie's face and body.

Four days had passed since I'd heard my best friend and my wife together, and I'd barely been able to look at her. She'd been uncommonly quiet and withdrawn – ravaged, I hoped, by guilt for what they had been doing behind my back.

I made a backlog of office work my excuse for spending time away from both her and the scene of their crime. But concentration was impossible and I'd sit at my desk, haunted by the noises they'd made behind our bedroom door. And although she'd desecrated my faith in her, my physical fury was directed towards Dougie.

I was unsure if I was more enraged by his devious, cowardly betrayal of our friendship or at my own naivety for never having doubted his loyalty. Catherine aside, I'd been closer to him than any of my friends. But he'd made a mockery of all I'd presumed, and try as I might to contain it, my anger refused to simmer until I'd made him feel as weak and vulnerable as I was.

I waited until the early hours of the morning when she was asleep before I walked to his rented house. Both the upstairs and downstairs curtains sealed off the inside from unwanted prying eyes, so I ventured to the rear and peered through his kitchen window.

The light was on and an unconscious Dougie was sitting inside on a plastic patio chair, his head tilted backwards, surrounded by empty beer cans lying like fallen soldiers. While my life was imploding, he'd been celebrating. My rage peaked.

He only became aware of my presence when I slipped my arm around his neck and jolted him backwards to the floor. Startled, his blurred eyes opened wide but the alcohol in his system made any attempt to reclaim gravity futile. I straddled him and rapidly recast the structure of his face into a tapestry of blood, hair and mucus. My knees pinned his helpless, flailing arms to the ground, but even bruising my knuckles as I broke his nose and jaw was not enough to curb my ferocity.

'Why her?' I spat. 'Why my wife?'

'I'm sorry,' he choked. 'Stop, please stop—' But I didn't allow him to continue: another blow thrust his front teeth to the back of his throat like pins in a bowling alley.

I dragged him to his feet by his stained shirt collar and held him against the wall. His head hit a clock and it fell, spraying glass across the lino.

'I don't know why,' he gasped, his breath reeking of booze and blood. 'I didn't plan to—'

'Shut up!' I snarled. 'You've destroyed us, Dougie. You and me, her and me, all of us. Everything . . .'

My voice had weakened, then faded into nothing. Hearing myself verbalise what he had done to me suddenly made the sheer enormity of it all too real. I let him drop to the floor and he curled up into a sobbing, bloody ball. I gawped at him like he was a strange, injured creature in the last throes of life. I questioned how I could have been so foolish as to have loved something that worthless.

I needed to get out of his house and stop breathing the same polluted air as him. I headed towards the back door, his wheezing growing quieter with every footstep.

I could have left him there to remain in his stink, but deep inside me, I knew it wouldn't have been enough. I stopped in my tracks and turned to face him.

His swelling, blackened eyes were already reduced to slits, so he was only aware of my shadow when it hovered over him. Even when he watched me take the bread knife from the sink, he didn't try to protect himself.

I slowly pulled back my arm and plunged the blade into his stomach once, twice, then a third time. It took surprisingly little effort. His face remained expressionless but the physical trauma forced his body bolt upright. There he remained conscious, but still.

I stood back to share his final moments. His last few shallow breaths merged with the sound of gases escaping through his wounds. He didn't try to clutch at them or fight for his life. He simply waited five long minutes before life drained from his carcass and his neck lapsed limply to one side.

We both knew what I had done was right.

I reacted to the events of the night with clarity.

Beth's family had removed almost every stick of furniture from her house when she sold it, so he had little to furnish his new hovel with. I searched each room for something suitable to put his body into. But all he possessed were empty takeaway containers, beer cans and free newspapers. It was a pathetic legacy.

I wiped his blood from the floor with newspapers and dirty towels. Then I bundled his body into the boot of his car. I drove through the village, passing our house, before I turned off the headlights and navigated by memory the lane by the woods.

I grabbed the spade and torch I'd taken from Dougie's garage and headed deep into the copse. The ground was frosty and hardened, so it took sweat and determination to dig. But after an hour, his makeshift grave lay ready for him. My arms, weakened and jarred by fury and determination, made dragging his bulky frame to the hole arduous, but I persisted until I'd rolled him into the earth.

I threw the stained towels and papers in, and without giving him a second glance, I shifted the soil back into the hole, trampled the ground to an even level and scattered fallen leaves to disguise my movements. I used an old blue rope that lay on the ground near the dried-up pond to mark his grave.

I left his car in a notorious area of town with the keys in the ignition, then caught two nightbuses home. I made my way to the bridge where I'd take the kids pretend-fishing, and washed his filth from my hands in the water below. And with my adrenaline spent, my physical pain began to manifest itself as sharp bolts of lightning. They ran from my knuckles up into my shoulders and made my chest tight. The letters I'd type to Roger and Steven on behalf of Dougie, explaining his sudden move home, could wait until morning.

With my fists locked tight, I could barely extend a hand to brush the tracks of my tears from my cheeks and chin.

27 April

I longed to hear Catherine confess and beg for my forgiveness. Because only then might she understand how far from my old self I'd shifted since I'd heard her and Dougie together.

She had asphyxiated the 'me' she thought she knew. Now she only lived with an impression of Simon Nicholson: a man so anaesthetised and glacial, the fluids inside him ran cold. I would never be the same man again.

I was so detached from everything that had happened before that week, I'd wiped Dougie from my history. Even having my best friend's blood on my hands had failed to humanise me. My actions were justified, I knew that. I had the strength to do what my father should have done to the many lovers Doreen had humiliated us with.

But dealing with Catherine was a different matter. I reckoned I'd gain more satisfaction from slowly snuffing out her flame than from any physical retribution. I wasn't sure how I'd do it, but somehow I would eke a confession from her. Then I'd make her hang with uncertainty for weeks while I pretended to make up my mind about our future.

And once she thought she could see a glimmer of hope in my open, forgiving arms, I'd abandon her and make sure my children and all her friends knew exactly what she had done. They would hate her like I did.

But I underestimated her. While I was allowing her to believe she had got away with it, she suddenly blindsided me.

14 May

I may have terminated Dougie's life, but he'd found a way to live on, inside my wife. Inside all of us.

It hadn't been enough for him to decimate our marriage while he was alive. Even one mile away from my house and six feet under the ground, he still rubbed salt into my open wounds.

Catherine wore the cloak of a troubled woman the night she put the children to bed early and ushered me into the dining room.

'We need to talk about something,' she began nervously, 'and I'm not sure how you're going to react.'

She dabbed her cheeks with a paper tissue before she spoke again.

'I'm pregnant.'

Then she leaned over the table and took my hand in her devil's claw.

'I'll need your help and it'll mean cutting back on some of your hours at work, but I think another baby could be just what we need.'

It was the last thing I'd expected to hear – another hammer blow to my fragile ego. I knew then she could never be honest with me. I'd have to rethink my plan to punish her.

'So what do you think?' she asked.

'It's great news,' I lied, and she immediately released the rest of her crocodile tears.

It was obvious that the evil seed inside her bore no relation to me. On the few occasions we'd made love, I'd had to summon up all the powers of my imagination to become aroused. It was soulless, remorseful sex between an adulterer and the wronged, and it never resulted in me climaxing.

Yet she was willing to pass her bastard off as mine now her lover, to the best of her knowledge, had cast her adrift and returned to Scotland.

I recalled her panicked eyes when Robbie had asked when Dougie was coming to dinner again. She neither lifted her head nor questioned me when I told him he wouldn't be. It made me wonder if she knew that I knew. But if she did, she played her cards close to her chest and said nothing. Inside it must be killing her, never understanding quite why he'd dumped her. I took some satisfaction in that.

She'd upped the ante and had been overcompensating for her wrongdoings by using every calculating trick in the book not to appear the desperate housewife. She'd wait until I arrived home from work late so we could eat together; she forced her way into every aspect of the children's lives and redecorated our verminous bedroom by herself.

On occasions when she thought she was alone, I'd see her skulk into the garage. And as I peered through the cobwebbed windows I'd witness her kneeling on the dirty floor, crying. I hoped she'd never stop.

19 August

As the months passed and the parasite in her belly grew, I resented it as much as the vehicle carrying it. I daydreamed about watching her fall down the stairs and miscarry, or of Dr Willows confirming the baby had died in her womb.

Yet despite everything I despised about her and how ghastly she made me feel, I wasn't able to confront her or pack up my things and leave.

All I'd ever wanted was a family of my own and I wasn't ready to leave my children like my mother had. Living with them all, I was miserable. If I walked out, I would be Doreen. Staying, at least for the time being, was the lesser of two evils.

So I played along with her charade.

25 November

She lay fast asleep in our bed, exhausted by a labour that had ravaged and contorted her body for much of the day and night.

I sat on the tatty green armchair in the bedroom cradling her son in a white shawl she'd knitted especially for his arrival. The midwife packed up her equipment and let herself out. She'd named him William after her late grandfather, and he was deep in slumber and only an hour old. His skin was still sticky and sweet-smelling, and covered in a fine, white, downy fur.

Once he'd been placed into my arms, I tried with all my might to imagine him as one of my own brood. But I wasn't able to press my lips to his delicate ear and whisper to him like I had the others.

I couldn't tell that little boy that I'd always be there for him and would never let him down. Because he was not my son and never would be. Even the product of an untruth didn't deserve a lie – I knew that better than most.

Weeks passed and I spent hours watching him, identifying traces of the father I'd killed in his smiles and frowns. He was the spitting image of Dougie, even down to his few strands of auburn hair.

He'd never experience a male role model who'd love him unconditionally, or a mother who'd be completely honest with him about his origins. So soon into his life, he was weighed down like an anchor by his conception.

However, my steely facade had begun to melt a little when I witnessed Catherine giving birth. In her vulnerability I saw pieces of the woman I'd loved, who'd already blessed me with three children of my own.

And for the first time in months, I'd even allowed myself to wonder if we could get through this. But while Billy was in our lives – a constant reminder of her transgression – I couldn't forgive her, I couldn't heal and we could never move forward.

His fragile existence meant nothing would ever be the same again.

◆ ◆ ◆

Northampton, today

8.00 p.m.

He struggled to draw breath.

His bleak, lethargic pupils fluttered to life like a loose-fitting lightbulb, then collapsed back into the murkiness of his irises.

On the surface he continued to offer little reaction to what she'd told him, but inside, he was fractured. Her disclosures had forced all one hundred billion neurons scattered about his ailing brain to shoot their electrical impulses in unison, rendering him disabled.

When he finally flickered back to life, his eyes bored deeply into hers, observing her from all angles with microscopic detail. He desperately searched her face for evidence that she was lying, but all he could see was the truth. What he'd too readily believed he had heard behind the bedroom door had created a chain of events that had changed and ended lives. Now he considered whether, deep down, he'd been waiting their entire life together to catch her out, and that had been the excuse he was looking for.

She had just demolished the framework of twenty-eight years' worth of assumptions. He could no longer blame his actions on her. It was Dougie's fault. It was Kenneth's fault. It was Doreen's fault. *It isn't my fault, it isn't my fault*, he kept telling himself.

So much distress and sorrow could have been avoided if only he'd turned the door handle another forty degrees. He could have protected her like a husband was supposed to protect his wife.

She had been a victim of the unresolved issues between two best friends and the parents who'd shaped them. And it broke the charred remnants of his heart when she explained how she'd sacrificed a justice she'd deserved for *his* sake. She'd even been willing to love a baby sired by hate just so she wouldn't upset him. He couldn't understand how someone could be that selfless.

'I – I . . .' he began to whisper but couldn't finish.

She remembered a time when words from this man mattered. Now they meant nothing.

Finally, the question that had harangued her for so long had been answered. A thousand times she'd asked herself what she'd done to make him cast her aside, and now she knew.

Nothing.

Absolutely nothing.

If the roles had been reversed, she'd have opened that door. She'd never have doubted him until she'd seen it with her own eyes. She also knew she'd have been a better person had she forgiven Dougie. And she had tried, so very, very hard. But it had been impossible, and now she knew he was dead, she felt gratitude, even if it had only happened as a result of misplaced pride.

But that gratitude was short-lived. She could never forget Paula's murder, the life of abandon he'd lived and the children he'd left behind. They'd all been dreadful things to hear. And nothing shocked her more than the depth of his dislike for a child he'd quietly rejected as his own.

'How could you have hated something so innocent?' she asked, determined to gain an insight into his thinking. 'You treated Billy like you treated your other children. I saw you with him. I watched you love him.'

'I didn't,' he replied. 'It was a lie because I knew he wasn't mine. I'm so, so sorry for what happened to you, but you have to remember, I thought you were having an affair. I was crushed.'

'Why didn't you open the door? Why didn't you open the bloody door?'

'I was scared of what I'd find.'

'You mean you thought you'd find Doreen. How dare you, Simon. How bloody dare you. That's what you always believed, wasn't it? That I'd turn out to be like her, because you think all women are like that. You even compared your daughter in Italy to Doreen. Your own daughter! You only see in people what you see in yourself – damaged goods.'

'I'm sorry.'

She wasn't interested in his apology. 'I don't know what's worse: that you thought I could cheat on you, or that you pretended to love your son.'

'That's the point, Catherine. Billy could never, ever have been my son, no matter how much I pretended. And if I'd have known how he was conceived, I'd have hated him all the more.'

'You and I created him!' she stressed, increasingly exasperated. 'He was *your* flesh and blood.'

'That's ridiculous. You know I never even completed the act with you those few times we tried. The odds are astronomically against him being mine. And he was so clearly Dougie's! I saw Dougie in every inch of him. He looked nothing like his brothers and sister, and even less like me.'

'No, again, you believed what your twisted mind wanted to believe. Take my word for it, Simon, you were his father.'

He dug his heels in.

'No. I only wish I could believe it like you want me to, but you can't promise me that. I understand why you need to think it but—'

'Please don't make me spell it out for you.'

'You're going to have to, because without a DNA test, I will never accept you're right.'

She held her breath and closed her eyes before she responded. She was too angry and humiliated to look at him.

'There is no possibility Billy could have been Dougie's child because he sodomised me.'

And there it was. His last remaining excuse for any of his subsequent actions disintegrated as fast as the ground beneath him.

She struggled to understand what he muttered as he clung tightly to the arms of his chair.

All she could make out were the words 'God' and what sounded like 'forgive me'.

CHAPTER
TWENTY-ONE
CATHERINE

Northampton, twenty-six years earlier

3 January

My gorgeous Billy giggled in delight as he threw his favourite toy from one end of the bath to the other and chased it on his hands and knees. 'Slow down!' I told him.

The blue and white plastic boat and its painted smiley face had been passed down from James to Robbie and finally to their fourteen-month-old brother. And like them, Billy never grew bored of picking it up and hurling it around.

His development was coming on leaps and bounds and he was often crawling around the house and trying to stand by himself like his brothers and sister. 'No, Billy,' I warned as he tried to lift himself up using the sides of the bath. He sat back down and then splashed me again with his boat.

Robbie was at an age where cleanliness was so far removed from godliness that he'd rather be playing dinosaurs with the devil than take his evening bath, and Emily always demanded that her daddy gave her one. And as James demanded privacy, Billy was the only boy who'd let his mummy share these precious moments with him. I relished every one of them.

I was shampooing the ever-increasing tufts of hair finally spreading across his crown when the phone rang. I'd been expecting a call from my friend Sharon to tell me how her wedding had gone a day earlier. I was so honoured when she'd asked me to make her three bridesmaids' dresses, as it was the biggest project I'd ever taken on. She'd invited us to the reception but Simon and I had been forced to turn it down at the last minute when our usual babysitter got chickenpox and couldn't look after the kids.

Sharon had promised to find the time to ring me tonight, before she and her new husband flew off on their Tenerife honeymoon.

'Simon!' I shouted at the top of my voice when the phone went. 'Watch Billy, please.'

Once I heard his muffled reply from another room, I dashed across the landing into our bedroom and picked up the receiver. By all accounts everything had gone like clockwork, but more importantly, my dresses hadn't fallen apart at the seams. I was momentarily distracted by a thud coming from outside the bedroom but I'd learned from experience that if no child's wail followed an unexpected noise, chances were all was well.

Sharon chatted for a few more minutes filling me in on her big day before we hung up. I was proud of myself and couldn't help but smile as I went back to the bathroom to tell Simon.

'Sharon says everyone loved them,' I began as I reached the door. 'It's a shame we couldn't . . .'

Only he wasn't there. But Billy was, lying in the bath, his face under no more than two inches of water.

His fine baby hair floated aimlessly, his body completely devoid of the life I'd given him. His boat was close to him, anchored in the bubbles, still smiling.

I froze until the full horror of what had happened sunk in, and then I screamed for Simon and dashed those few feet from the door to my baby. I threw my arms into the water and grabbed at him, picking him up by the waist and placing his body onto the fluffy bathroom mat.

The children appeared from nowhere and stared from the doorway in confusion. Robbie yelled 'Daddy' and I heard his heavy feet pounding towards us.

'Oh God, oh God, oh God,' I repeated as I picked Billy up again and held him in front of me. His neck flopped forwards.

Simon pushed me away and took charge. He lay him on the floor, tilted his head backwards, pinched his button nose and gave him the kiss of life. I knelt by his side, helpless, my arms as wet as my eyes, sobbing as his dad pushed down heavy on his chest to encourage his heart to beat again. I heard the crack of a rib under Simon's pressure and it felt like it was my own.

'Call an ambulance,' Simon kept repeating, but I remained deadlocked and torn between hope and despair. James must have heard his pleas and ran. I listened to Simon's warm breath as he blew hard into our son's mouth; saw his palms sliding across his wet body; heard the crack of a second rib and the brush of his spine against the mat with every push.

I reached out to grab Billy's still-warm hand and begged God to give him the strength to move his fingers and clasp one around mine. But God had neglected my son when Billy needed him, just like I had. Robbie and Emily were crying behind us when James returned and led them away to his room.

Simon wouldn't give up, even when the paramedics arrived and tried to take over. They had to pull him to one side, but there was nothing they could do that he hadn't tried already.

Eventually they looked at us with empathy and shook their heads apologetically.

Despair dragged my body to the floor and I clawed at my chest to take the weight off my heart. I reached for the mat, desperate to grasp something after losing so much. I tried to pull myself closer to my baby but my body was stuck to the floor. Simon scooped my head onto his thigh as I screamed so hard my eyes and throat burned.

'It's my fault, I'm sorry,' I wailed. 'It's my fault . . .'

'No, don't blame yourself,' he replied as he stroked my hair. But we both knew it was.

'I thought you were here with him,' I cried. 'I shouted for you.'

'I was downstairs.'

I begged the paramedics not to take Billy away from us, but Simon quietly explained it was time to let him go. I tenderly dried his body and put him in his Mr Men pyjamas before they carried him downstairs. I couldn't bring myself to watch as he left our home for the last time.

Instead, I lay with my cheek pressed to the cold lino, holding on to his toy boat and wishing it could sail me back an hour in time, before I left my baby to die.

7 February

My bedroom was a tortured sanctuary. I wanted to seal off the door and windows and turn it into a coffin, like the one my little boy lay in, deep underground.

Days had passed before I could even stand up unaided by Simon. Each time I tried it alone, the ground swayed beneath me and I'd go back to my bed dizzy and defeated. The phone rang so often that he unplugged it from the wall socket so it didn't disturb me.

I'd hear the muffled voices of friends stopping by with food parcels and offers of support, or to take the children out of our mausoleum to play with their friends. I was glad when they were out of the house because it meant they were safer than when they were with me.

But I couldn't stop them from quietly opening my bedroom door, crawling under the quilt and curling their warm bodies around mine. I'd wrap my arms around them and hold them tight before I realised what I was doing, then I'd reject their love and send them away. They were too young to understand why their mummy didn't want to be with them. It was for their own good: I didn't deserve them.

Simon became both mum and dad and told them that, although I was very sad, I still loved them and I'd come out of my room when I was ready. But until then, they had to be patient.

Throughout Billy's funeral, Simon had never let go of me, holding my head against his shoulder as my mascara melted into the lapels of his jacket. And when we arrived home, he let me stay in our bed for weeks without complaining.

I always felt worse when I woke up than when I tried getting to sleep. Because for the first few seconds of consciousness, I'd forget what had happened. Then it would all come flooding back to me and the grieving process would start again from scratch.

When I tried to focus on anything else, I'd recall the moment I found Billy's body and it hijacked all other thoughts. Some nights I was convinced I could hear him crying, and on motherly instinct I'd jump out of bed and be by the door before realising I was hallucinating.

My body and mind operated separately. My head knew I'd lost him, but my breasts punished me further by continuing to produce milk.

I missed Billy's babyness and longed for the cherished droop of his head on my shoulder as he slept. I missed wiping the sleep caught in his eyelashes. I missed how he'd made me feel like a woman again after what Dougie had done to me.

No matter how much Simon tried to reassure me it had just been a terrible, terrible accident, deep in his heart he must have hated me. How could he not? I did.

12 April

Simon's support never ended, but no amount of reassurance was enough. I even took my self-loathing out on him, blaming him for not being in the bathroom where I'd expected him to be.

But he never took the anger he must have felt out on me. He dealt with his grief in his own stoic way. And he was always there for me when I needed to roar or bawl. He was the perfect husband.

I'd always said Billy had the smell of pink roses about him. So Simon dug up a patch of land under the kitchen window and planted six rose bushes there. It was a place where I later grew to find peace, by just sitting near or inhaling through the open window while I washed the dishes. It was just what I needed for my healing to begin.

22 October

When I was so completely, utterly empty and there were no tears left to fall and nothing left of myself to hate, there was only one direction left for me to go.

So I gradually opened my eyes and allowed myself to slowly fill up with the love that had surrounded me for months, but that I'd shunned.

The love from my family; the love from my friends; but mostly, the love from my husband.

◆ ◆ ◆

SIMON

Northampton, twenty-six years earlier

3 January

I paused under the architrave behind Robbie and James, riveted by the pain that forced her body into awkward angles as she endeavoured to bring life to a little body for the second time in fourteen months.

Billy lay wet and motionless on the floor; his eyes held their sparkle but his body was lifeless. I'd often caught myself looking into them and wondering what they saw when they looked back at me.

It was the second time I'd been in the bathroom in the space of a few minutes.

When she'd called me to keep an eye on him, I'd been in Emily's bedroom helping to dry her hair after her bath. I heard Catherine's muffled conversation behind our bedroom door as I made my way to the bathroom. Billy was playing with his smiley-faced boat when he saw me and offered a gummy grin. I gave him nothing.

I watched him throw the boat too far to reach with ease, and he looked at me, expecting me to sail it back. I didn't move. Frustrated, his arms, still just doughy rolls of skin, reached out to bring it closer. When he failed again, he clambered to his feet, holding the sides of the bath with his hands for support. Then, as he shuffled along, he lost his footing and slipped, spinning as he went down and smacking the side of his head on the tap and then again on the brutally hard porcelain. As I watched, his body came to rest face down in the water.

After a long, still moment, he startled me by lurching to life, arching his back and trying to force himself free of the water, but when he opened his mouth to scream, it filled with water and bubbles. His arms flapped as he tried to prop himself up but he possessed neither the strength nor the coordination to push himself back up.

And then I waited for the inevitable.

I remained stationary, as almost two years of fogginess began to clear.

I knew what I was supposed to do, what anyone with an ounce of humanity would have done. But I was no longer that person. Catherine had drained me of my compassion and left a cold, cold man in his place. Billy and I were both her victims.

My reaction was the fault of Billy's abhorrent chromosomes. And I couldn't live with him in my home, pretending to be like those I loved any longer. So I watched as he slowly and quietly drowned; the helpless leaving the helpless to flounder in a fight only one of us could win.

As the last bubble of air left his lungs and bathwater seeped in, I glided out of the room as quietly as I'd arrived.

18 January

In the weeks following Billy's death, I would lie with Catherine in the darkened cocoon she'd created in our bedroom, listening to her agony until she fell asleep. Then I would replay the moments in my head that had destroyed her.

'Oh God,' she'd repeated after yelling my name. 'Oh God, oh God.'

I'd run along the corridor and stood behind Robbie, James and Emily as the consequences of my inaction became clear. I panicked, and needed to take back what I'd allowed to happen. I pushed the boys out of the way and began CPR, attempting to take back the madness of those five minutes and to repair my damage.

Billy's mouth tasted like washing-up liquid as I struggled to get a firm pinch on his nose and give him back the life I'd allowed to slip away. I felt sick with adrenaline and fear as his first rib broke in my heavy-handed desperation.

You were wrong, I heard my inner voice tell me. *You could treat him like your own.* A second rib snapped. *It will take small steps, but you could spend more time with him; buy him a bigger and better boat; teach him how to ride a bike like you did with the others; watch him from the sidelines as he scores the winning goal for his football team . . . Yes, you could do all of that if you were given a second chance. But you won't be.*

In the time it took me to watch him die, I had mapped out our next sixteen years together as father and son. My son. Not biologically, but my son nonetheless.

Even when the ambulance men appeared from nowhere, I refused to admit failure. But inside I knew it was too late. Billy was dead and I had let it happen.

I'd stroked Catherine's hair as she lay deep in the floor sobbing her heart out, her baby by her side. Her world had been shattered and she was reduced to rubble and ruin. The hurt she had caused me was nothing compared to what I had done to her.

20 March

For weeks Catherine did little but blame herself, my decision condemning her to an intolerable purgatory. And my inability to reveal the man she loved had been responsible for her son's death cast a shadow over all our lives.

Each time she chose sleep over reality, I'd put on my running shoes and sprint as fast as I could until my legs folded beneath me. I deliberately chose hard surfaces so I could feel every jolt of concrete jar my knees and spine, because the physical pain eased the mental one.

Each time I hurt myself, I'd hope it would take some of hers away, but there was nothing I could possibly have done for that to happen.

12 May

To the outside world, I was the portrait of a consummate husband. But inside, I was in bedlam. I dragged myself through the motions to keep the family engine running. I became an expert in forging smiles and convincing the concerned that everything would be all right in the end, given a little time.

I made myself responsible for all the children's needs while Catherine was too empty to cope. I was the face that friends saw when they turned up on our doorstep to see how we were.

I took a leave of absence from the business to take charge of the everyday tasks like shopping, housework and gardening. I cooked all our meals, made sure the children had clean school uniforms and kept them occupied when their mum needed to be alone.

We spent hours together pretending to fish in the stream near the cottage. Sometimes I'd stare into the water, convinced I could see Dougie's blood caught in a whirlpool and unable to dissolve. We took drawn-out walks through the fields searching for snaggle-waggles or spent time in the garden playing board games. At a time I should have been close to them, I'd never been so far away.

I juggled so many balls at once and only I knew what the repercussions of dropping them would be. I saw the consequences of my actions in my wife every day. And it helped me to understand that it wasn't just remorse over Billy's death I was feeling, but towards the death of our marriage. Opportunity had presented me with a chance for revenge I'd never considered. Yet once my mission was complete, I felt nothing. It hadn't healed me like I'd hoped it might; we were broken, with or without him.

I'd been weak when I'd tried to bring him back to life. Filling his lungs with a stranger's air would not have helped me long-term. Even with his blood on my hands, I still felt the same kind of rawness as when

I'd discovered Catherine's affair. All I'd done was force four people to feel as worthless as myself. And my misery didn't love company.

I frequently had to remind myself it was her duplicity that provoked my reaction. She had brought this on us. I watched in silence as she floated without aim through the house, unable to associate herself with the world. Now she knew how I'd felt when I found out about her and Dougie.

The pressure on me to keep up my facade was immense, as I had nobody to confide in. So I took to sitting in the woodland near to the man buried below the blue rope. It was the only place where things made sense.

I'd talk to Dougie like I did when we were innocents. He understood me and I believed that wherever he was, he knew what he'd done to me was wrong. I became envious of how easy it was for him to accept it and how uncomplicated things were for him now he was resting beneath a carpet of dirt.

It would be so much simpler if I, too, were six feet under.

22 October

For nine long months, Catherine remained in darkness. Then, gradually, the sun began to reveal itself and she rose from the bottom of the hill and navigated her way back up it.

We were sitting watching *The Two Ronnies* when she unexpectedly laughed at a sketch. We all turned sharply to look at her, as it was a sound we'd not heard for so long.

'What?' she asked, surprised by our attention.

'Nothing,' I replied, and I knew my time was coming.

As she slowly healed, my disintegration was close to completion. My wife was on her way home, but in doing so, she was leaving me behind. She had learned to live with what she thought she'd done. But I couldn't live with what she'd done to me.

Christmas and New Year passed, and as winter merged into spring and then summer, my trips to the woodland copse grew more frequent. I'd pick up the rope from the ground and feel my way around it, tugging it between both hands until it was taut. Then I'd face the canopy to search for the strongest, sturdiest-looking tree branch. Several times I thought I was ready to kill myself, then I'd make an excuse as to why it didn't feel like the right day to complete my mission. Each time I'd walk back home, cursing myself for not having the strength to go that extra mile.

Tomorrow, I'd tell myself. *I'll be able to do it tomorrow.*

And eventually tomorrow came.

◆ ◆ ◆

Northampton, today

8.20 p.m.

She shook her head vigorously. She was adamant that the horror story he'd told her about Billy wasn't true.

'No, your Alzheimer's is making you confused,' she began faintly. 'Let me call Edward. He can come back from the golf club and help you.'

To this point, making anyone else aware of his secret existence had been the last thing she wanted to do. But now her need to prove that his confession was actually confusion became a much higher priority for her. Edward could examine him, test him. Allow her to dismiss the abomination he'd just admitted to committing.

But Simon fixed a watery gaze upon her and slowly shook his head. Her stomach began the first of many somersaults.

'I was there, don't you remember?' she continued, gently coaxing him. 'I left Billy alone, not you. I was the one who found him and shouted for help. It wasn't your fault: it was mine, wasn't it? Remember?'

He gave her the weakest, most apologetic look she'd ever seen, but still she could not believe him. She did not want to, because over time, she had learned to accept her pivotal role in Billy's death. It had been an accident.

For it to have been deliberate . . . for her husband – the boy's father – to have allowed him to die . . . that was so much worse than her negligence. It was evil. And she had loved this evil man. She raised her voice in a last-ditch attempt to persuade him to concede he was muddled.

'I accept you've done a lot of wicked things,' she continued, 'but the man I adored back then would never have let that happen. You could never have held me and dried my tears and kept our family together like you did, knowing it wasn't my fault. So I'm begging you to tell me now that you're confused and that you didn't let Billy die.'

He couldn't have answered even if he'd wanted to. The stranglehold guilt had on him was so tight it barely allowed him to breathe. He couldn't move, yet he swore he felt his body convulsing.

She sank deep into her armchair while she evaluated what it all meant. She had never got over Billy's death, because no parent ever does when something so tender and innocent is wrenched away from your arms without warning. But gradually, the image of his lifeless body in the bath wasn't the first that came to mind when she thought of him. It was of his warm, toothless smile in photographs she'd taken during his first and second Christmases. She'd pored over them hundreds of times since.

And every year on his birthday, she'd lock herself in her bedroom away from everyone, take his tiny blue satin booties from the crushed-velvet box in her wardrobe, and rub them gently between her fingers like she'd done as a child with her mother's clothes. She'd hold them to her nose and inhale deeply in the hope of picking up a long-faded scent.

Only, now she'd learned Billy hadn't died because of her careless parenting, but because of the insanely misdirected spite of his own father. She pictured him standing over Billy like the Grim Reaper, captivated by the panicking infant drowning before him.

It enraged her. She wanted to kill him.

He was oblivious to the escalating fury before him. He'd been used to finding ways of justifying his aberrations by blaming other people. But now there was no one left to blame. Kenneth had been right when he told his only son he was a monster.

The first physical contact in twenty-five years between Simon and Catherine Nicholson came after she jumped from her chair with such speed for a woman of her age, it terrified him.

'You bastard!' she screamed as her fists pummelled his head, over and over again. He had little time to raise his arms to protect himself from her blows. He struggled to push her away at first, but when he succeeded, she came back more ferocious than before.

He grabbed her arms, so she kneed him in the groin. He bent double in excruciating pain as an onslaught of slaps and scratches began. She caught slivers of flesh from his cheeks under her fingernails. Finally, he was able to muster up the strength to grab her arms and twist them behind her back. She shrieked in pain.

'Kitty, Kitty, please,' he begged, trying to catch his breath and calm her.

'Get off me!' she screamed, and squirmed to release herself from his grip, but to no avail.

'I'm sorry for what I did to Billy and for not trusting you. You have to know that.'

'Don't you dare use his name! You aren't fit to use his name!'

'I know, I know, but I had to tell you the truth before my disease made it impossible.'

'Am I supposed to be grateful? How could you let me spend my life believing it was my fault when it was you who'd killed him? His own father!'

She tried to jab her elbow in his stomach but her arm wouldn't budge against his clutch. The last time she'd been forcibly restrained by a man, she'd eventually given in and accepted her fate. She would not make that mistake again.

'Please, please forgive me,' he cried. 'Don't let me die knowing you couldn't find it in your heart to accept my apology.'

His desperate hope filled the room as it fell silent. Finally, she replied in a voice so fuelled by venom, he barely recognised it.

'Never.'

Her response immediately drained him of his energy and she wriggled until one of her arms came free. It flailed around behind her, trying to hit anything that felt like him. A fingernail scraped across his eyeball, and instinctively his hand reached to cover it.

While he was temporarily blinded, he failed to notice her grab a metal picture frame of his children before it smashed against the side of his head. He fell to the sofa, dazed, but moved just before the orange glass vase from the fireplace shattered against the wall above him.

'Kitty, please!' he yelled, but she would not listen. A man capable of such evil did not deserve to be heard.

As he opened his mouth to beg for her forgiveness one last time, she reached for a brass poker from the fireplace and swung it above her head. He backed away but not fast enough to avoid the brunt of its force on his wrist. They both heard the bone crack, but he felt nothing as he fell to the floor.

Then, as she raised the poker again, he didn't flinch or try to protect himself. Instead, he lay there, sodden and shaking, accepting his fate, as weak and pathetic as she'd ever seen a man. With a final lift, the poker was as high as she could carry it.

Then she threw it against the fireplace with all her might.

'You don't deserve the easy way out,' she spat. 'I want your disease to slowly eat away at you until your one and only memory is of the son you killed. Now get out of my house!'

He used the wall to support him as he slowly rose. He backed away from her towards the door, while blood poured from the open wound to his head. He touched his temple to stem the bleeding and pricked his finger on a shard of glass that jutted out from it.

He opened his mouth to make one final apology but his vocabulary was barren. And when she glared at him with such menace, he knew there was nothing he could say with his hollow words that would make any of this better.

So he fumbled for the handle, opened the door and stumbled down the gravel path, his heavy feet shunting stones in all directions.

He didn't hear the door slam behind him, or see her slump to the floor and wail like no other person had wailed before.

EPILOGUE

Northampton, today

8.40pm

Simon steadied himself against the church railings as he lurched through the village, his body as traumatised as his mind.

He failed to notice the school he'd once attended, the Fox & Hounds where he'd tasted his first pint of beer, or the village green where he, Roger, Steven and Dougie had spent so much of their youth playing.

Finally, when he reached the graveyard, he could breathe again. He scrambled as best his shaking legs would allow from grave to grave, hunting for the plot that housed the unhinged soul so many had thought they'd known. But they'd never understood it had abandoned his body long before he'd left them.

His eyes prickled from the tears of regret he shed for lives lived, lives wasted and lives taken. And he cried for the forgiveness he had no right to expect and would never receive.

Catherine had deserved the truth no matter how much it had hurt her. He'd wanted her to apologise for what she'd done and for her to understand why he'd allowed Billy to die. Before he left Italy, he'd convinced himself that when she learned she was equally to blame, then she would understand. Then he would return home to his children Sofia and Luca and await the day he could take Luciana once again in his arms.

But now he knew what a stupid old fool he'd been. Because he had never considered in all that time they were apart that he might have got it wrong. And in the end, he had been savaged by the truth just as much as her.

Eventually he found the charcoal-grey granite headstone he was searching for. The sandblasted lettering on the epitaph was as brief as that written on his mother's marker.

Simon Nicholson – loving father, gone but never far.

It was an ambiguous tribute and open to interpretation, but only he and Catherine knew that. Oh, and Shirley of all people, thanks to Catherine taking her into her confidence. Whatever her considerable faults, his stepmother wasn't one to blab for blabbing's sake.

He inched his aching limbs towards the ground and knelt. With few burial spaces remaining in the three-hundred-year-old churchyard, he wondered if another corpse lay beneath where his should have been. It would've been apt if so, he thought, as wherever he roamed, a dead body was never that far away.

He removed the silver hip flask Luciana had given him for his fiftieth birthday from his jacket pocket. He frequently topped it up with Jim Beam to take away the bitterness of his medication. It also helped to relax him on the days confusion made him feel like a tightly balled fist.

He took out both packets of pills. He knew the ones designed to slow the pace of his advancing Alzheimer's were no longer powerful enough, and he'd barely touched the antidepressants. But he hoped there were enough of them combined to put him out of his misery. One by one, he popped them from their blister packs into his bloodied palm and then to his mouth. After each four or five, he took a swig from his hip flask and swallowed hard.

Then he sat motionless, numb to everything but the sensation of the tablets as they slipped down his throat and settled in his empty stomach.

Nobody in this world had understood him like Luciana, and if God were willing to show him just one act of mercy, he would soon be with her. But he knew it was a lot to ask, considering all he'd said of the Lord and the torment he'd inflicted on the undeserved.

Finally he accepted it hadn't been God, Doreen, Kenneth, Billy, Dougie or Catherine who had caused his suffering, but himself. He'd been so hasty to blame everyone else for not living up to the perfection he'd expected from them, yet he was the least perfect of them all. He'd been the architect of his own misery.

He began to think about his death and the complications it would create for those he loved. Luca and Sofia would be financially secure for the rest of their lives. But when they were to learn of his passing, they would surely have questions only Kitty could answer. He hoped that when they finally traced her, she might respond to their confusion and grief with kindness.

As for his other children – well, keeping his return a secret would be too tall an order for her. His body, less than a mile from her home, would be impossible to conceal. He hoped they wouldn't hate their mother for lying to them for most of their lives.

Conscious there was nowhere left for him to hide, he wished he'd hanged himself from the tree in the woods when he'd had the opportunity, all those years ago.

'You know what to do,' came the voice that only appeared when his options were few and far between. 'This is the place. Right here, right now.'

'I do,' he said out loud. It was a solution that would help everyone. He could bury himself where no one would think to find him – in the ready-made grave below. If he could disappear once, then he could do it again.

So he lifted his aching head and began to dig.

As he clawed his way through the sharp turquoise gravel chips, he failed to notice the blood that dripped from his cracked fingertips and temple was making the soil underneath syrupy. He tried to ignore the numbness of his broken wrist and that made digging much harder.

He just needed to scrape a little deeper, he imagined, and then heap the earth back upon himself, and nobody would be any the wiser.

'Focus, focus, focus,' he repeated, determined not to be defeated by an ageing body that ached to admit defeat. But his arms smarted and his knees grew weaker.

He began to topple forwards until he steadied himself and then made one last frantic attempt to scoop away the broken earth and push it to one side. But it was no use: he no longer had the strength to support his weight.

I'll rest for a minute then continue, he reasoned, and with all his remaining strength, he pushed himself onto his back and lay on a blanket of grass. He watched carefully as the burnt-orange sky gradually faded to a darkening twilight.

And with a final anxious sigh, he closed his eyes and wondered if God would listen when he apologised for all he had done.

ACKNOWLEDGMENTS

I offer my heartfelt gratitude to those friends who read early versions of this story and were then subjected to a barrage of questioning.

Thanks to my mum, Pamela Marrs, the biggest reader I know and who inspired my love of books. Thank you to Tracy Fenton from Facebook's THE Book Club for discovering this story and helping it to take on a life of its own. And in alphabetical order, thank you to my early readers Katie Begley, Lorna Fitch, Fiona Goodman, Jenny Goodman, Stuart Goodman, Sam Kelly, Kath Middleton, Jules Osmany, Sheila Stevens and Carole Watson. Also thanks to John Russell for his constant encouragement and Oscar, my four-legged friend, for sacrificing walks around the park for this book.

My gratitude also goes to Jane Snelgrove who found this story, out of the millions and millions of books out there, and started a whole new chapter in my career. Thanks also to my editor David Downing for his eagle eye, superb suggestions and advice on tongue biting.

Finally, thank you to the woman who inspired this novel. I don't know your name, where you are from or if you will ever know that this story was inspired by you and the struggles you faced. I'll always be grateful to have read your story and I will never forget you.

ABOUT THE AUTHOR

Photo © 2016 Jocelyn Woo/Everly Studios, New York,

John Marrs is a freelance journalist based in London and Northampton. He has spent the past twenty years interviewing celebrities from the worlds of television, film and music for numerous national newspapers and magazines. *When You Disappeared* is his third novel. Follow him on Twitter @johnmarrs1, on Instagram @johnmarrs.author and on Facebook at www.facebook.com/johnmarrsauthor.